FIRST KISS

"I don't believe you are a criminal," she said in a whisper.

Valentine swallowed, noticing that her fingers were now curved around his hand. "No?"

She shook her head.

"What has caused you to change your mind?" he asked.

The only sounds in the room were the crackling of the fire and the hush of the rain beyond the stone walls. He could feel her pulse quickening beneath her skin.

Then she stood up from her stool without withdrawing her hand and stepped toward him. Valentine rose automatically as she came into his arms and raised her face. He lowered his mouth to meet hers as if it was a dance they had rehearsed a thousand times, and their lips met perfectly. Maria's right arm came up around his neck, his left went easily around her waist.

Valentine heard the roar of a warm sea in his ears, tasted the sweet saltiness of her mouth, smelled the garden of her hair. His heart pounded in his chest like hoof beats, his body pulsing with this sudden onslaught of unmistakable desire. . . .

Books by Heather Grothaus

THE WARRIOR

THE CHAMPION

THE HIGHLANDER

TAMING THE BEAST

NEVER KISS A STRANGER

NEVER SEDUCE A SCOUNDREL

NEVER LOVE A LORD

VALENTINE

HIGHLAND BEAST
(with Hannah Howell and Victoria Dahl)

Published by Kensington Publishing Corporation

Valentine

The Brotherhood of Fallen Angels

Heather Grothaus

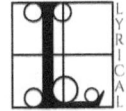

LYRICAL PRESS
Kensington Publishing Corp.
www.kensingtonbooks.com

LYRICAL PRESS BOOKS are published by

Kensington Publishing Corp.
119 West 40th Street
New York, NY 10018

All Kensington titles, imprints, and distributed lines are available at special quantity discounts for bulk purchases for sales promotion, premiums, fund-raising, educational, or institutional use.

Special book excerpts or customized printings can also be created to fit specific needs. For details, write or phone the office of the Kensington Sales Manager: Kensington Publishing Corp., 119 West 40th Street, New York, NY 10018. Attn. Sales Department. Phone: 1-800-221-2647.

Lyrical and the L logo are trademarks of Kensington Publishing Corp.

First Electronic Edition: June 2015
eISBN-13: 978-1-60183-396-9
eISBN-10: 1-60183-396-2

First Print Edition: June 2015
ISBN-13: 978-1-60183-397-6
ISBN-10: 1-60183-397-0

Printed in the United States of America

For JRG
I took your advice.

And for DLB
Sometimes all you need is a good potion.

Prologue

September 1179
Jacob's Ford, Syria

He had slept in worse places before, certainly.

Valentine Alesander shifted in his saddle as the late-afternoon sun blasted down on him, caught between the white-bleached sky above and the heat glowing up from the sand beneath his horse, making him glad of the protection his long keffiyeh afforded his neck and head. He had hoped the news of the complete destruction of Chastellet had been only exaggerated boasting from the triumphant Muslims. From his view atop the hill across the river, the reports were dreadfully accurate.

The compound lay in hazy ruin, the smell of charred wood still wafting on the hot breeze even some five weeks after the battle between the Templar defenders and Saladin's army. Surely there was nothing left—perhaps not even shelter.

Valentine squinted up at the sun—so bright that its orb was indiscernible in the blinding Syrian sky. Night fell quickly in this country, and though he now regretted the reckless curiosity that had prompted him to leave Saladin's festive and generous court, he could reach no other city before darkness—and thieves—swept over the land.

Valentine perhaps would have been one of those thieves himself, but no one of any means would be making his way via Jacob's Ford this late in the day, and he now suspected that there would be little of value to scavenge here beyond what the black birds perched atop the walls had not already helped themselves to. There must have been a score of the vile things.

A gust of wind charged through the scrubby brush of the hill, showering Valentine with a fine spray of sand and causing his horse to shift and toss its head toward the dull glimmer of the Jordan below. Valentine sighed. He had no choice but to pass the night at Chastellet—or at least make camp nearby. He kicked lightly at his horse and started down the well-worn road toward the river.

Valentine did not dismount as he let his horse pause for a drink at the river's edge; there would be time aplenty for the recently acquired gray beast with handsome black mane and tail to leisure once Valentine had determined where he would make camp. Instead he looked to the ruined northeast corner of the fortress where Saladin's army was rumored to have breached the Templar defenses.

Great blocks of stone appeared to have been tossed about, half-hewn, laying tumbled down the hill as if they were mere pebbles. Massive vats in which mortar had been mixed weeks ago now sat abandoned, dried into symmetrical boulders. The endless wind scrubbed at the gold-colored walls, already softening their edges. Chastellet, the famed fortress intended to preserve all of Christendom, defeated before it had truly been complete, surrendering itself to the sand and the sun and the lonely wind, sinking slowly into the tomb of history.

The thought made Valentine shiver.

His horse temporarily satisfied, Valentine urged his mount through the shallow river and up the bank on the opposite side. He rode wide of the spot where Chastellet's wall had been sapped and moved warily toward the gaping hole where surely a mighty gate had once stood.

The silence was complete outside of the scraping of the horse's hooves as he passed through the twenty-foot-wide opening. Even the scavenger birds gave no cry of outrage against their brethren, and Valentine realized why when the hot wind shifted suddenly, blasting through Chastellet's bailey and rolling over him.

Valentine grabbed the hem of his long keffiyeh and drew his forearm up, burying his nose in the crook of his elbow as he gagged.

There was no reason for the birds to fight. They were all full.

Thankfully the wind turned again, dragging the suffocating stink up with the shimmery heat. Valentine urged his horse onward, deeper into the bailey, although the beast was now reluctant and showing his nerves with a sideways gait.

"Ch-ch," he whispered. "*La taqlaq.*" *Don't worry.*

He hadn't had the horse long enough to gain its complete trust, so it was important the animal not get startled. Valentine had little coin to spare for another, and horse thievery was an offense punishable by death in this part of the world. He didn't plan on swimming to Constantinople.

Even as he continued to soothe the horse beneath him, an eerie chill stiffened Valentine's spine. Perhaps it was the idea that somewhere within Chastellet, hidden from his view, countless corpses lay rotting. Perhaps it was the idea that such a massive slaughter had so recently taken place here. Or perhaps it was just the usual wariness of a man who is no longer of any country, allegiance, home or family. The unease of a wanderer so far from anything familiar that everything has the violet hue of danger, emphasized by the sinking sun and indigo shadows growing in the stone corners of the ruined Chastellet.

But Valentine didn't think so. He could feel living eyes upon him. He was being watched, and not only by the carrion birds above.

He drew his mount to a gentle halt and tugged on the reins, seeking to turn the horse and depart the bailey at once. He would sleep in the open, across the river, rather than be trapped in this haunted place.

"*Jayed, la taqlaq,*" he murmured. He clucked gently, and then with the horse's next step the world seemed to explode.

It was some piece of broken metal hidden in the packed dirt—perhaps from a breastplate, perhaps some tool discarded upon the breaching of the walls—but when the gray kicked it and sent it clanging across the bailey, it was the beast's undoing.

The horse reared and screamed, sending wave upon wave of screeching birds from Chastellet's walls—hundreds more than Valentine had seen earlier, emptying seemingly from the very bowels of the compound. Their shadows joined and twisted, darkening the bailey as if it was already night. Thousands of wings joined, creating thunder overhead and sending the horse into a blind, spinning frenzy. Feathers and guano fell like stinking rain, the stench of avian wet and putrid corpse blooming like a rotting garden.

And then from the corner of his eye, Valentine caught the blur of a white mass escaping from shadow and hurtling toward him, a lengthy, black-crusted sword clutched in its grip. A wordless scream from the ghoul cut through the thunder of wings, echoing beneath the blanket of scavengers.

"*La!*" Valentine shouted, reaching down into his boot for the hilt of his dagger while still fighting to gain control of the horse. But the white monster was coming at him too fast, the horse spinning too wildly for Valentine to free his weapon, and the blackened sword seemed to fly toward him. In but a moment he would be skewered.

The gray chose that moment to rear again, and Valentine used the upward momentum to spring backward from the saddle, landing mostly on his feet in a crouched position as the horse sprang free and bolted toward the bailey's gate—all Valentine's supplies still strapped to its saddle. The creature with the sword never broke stride, still giving its hellish scream. Valentine at last freed his dagger from his boot and rose, his arms outstretched, his weapon ready.

"La! Stop! *Detenga!"* he shouted at the devil again, and as the attacker skidded to a halt perhaps five paces from him, Valentine saw that the beast was—or had at one time been—a man.

A man well over six feet tall, even with his hunched posture, with shoulders and a chest that would have rivaled the horse that had just fled the bailey. *Laborer.* His head was large, blockish, the hair on top cut close to the scalp and showing white through the flaking black filth that was streaked down his face. *Not aged, though.* His eyes were shocking—pale blue in red-shot whites; his lips colorless and cracked. *Foreigner, most likely Norse. Dehydrated.*

The man's massive right bicep and forearm—bared by the rough-woven brown tunic he wore—still pointed the sword at Valentine, the blade shuddering as if the man stood atop a rolling cart. The sizable weapon looked no bigger than a twig in that mighty grip, and so Valentine doubted it was fear that caused the man to shake. Valentine thought of the weeks that had passed since the battle, the carrion birds belching from the innards of Chastellet, the stench that was likely so much lessened at this point.

The blond beast gave a sound that was like a growling whine. *Mad. Or nearly so.*

"Do no do this, my friend," Valentine warned in English, keeping his tone low and even. "I can see that you have had some trouble, and I do no intend to harm you."

The giant blinked twice, as if Valentine's words had shocked him back from whatever brink he'd been about to throw himself over.

"You . . . you speak . . . English?" he rasped.

"Yes, of course," Valentine replied in a mild tone. "And you also speak English. So then we have at least that in common. Perhaps we will be friends, yes? Friends do no threaten each other with weapons."

The man paused for only an instant, his gaze jumping as he thought, and then his expression hardened again as his eyes swept Valentine's keffiyeh and flowing robes.

"You trick me," he accused, taking a menacing step forward and raising the sword tip higher. Valentine was dismayed to see the trembling of the weapon had lessened. "It is clear that you have returned to finish the work of your friends. I will avenge Chastellet!" He moved forward another pair of steps, and Valentine saw that the man's left arm, held behind him, hung limp, painted with the colors of old bruises.

Dislocated shoulder. Perhaps a broken arm, as well.

Valentine stepped back quickly an equal number of paces and tightened the grip on his own blade. "No, no! Easy now—you merely mistake my costume," he said. "I am but a lowly traveler, seeking shelter for the night."

Again the man stepped forward, his jaw working as he ground his teeth together, his white eyebrows lowered. "I don't believe you."

Valentine retreated yet again. He would need to act quickly, and on the man's lame side—if the giant managed to lay hand to him, he could crush Valentine's throat in his one massive fist.

"I hail from the Spanish kingdom of Aragon," Valentine explained, working his way almost imperceptibly to the man's left. "I only obtained this suit of clothing in Damascus, to ease my journey through such an inhospitable land. On the morrow I shall continue on to the Mediterranean. I assure you I claim no part in the slaughter here."

The man's posture straightened and the confused expression came over his face again. "Damascus?"

"Yes," Valentine said in a friendly tone, edging ever closer to the man's left side. "I took rest there for several days. Although this is not the country of my birth, I make friends easily. It serves me well when outfitting for my travels."

"You have friends in Damascus?" the man repeated, his gaze narrowing. "Wealthy friends?"

"No as wealthy as they were when I came into that city," Valentine admitted. He was almost close enough now. "Only some guards. No one of status." He readjusted the grip on his dagger.

The man threw down his sword and rushed at Valentine. With reflexes quicker than Valentine ever would have guessed considering the man's injuries, he swatted the dagger from Valentine's hand and then seized his left bicep, half-lifting Valentine from the bailey's crusted dirt.

"You will take me there now," he said.

Valentine ground his teeth together. "That is no possible. I can appreciate that you have been here for some time alone, and so I will forgive this one time your handling of my person. Release me."

The giant behaved as if Valentine had not spoken. "You will take me to your guard friends in Damascus. I will go get my things." He shoved Valentine away and then turned from him, walking back toward the charred and tumbled-down wall from which he'd emerged.

Valentine retrieved his dagger from the dirt and then started walking in the direction in which his horse had disappeared, keeping his eye on the spot where the giant had vanished. He had only taken a handful of steps when the enormous man ducked back out into the bailey, a pair of rough sacks in his right hand, a pack across his back, and on his shoulder was a—

Valentine halted and stared.

A falcon?

The giant walked determinedly toward Valentine, the bird sitting easily on the massive perch of the man's shoulder and wearing the typical hood and leather tie about one of its legs.

"We must find your horse," the man said. "It is too slight to carry me, but I am a fast walker and you are likely already fatigued from your journey, so you may keep it." He swept past Valentine without a glance, leaving his sword lying in the dirt.

"Perhaps you did no hear me," Valentine called after him. "I am no returning to Damascus."

"We go tonight," the man said, continuing in his walk toward the bailey gates.

"No," Valentine insisted.

The giant stopped abruptly and turned. "I watched hundreds of men slaughtered," he said, retracing his steps. "I pulled arrows from eyes, hearts, necks. Do you see the black dirt of this bailey? 'Tis not dirt—'tis dried *blood*. After my arm was nearly ripped from my body, I could only hide like a woman and watch as every last man at Chastellet, save me, was either killed or captured." He came even with Valentine at last. "Two of my friends were taken prisoner and marched to Damascus. I will free them. Or I will die trying."

Valentine smirked. "Then you will die, my friend. A man such as you walks into Damascus, the hair, the size—they will cut you down without inquiry."

"That is why *you* will go. To your guard friends."

"And ask them to please release Saladin's prisoners?"

The giant shoved one of the sacks he held into Valentine's chest, nearly knocking Valentine from his feet.

"Pay them," he growled.

Valentine took hold of the sack's rough, limp neck as the giant's hand fell away.

It was heavy. Very heavy.

Valentine shoved the sack back at the man, holding it against the wall-like chest when the giant made no move to reclaim his possession.

"I am afraid no. I ran into a little trouble there before I left. It is likely that your friends are dead any matter—many of the prisoners became diseased on the march to Damascus, and the road is littered with their skeletons. So you would lose whatever it is of value that this sack contains and I"—he shrugged—"well, should I encounter a certain friend of mine who feels he was perhaps no treated so fairly, I would be without the use of my legs for some time."

The giant only stared down at Valentine, while the falcon on his shoulder cocked its head, as if listening to the exchange it could not see.

"Take the sack," Valentine demanded.

The giant shook his head. "No."

"Take it." Valentine thumped the weighty bag against the man's chest.

"If you help me," the giant said, motioning with the hand still hanging by his side, "the rest is yours to keep. More than what you now hold."

Valentine sighed. This was madness.

"Please," the giant entreated. "The men I seek are of great importance to King Baldwin, and you will be remembered kindly to him if you help me."

"My friend, the only men who survived the march are well known to be the traitors of Chastellet. It is likely that anyone I managed to free would only slit your throat in thanks."

There was no response from the blond beast, and the sack seemed to be burning the palm of Valentine's hand.

It couldn't hurt to look. It was likely only smelting scraps any matter.

He drew the sack back to himself with another sigh and loosened the neck to look inside. His eyes widened.

Coins. *Gold* coins.

Valentine looked back into the giant's face, and as if the man saw the question Valentine was too shocked to ask, he supplied the answer.

"Chastellet's wages. I am—*was*—the master stonemason here." He held out his good arm to indicate the bailey. "I built this place. And now all my laborers are dead. Except you."

"I am no laborer," Valentine said as he looked back down into the sack. It was a fortune in gold—a year's wages for ten men, at least. If, as the giant promised, the other sack contained an even greater wealth, Valentine could travel anywhere in the world he chose, in the greatest comfort.

Valentine looked up at the colossus again, his mind turning. "What if they are already dead? Then I would place myself in great danger for nothing."

"I still pay you."

"Mm-hmm." He pursed his lips, staring at the man. "What if they are no already dead, but they are the traitors?"

"They aren't. But still, I will pay you what I promise."

"Even if dead, even if traitors?"

"Yes."

Valentine crossed his arms. "They are soldiers?"

He shook his head. "A general, and a man of learning."

Valentine frowned. "Franks?"

"English."

"Well, I suppose that is something," Valentine muttered. He straightened. "All right. Give me the other sack and I will think about it."

"No. When you return with my friends, I will give you your payment."

It had been worth a try.

"I could very well lose my own life in this business, you understand?"

"All the more reason to keep the remainder of the coin with me."

So he was not as dim-witted as his appearance would lead one to believe. Before Valentine could comment further, the giant spoke again.

"You know the pagan language, and your coloring is akin to theirs. But if you feel you cannot succeed, only take me to Damascus and leave me at the gates. I will do it myself."

"What would I get in return for that?"

"Ten pieces."

"Ten pieces?" Valentine laughed. "There is a fortune in those bags, my friend!"

"Which can be yours in exchange for one simple task." The man paused. "I would have no way of knowing if you somehow managed to make your way into the prison without the bribe. . . ."

Valentine stilled as the man's meaning fell upon him: he could keep both sacks of coin.

He looked up at the purpling sky. It would be full dark in an hour. If he was sly, if he utilized all of his tricks, all of his charm, in twelve hours he could be away from Damascus again, this time as wealthy as a prince.

"You can no accompany me into the city," Valentine began, tying the neck of the sack to one of the belts in his voluminous robes. "There are some caves in a nearby hillside that face the gates. You will wait for me there."

"Very well."

"And that is if we can even lay hand to my mount—surely he has run all the way to Tiberias by now, and I will no attempt this madness after the sun has risen." Valentine turned and began walking once more toward the gaping entrance. "If I can no find my horse, you will pay me his full value, and for the worth of my supplies, which he carries."

The giant followed along. "Of course."

"If we are approached on the road by Saladin's men, they may no be as accommodating as I," Valentine warned.

"I will kill them all myself."

Valentine threw back his head and laughed as he came to a stop and turned. "No in your condition, my friend." He held out his hand. "Fine. We have a deal. I am Valentine Alesander."

"Roman Berg."

They shook hands, and then Valentine unlooped one of the long belts from his middle. "Kneel down and loose your feathered friend, Roman Berg. I will fix your shoulder for you. It does no appear to me that your arm is broken after all."

Roman hesitated.

"Come now, you could kill me by falling on me. I have nothing more ominous in my hand than a little strip of leather." Valentine waited.

At last the giant knelt in the dirt, setting his bag of coin and rough pack aside and gently lifting the fiercely colored hunting bird from his shoulder.

"Lou," the man mumbled.

Valentine leaned slightly forward. "Pardon?"

"The falcon. I named him Lou. I don't know what he was called before."

"I see. Well, the pleasure is mine, Lou." Valentine looped the ends of the strap around both palms several times, leaving a long length dangling between his fists. He captured Roman with the snare, drawing the strap tight under the deflated bulge of the man's left bicep and pulling the giant's right side flush against Valentine's own braced thigh and hip.

"Now, Roman, are we agreed that once this little business is over, we shall part ways? No further conditions once I've given you what you ask for? No demands for me to carry you back to the land of sea monsters and longboats before I am paid?"

The man glared up—only slightly up—into Valentine's face. "I keep my vows. What further use have I for a sneaking Spaniard? If I never see your swarthy face again, it shall be too soon."

Chapter 1

May 1180
Beckham Hall
Kent, England

L ady Mary Beckham took a deep breath of the fresh, warm air and
rested her chin in her hands as she adjusted her elbows on the
stone windowsill. The view of the village in spring always made her
smile as she watched the people scurrying about below, small as
birds when seen from the third floor of the keep. Occasionally Mary
would see people she knew by name, but they never took notice of
her—she might as well have been a tapestry hanging on the side of
the castle, a woman in a window rendered in embroidery.

It was the many persons she didn't know whom she most loved to
watch. She could give them her own pet names: Woolhead and Limpy
Hip and Lady of Sausage. And she could create her own stories of
their lives and personalities based on the small details she noticed
from her observation point, high above the ground. Sometimes she
had to watch for days to see some of her characters, but that suited
Mary well enough. She had nothing else to do.

But her game had become more difficult the past several months, as
the increase in Crusaders and pilgrims arriving and departing from the
port of Beckhamshire caused temporary surges in the population of the
town below. Mary would watch an individual for perhaps a fortnight, deciding on a name, a background, and then suddenly, with the ship
departing to somewhere beyond the horizon, her character was gone and
her story was dashed. This was particularly vexing with the soldiers, as
they seemed to come and go from so many different lands, calling out
with strange accents and wearing even stranger clothing.

Most vexing of all was that the majority of the fighting men would await their voyages in the lower levels of Beckham Hall, beneath Mary's very feet, and yet she would never set eyes upon them while they were within her home.

"Well?" Agnes asked, her ever-present smile obvious in her voice. "Who's out adventuring this eve?"

Mary glanced over her shoulder at her nurse, who was indeed smiling indulgently as she folded some freshly laundered linen at the table where Mary had taken her supper not even an hour before. Although Mary was a score and six years, Agnes still maintained her insistence that Lady Mary dine early, as she had since she was a child. Mary didn't mind. After all, it left more time before bed to watch the comings and goings below as the soldiers attended to their duties.

"Yes, let's see then," Mary said, turning her attention back to the view below and scanning the milling crowd. "Grandfather Crumb has just come across the green, and he is brandishing some sort of pastry. A treat for a sweetheart, perhaps."

"Likely a stale trencher to chuck at some lad who dares cross before him, I suspect," Agnes chortled.

"Oh, no, I can't believe that. He looks so kind—he's always smiling."

"He's a curmudgeon. It's a grimace."

"Whose adventure is this any matter?"

Agnes laughed. "What of Lady of Sausage? It should be nigh hour for her to pack up her wares."

"I've not seen her," Mary admitted, scanning the villagers for the portly old woman and her long stick full of swinging meats. "Oh! But there's Princess Lard."

"Her mother must've already come through, then. Who's the lucky prince today?"

"I can't tell exactly, bent over the way he is. Perhaps the Merman."

"For goodness, Lady Mary—likening that warty scavenger to a fantasy creature."

"Princess Lard cannot resist his siren's call," Mary teased. "Perhaps he's brung her a magic seashell."

"More likely a penny," Agnes muttered.

Mary grinned to herself and sighed again. Birds sang, and the air was sweet, indeed. Beckham Hall's upper two floors—where Mary had lived her entire life—were as lonely as ever, but she smiled because they would not be lonely for very much longer.

Besides Agnes and a handful of servants, the official Lady of

Beckham Hall had no friends, no family, and no companions of any sort. Hadn't since she was a baby and her parents had been lost at sea. Mary's father had been the warden of the Cinque Ports of England, governing the ingress and egress of ships for England's southern shores and providing a substantial navy for the king. Upon his death, Beckham Hall—and Lady Mary's guardianship—had fallen to the Crown and been held in that manner until a suitable replacement could be found for her father.

Lady Mary suspected that the king had used the lengthy search for a new warden as merely an excuse to more closely monitor the wealth going in and out of the town, and to use Beckham Hall for his own purposes; it was largely a garrison and storehouse for the endless river of fighting men. Her presence had been but an aside, and Mary assumed the king had quite forgotten about her existence until just before last Christmastime, when a ship of returning Crusaders had landed in the town and been forced to take shelter at Beckham Hall by a sudden and unusual ice storm.

That's when she had met him—her future husband, her betrothed. He'd come up the stairs from the main floor—a passage that was usually barred from the inside to protect Lady Mary from the irascible ilk of the soldiers below—seeming intent on exploring the whole of the castle. He'd been quite shocked to find Mary before the hearth in her small private hall, tending to her handwork, and her heartbeat had increased at the sight of him. He'd worn a studded, dark leather hauberk with a cross burned into the hide, his weapon still on his hip, his flowing red hair cascading in waves from his high forehead.

"A thousand pardons, my lady," he'd gasped with a low bow, and Mary's heart had trilled in her chest. "I was unaware this floor was occupied. I shall leave you posthaste."

"No," she'd called, her voice shaking with fear and excitement. She'd glanced over her shoulder to the stairs, which led to the uppermost floor and Agnes's sleeping chamber. "Please stay, if you'd care for company. I know I would."

They had talked the moon into bed that night, and Mary had only crawled beneath her own covers when the sun sparkled through her icy window and Agnes had come in bearing the breakfast tray. For the next several days, they kept the same routine—Mary would unbar the door after Agnes was abed, and she and her brave knight would talk away the hours, speaking of her lonely childhood and deceased parents, of Beckham Hall and the surrounding village, and of his heroic escapades in the Holy Land. He even carried a fantastically embroidered coin purse hidden in an ingenious flap in his leather tunic, heavy with coin.

His company had departed within the week, and it was with bitter tears that Mary had watched her soldier go, waving at him from her window high above. Only after he was gone and Agnes would not ignore the heartbroken sobs of her ward did Mary confess her late-night activities. The nurse had been scandalized and outraged and questioned Mary mercilessly after her honor, but Mary answered honestly that her virtue was still intact, for not even a kiss had her lost hero bestowed upon her.

If she had been morose during all the lonely years of her residence at Beckham Hall, Mary soon became despondent. She didn't look out her window. She'd lost all imagination for her game.

But then, on the first day of the new year, when Mary was sitting before her hearth alone, there came a rapping at the door to the lower floors. It was just past midnight. Hoping against hope, Mary had once more disregarded Agnes's primary rule and dashed down the stairs to struggle with the bar. She flung open the door to find—

A strange soldier, dusted with his road travels and a light sprinkle of snow.

"Message from the Crown for Lady Mary Beckham," the soldier had stated, thrusting a folded and sealed parchment at Mary.

She took it and secured the door once more before flying up the stairs to her chair before the hearth. Pulling the wax away with trembling fingers, she'd opened the message and read, her heart pounding in her chest.

Then she'd looked up from the royal decree and given a shout of laughter. The king had found his man, and apparently so had Mary, for she was to be wed that very year to her knight in burnished leather.

"You'd better come away now and prepare for your lessons with Father," Agnes called, stirring Mary from her delightful reverie. Mary turned and regarded the nurse as she lifted her willow basket onto her substantial hip. "I'll come back in an hour with your pudding and warm milk."

"Yes, Agnes," Mary said. And as she did as her nurse asked, Mary thought happily that the woman would soon find new purpose in caring for Mary's own children, which would surely number more than the fingers on both her hands.

Perhaps her toes as well.

Mary was waiting in the tiny chapel tucked in a corner of the same floor as her private hall when Father Braund rushed in through the arched stone doorway. He gripped his leather-bound book in both hands and, after looking around at the hall behind him frantically, began to push the rounded wooden door closed. He apparently did not trust his eyes, for he opened the door again, leaned out, his head swiveling in either direction, and then shut the door firmly. He seemed to scan the closed door, as if looking for something.

Mary smiled at the usually calm priest's odd behavior, and then her eyebrows rose as he seized the back of a plain wooden chair nearby and wedged it against the door, its back legs dropped securely into a gap in the wooden floorboards.

He'd been searching for a lock. But of course a private chapel would have no need for such secrecy, and Mary wondered why Beckham Hall's priest suddenly did.

He spun around to face her at last, his flap of graying blond hair rising like a sail over his pate; and his eyes seemed to examine the very corners of the chapel, which was no more than twenty feet squared.

"Good evening, Father Braund," Mary began. "Is something amiss?"

"Where is your nurse?" he whispered, his gaze flitting about the chamber.

"Well, I don't know exactly," Mary said, nonplussed.

"She isn't here, is she?" the priest pressed, bending at the waist and peering beneath the benches as if he expected the portly woman to spring forth, shouting "Ah-ha!"

"No," Mary said, half-laughing. "I don't expect her until our hour is complete. She is insistent that I fully comply with my instruction before becoming a married woman, and I would wager she would rather spill a chamber pot across the floor than interrupt our lessons."

The young priest shook his head, his flap of hair flopping, his eyes wide. Mary noticed he was gripping his leather book to his chest, as if clinging to the true cross itself. "No more lessons," he said. "I've information of a much graver nature to impart to you this eve."

Mary brightened. "I've completed all the lessons already?"

Again he shook his head, and his brows knit together in a pained expression. "You may not get the chance to put them into practice."

The first inklings of concern tickled at the nape of Mary's neck. "What do you mean?"

Father Braund swallowed and his eyes flicked down to the book in his hand. "Come," he said at last, scurrying to a tall, shallow side table against one of the walls. He set down his book as Mary appeared at his side.

"As you know, I must compile a document of your birth and lineage, and that of your parents', to be recorded in preparation for your marriage. Because your betrothed would gain not only your hand and Beckham Hall but also a noble position within the king's court, it is imperative that records of your pedigree be complete, for they shall be thoroughly examined by the king's advisers before your wedding takes place in the autumn."

"Yes," Mary said, "but I don't see how that could possibly give you cause for such alarm. My father's lineage is well documented here, where he and his predecessors were born for hundreds of years. And my mother's family is well known as one most loyal, even as long ago as to William. I was their only child, of that there can be no question."

"No, no—no questioning any of that at all," the priest agreed, still speaking in a raspy voice, as if he feared they would be overheard through the thick stone walls. "It's what was recorded *after* your birth that is so troubling."

Mary frowned. "After my birth?"

"Your baptism!" the priest hissed ominously.

Mary waited for further clarification from the agitated priest, but none came. "I don't understand. I was born unexpectedly at sea, on one of my father's ships, during a storm, and so the baptism was performed at a place other than Beckham Hall. But Father de Moy found nothing out of order when we at last returned home, obviously, else he would have performed the ceremony again. And he certainly never mentioned to me that anything was amiss before he died last year."

"You did receive the full sacrament, and it was recorded precisely," the priest whispered, and then leaned closer to Mary's face. "Along with another important agreement, documented here in Father de Moy's own hand." He opened the book, rifling through pages for a moment before spreading both halves flat and pushing the large tome toward her. "You can't marry your knight, my lady."

Mary was becoming worried, and that emotion wanted to manifest itself as anger. "Why ever not?" she demanded, taking hold of the book's edges and tiptoeing to lean close to the tiny scrawls, her eyes scanning the jagged marks made by Beckham Hall's longtime—and now deceased—priest.

Her eyes skipped along the unbelievable information just as the priest whispered at her shoulder.

"You're already married."

Mary read the lines scratched in the book perhaps fifty times before she straightened and looked at Father Braund. "Well," she said, "obviously I was promised in marriage shortly after my birth. But this document cannot be binding as the man has never come for me. All we need do is send a message to this family and demand that the agreement be annulled. Surely he has already married by now, or perhaps he is long dead and that is the reason we have had no word of him. His family has simply forgotten all about me."

The priest shook his head. "He's not dead."

"My goodness, how could you possibly know that?" Mary peered at the book again. "I realize I'm rather sheltered here, but I've not heard mention of any Spaniard—this . . . this Valentine Alesander." She straightened.

Father Braund swallowed.

"How do you know, then?" she demanded. "Tell me, because I will not have this man, whoever, wherever he is. I refuse to be married to *him*. I don't want *him*!"

"Well, I should hope not," the priest said. "He's a criminal wanted by the Crown."

"A *criminal*?" Mary shrieked.

"Shh!" Father Braund clutched at her arm and looked around the chapel fearfully before returning his gaze to her and continuing in a whisper. "A group of pilgrims returned from the Holy Land only a fortnight ago, bringing further word about the king of Jerusalem's defeat at his mighty fortress. It's been determined that the siege was enabled by a small group of traitors in the king's own company, and that this Alesander was among the betrayers. Four men in total—Gerard, Hailsworth, Berg, and your Alesander—all on the run, and now sought by every bounty hunter and Christian ruler the world over."

"He's not *my* Alesander!" Mary hissed. She collapsed on a bench and threw a hand over her eyes. "No! No, no, no! It was all so perfect!" After a moment she dropped her hand and turned on the bench to face Father Braund. "Surely the king would see this farce terminated. He would not hold me to such an evil agreement."

"There's more," the priest admitted. "Alesander's family was once wealthy nobles—some of the most respected and powerful in the kingdom of Aragon. But there was a rebellion, and this man—your husband—double-crossed his family and absconded with a vast portion of their wealth. It is rumored he murdered at least one of them. His kin have been searching for him for years. If they—or he—should discover his connection to you, and that you are soon to wed another, it is completely conceivable that they could come looking for you and insist that the match be honored for the dowry to replace what was lost to them, and Alesander could then lay claim to Beckham Hall." Father Braund paused, seeming to consider. "That is, of course, if he was not hanged first, leaving you a penniless widow with no home."

"He is *not . . . my . . . husband!*" Mary insisted. Her stomach knotted and her mind raced. If her betrothed—a man profoundly loyal to the Christian king of Jerusalem, who had nearly lost his own life in the Holy Land protecting King Baldwin—found out about this ancient agreement with one of the traitors, he would absolutely call off the wedding. Perhaps he would even be granted Beckham Hall for his trouble and embarrassment.

He could never find out. Never.

Mary looked up at Father Braund. "What can I do?"

The priest gave a deep sigh. "There is only one possible solution, and it is highly unlikely you would succeed."

"I don't care. I must try."

The priest nodded and then came to sit next to Mary on the bench. "Through my religious connections, I have heard of an abbey that has taken on the task of gleaning information that would bring justice to the four traitors." He reached into the folds of his robe and pulled out an object that he kept clenched in his hand. "You must visit that abbey and enter into a confessional with a red curtain. Once there, give the priest this."

He held out his hand; lying in the center of his palm was a single gold coin.

Mary picked it up with a thumb and forefinger, noting the rough edges and Latin inscription.

Father Braund continued. "Tell the priest—Father Victor—tell him everything. Tell him the name of the man you are looking for. If there is any help to be had, he will be the one to provide it. We are fortunate that your wedding is yet months away—it is common for those engaged to inter themselves at a religious house for a period of intense instruction. It should raise no suspicion with your betrothed, but we must not reveal your exact destination. To anyone. Not even to Agnes."

"Then I don't see that this is so very difficult a task after all," Mary said. "I only have need of a conveyance to carry me to whichever part of England the abbey is in, and—"

"Not England."

Mary paused. "Scotland?"

Father Braund shook his head. "Austria. On the Danube River."

"Austria?" Mary shrieked. "How am I to get to Austria? I've never even been to London!"

Father Braund stared at her for a moment. "Are you ready for a real adventure, Lady Mary?"

Chapter 2

July 1180
Melk, Austria

Valentine Alesander pretended to peruse the wares at the market stall as he circled around in pursuit of his quarry. He picked up a strand of garlic, seemed to consider it as he gave the stall's proprietor a sage nod of admiration, and then returned it to the pile. Two more slow, sidling steps to the right to the next stall, which offered a selection of cheeses.

The woman was stopped, considering a large wedge wrapped in cloth with great concentration before putting it down and picking up another, smaller piece. *Eldest daughter; many mouths, little coin.* Valentine leaned his left forearm along the stall's half wall.

"Good day," he said. "Beautiful weather for marketing, yes?"

The woman glanced up with a frown, and then her face softened as her eyes took in Valentine's person. Her lips and fingertips were stained berry pink. *Fruiter's daughter.*

"Indeed," she replied. "God is admiring his creation."

"As am I," Valentine replied, taking in the young woman's abundant curves. *Perhaps eighteen.*

Her brow wrinkled. *Steady suitor, arranged marriage.* "Well, certainly. It is your duty always to point to his wondrous deeds. Everyone appreciates your dedication."

"Is that so?" he asked, taking a half step closer. "Perhaps you would like to express your appreciation in a more . . . personal manner?"

"I—" the woman started, her frown increasing into an expression of distaste. "I must go. Good day, Brother."

"Wait," he called after her, straightening from the stall, but she had already fled through the milling crowd of the village. "Damn."

"I do believe you are losing your touch, Brother Valentine," the deep voice said from behind him. Valentine turned to see Roman Berg, a bouquet of long loaves beneath one massive arm, his voluminous robes making the man seem twice as wide as he already was.

"I am no losing my touch—it is only this damned gown," Valentine muttered, jerking at the brown cowl sagging against his chest.

"Certainly it is." Roman chuckled. "The women of Melk would not risk hell by dallying with a man under holy orders—not even one with your pretty lashes. And Victor has warned you about your forwardness with the women villagers."

"Bah, Victor. I hate this place." Valentine turned and joined Roman as the man began to walk back through the village.

"'Tis better than a Damascene dungeon."

"I will only concede that the climate is milder," he answered. "In truth, we are as trapped here as if we were still beneath Saladin's hand."

"Perhaps," Roman said. "But I still prefer this locale. And that we are not dead. Any matter, something to distract you for a bit—Stan says a large group of pilgrims has come to Melk today. I know not from which direction they hail, but perhaps they carry some bit of news. I've not seen Victor since Lauds—which you were absent from. Again."

"I am *pretending* to be a monk, Roman. *Pretending*," Valentine enunciated. "I am glad you find some enjoyment in the role, but me? Pfft!" He threw up his hands and noticed crossly how the movement caused the villagers he and Roman passed to bow their heads.

Roman smiled and raised his right hand to make the sign of the cross in the air before them. "God's blessing upon you."

Valentine only smiled stiffly until they had passed the pious group. "I suspect Victor would have us all become monks in truth!" he continued his rail. "It is Brother This and Brother That all the day—and that is when we are even allowed to speak! But do you know the worst part?" he demanded of his friend.

"No women?" Roman guessed.

"No women," Valentine said. "No a maid, a laundress—nothing! Only men!"

"Melk is an abbey of monks," Roman pointed out. "I don't know why you do this to yourself every time. Perhaps you should stop coming to the market."

"And go completely mad?" Valentine kicked at a rock in his path, very aware that the action was childish. "I hate this place."

"Well, one thing is certain—there is nowhere else for us to go in the foreseeable future, lest we yearn for stretched necks. The bounties on our heads are such that every man with a sword and a too-light purse is looking for us."

Roman came to a halt in the dirt road, having reached the end of the market and the fork that led either deeper into the village or up the long and narrow path to the monstrous abbey on the cliff overlooking the Danube River. Valentine paused to listen to his friend.

"I know you are unhappy here. But there is nothing to be done about it. I for one am not sorry that you came upon Chastellet, else Stan, Adrian, and I would all likely be dead."

The giant's words kicked at Valentine's conscience. "I am no sorry for that either, my friend. Forgive me. I am no myself today."

"I think you are very much yourself." Roman grinned and clapped Valentine on the shoulder as he nodded past it pointedly. "Cheer, Brother—it seems as though a lovely pilgrim has need of religious assistance. And since I must return to Lou in the mews, I shall leave you to her. And I shall not tell Victor. See you at supper." Roman stepped away with a wave and then turned up the path toward Melk.

"Tomorrow is my birthday," Valentine said to Roman's back when his friend was far enough away that he could not overhear. He sighed and turned to look down the path where Roman had indicated.

She approached swiftly, glancing about her, but Valentine could not tell if she was wary of someone following her or disconcerted by her surroundings. Her gown was clearly English, simple but well made. Her kirtle was a drab brown with gold braid trim and belt, revealing a plain, creamy underdress with wide bell sleeves. Her hair was the color of chestnuts, hanging long over one shoulder and twisted with ribbons. Her complexion was the epitome of an English lady of sheltered and privileged life, like the petals of a peony, a dusting of pink across her cheeks and nose. She was striking in her distress, and her eyes were locked on Valentine as her little slippered feet carried her closer.

Valentine grinned.

Happy birthday to me.

* * *

"Excuse me, man of heaven, excuse me. Good morning. I need you to helping me," Mary called out, struggling to find the right words in the language of Melk. Miraculously, the man in the brown robes seemed to be waiting for her at the top of the steep path.

She was so tired. Exhausted. The last leg of travel to this little Austrian village had nearly been Mary's undoing. Her legs and back were stiff from the long ride up and down the endless hills, and now that the horses were stabled and out of her reach, Mary had no choice but to traverse the rolling streets on foot. The natives must be part goat.

But she must hurry. If her chaperones discovered she was missing before she could reach the man she sought, a cry of alarm would be raised and she would be locked in her room at the inn until the pilgrim party moved on in the morning. She might have only minutes.

She reached him at last. "Good morning," she said with a gasp.

"Good afternoon," the monk corrected in a smooth voice, and as Mary tried to catch her breath, she noticed that this had to be the most handsome monk who'd ever donned a habit. His tanned skin fitted perfectly over the angular planes of his strong jaw. Dark brown eyes sparkled from beneath lashes that seemed too lush to belong to a man. His dark hair was cut short to his head, and although the copious brown wool hid his physique, his shoulders were broad, the tight cincture of his robe hinting at a lean frame.

"Afternoon? Excuse. I have no speaking," she apologized. "I want a man quickly."

The monk's lips parted in a grin that could only be described as devilish, his teeth shockingly white and even against his sun-kissed skin.

"Hello," he said, his English flavored with an accent that was not of this little Austrian village. "Certainly I am that man for you, my lady."

Mary gave a tremendous sigh of relief and turned her face toward the heavens. "Oh, thank God!" But she had no time for extended thanksgiving . . . they would be looking for her soon. "Are you Victor?"

The monk frowned. "Victor? No," he hedged, and then his sultry smile returned. "But you may call me Victor if it pleases you."

"No." Mary shook her head and glanced over her shoulder. "I

need Father Victor. Please, oh please, tell me that he resides in yonder abbey. I've come such a long way and my time is short."

"Well," the monk drawled, "perhaps . . . perhaps I know of a man named Victor. Indeed, I do. And perhaps," he took a step closer and reached out to touch a curl of her hair, "I could be persuaded to introduce you to him. Although I can no think how he could be of assistance to a lady as lovely as you."

Mary was near to losing control. If she did not get what she needed here in Melk, she would be swept off in the morning with the group. She closed the short distance remaining between them and grabbed the monk's cowl in both fists.

"Is he there or not?" she demanded through her teeth.

"You." The monk chuckled. "Such passion!"

Mary screeched in frustration and released him. "Never mind," she said, picking up her skirts once more and starting toward the path to the abbey. "I shall find him myself! You should be ashamed!" she tossed over her shoulder.

"Wait!" she heard him call out from behind her, and then the sound of his footfalls on the path. "I am ashamed, yes!" He came even with her once more as she tromped up the hill. "Please, do no run away. I am sorry to have disregarded your plea in my admiration. I shall take you to Victor, of course. He is right this way."

She glanced at him, thinking that perhaps she had judged him too hastily. After all, it was likely the religious behaved differently in other parts of the world.

"Thank you," Mary replied. "He must hear my confession immediately, so if you would be so kind—"

"Confession?" the monk repeated. "If that is what you seek, perhaps we should . . . share a meal first, and I could counsel you that you might completely purge your conscience."

Mary stopped in the path and gaped at him. "What kind of monk are you?"

He shrugged and gave her another grin.

"I have come all the way from England to meet this priest. I have endured weeks of road travel, sea travel, infestations of lice. I've shared a bed with an old woman who can't keep her hands to herself. I've essentially run away from home, and my nurse is likely out of her mind with worry. I am very happy that I will marry a great knight later this year, and I don't have time for your nonsense! Unless I accomplish what I set out to do *this very day*, my entire life will be ruined!" She shoved a finger into his chest. "And if it is because of *you* that I miss the opportunity to see Father Victor, I will personally see to it that you are defrocked."

His smile widened. "You wish to defrock me?"

"Argh!" Mary screamed, and once more took up her march to the abbey.

"Fine! Fine!" the monk acquiesced with a laugh. He easily matched her pace. "So determined! I do hope your betrothed knows what he is getting himself into by marrying you. I will take you to Victor."

She spoke not another word to him as they climbed the path together, and it took all of Mary's self-control not to burst into tears. As they neared the monstrous compound, she was distracted by the beauty and scale of the abbey. Imposing winged cherubim stood watch on both sides of the wrought gates, and inside the bailey, Mary was surprised by the cultivated gardens, fountains, and pools, and the numerous statues that gave the area the feel of a luxurious royal enclosure.

Everywhere she looked, men in brown robes seemed hard at work at some task, or floated past her en route to another part of the massive structure. The long, rectangular courtyard was edged against the steep walls by a covered walkway, where delicate columns upheld graceful arches, and within the shadows she saw even more brethren. None seemed to pay any attention at all to her arrival. Her ears were filled with the sounds of bubbling and splashing water, sweet birdsong, distant bells, and . . .

Nothing else. She guessed there must be over a hundred monks within earshot, but there was no laughter, no conversation, no calls.

She turned to her reluctant escort. "Is this a silent order?"

He only gave her a sideways look of exasperation.

Mary allowed herself a little smile. "That must be quite uncomfortable for a brother of your . . . loquacious nature." Another glance confirmed her observation was accurate by the tight line of his finely shaped lips. He couldn't speak here.

He guided her through one of the arches by taking hold of her elbow, but Mary shook him off, choosing to follow at the hem of his swishing robes. They entered the abbey proper through a set of vestibules, ever increasing in size, and then through a maze of wide corridors, until they came into a long, narrow hall.

A bank of shallow windows were set up against the ceiling, perhaps thirty feet above Mary's head, casting dusty beams of late-afternoon light against the opposite wall. Row upon row of skinny benches ran parallel to a bank of curtained confessionals, the wood ornately carved into splinter-intricate designs. The heavy drapes were pulled to the side of each one, showing that each closet was empty. Mary's eyes scanned the small enclosures.

The curtains were all green.

She turned to the monk at her side, already shaking her head. "This isn't the right place."

His eyes glanced around the empty room before whispering in reply, "If it is confession you seek, I assure you this is where it is done."

"No!" she half-shouted, the word echoing against the stones. She spun around. "There must be another—" Then her eyes landed on the single wooden box nestled in a far corner, separated from the bank of confessionals by a small arched passageway.

The curtain was red.

Mary half-ran to the solitary confessional, her dubious companion hurrying to keep up.

"No!" he hissed. "No that one!"

She reached the box and spun on her heel just as the monk caught up with her. "Fetch Father Victor. I'll wait for him here."

"You can no use that one," the monk repeated. "It is for the bishop. Or the king. Or . . . I do no actually remember," he admitted. "But no one may enter without permission."

"I have permission," Mary assured him, "and I'll wait here as long as it takes." She spun again to duck inside the confessional and flopped down on the narrow little bench hovering over the kneeler.

The monk stood there for a moment, his dark eyes glancing around the long hall again before leaning slightly into the closet.

"May I . . . join you?" he asked.

Mary extended her arm, placed her palm against his chest, and shoved. Then she grabbed the edge of the red curtain and whisked it closed, ensconcing herself in murky darkness.

"I can wait here if you wish to think about it."

Mary rolled her eyes. "*Victor*," she reminded.

She heard the monk's defeated sigh from beyond, and then his reluctant footsteps fading away.

With the tomblike silence settling around her like the lingering smell of old incense, Mary began to tremble. And then, as if at last she had awakened from a very long nightmare, she acknowledged the reality of where she was, how very far from home, and what she had done. She reached into a fold of her kirtle and found the little gold coin, tied into a knot of belting, and gripped it in her sweaty fist.

And then Mary went to her knees on the hard wooden ledge, leaning her forehead against her hands folded around the coin, and began to pray.

Chapter 3

It had taken Valentine nearly a half hour to locate the skinny old abbot, and then nearly that amount of time again before Victor would pay him any mind. In the end, Valentine had had to resort to calling in a low voice before the head of the abbey turned to him with a cross expression. But once Valentine had begun to explain that there was a strong-headed young Englishwoman who had insisted on taking up residence in the red confessional, all traces of annoyance were gone. In fact, Victor had abruptly left Valentine standing in the corridor with no more explanation than a hasty thanks.

By the time he came into the dining hall for the last meal of the day, Valentine was extremely cross. It didn't help matters that his late arrival forced him to take the only empty seat available, at the table of the abbey's misfits.

That the seating arrangement also included two of his own friends did not appease him.

He stepped over the bench and then sat down between Roman and the albino with a grimace, shaking his head slightly at his giant friend's inquisitive look.

How'd you do?

Do no ask.

Then Valentine gave a grumbling sigh and ran a hand up over his face as the stench of Brother Wyn climbed his person like the attentions of an unwanted whore.

"Gah." He gasped into his sleeve.

"Shh," came the admonition from behind, and Valentine glanced sideways as Stan reached around him to set a long wooden bowl of sliced bread in the center of the table. Valentine had forgotten that it was Stan's turn to serve, and it only made his mood darker—only two more days before Valentine would be forced to slave in the kitchens for an entire week like some tavern wench.

Stan moved to the next table as another monk came down the line, setting platters of fish and potatoes before each diner, followed by another monk with the water pitchers. Across the table from Valentine and to the left sat one of the twins, either Vladislav or Ladislav, then Valentine's friend Adrian, who seemed even more sickly outside of the library. The other twin flanked Adrian on the right. That, at least, was something to be grateful for; Valentine would not be forced to contend with the twins reaching across his own trencher, each trying to give his food away bit by bit to his brother with increasing forcefulness. Valentine hoped it wouldn't deteriorate into yet another hour of bits of herring being flung about.

Then the mucousy clearing of a throat sounded, and all eyes dropped to the table top—except Valentine's, who dared to glance at Victor's second in command, the fat Brother Hilbert. As if the rotund monk knew that Valentine would dawdle, his beady eyes landed on him. Valentine complied by bowing his head, if only to get to the mediocre meal faster.

The blessing went on for a quarter hour. At the last "Amen," Valentine swooped his hand around in the air before his face in a sacrilegious farce, and then pulled his trencher toward him as the dining hall broke out in conversation at last.

"You lost your little bird, I suppose?" Roman queried matter-of-factly as he tucked into his fish.

"Oh, no, my friend," Valentine argued. "Indeed, I know exactly where she is. I brought her back to the abbey with me."

The big blond man coughed as if he would choke. He chewed quickly and swallowed. "You brought her *here*?"

On Valentine's other side, Brother Wyn's attention had been drawn at the mention of an animal.

"Bird, you say?" he demanded, his sudden movement bestirring the stench of him. "What species?"

Roman leaned forward to look past Valentine at the albino. "You wouldn't be interested. Quite common."

"It's not a white-throated needletail, is it?" Brother Wyn insisted. "I've males but no female."

"Shocking!" one of the twins gasped, and then the brothers twittered and snickered.

"How precious," Adrian slurred as he pushed his food around his trencher. "The pair of you can take your birds for air together, tuck them in at night, sing them lullabies. . . ."

Now Valentine wished they had been forced to keep their silence. "It is only a pilgrim, Adrian, insisting Victor hear her confession in the red—"

But before he could finish his sentence, Roman had swung his beefy left forearm into Valentine's chest, knocking him backward from the bench to land on the stone floor. His cup went flying from his hand, his robes up around his knees.

"What the—" Valentine began, but Roman was already at his side, helping him to his feet.

"My apologies, Brother," he said, and then as he yanked Valentine from the floor, Roman turned his back to the table. *Shut up,* he mouthed. "My arm must have slipped. It still pains me at times."

Valentine was straightening his robes when his eyes caught sight of Adrian between the snickering twins. Adrian looked as though it had been he who had been knocked on his arse. Valentine shook off Roman's attempt at help.

"Pilgrims *are* quite common," Brother Wyn agreed, waving his hand and dismissing the whole display as uninteresting.

Before Valentine and Roman could take their seats once more, Stan came striding through the hall toward them. He slid his still-laden tray of fruit onto a table but did not look at his friends.

"Let's go," he said in a low voice as he passed.

Across the table, Adrian stood up and limped away without a word, and Vladislav and Ladislav descended upon Adrian's abandoned trencher like vultures.

"Brother, you must take this food."

"No, you most certainly should have it."

"I could not sleep knowing you had gone without. I insist—"

"No, *I* insist."

Valentine looked to Roman, who wore a grim expression as he said, "You heard Stan. Let's go."

"What is this about?" Valentine demanded as he and Roman followed Adrian's hitching gait through the passageways of the abbey. Certainly their destination was the library, but why would Stan call them from the meal so conspicuously?

"You shouldn't have spoken of the red confessional in the hall," Roman admonished.

"And Stan has enchanted hearing that he would know of my indiscretion?" Valentine scoffed. "It is a confessional in an abbey—why is that a secret?"

"Do you hear nothing Victor says?"

"I try no to," Valentine admitted.

Before his friend could chastise him further, they reached the double doors at the end of the long corridor. Adrian had already pulled one open just enough to slip inside, and Valentine and Roman followed, the latter being certain to close both doors behind them.

They moved through the long, silent room that was the abbey's official library. Perhaps sixty feet in length and thirty in width, the ceiling reached upward of twenty feet at the height of its arch. The walls were lined with shelves from the richly carpeted floors to the elaborate ceiling, and contained thousands of tomes in a hundred languages. In this room one could find material on any subject imaginable, and many had been transcribed by Melk's brethren.

Between the laden shelves were long, narrow floor-to-ceiling windows, leaded and cased with stone, the panes tinted in various colors similar to those in a cathedral, to protect the library's interior from the harsh light of the sun while still being bright enough to allow for reading without the danger of open flames. The effect was such that the room's atmosphere was as muted as the light, hushed by the upholstered chairs, the dim gleam of the tables.

It was suppertime at the abbey, and so the library was empty, fortunate for the friends as they crossed to the particularly wide bank of shelves in the center of the right wall of the library—the only section that was not uniform with the rest of the room's design. If one should look up at the exterior of the wall from the hill outside the abbey, it would appear that this section of Melk abutted the gatehouse directly.

Valentine and Roman were at Adrian's heels as he reached up with one arm—the sleeve of his robe sliding back to his elbow and revealing the misshapen muscles in his forearm—and pulled out a tome that seemed as anonymous as the ones stretching to either side.

But at the book's tilt, a soft click and then a softer creak sounded and a section of the bookshelf shifted. Adrian reached along the bottom of one of the shelves for the shallow handhold and pulled the secret door open.

Then the trio stepped into one of Melk's greatest treasures—the abbey's *true* library, and the place that had been Valentine and his friends' private refuge since their arrival late last October.

This room, too, was filled with manuscripts, but unlike the ones that lined the shelves in the outer library, these books were not copied texts produced by the monks; they were original manuscripts written in the hands of their authors. Works on astronomy, mathematics, anatomy, architecture; writings of saints, popes, emperors, and kings—priceless firsthand accounts from the greatest geniuses who had ever lived.

Victor and Constantine were already within, seated at the large, square table in the center of the room; Valentine thought they must have come up through the gatehouse. Adrian went to his high-backed chair set at an angle to the long, deep window that, from the outside, appeared to be nothing more than an arrow slit.

Victor wasted no time. "We have a problem, gentleman," he said, and his eyes locked on Valentine's.

Valentine sighed and then spread his arms wide and sank into a bow. "I am very sorry that I allowed the woman to breach the sanctity of the little wooden box." He arose and let his arms fall as he looked around at his friends. "But I can assure you that I had no choice. She was determined to wait for Victor there, and I dared no refuse her lest she scream down the walls and disturb your holy silence."

Stan shook his head. "That's not the problem, Valentine."

Roman took a seat across the table from the abbot, but Valentine preferred to stand. Close to the exit. He was not certain that this little meeting would not yet find him at fault.

Victor continued. "You acted correctly in showing the lady to the red confessional, although I do wish you had paid more heed to my instructions for its use."

"Again, I apologize. I do hope the sack of coin we gifted you at our arrival helps to offset your annoyance with me," Valentine said, speaking of the Chastellet gold carried by Roman on the men's long flight from Damascus—the portion that had not been lost to Saladin's guards.

"It is in speaking of that coin that I have my own confession to make," Victor continued.

Valentine's interest was piqued, and so he pulled out his chair and sat at last.

"Perhaps a month after your arrival here, I entered into a deep introspection, not only of the facts that Constantine and the rest of you had presented to me about the charges against you all, but of my own soul and conscience."

Valentine glanced at Stan. How much of this explanation did Constantine already know? Likely all of it, Valentine mused. But that suited him well enough; Constantine Gerard was the general, after all. If anyone knew now how to be deliberate in actions and planning, it was he.

"I worried that beyond giving the four of you asylum at Melk, there was little I could do to help you extricate yourselves from these wicked accusations. I want nothing more than for your names to be cleared. For Constantine to be reunited with his wife and son; Adrian, his family; Roman, his good name and livelihood returned." He paused when his eyes fell on the last man, and a prickle of irritation tickled at Valentine's spine. "And for you to have back the life that you wish, Valentine."

Not even God himself is capable of that, Valentine thought.

"I at first intended to use the coin to further Melk's ministries," Victor continued, "but, after reflection, it seemed neglectful, when I had the four of you here, whose futures were so imperiled." Victor took a deep breath. "And so I dispersed the coin from Chastellet."

Valentine leaned forward in his chair. "I beg your pardon—you did what?"

"I gave it away," Victor said. "To trusted religious contemporaries at houses in all corners of the earth."

"You gave away the coin," Valentine repeated.

"Wait, Valentine," Stan requested.

"Yes. With instructions that requested any monk, prior, abbess, sister, priest—anyone connected to me or to Melk—to send any with your names on their lips to me here, with the stated intention of 'bringing justice to the traitors of Chastellet.'"

From his chair near the window, Adrian Hailsworth muttered, "That's brilliant, Victor."

"Indeed," Roman chimed in. "For where else could one go with information of such a dangerous nature if not to his trusted priest? And then word could be sent safely here to you, and to us."

"Exactly," Stan said. "And now it seems as though Victor's efforts are at last beginning to bear fruit."

The abbot nodded. "It has taken a bit longer than I'd hoped, and this first encounter was not at all what I expected." He looked up at Valentine again. "We have a problem."

"So you have said," Valentine replied.

"The woman you brought into Melk is betrothed to be married in only a few months, but the family priest—a man I indeed know personally—has discovered that the marriage cannot take place because of an agreement entered into by the woman's parents shortly after her birth."

"A childhood marriage?" Roman guessed.

"Yes," Victor confirmed. "Her parents died less than a year after the agreement was made. The woman has no choice but to track down the man to whom she is bound and have the record expunged. There can be no trace of the man's name connected to her, lest the match be lost."

"I fail to see the correlation," Adrian mused from his chair. "Why would your priest friend send her to us? Are we to locate her wayward spouse?"

"She's already found him," Victor said. "The conundrum she faces is returning with him to England to annul the agreement."

"I, too, fail to see our part in this," Valentine said.

"The man is wanted for conspiracy, with a great price on his head."

Valentine shrugged. "Yes, well, I can sympathize with him."

"He is thought to be in hiding."

"Of course." Valentine hoped he looked as unimpressed as he felt.

"He is also being hunted by his own family."

Valentine frowned. Then he glanced around the table at his friends. They were all staring at him; Roman's blond eyebrows were raised.

Victor's next words drew Valentine's attention once more. "The same family who witnessed the agreement, which was entered into a score and six years ago, in the Spanish kingdom of Aragon."

And then memories that he hadn't visited for years bloomed in Valentine's mind:

Playing on the damp shore, watching the black clouds race off toward the horizon. The small wooden ship floundering on the reef, listing dangerously. The big bearded man rowing ashore, his words foreign but his anxiety clear.

"The man she seeks," Victor said, interrupting his thoughts of the past, "is none other than Valentine Alesander."

"Valentine is married?" Roman asked, his disbelief clear in his tone.

From his window seat, Adrian Hailsworth chuckled. "To a lovely English lady, no less."

Valentine still could not find any words. The woman in the red confessional had come all this way to find *him*? And she was his *wife*, who needed him to accompany her back to England?

She needed him to accompany her back to England.

"Valentine?" Stan prompted. "What say you? If we refuse the woman, surely she will raise a hue and cry and betray our location."

"And divulge to her betrothed the sordid details of her marriage to a criminal?" Adrian challenged. "I do doubt it."

Roman held out a large palm. "Perhaps Valentine should not have the arrangement annulled. What if he were to remain married to her? Perhaps it would alleviate his boredom with our captivity, and, if she is wealthy, any resources she possesses might benefit us."

Adrian snorted. "Oh, yes, let's do keep her. Like a *pet*. May we, Victor? May we?"

"She cannot stay here," Victor said, choosing to ignore Adrian's snideness. "She is missing from her home, and now from the group of pilgrims with whom her priest arranged for her to travel. Should she not return before her wedding, her betrothed will surely retrace her journey to Melk. It would not do to have authorities from the Crown sniffing about the abbey."

"Valentine?" Stan prompted again.

"What can I say?" Valentine said, forcing a great sigh and holding out his hands. "I must go."

"The journey will be dangerous," Roman warned.

"No worry, my friend—I am a dangerous man myself." He looked to Victor. "She will pay me for my trouble, yes?"

"That I do not know," Victor said. "Perhaps once the agreement is terminated, she might compensate you for your return journey. I've given her a chamber for the night so that she might evade the group she came with, and she has agreed to leave at first light so as not to be seen. I have prepared a letter for you that you might take to some friends of mine in Vienna to outfit yourself properly for your journey.

You'll continue on to Prague from there, I assume. It will be cooler in the north."

Valentine looked at the priest and raised an eyebrow. "You were so certain of my cooperation?"

"Yes."

Valentine felt his mouth pull downward at this admission, but he had to agree. Stay at this damnable abbey for an unknowable amount of time or accompany a beautiful woman on a journey across the map—leaving tomorrow, no less? No choice at all.

Happy birthday to me, indeed.

Chapter 4

Lady Mary Beckham waited in the abbey's great courtyard in the darkness before sunrise, the mount beneath her and the quiet abbot her only companions. Her nerves jangled as she checked and rechecked her seat on the saddle of the small horse she'd bought from the religious house, adjusted her skirts, patted her purse beneath her kirtle, looked over her shoulder at her small satchel strapped behind her.

Valentine Alesander was here. Here, at Melk.

And in a few moments she would at last come face to face with the man she had traveled a thousand miles to find. She should have been triumphant at her amazing good fortune, but instead she felt only like a bundle of raw nerves. A notorious criminal. A disgraced Spanish noble. For the next several weeks, her husband.

She wondered what he would look like.

Then her heart leaped into her throat as a shadow emerged from the darkened arch near the abbey's wide gates. Two shadows; three.

The men moved into the light cast by the torch attached to the nearest support column, and one by one Mary took measure of them:

The first man was stocky, well built, his expression serious beneath his mane of tawny hair. He moved with the confidence of a noble. But this was no Spaniard.

Mary came to the same conclusion as the wide black shadow that followed revealed itself to be a mountain of a Norseman, with white-blond hair and a hooded falcon, of all things, perched on his shoulder.

She held her breath as the third shadow limped into the circle and revealed itself to be a long-haired man of aquiline visage, his gaze upon her blatantly suspicious. His skin was ashen, his eyes circled from either lack of sleep or heavy mental burdens, and Mary thought that if it were true, what the abbot had said—that Valentine Alesander and those he traveled with had been unjustly accused—then this man certainly had reason to lose sleep.

The first man stepped to her side and bowed. "Lady Mary, I am Lord Constantine Gerard, Earl of Chase. It is a pleasure to make your acquaintance."

"How do you do," Mary responded, startled. "Chase? I do believe we are neighbors."

"Indeed," Constantine Gerard said, and something like hope flickered across his face. "Are you familiar with Benningsgate Castle, Lady Mary? Or perhaps my wife, Patrice? She is known far and wide as a most generous hostess."

"I'm sorry, no," Mary replied. "I've not gone farther than our village more than a handful of times. I have heard of your wonderful estate, though."

The giant man stepped forward, Mary thought to cover the earl's almost palpable disappointment. "Then you most certainly are having a grand adventure, are you not?" The man bowed, and his falcon twitched its wings to steady itself. "Roman Berg, my lady. I consider your"—he paused and seemed to reevaluate his words—"Valentine is my closest friend."

"How do you do?" Mary said, giving the man a slight smile, but she could not keep her gaze from flicking to the shadows, waiting for a fourth man to emerge. She looked to the abbot. "Perhaps we should send for him? The sun will soon rise and—"

"Fear not, my lady," the third and heretofore brooding man said. "He shall arrive at the very last moment; it is his signature. Adrian Hailsworth, at your service." But he inclined his head only slightly.

"Indeed, last-moment arrivals are Valentine's specialty," Constantine Gerard said, having apparently regained his composure. "His . . . *expertise* has been invaluable to us. There is no one better able to guide you unseen back to England."

"He saved our lives," Roman Berg volunteered.

Adrian Hailsworth shook his head once, a mere flick. "I do believe that distinctive honor lies with you, Roman."

"I could have never come to Damascus without Valentine," Roman argued. "We would have never known of Melk."

"He is a man of honor," Constantine agreed. "Although oft times that is not the appearance he presents. You would do well to remember that when perhaps he behaves . . ."

"Badly," Adrian Hailsworth finished in a flat tone.

Now Mary was thoroughly confused. Her nerves were so fresh already, and she suspected the hardest part of her adventure had yet even to begin. Was this Alesander a criminal or not? Father Victor had assured her that she had nothing to fear from this man, and as the priest had once been a close friend to her own Father Braund, Mary had no choice but to put her faith in him, as well as in Valentine Alesander.

If he ever arrived . . .

"Perhaps he has changed his mind?" Mary fretted to the group.

"And forsake the opportunity of a journey with a woman of such remarkable beauty and passion?" The voice came from beyond the circle of light.

That accent. She'd heard it before. A tingle raced up her spine. *No, it couldn't be . . .*

Then he stepped from the shadow, and Mary was shocked into silence at the embroidered tunic of blue and gold, his silken, fringed belt, the tight breeches, which fit his lean legs like a second skin, the fine tooling of his boots. Her eyes traveled back up and saw once more the angular jaw, the sparkling eyes, the dark, silky-looking hair.

"I would never." He smiled at her and then swept into a grandiose bow. "So we meet again, my lady."

"You?" Mary said. "You are Valentine Alesander?"

He inclined his head and brought one hand to cover the area of his heart. "It is my most sincere pleasure to meet you properly at last."

Mary felt as if there was a tight band constricted around her chest. "Where are your robes?" she demanded, half in a panic. She could not be expected to travel any distance with a man of such obviously forward appetites.

He raised a slender eyebrow but replied good-naturedly. "They are in my bags. I would no risk being recognized as we leave the village. The people here know me only through my connection with the abbey."

The morose Adrian Hailsworth snorted. "And Brother Valentine certainly could not be seen associating with a young lady."

Mary frowned through her blush at the implication of Adrian Hailsworth's comment. This was not going at all the way she had planned, but she could not determine if the surprises were of the better or disastrous sort.

Before she could ask any further questions, a monk so pale as to be almost transparent brought Alesander's horse to him, already laden with satchels. The Spaniard took the reins and swung easily onto the beast, and Father Victor put his blessing upon them while the albino monk disappeared without a word into the blackness of an archway.

The sky was lightening. Pale gray, the clouds overhead rippled like steam.

"Well, then," Constantine Gerard said and then turned to Mary, giving her a shallow bow. "God's speed, my lady." He shook hands with Alesander. "Remember, you have our lives in your hands yet again."

"I shall do my best," Alesander vowed.

Adrian Hailsworth clasped hands with him next, quickly and stiffly. "Good-bye." He inclined his head toward Mary once more but said nothing, and then limped off into the shadows alone.

Roman was the last to wish them farewell, and he held his friend's wrist longer than the others. "Come back to us, Val," Roman said. "I shall not be able to endure Brother Wyn without you."

"It would be a long time to hold your breath," Alesander replied with a smile. "Give the villagers my love should they miss me."

"I'm certain they shall." Roman laughed. He released his friend and stepped away, bowing to Mary. "My lady."

Father Victor had already slipped away on his quiet monk's feet; Constantine Gerard and Roman Berg moved back into the shadows. From the corner of her eye, Mary saw one-half of Melk's wide gate open slowly—that was where the abbot had gone, she realized as she saw his long, bell-like shadow.

She turned to Alesander and discovered that he was regarding her with a charming grin. She wondered if he had any other expression.

"Shall we, my lady?"

"I'm afraid I'm not at all sure," Mary blurted out.

Valentine Alesander threw back his head and laughed, the merry sound filling the abbey's bailey. Then his eyes seemed to sparkle even more brightly as he met her gaze and kicked at his horse's sides.

"Vamanos!"

* * *

Valentine took a deep breath of the cool, humid air wafting up from the Danube as if he had never smelled it before. Indeed, it was different air—air he would not breathe again for months, perhaps. He leaned back in the saddle as his horse started down the narrow path toward the growing dawn and the crossroads of the village, Mary Beckham following along behind him.

"We don't dare go into the village," she called out.

"Of course no," he assured her, unable to keep the smile from his mouth. The day was just so . . . fine.

He urged his horse to the left of the path, cutting through a sloped field of tall grass that abutted the abbey's steeper motte, and headed north toward a small tributary of the river.

"How long will it take us to reach Vienna?" she called out again.

"Three days. Perhaps four," he answered.

"Four days?" she repeated. "To the east?"

"Mmm," Valentine confirmed. Could she not simply relax and enjoy this time?

Apparently not, for he heard the clip-clop of her horse's hooves as she urged the animal alongside his.

"That's too long," she said. "Too long, in the wrong direction. If it takes us four days to get there, that means we must travel four days west to make up for it. That's eight days."

"Yes. It is," Valentine agreed. "Unless we run into bad weather, of course. But it can no be helped. It is a glorious morning, yes?"

"I don't think you understand. I am in a terrible hurry."

"I do understand, I do," he insisted. "But success on our journey begins with being properly equipped, and then joining with the best road. There is a major route between Vienna and Prague—well traveled, so generally passable most of the year. We will be safer, and travel faster, even considering the four days it may take us to reach Vienna."

To his amusement, Mary Beckham reined her horse to a halt. He obligingly did the same and looked back at her with a smile. She was completely lovely in the sunrise.

"Can we not simply head north now and intersect the route between Vienna and Prague?"

Completely lovely when her mouth was closed.

"No," he answered.

Her horse danced, sensing her frustration.

"Why not?"

"Primarily because we need the sort of supplies that we can get only in Vienna. Secondarily, there is currently a little river between us and the route. Perhaps you have seen it, yes? We can no cross it except by ferry."

He saw her frown deepen as she looked past him. "There is a ferry in Melk."

"Yes, there is," he acquiesced. "You wish to wait for the ferry master to awaken, and take the chance of alerting the party you arrived with?"

"No." She sighed.

He turned forward in the saddle and kicked his horse. A moment later, he heard her follow.

"Why can we not follow the Danube south? Perhaps meet the Rhine and then proceed through Normandy?"

"Too crowded," he explained. "This time of year is popular for travel, and in all likelihood we could no keep our horses with us. There are few barges that make a leg of any length that could accommodate mounts. It is tournament season in Normandy—it will be full of the nobility and even royalty. Wise to avoid in our situation."

"I didn't actually mean to suggest that we travel on the rivers themselves. I don't do well on the water," she said stiffly and then was silent for a moment. "You seem to know an awfully lot about . . . well, everything," she said.

"I have traveled extensively," he admitted.

"While trying to evade your family?" she asked.

He turned to look at her—she had come even with him again. It was a distasteful topic, but Valentine thought there was a chance it would come up at some point during their journey. Perhaps it was better to get it out of the way now.

"Yes," he said patiently. "It is true that there are some members of my family who . . . are pondering my whereabouts."

"Who?" she pressed.

Valentine paused at her forwardness. "My brother. A cousin, perhaps. You are very interested in my past—a topic I prefer to keep more or less private."

She smiled at him, and he was charmed at the transformation of her face. "More or less?"

"Private," he repeated.

"I *am* interested," she admitted. "I have no family of my own, and this is the first journey I've ever made from my home, not to mention alone with a strange man. Whether we like it or not, we must accept each other as part of our own pasts."

"Very true," Valentine agreed, his mouth turning down at the corners as he considered her observation. And since it had been she who broached the subject of their histories, he asked, "No family at all?"

"None. Only a nurse."

"Does she know where you are?"

Mary Beckham shook her head. "Our priest told her that I have gone on a prenuptial pilgrimage. I'm certain she is mad with worry."

"What of the people you journeyed to Melk with?" Valentine asked. "Who are they?"

"A group of elderly nobles eager to see the world, now that their children have taken over the duties of their estates. My personal companion was a dowager countess called Lady Elmsbeth. Very nice woman."

"I thought you said she was . . . pluckish?"

Mary Beckham blushed. "You must understand the desperation I felt when we met yesterday. Our party needed to travel so very slowly to accommodate our aged members, and I feared I had come all this way for naught—that Victor would have no answers for me, if even he was at the abbey at all. Lady Elmsbeth is only lonely, and seeking someone to look after."

"Then she is likely despairing at your sudden disappearance."

"Likely," Mary said, looking back in the direction of the village, which now had sunk nearly out of sight between the hills of the shallow valley. Valentine could see the guilt Mary Beckham felt as clearly as if she had been clothed in sackcloth and ashes.

"You will perhaps use the time between Melk and Vienna to practice guarding your emotions," Valentine advised.

"What do you mean?"

"We shall likely have to . . . tell some untruths so as to remain anonymous. For instance, in Vienna, perhaps we are brother and sister. Do you think you can imagine being someone you are not?"

She gave him a smile that was more than a bit enigmatic and, try as he might, he could not decipher its cause in her eyes.

"That does sound like a rather interesting way for one to pass the time."

They rode until the sun was high in the sky before stopping to give their horses rest. Several smaller paths converged on the Vienna road at a bend in the river, where a small grove of gnarled, low-branched trees protected the bank. Valentine swung from his horse and then did not hesitate in turning to help Mary dismount. He took swift charge of their animals, leading them to the river and letting them dip their heads while he unstrapped one of his bags and a blanket roll from his saddle.

Mary went upstream from the horses to splash her face with the refreshing water and then cup her hands for a quick drink. She paused, watching her companion as he unfurled the blanket beneath the widest tree. Every move he made was confident, deliberate, efficient. He didn't seem fatigued at all from the morning's journey, and in fact even his costume was still pristine. Mary guessed it was from the obvious quality of the material, and she wondered how he'd acquired such fine garments. She was a titled lady, after all, and yet her entire ensemble was worth perhaps only one quarter of Valentine Alesander's tunic.

She had to admit that he was handsome. Not only handsome—his features were captivating. And when he spoke, the flip of his accent was soft on her ears, warming to her skin, like the glow of good spirits in her belly on a cold night. She couldn't prevent herself from drawing comparisons between Alesander and her future husband: her betrothed was English—white, polite—almost hesitant at times. But he was direct and he had never done anything to compromise her reputation.

On the other hand, she was very certain that Valentine Alesander had sought to compromise her reputation at their first meeting on the path to the abbey, while he had been wearing monk's robes. He'd made no overtures since they'd been properly introduced, though, and so Mary hoped he would remain well behaved.

He rose up from the blanket he'd been kneeling on and hailed her with a long arm.

"My lady," he called. "Would you care to dine?"

Mary realized she was starving.

He had laid a feast for them on the blanket: stuffed cabbage leaves, a small round of dark bread, a hefty wedge of fragrant cheese, and a finely woven sack filled with dried figs and dates and raisins. A short, fat, leather-wrapped bottle sat near the food, its chained cork dangling, and two silver cups stood at the ready.

"I'd no idea the brothers ate so well," she said with a smile as she sank to her hip on the far side of the blanket from him.

"They do no," Valentine said, picking up the bottle and pouring. "I liberated the ingredients from the abbey's larder and prepared it myself after I learned of our journey last eve."

Mary blinked. "You made all of this?"

"I have many talents," he said, handing Mary a cup and then raising his own to her in a silent salute before drinking. He sighed with relish. "It is very good, yes?"

She swallowed a mouthful of cabbage and lamb and spices. "Yes, it's delicious!"

His smile broadened and he set his cup aside to pick up one of the rolls. "Since we are to be in each other's company for many weeks, shall I call you Maria?"

"My name is Mary," she clarified, a little stung that he had so quickly forgotten.

"Oh, yes, I know," Valentine assured her. "But in my country, you would be Maria." He half-sang the word, and the way it danced for him made Mary's cheeks heat.

"In your country, you would likely be dead," she pointed out, trying to cover her flush.

He laughed and drank again. When he set his cup down once more, it was slightly closer to Mary's. He leaned far across the food to grab a handful of fruit from the sack, and when he settled back onto the blanket, Mary noticed he was perhaps twice as close to her as he had been only a moment before. She wasn't sure how he had managed the move so slickly.

He kept the smile on his face as he popped a few pieces into his mouth. "You may call me Valentine, of course. In my country, we say Valen*teen*, but you may pronounce it however you wish."

Mary fussed at her skirts, avoiding his warm gaze.

"I have yet to hear my name from your lips—will you indulge me?"

"Valentine," she said distractedly, looking over his shoulder.

"Very nice," he praised, drawing even closer to her.

"Valentine?" she repeated.

"Yes, that is right. Did you know that today is my bir—"

She put her hand over his mouth, her fingers flattening his nose and stopping his advance. *"Valentine, someone's coming."*

Chapter 5

Not someone, some*ones*.

A trio of riders came onto the Vienna road from one of the smaller paths. Men of some means, by the look of their fine horses and sheathed weapons. One even had a small leather shield tied behind him. They had apparently spotted Valentine and Mary from the road and were slowing their horses, turning toward the grove of trees.

Damn! He'd allowed himself to become so distracted by the lovely English flower at his side that he hadn't heard even a whisper of their approach. Valentine slid a respectable distance from Maria and casually felt inside the top of his boot; his dagger was there.

"Now seems as good a time as any," he remarked to the woman beside him, whose eyes were wide. "Remember, brother and sister. Only follow my lead."

She murmured assent.

"Ho there," one of the men called out. He walked his horse closer to where Valentine and Maria sat, and his face was openly curious. "Good day! How do you find the road to Vienna?"

"Good day to you," Valentine said. "It is well, although my lady sister does no care for the dust."

"Isn't it the same for most? Good day, my lady." The traveler smiled at Maria before surveying the items on the blanket. His eyes went from Valentine to Maria again, more cautiously. It was not completely unlikely to find siblings who appeared to be so unrelated. Not common, though.

Valentine sought to distract the man. "Have you made a long journey?"

"Not half as long as it shall be at its end," the man confessed. His gaze lingered on Maria, and Valentine decided he did not like the interest he saw there. "We are en route to Vienna, and then on through the Continent to Constantinople. What of you?"

"Also Vienna," Maria chirped.

"Brussels," Valentine offered in the same moment. He winced inwardly as Maria's gaze flew to his.

The man's forehead wrinkled. "You mean you've come from Brussels to Vienna?"

Mary nodded hesitantly.

"No." Valentine laughed.

Now the traveler frowned outright.

"You must forgive my sister," Valentine offered with a rueful glance in Maria's direction. "She is easily confused. This is her first journey of any length, and she is somewhat of a fool when she is at home."

At his side, Maria gasped.

But Valentine didn't look at her, and the traveler laughed. "I have two like that of my own," he said, but his attention was more concentrated than ever, and Valentine did not like to be marked in the man's memory. "It is unusual to see a brother and sister who do not compare in the least," he remarked in a leading tone.

"We are related by marriage," Valentine said, dropping his smile.

"I see," the man said, but Valentine could tell that he was unconvinced. The traveler glanced over his shoulder at his companions, who were talking in quiet voices, their eyes seeming to examine Valentine. "We will just avail ourselves of the river then." He nodded to Maria, and then urged his mount onward to the bank, his friends watching Valentine and Maria brazenly as they followed.

Valentine watched them back.

When the men were a fair distance away, Maria leaned toward him and hissed, "I am not a fool"

"Why do you care what they think of you?" Valentine demanded, picking up his cup. "Perhaps you could pretend to eat something until they are gone? We will talk about it later. No, no—do no turn around to look at them."

He could tell she was steaming from his reprimand, but to her credit she picked up a cabbage roll and nibbled at it and did not turn around.

Valentine watched the men gather in a close knot to confer with one another, casting glances in his direction the entire time. Valentine sipped his wine and hoped he would not have to kill anyone so soon after leaving Melk, and so close to a main thoroughfare.

But they remounted a quarter hour later, riding close past them again and nodding. "Safe journey to you," the leader called out. "Perhaps we will meet again. My lady."

Valentine lifted his cup.

He waited, saying nothing, until the band of riders had dipped below a hill in the road, appeared on the next incline, and then were gone into a stand of trees that enclosed the road perhaps a mile away. Then he got to one knee and began gathering the uneaten portion of what was supposed to have been a romantic meal.

"Get up," he said. "We must be away quickly."

"Are we to follow them?" Maria asked.

Valentine paused and looked at her, trying very hard to hold his tongue. "No," he said. "We do no want them to follow us. Most likely they are waiting for us to pass through yonder trees, and when we do no oblige, they will return."

"Why?" she asked, placing the items he handed her in the satchel without direction. "To rob us?"

"That, and to perhaps detain me."

"Why?" She rose to her feet and snatched up a corner of the blanket before following him as he strode to gather the horses. "They can't possibly know who you are."

"*Why, why?* They are suspicious," Valentine said, reattaching his satchel and blanket roll to his saddle. "Thanks to *you*, Maria."

"Me?" she squeaked as he all but threw her into the saddle. "You told me to follow your lead and I did. It's not as if I told them our names."

"You should have let me answer the questions," he said, adjusting her seat and then handing her the reins. "Surely you have been taught that ladies are to be seen and no heard?"

She gasped her outrage and jerked the leads from him. "Well, I'm sorry! But I've not had the experience of lying for my living as you have. You found no fault with my speaking before they arrived, and you were trying to find your way into my skirts!"

He paused then, looking up at her in surprise. "So you are no as innocent as you would lead one to believe. Have you had many in your skirts?"

She kicked at him, but he moved away just in time. "I have been warned of men the likes of you."

"You have, have you? By whom? Your priest?"

"My nurse," she snipped.

"Oh yes, *your nurse*." He rolled his eyes and stalked to his mount, then swung himself up. "But no a child at all, are you?" He wheeled his horse around and kicked at its sides.

Maria followed. "Where are we to go now if we cannot follow them to Vienna?"

"I suppose we are going to Prague!" he shouted over his shoulder. "Is that no where you wanted to go in the first place?"

"Yes! It is!" she shouted back. "Good!"

He pulled his horse to a stop. "No, Maria, no good. We were to outfit ourselves in Vienna. Now we have only what we carry and can piece together along the road. I wished for a proper bed, a proper drink, and proper provisions before we set out on this mad journey. I have been locked up in one prison or another for nigh a year and *today is my birthday!*"

"Well, many happy returns," she snipped. When he kicked at his horse and started up the slope once more, he heard the vile name she added under her breath, and the vulgarity of it nearly caused him to laugh despite his anger.

"Did you learn that from your nurse as well?" he tossed over his shoulder.

"No," she called out. "I learned *that* from my priest."

Mary glared at the back of Valentine Alesander's head for the next hour as he set their pace just beyond a trot. She was still embarrassed by the things he'd said to her, but she was also feeling guilty now, as she looked back and realized the faux pas actually had been hers.

She would do better next time.

Valentine abruptly left the much narrower road to navigate around a bramble patch into a thin stand of trees. She followed him.

"Have you another set of clothes?" he asked as he swung down from his horse and undid one of his many satchels.

"I do," she said, not wanting to admit to him that she'd saved the gown she wore now to meet her long-lost husband. "The kirtle I wore when first we met."

"That is all?" he asked, pausing in his search of the bag to turn a surprised face to her. "Two gowns?"

"I was in a bit of a hurry when I left," she defended. "I only had time enough to pack one bag."

"Oh, for the treasures of Vienna!" He sighed. But then he shrugged and began digging in his satchel again. "We must remedy that as soon as we are able. In the meantime, it can no be helped. So if you would, change, please. And cover your hair."

"All right," she said warily, and dismounted on her own. "May I ask why?"

"If the men we encountered retrace their steps and ask after us to anyone they pass, we do no want to be wearing the same costumes," he explained, pulling lengths of brown cloth and rough leather strips from his sack. "And should we seek to beg shelter from some simple farmer, he will extort us shamelessly should he think we have any means at all. Travelers are of great profit to those who live along the roads."

"I see," she said, reassured by his foresight, and by the fact that he no longer seemed put out with her. She dug the drab brown traveling gown and a long white linen scarf from her only satchel and then struggled through the tangly grass for the privacy of the trees some distance away. She most definitely did not think Valentine Alesander was above peeking at a lady while she was dressing.

It took her several minutes to change, having no maid to assist her. When she finally came forth from her spindly cover, she froze with a gasp—they were already being robbed!

A peasant dressed in brown with tall laces over his leggings was attending to emptying a saddlebag, the lappets of his head cap covering the sides of his face. But wait—those weren't even their horses. Had Valentine left her?

The peasant turned around then and spotted her, and Mary's heart rose into her throat at the thought that she might soon be attacked.

"What is it, Maria? Why do you no hurry?"

"Valentine?"

"Yes?" he asked, giving her a sideways look. He appeared to be no more than a dark-skinned field worker—even his posture seemed different.

Then she looked to their mounts again. Where once two sleek

brown beasts stood, there were now a pair of tired, grayish nags. "What did you do to the horses?"

"Are they different? Good," he said with satisfaction. "It is much harder to tell when you are close, and if you apply too much, it will only come off in a cloud as we ride. No so effective. Come and I will show you."

She reached his side and he held forth two small bags, the gaping neck of one revealing long chunks of black charcoal, the other white ash.

Mary looked up at him in surprise. "You painted the horses?"

"A bit, yes. Do you see?" He ran his hand over the side of Mary's horse, indicating as he explained. "The dark—the charcoal—between the bones here and here, between the ribs and at her hips, creates depth. This horse, she is bony. She is hungry. There has been no food for her." He stuck out his lower lip and pulled a sad face. "And the white—the ash—lessens the gloss, but still reflects the light. This poor, poor horse—she is old and tired and should be someone's stew."

"That's amazing," Mary said.

He bowed, the strings of his lappets nearly grazing the ground. "Thank you. But we should be going; the horses do no much like this and at the first opportunity they will seek to roll it off."

Valentine took her folded gown and returned it to her satchel, and then he drew a thin, roughly woven linen sack over the leather of the saddlebag and cinched it closed with hairy twine. Now it appeared to be nothing more than the bag of a peasant. She saw that all of Valentine's own bags were already disguised in the same manner.

Mary was impressed.

Valentine helped her into her saddle and then mounted his own horse. He pulled it around in a circle and then nodded toward the road.

"You should precede me. Even though your gown is no much to look at, it is still a little bit finer than my garb at the moment. You shall be my lady and I your servant. A very poor lady," he added. "Impoverished."

"I'm not certain if I should be pleased that I am to play your better or offended that you insulted my clothes," she said as she urged her horse past him and onto the road.

He only gave her one of his charming smiles, made even more

so by his simple costume, and sank into a mockingly deferential seated bow.

"You have not mentioned the very reason why we are on this journey together," Mary called over her shoulder once they had gained the road and were again heading north.

"That we are married?" he answered. She turned around in time to see his casual shrug.

"Yes," she said. "Weren't you surprised?"

"No really," he said. "I assume you were?"

Mary laughed at his indifferent attitude. "Well, yes, quite. It's not every day one discovers she was promised in marriage as a baby."

"It does happen, though. Quite a lot where I come from. I suppose that is why I was no so very surprised. I had forgotten all about it."

"You knew?" She slowed her horse now, too rapt by their conversation to care who should see them. They hadn't passed anyone since altering their appearances, any matter.

He was at her side when he answered. "Yes, of course. I believe I was to collect you when I was . . . twenty and three? Five?" He seemed to think upon it, and then gave one of his shrugs that Mary was beginning to understand were part of the way he communicated. "That was some time ago, of course. Ten years or more."

"Why didn't you . . . *collect me*, as you put it?"

He grinned at her. "Do you regret that I did no?"

"Well, no!" she said, and felt the tips of her ears burning. "What I mean to say is that, had you—had we—" she pressed her lips together and took a quick, deep breath. "I never would have met my future husband."

"Ah, yes. That is true," he conceded, but his smile belied his matter-of-fact agreement. "Perhaps if I had known the beauty that was promised to me, I might have pursued the agreement. Perhaps it would have redeemed me, kept me out of some of the trouble I made for myself. But, alas, yes?"

Mary felt the redness on her ears creeping down to her neck. He thought her beautiful? She'd only ever heard a compliment on her appearance from Agnes. She sought to push his words from her mind.

"Did you not think that it was wrong to run away from such an agreement?"

"I was no running away from the agreement, Maria," he said. "But no, it did no trouble me. I assumed you would marry another."

"I *shall* marry another—but the agreement must be annulled first," she said pointedly.

"You English and your contracts," he said indulgently. "Where I am from, loyalties, rulers, religions, borders—they are always shifting, changing. If everyone held to every contract that had ever been written, well, all of Spain would likely be related to one another by now."

"You just . . . ignore the ones you don't want?" she asked, blinking.

"Yes!" he said, holding out his hand and smiling at her. "We *ignore* them! And then we do whatever it is we truly want to do."

"That seems . . . frightening."

"No, no! Liberating," he insisted, and gestured toward her with his hand once more. "You—you were forced to come all this way, such a dangerous journey, only to fetch me back so that I might scribble on a document before you could live your life as you wish." Then he placed his hand on his chest. "Do you no see my freedom? I go where I like, do as I please."

Mary raised her eyebrows at him. "People want to kill you."

He laughed. "Yes, well, if we had become man and wife in truth, those people would likely be you by now, so it makes little difference." He paused, and she could almost feel his gaze as he took an obvious perusal of the outline of her leg through her gown. "Although I am certain that the passing of time with you would have been much more enjoyable."

Her neck felt afire again, and Mary turned her eyes to the road. Thankfully, he changed the subject.

"I am surprised you only found out so recently," he said. "Did no one think to tell you when you approached the age to be married?"

"There was no one to tell me," Mary admitted. "My parents died when I was still an infant. As I said, I have no family."

His brows drew together then, his expression becoming serious. "That is too bad." He was quiet for several moments. "I remember them."

Mary's head whipped around to look at him. "My parents?"

Valentine nodded. "I think so. Vaguely. Do you know—did your father wear a beard?"

"He did," Mary said, a little breathless. She knew of no one alive save Agnes who had known her parents.

The Spaniard nodded again. "Yes. I remember there was a storm, and the ship had floundered on the rocks. Your father rowed to shore himself. I was playing on the beach with my cousin when he landed. We were very frightened of him."

Mary smiled, and her heart squeezed a little at the thought that this man had actually seen her father, knew what he looked like. Mary never would.

"We did no speak his language, of course, and so we ran like rats to the villa, fetched our mothers. I do no know how it was arranged for your mother to be brought ashore." He paused and looked at Mary. "Did you know you were born in my house?"

Mary's eyes widened. "No. I mean, I was told it was aboard ship."

"I do no remember seeing you," Valentine admitted. "Or if I did, I paid you no attention. I was perhaps only six or seven. And then you were gone, and that was that." He smiled at her again, and his charm had returned full force. "Until you came across the world to find me."

"I had no choice," Mary defended, wondering if she was going to be in a state of embarrassment the entire way back to England. "It's not as if I sought you to enforce the marriage agreement." She huffed a laugh. "You're not exactly eligible."

"Ah, you wound me, Maria," he said with a smile, but Mary thought the twinkle in his eye had dimmed the tiniest bit as he sat in his serf's clothing atop his painted horse.

She found herself sorry for what she'd said, although she didn't apologize.

Before that moment, he'd been a nameless, faceless criminal, a monk, an exotic noble, and a peasant. Now, for the first time, Mary wondered who Valentine Alesander really was.

Chapter 6

They reached the little town of Spitz by afternoon. Valentine had never been to the village, on a big bend in the river, and although Maria looked longingly toward the center of the town as they skirted fields of grapevines and yellow grain, he could not allow them to pause. It was too close to Melk, and still on the wrong side of the Danube. Valentine would not be comfortable until they reached a town with a much larger population.

As if fate approved of his decision toward haste, there was a ferry in operation on the edge of the village. A large, bearded brewer and his strapping sons ran the raft, by both rowing and pulling it across on a thick rope. There was some argument about taking both horses at once, but Valentine was loath to leave the beasts unattended, and he certainly would not leave Maria alone on the opposite bank—such a beautiful and innocent woman would make an easy ransom. The brewer charged an exorbitant amount for their crossing, any matter.

The slow, precarious river journey was nearly the end of the English flower as it was. Valentine concluded she had significantly minimized her intolerance for water travel when she began retching even before they had departed the shore. Maria rejected his attempts at assistance, even on those several occasions when he feared she would be thrown off the edge of the raft as it undulated across the river. That she managed to hang on was a testament to her strength, although her gown was completely drenched by the time they landed on the opposite shore. She was forced to accept his help then, as the sheer weight of the wet wool of her skirts combined with her nausea-induced weakness nearly prevented her from standing.

Maria kept her greenish cast even after changing into her only dry gown. She refused his offer of food, and they made the rest of the day's journey into a late sunset without conversation. Valentine was oddly sorry for that—quite a change from the morning, when all he'd wanted was her silence.

They sheltered for the night in an empty hay shed, the grass still tall and uncut around the crude structure and hiding them from the road. Maria again refused the light supper he offered, taking only some small sips of water before she curled up on a blanket in the corner and was asleep before the sky was completely black.

And so Valentine had only a bottle of very good wine for company as the anniversary of his birth slipped away.

The sun came up in a haze of red, and although the air was humid, it was still cool. Valentine suspected there would be rain soon, and he was eager to gain the road. He had no need to wake Maria, though, as she greeted him with a smile when he emerged from beneath the low, sloped roof.

"Good morning," she chirped, pulling her gown from the side of the shed, where she'd hung it to dry the night before. "I've already packed the horses. I left some bread and wine aside, though—what wine there was," she said pointedly but with a smile. "I need only to change." She passed him and went into the little shelter.

Valentine mumbled something akin to a greeting and went off to seek a bit of privacy. Obviously Maria enjoyed an agreement with the dawn that Valentine did not share.

She kept up her chatter as they gained the road. "I'm sorry about the ferry yesterday," she said with a sheepish flush. "Terribly embarrassing."

"One would think you to have a better forbearance for water travel, being the daughter of a sea captain," he responded, hearing the gruffness of his tone but unable to do anything about it this early in the day. If she insisted on conversing, she would have to be satisfied with what he offered.

"One would, wouldn't one?" she replied, losing none of her cheerfulness. "Ofttimes, even traveling by cart is a harrowing experience. Perhaps I should have been more insistent with Agnes that I journey from the keep more frequently."

"Did you never leave your home?" Valentine asked, surprised that a lady of any means would deign to stay a prisoner of her nurse.

"Oh, yes," she assured him. "I went into the village every week."

Valentine turned his head to look at her. "Just to the village?"

"Yes," she said, completely unperturbed. "I told you I'd never been anywhere."

"You did," he agreed, "but I thought you meant you'd never been beyond England."

To his surprise, she laughed, the sound of it mingling almost seamlessly with the birdsong fluttering up from the fields to either side of the road.

"Well, I never *had* been beyond England. I've yet to see London."

"I do no believe it," he said, shaking his head.

"It's true," she insisted. "After my parents died, the king became my guardian. He invited me to his home some years ago, but Agnes advised against going."

"Why?" Valentine asked. "Certainly he would have provided well for you."

"Certainly. But Beckham Hall is the seat of the Cinque Ports. Agnes feared that if I left, the king might conveniently forget that I was part of the estate and I would lose my home forever when he appointed a new baron. He seemed to forget about me for years as it was."

Valentine's respect for this nurse grew. "I see. That was perhaps a wise decision, then." He paused, debating on whether to sate his curiosity with his next question. And because he had never been very good at self-denial, he proceeded. "So, your new husband, he will become the baron?"

"Yes." She seemed to smile the answer. "It is a position of great honor and responsibility. The king thinks my lord worthy after his service in the Holy Land. He saved the king of Jerusalem, you know."

"I did no," Valentine said, sorry he'd asked, and not really caring to hear about the brave exploits of the man who was to wed the beautiful innocent riding at his side. "Although I have heard that Baldwin is a leper. Perhaps your betrothed only saved part of the man, yes? That news may no have gotten around. If it was only a finger, or what have you."

Maria gasped as if scandalized, but Valentine saw her struggling to suppress her smile. "No, my lord saved the king's entire person. Of course, you might not have heard about it, being . . . well . . . on the opposing side, I suppose."

"Opposing side?"

Maria winced. "You know—you're one of the traitors."

"I am no," he said firmly. "Maria, despite what you may have heard, I had nothing to do with the goings-on at Chastellet."

Her expression conveyed her doubt, and for some reason that bothered Valentine very much. "I did no," he insisted.

"You were imprisoned by Saladin with those other three men, were you not? And then you helped them escape."

"Other *two* men," Valentine clarified. "Constantine and Adrian. I met Roman—he is the big one, the monster—at Chastellet weeks after the fortress fell. He offered to pay me quite handsomely if I would take him to where his comrades were being held and bribe Saladin's guards to release them."

Maria's eyes widened. "You freed them?"

Valentine squirmed in his saddle. "No so much. The bribe did no work."

"So the other man, the lame one—Adrian? He was correct when he said that Roman was the one who actually helped them escape."

"Yes, although I am still no certain how he did it. He simply walked in—his falcon on his shoulder, mind you—and in moments, the guards were all dead. We walked out." Valentine snapped his fingers.

"It marked you as in league with them, all the same," Maria concluded.

"Apparently." Valentine looked around the countryside they were passing through; it was so beautiful here. The colors of summer, the endless fields of ripening grapes, the gently sloping hills creating endless hidden valleys. He wanted to pause here, sketch it in his book so that he would remember it.

Maria's voice interrupted his appreciation of the scenery, but Valentine found he didn't mind.

"But if you and your friends are not the traitors you are rumored to be, then who betrayed Chastellet?"

"A lesser officer, eager to make his name by destroying his greatest rival: Constantine."

"He sent hundreds of soldiers under his command to their deaths only to have a moment's revenge on one man?"

"It has become a very long moment, yes? But he is English. As I said, you come from a people who take their oaths very seriously."

"I wonder what my lord knows of this," Maria mused.

"Of course you can say nothing," Valentine warned. "How would you explain how you came by your knowledge?" She seemed to consider this while he continued. "Any matter, once we have parted, there will be no way for us to communicate, and no reason to do so."

"But what if I hear something useful?" she asked. "Couldn't I at least send word to Father Victor?"

"There can be no connection between us after our journey, Maria," Valentine reiterated, and this time he was sure to convey his seriousness in his tone. "It would be too dangerous, for you and for all of us."

Maria pressed her lips together and spoke of it no more, but Valentine could tell that she was not satisfied with his answer. He hadn't meant for their conversation to cast a shadow on such a lovely morning.

"Besides, once we are parted, you will be consumed with your new life as a bride and will think of me no more. So let us enjoy the time we have together. To repay you for temporarily freeing me from my prison, I will perhaps show you a bit of the world before you are forced to return to yours, yes?"

She turned to him with a smile, then. "As long as I return to Beckham Hall as innocent as when I left it."

He shrugged and returned her smile. "I can no promise you that."

They passed through the unguarded opening in the wooden palisade at the town of Zwettl just as warm, fat drops of rain began to make dusty craters in the road. The town was situated in a valley where two rivers converged, and as they trotted toward the center of the village, Mary breathed in the now familiar scent of fermenting grains melting with the metallic air of the summer shower, and noticed the center of the road ahead was marked with stone wells every hundred feet or so. The street was deserted in anticipation of the rain that was steadily falling faster, and Mary, too, was eager to find shelter before her gown was soaked. Which was why she was surprised when Valentine stopped his horse at the first well and jumped off.

"What are you doing?" she called as he swept off his peasant cap and shoved it into his belt, and then threw both the tethered buckets into the well. He began working both handles furiously.

He didn't answer her as he pulled the now full vessels onto the stone ledge. Valentine poured one bucket into the trough below the horses, who lowered their heads at once, and then tossed the empty bucket back into the well. Then he carried the other to his own horse and began pouring the water carefully over the horse's rump. The now mottled colors ran off in an instant, revealing glossy brown once more. He went swiftly to the well again and cranked up the first bucket, treating Mary's horse to an impromptu bath.

After setting the bucket back at the well, Valentine went first to her horse and then to his, swiping off the makeshift coverings from their saddlebags as he walked. He shoved them into one of his own satchels and then reached inside a different bag up to his elbow. In a blink he pulled out a long length of ivory-colored cloth and slipped it over his head, revealing it to be a long, embroidered surcote that completely hid the peasant lacings of his leggings and complemented the brown sleeves of his tunic, which showed. He reached into the bag a second time and withdrew a thin, rolled leather belt and a small sheathed dagger, strapping the belt twice around the surcote, then fastening the dagger at his waist. In an instant, Valentine the peasant had become Valentine the wealthy foreign traveler.

"How many costumes have you in there?" Mary asked as he swung back onto his horse.

"No enough," he replied, pulling on the reins to move his horse from the trough and farther down the street. He looked over his shoulder at her. "We are cousins. But you are foreign and do not speak the language."

"I *am* foreign and I *don't* speak the language," she reminded him as she followed him down the street.

"Then stop speaking," he ordered curtly. "This is our best opportunity to outfit before Prague, Maria, so please, do no ruin it."

Mary felt her head draw back at his abrupt change in manner and she frowned at his tapering back.

As if he felt her disapproving gaze, he tossed back, "Be angry with me, yes. That is good."

Whether she had permission or not, Mary was unused to being spoken to so abruptly—actually, she was unused to being spoken to at all—and she couldn't help the sting she felt.

She followed him to a building that opened directly onto the street, its double doors standing wide, a goat presently taking up occupancy in the doorway. It bleated at Valentine as he slid from his horse and took Mary's reins, tying them to a post near the building's daubed façade. He helped her down and then grabbed her roughly by one elbow, all but dragging her through the doorway after him.

Although she too wished to be out of the rain, she couldn't help but dig her heels in a bit, pulling against his grip.

"Let go," she gritted between her teeth and yanked her arm free as they ducked into the darkness of the building. "You're hurting me."

He spun on her and put his face close to hers. "Stay here," he replied, grasping her upper arms and pushing her back firmly until her shoulder blades bumped against the door frame. He jabbed a finger toward the horses, waiting placidly in the rain. "Watch our things."

Mary sent him a glare and rubbed her arms where he'd grabbed her as he walked away. She noticed several pairs of eyes watching her and Valentine as he made his way to the back of the room, where a long table was set against a steep set of rickety-looking stairs. The rest of the room was crowded with little round tables and stools, where several men and a few poorly dressed women lounged with metal steins and trenchers of food. Mary noticed three more goats besides the one currently her neighbor. The whole place smelled of stale brew, sweat, and dung.

The patrons regarded her with bold curiosity, and Mary turned her gaze elsewhere—to the low beamed ceiling, the gaping planks of the walls, the littered and dirty floor—to avoid their appraisal.

Her attention was drawn to the back of the room as Valentine gave a merry shout of laughter, and a bald, portly man talked through a wide smile. Valentine and the man shook hands, and then the man turned and stomped up the stairs while Valentine strode toward her once more.

"Come." He hooked her elbow with his hand as he headed past her, pulling her from the doorway and into the street once more.

She didn't manage to shake free of him until they were standing between their horses, and he had let go of her, any matter. Valentine began unstrapping the numerous bags on his saddle.

"What is wrong with you?" Mary demanded of him before turning and starting to pick at the knots of her own bag.

"Do no talk," he ordered.

Mary slid her pack free and turned, and was nearly hit in the face by the three bags Valentine had shoved into her arms atop her own. She had to scramble not to drop them as she staggered to follow him back into the foul-smelling common room.

"I can't see!" she hissed.

He apparently stopped abruptly for she ran into his back.

"Then you should no have brought so much," he said in a loud and quite cross voice. "I'll no cater to you as your father did. You shall carry your own things. Now come along, and no more whining lest I take the strap to you again."

Mary felt her face heat and her mouth drop open as Valentine summarily dismissed her by striding away. The patrons' eyes were heavy with interest on her and she had little choice but to follow him up the narrow and creaking stairs, her cheeks flaming.

The bald man was waiting for them in the cramped corridor, next to an open doorway. Valentine called out to him in a smooth rush of foreign words, and the man roared with laughter before answering in the same tongue.

The proprietor indicated the open doorway and Valentine turned to her.

"Go on," he demanded in an exasperated tone.

Mary glared at him as she passed into the sweltering room set beneath the eaves, with only one small round window nearly level with the rough floor. Two crude bedsteads were pushed beneath the steep ceiling on either side of the window. There was a small table that held a single half-spent candle and a wide, dented metal bowl. Beneath the table hid a small pot next to the door, which opened against the other wall.

It smelled suspiciously of goat.

She turned to watch Valentine follow her into the room, his eyes never meeting hers. He strode to one of the beds, dumped all but one of the satchels there, and then turned immediately back toward the door.

Mary's eyes widened as she realized he intended to leave her alone in the stifling, stinking room.

"Va—" she began but caught herself before speaking his name. The bald man was watching her with wary curiosity, as if she were some exotic species of animal. "*Cousin*? To where do you hie without me?"

"That is no your concern," he said, taking the key the inn's proprietor offered him. "I shall return when I return. Do no do anything foolish." He looked at her, the briefest glance. "I am certain you can find a crumb of something in your many bags to sustain you."

Then he grabbed the handle of the door and slammed it shut with what was, in Mary's opinion, unnecessary force. She heard the loud scrape of the lock being engaged, and then tromping footsteps fading away, the fat proprietor's laughter echoing ghoulishly.

Mary blinked and realized she still stood in the center of the small room, her mouth open in shock, her arms laden with Valentine's things. She let them fall to the floor, and the muffled crash caused the flimsy wooden boards to tremble.

For the second time in as many days, Lady Mary Beckham used a very naughty word.

Chapter 7

Mary soon recovered enough self-interest to rush to the small window. She was forced to crouch near the floor in order to see out of the oddly-placed opening, and what she saw did not make her feel any better about her situation.

There was Valentine, riding through the now steady rain away from the inn, Mary's own mount tethered to his saddle.

The window was so small that she could see only the smallest section of the road directly in front of the inn. Valentine disappeared to the right, farther into the town.

Mary raised up and immediately bumped her head on the sloping ceiling, causing a shower of filth to rain down on her from the ancient roofing. She ducked back down and half-crawled to a spot on the floor more central so that she might stand up properly. She then proceeded to take down her hair at once, combing the vile mess out with her fingers as best she could to prevent the settling in of whatever particular insects lived in the roofing in this part of the world. She squealed and shuddered, flapping her hands in revulsion as she bent to the pile of bags and pulled out her own.

Mary would not have sat on the beds had her betrothed himself asked it of her, and so she went instead to the battered chair and table, setting her bag upon the latter and her bottom—barely—on the edge of the former. She found her comb among her few possessions and set to attending to her hair properly. Her hair as clean as she could manage and twisted into a neat side plait, she had no choice but to use the filthy pot on the floor. There was no water in the basin to wash with, and she dare not beat on the door for "service." The lock could be broken for all Mary knew, and the door might swing wide at her first attempt, but she would never venture to the hostile and foreign common room below alone. She would simply wait for Valentine to return.

If he did return.

"Of course he will return," she muttered chidingly to herself.

She drummed her fingertips on her knees.

Maybe he won't return. After all, what has he to gain by helping me? Freedom from Melk, I suppose, should he choose not to go back to his friends.

So perhaps he already has what he really wanted.

But he left all his things here.

Not all *his things. He took one satchel with him.*

Mary stood up from the chair and walked to the window again, smoothing her hands over her bottom so that her gown wouldn't pick up any more filth from the floor as she crouched down. The rain was still falling, turning the street below to mud. Mary saw no one about, not even the goat.

She walked back to the chair and sat down, her hands clasped in her lap.

A chorus of laughter erupted through the floorboards, causing Mary to jump. Unable to sit with her jangling nerves, she sprang from her chair again and picked up the rest of the bags from the floor, setting them together on one of the beds with a deep sigh. She opened the first one and began to rummage through it.

Various articles of clothing, most of which she could not identify. Lacings of different lengths and materials. A handsome feathered hat. Gloves.

She shoved the loot aside and pulled another of Valentine's bags toward her.

A monk's habit. Sandals. A knotted cord of rope—perhaps a belt of some kind. She held up a bowl-like piece of metal.

"Helmet?" she wondered aloud. She tossed it onto the bed and kept searching.

The bags of charcoal and ash; a sling; two sets of braies, the handling of which caused her to blush; a length of plaid; three shirts; four tunics; a large, ornate brooch with a golden clasp; a long cloak; a woman's comb; some toweling; and a short red cape.

She opened the last bag with another sigh, knowing at least that it would contain something to eat.

And a variety of knives, she noted as she dug through the little food left in the pack. She found the drawstring bag of dried fruit and the last of the wine, but before setting them on the table, Mary made use of one of the rougher shirts as a tablecloth. Then she retrieved a metal cup and one of the knives—just in case—and sat down to her pitiful meal, chewing some raisins slowly and gazing upon the detritus that had been contained in Valentine's bags.

She thought about what she would do if he didn't return. He'd taken both horses with him, so she would be forced to buy one, if anyone would even sell to her. Mary had discovered the hard way that there were parts of the world in which women could not negotiate a purchase without the express permission—and presence—of a father or husband. She might be able to afford a horse with what little coin she had left.

But then where would she go? Back to Melk, to tell Father Victor that she'd been abandoned? Even though Mary thought she could make her way back to the Danube well enough, there was still the river itself to consider. Then Mary thought about the three men she and Valentine had encountered soon after beginning their journey, and a shiver raced up her spine. She would make easy prey alone on the road.

How long was she willing to wait in this stinking chamber? Until morning? The next day? Then what? She briefly fantasized luring one of the goats to her room, butchering it with one of Valentine's knives, and then roasting little bits of meat over the candle.

Mary gave a snort of laughter. She'd just as soon set the verminous roof afire, then make a mad escape through the common room while the whole wretched thing burned to the ground—that rude, bald-headed innkeeper with it.

She would not return to Melk. She was not going backward. If Valentine didn't return by morning, Mary decided she would head for Prague on her own, as dangerous as that would be. Once there, she would pay or promise whatever she must to buy passage back to England. Then she would perhaps lie. She would tell Father Braund that Valentine Alesander was dead.

But the marriage would still be of record, she thought.

"Then I will just burn the record," Mary said aloud, giving one of her shoulders a little shrug. She realized she was copying the movement from Valentine, but for some reason it felt good to her. Right.

"I do as I please," she said to her cup, trying out the phrase in a

Spanish accent. It made her feel much better—her spine grew taller, her chest expanded. Then she announced to the room in general, "I go where I like."

And she recognized that it was true. No one knew her here. She didn't have to be Lady Mary Beckham, orphan of Beckham Hall, poor girl. She could be Maria.

She could be Maria Alesander, the bride of an infamous Spanish noble.

Mary stood up and walked to the bed where Valentine's things lay strewn. She picked up the feathered hat and placed it on her head, cocking it at a jaunty angle. Then she swung the short red cape over her shoulders. To complete the ensemble, she added one of the thin belts, and a knife in a simple leather sheath. Then she placed both hands on her hips and twirled around on her heel, her skirts billowing about her dramatically.

She recalled all the chastisements from Agnes, warning her about the assumptions Mary had made of the strangers she spied on from her tower window, cautioning her that people were not usually as they appeared to be. Mary realized she could be one of the characters that others passed on the street, looked upon from windows above. She could present herself to be anything or anyone she chose.

As her skirts swung to a stop about her ankles, Mary wondered what Maria Alesander would do in this situation.

"She would patiently await her husband's return, for she is such a woman that no man would ever abandon her," Mary said aloud. "In the meantime, she would gather their things together and be ready to depart, for this establishment is not suitable lodgings for Maria Alesander." She nodded to herself and then set to work, the feather on her hat bobbing.

Valentine crept up the stairs, keeping close to the wall. The inn's proprietor was asleep on the bench behind his table, as were a pair of his patrons, having indulged in too many tankards. It was well past midnight and the horses were tethered just outside, their saddles loaded with the booty Valentine had been able to procure. He was satisfied with the accomplishment of his mission.

Now all he had to do was wake Maria.

The key was ready in his hand as he approached the door on silent feet, all his senses alert to the slightest change in his environment. He slid the key into the lock, turned, winced at its dry scrape. He pushed the flimsy door open without a sound, thanks to its old leather hinges, and prepared to be greeted by a darkened room.

And so the candlelight was a surprise. As was the woman who appeared to have just stood up from the chair facing the door, a knife in her hand pointing at Valentine's face. She was wearing his feathered hat.

Maria dropped the blade down by her thigh. "Where have you been?"

"Shh!" he urged, pushing the door shut behind him. "The common room is no empty, although its occupants sleep."

"Where have you been?" she asked again, this time in a whisper, and she rounded on him as he walked the short distance to the beds. "You've been gone for hours."

"Gathering our supplies." He looked, nonplussed, at the satchels lined up like soldiers atop the rotten blanket, their tops cinched tightly. He looked behind him at the table—empty. "Maria, did you do this?"

Her chest rose as if she took a deep breath and he noticed that she was also wearing his red cape, which nicely framed her breasts. She squared her shoulders, and his view of her figure was improved even more. "Valentine, I am sorry, but I cannot stay here."

He grinned at her, shrugged. Then he half-turned, picked up one of the satchels and swung it, tossing it to Maria. She caught it.

"Then let us go."

She blinked, hesitated for only a breath, and then her mouth broke out in a smile as she stepped to the bed and began scooping up the remaining bags along with Valentine.

"Have you paid the innkeeper?" Maria asked.

"I would no give that pig a farthing for such a hovel," he said. "Seeing your beauty is more payment than he deserves. So we must be quick and quiet. Ready, Maria?"

She nodded, her cheeks rosy under the wide brim of his hat, and then bent to blow out the candle.

"Stay to the wall," he whispered into the darkness as he grabbed the door handle. "Once we are past the hearth, quickly is better than quietly."

"What if someone wakes?"

"Run," he said. And then Valentine opened the door.

He was not sure how they made it across the common room unde-tected, except that perhaps the sleeping patrons were used to the sounds of very large rats scurrying through the litter on the floor. Nevertheless, he was impressed with Maria's gameness for their es-cape—she didn't so much as squeak when Valentine threw her up onto her saddle. Then a gust of wind grabbed half of the inn door and threw it against the exterior wall with a crash that seemed to shake the entire building. Alarmed voices, heavy with sleep and drink, could be heard within.

"Vamanos!" Valentine shouted as they wheeled their mounts to-ward the gates of the palisade and the horses jumped into a run down the street, flinging up wild sprays of mud.

He swung one leg over the side of his horse as they approached the gate, hanging from his mount like a performer at a tournament. He kicked at the stay that held the long, diagonal brace as they rode by, and the timber fell as though it had once again been cut where it stood in the forest, screeching across the wooden gate.

It was going the wrong way, though, Valentine noticed as he swung back onto his horse. The log splatted into the mud across the road and began to roll toward the riders even as half of the gate swung wide in the rain, freedom beckoning to them.

"Get down!" Valentine shouted over his shoulder as he himself leaned close to his horse's neck and raised up from his seat as he felt his mount gathering beneath him and heard its distraught shriek.

He hoped Maria's horse would jump.

He hoped Maria stayed in the saddle.

Valentine's horse cleared the rolling obstacle easily, and he looked over his shoulder as he was carried through the gate. He saw the mo-ment Maria's horse too, leaped over the log, and she gave a dainty scream, one pale hand atop Valentine's feathered hat.

He would have laughed with relief had he not seen his leather bag being flattened by the log and then lying in the muddy street as the brace rolled away.

"Damn," he muttered as he pulled on the reins, fighting his horse, who wanted only to completely escape the madness it had just en-countered.

Maria pulled even with him, and her smile was wide, breathless—

breathtaking. "What are you doing?" she asked. "They're coming—let's go!"

He looked back toward his bag again, and indeed, a trio of figures with torches was running through the slop toward them, shouting.

It was the only bag he could not lose.

"One moment, I beg, Maria," he said, and then wheeled his horse back through the gate.

"Valentine!" she called after him, her voice high with alarm.

Valentine hooked his left boot through a strap on his saddle and let the reins go loose in his left hand. As he neared the bag—and the angry villagers—he flexed his foot, kicked out his left leg, and slid off the right side of his horse, his right arm outstretched. He would have only one chance.

His face was instantly splattered with mud so that he was forced to close his eyes. His fingers opened, his arm reached—

And he felt the leather strap slip up to his wrist, dragging his arm back with such force that his shoulder sang.

He pulled himself up with the muscles of his abdomen and left leg, already jerking at the reins, turning his horse, and he almost fell off after all when the beast rose up and pawed at the air in protest. Valentine looked down upon the bald head of the innkeeper, shining and red in the torchlight, as the man shouted profanities and threats, his friends reaching up to grab at Valentine and his horse.

Valentine swung his heavy leather bag into the side of the head of one and then kicked the other squarely in his soft chest, sending both men to the mud on their arses. And then he was racing back toward the gate, where Maria waited just beyond, her horse dancing in agitated circles.

"Go! Go, go, go!" he shouted over the pounding, squelching hooves.

Valentine caught up with Mary at the road, passing her for only a moment before Mary encouraged her mount on faster. Then the two of them kept stride with each other in the rain and the night, the wind and her horse's heavy breaths catching and hanging in her ears, the damp pulling at her clothes, sizzling against her skin. Every nerve in her body seemed to sing; the air she breathed was shockingly sweet, her heart pounding out a war rhythm that her horse kept time with.

It seemed as though they rode the wind for an hour, although she knew it couldn't have been that long before Valentine began to rein in his mount and they slowed on the road. Mary followed him when he veered off toward the river and the blackened silhouette of a mill.

They stopped under the wide branches of an old tree whose girth had over time toppled part of a stone wall. The heavy blanket of clouds obscured the moon and drizzled halfheartedly as they dismounted, filling the air with little snapping sounds as the raindrops flicked the canopy of the tree above them. Mary was shocked to discover the bags she'd carried from the inn were still looped over her arms, and her elbows seemed to creak as she lowered her hands, allowing the satchels to slide off onto the top of the wall.

She gave a little groan and rubbed at the deep creases she could feel beneath her sleeve and then turned to Valentine.

He was staring at her, an enigmatic smile on his full lips. She felt the roots of her hair tingle, the telltale flush beginning to creep up her neck.

"What is it?" she demanded, trying to sound as though she jumped horses, skipped out on notes, and fled in the dead of night every day of the year.

Valentine said nothing, only dropped his reins, letting his horse join hers at the river's edge. He walked toward her slowly, and Mary forced herself to stand her ground.

He was before her now, and she could feel the warmth of him even in the humid night air and through her gown and borrowed cape. His smile grew into an intimate sort of grin. He reached out with one hand and swiped a warm thumb against her cheek.

"You have mud on your face," he said.

"So have you," she chirped, although her skin felt as though it was on fire where he'd touched her.

He continued to stare into her eyes, as if considering her. And Mary had the strange and sudden urge to know what it would be like to lean up and place her lips against his, if they would be as warm as his thumb, as his gaze.

"I am very impressed by you tonight, Maria," he said. "And, under different circumstances, I would kiss you."

She blinked, startled. It was as if he had read her mind. "But you won't, because I am to be married," she stated dumbly.

His grin grew more sultry, almost mischievous, as he leaned his face close to hers. His breath fanned her lips. "You are already married," he breathed. "I am a lucky man, yes?"

Then he turned away, talking to her as he went into the shadow cast by the dark stone building, but his words held none of the magic of a moment ago, as if he had not felt the heavy vibration between their bodies that Mary had.

"Let us change into something dry and then have a light meal before the sun is up. I have some delicious things for us." Mary heard heavy crashes, like a boot against wood, and then a splintering creak. "There you are," he said, reemerging from the gloom. "It is quite empty. Now you may change in some privacy."

Mary was so disconcerted she didn't know what to say. And so she said the first thing that came to her mind.

"Do you want your hat back?"

He paused in going through the bags hanging from his horse and looked at her over the saddle. "I think no," he said. "It looks much better on you."

His smile sent the heat racing up from her chest and over her face so that Mary turned away and picked up her own bag.

She thought to herself as she ducked through the busted doorway that Maria Alesander still had a thing or two to learn.

Chapter 8

Dawn never really came, only more rain. Valentine stirred nearly as early as Mary, and he spent his waking-up period walking through the deluge to the road. Mary could tell by the sour look on his face at his return that what he'd seen had not lightened his mood.

"The road is a river," he growled, coming in through the ruined door of the mill and flinging the rain from his cloak as he swept it from his shoulders and jammed it on one of the many pegs set in the mortar between the stones. "We might as well have a fire. Even should the rain stop within the hour, the road will be impassable today. It is better that we should be held here than in the open."

"But what if the miller comes?" Mary asked his back as he walked to the small corner hearth and crouched down.

"No one will be gathering grain today, Maria," he said curtly.

She raised her eyebrows and pulled a face as she turned to her muddied gown of yesterday, thrown across a wide table with unusually short legs. She would spend the morning washing her clothes and letting them dry, then, so as not to waste the time. Although once that was finished, she didn't know what else she would do with herself. She certainly didn't want to pass the day with Valentine the Irritable.

"Why did you leave me yesterday at that wretched inn?" she asked as she moved to the cistern to draw some water. "I didn't trust that innkeeper."

"Nor did I," Valentine muttered, pausing between leaning low to the floor and blowing up small flames in the kindling. The fire crackled to life and Valentine sat back on his haunches, brushing his hands against his thighs. "You were safe enough until my return. It would have taken him until morning before he had worked up the courage to approach you. He is a coward."

Mary dipped her wide brush into the water, then set to scrubbing her gown one small section at a time, squinting at the fabric in the gloom of the stone room. "Why would he have to work up the courage?"

"Because you were a murderous widow," Valentine said matter-of-factly, going to the cistern to draw himself a drink. He swallowed several times and then sighed. "But too beautiful for him to resist for long. This"—he tapped his temple—"I could see."

"I beg your pardon?" Mary's arm froze, holding the brush in the air above the soiled skirt. "I thought we were to play at cousins."

"Oh, yes, we were cousins," he conceded, moving to his bags and withdrawing his own muddied garments. He walked toward the table. "But you see, you had run away from your husband, to be with your lover in Vienna. Your absence was only discovered after your husband's body. Everyone knows you poisoned him, of course." He looked sideways at her and tsked, then set his bundle of clothes on the table. "Would you mind, Maria . . . ?" He gestured toward his filthy surcote.

Mary knew her mouth was hanging open and her cheeks sparkled with heat. She closed her mouth and rolled her lips inward as she set to scrubbing once more with considerably more vigor.

"You could have told me what you were playing at. And you shouldn't have left me there in the first place," she scolded. "Wash your own clothes. I'm neither your cousin nor your laundress."

"But you *are* my wife," he goaded, sifting through another of his bags and shooting her a rakish smile.

At least his mood is improved, Mary thought.

"Oftentimes you can no plan these sorts of things. I must—how do you say? Let them come to me. I am inspired by the moment. Any matter," he continued, pulling out some garments and appraising them, then spreading them out, "I needed to move quickly, and I could only do that alone. You were much safer locked in that cell than you would have been with me."

It was only a moment before she couldn't help but demand, "How was I safer? If several hours is you moving quickly, I would hate to wait on you when you were at your leisure."

"I told you, I was securing our supplies."

"Valentine, I am a woman. I can very easily stand in a shop and peruse wares for hours with no danger to anything about my person save my purse."

"I needed to . . . negotiate several things." He held up a long length of rich wine-colored velvet. "Such as this. You like this, yes?"

Mary's eyes widened. "That's for me?"

He shrugged. "You needed a fine gown. You are a lady, after all, and should the need arise, you may perhaps wish to look the part."

Mary frowned. "Don't ruin it." She wanted to dry her hands and take the material between her fingers, but she didn't want to appear easily enticed.

He next pulled a pair of tall, buff-colored boots from the bag and draped them over his forearm for her approval. "Shoes to match, my lady?"

"Oh!" she exclaimed, no longer caring. "They're lovely! Valentine, how could you aff—"

"Ah-ah," he interrupted, laying the buttery boots aside and reaching into his bag again. This time he withdrew a long length of black lace—so long, he pulled and pulled and looped it over his arm before it was all revealed. "For your hair."

Mary gasped and then tossed the brush into the bucket with a splash. She stood, shoving her old, muddy gown onto the table before wiping her hands on her skirts and taking the delicate lace into her arms.

It was knotted so finely, Mary feared breathing on it would rend the fine threads. Designs of flowers and leaves and birds swirled all the way to the triangle points, where twisted fringe crowded together like a silken mane.

"Valentine," she breathed. "This is the most beautiful thing I've ever seen." She raised it carefully and spread it over the crown of her head and then looked up at him. "What do you think?"

"No, no—that is all wrong," he chided, stepping to her and removing the veil. He shook it out, spread it fully, and then raised it over her head. He arranged it around her face and shoulders, bringing the ends crisscrossed before her throat to hang down her back. The he stepped away.

"There," he said. *"Bonita."*

"I wish I could see it," Mary said, fingering the material next to her cheek and then pressing it to her skin. "This must have cost a fortune!"

"Eh, no so much," he said, the corners of his mouth dropping down.

Before she could question him further, Valentine drew another bag toward him, and Mary soon realized it was the satchel that held their foodstuffs by the items he was withdrawing. What he produced was not the cold pheasant they'd dined on last night, though, but a rainbow of delicious items.

Smoked ham, mincemeat, dried mushrooms, carrots, turnips, cabbage, lentils, a small bit of cheese, a round of dark bread, a miniature pot of honey, a jug holding what Mary could only guess was some home-brewed drink, and what appeared to be a long, hard-looking sausage.

But that was not all. Next Valentine pulled forth a fine, forged metal stew pot and a long ladle, as well as a bag of coarse, dark-colored salt.

"This is a feast!" Mary exclaimed.

"It must last us until Prague, but yes, I think it will meet our needs very nicely," he conceded with unusual modesty.

She picked up a few of the items in turn, examining them with wonder before returning them to the low table. "How is it that a man who is wanted for stealing a vast fortune, who is in hiding from bounty hunters, and claims to have little coin for a river crossing can afford such luxuries?" Mary questioned boldly.

"Well, as I said," Valentine hedged, "I needed to negotiate. And the merchant—he was . . . no a nice man."

"How much do you have left?" Mary demanded. When Valentine seemed loath to answer, she pressed. "I must know what our resources are for the remainder of the journey. I have little left myself."

Valentine shrugged. "Do no worry, Maria. I still have my coin."

"All of it?" Mary demanded incredulously. "He *gave* these things to you?"

"He was a bad man," Valentine said, frowning. "He deserved no coin. If you had only seen his wife, Maria—so sad."

Mary felt her brows lower. "I can understand your reticence to pay the innkeeper, but Valentine, these things are worth a good deal. What did you do?"

One of his shoulders raised.

"No, don't shrug at me," she insisted.

"The prices he asked were robbery. There was a pit behind his shop—mounds of food, wasted. Rotting." He flung a hand into the air in disgust.

"Valentine . . ." Mary said.

"I was very fair. I chose the things I wanted and then made a wager with him over a game for the price. If I won, I would receive what I wished for the price I offered. If he won, I would pay what he demanded." He leaned toward her in a conspiratorial manner. "I would never have paid that amount."

"So, you won?" she asked.

"He cheated. I plainly saw him draw another piece from inside his tunic."

Her eyes widened again. "What did you do?"

Another little shrug, as if it were of little consequence. "I showed him the folly of his actions by way of his own pit. Then I gathered my winnings and came to fetch you. *El fin.*"

"You threw him into a pit?"

"Well, a small one, yes. A small pit. Very small. A large ditch, really. He is likely already out by now."

Mary threw up her hands with a little cry. "No wonder you have men hunting you!"

"Maria, Maria," he cajoled. "He got only what he deserved. Plus, before I left, I gave his wife one of my own blades so that she might defend herself in the future. A beautiful dagger, a ruby in its hilt. So I *did* leave payment, one I hope is put to swift use. Now, do you like your new costume or no?"

"Was he really a bad man?" Maria asked, squinting at him sideways.

Valentine leaned his face toward hers, his expression grim. "The worst sort." Then his full lips quirked a bit, causing Mary's stomach to flutter. "The boots, though, yes?"

Mary couldn't help her grin. "May I try them on?"

Valentine very much enjoyed watching Maria preen in her boots, the ends of her veil dropping down past her hips behind her. The wine shade of the new gown would perhaps prove too muted for her coloring, he thought, but it wasn't the drab browns and grays she'd been wearing, and the sheer delight she'd shown at his gifts gave Valentine a satisfied feeling in his core. He was reminded of the noble, Spanish *damas* from his childhood, could almost hear the music of the qitara and smell the warm salt of the sea as Maria twirled.

He had lied to her a bit, yes. But he could not think how to tell Maria that the trader's "wife," as he'd called her, had been little more than a girl—not yet with proper breasts. And likely not his wife either, but a young, olive-skinned slave who had been bartered at some time by her keepers for supplies. The child hadn't spoken to Valentine, either too terrified or a mute, or perhaps Valentine had simply not possessed the words of her language, but her eyes and bruises had told him enough.

Valentine had wanted to kill the merchant, but it was one thing to be wanted for thievery in a small trade-route town, quite another to be charged with murder. He could not add that taint to his and Maria's already perilous journey. And because Valentine could not take the girl with him, he had done the best he could for her—giving her the means to protect herself, and the opportunity to gather what she needed before making her own escape. He wished her well.

In the meantime, he was preoccupied with getting himself and Maria as far from Zwettl as possible, and quickly. The quagmire of the road would put off any pursuers only until later in the day perhaps, but if they were intent enough to journey as far as the mill—seeing the wet, trampled grass from the horses' passing last night—there would be trouble. He and Maria would have to leave with the dawn, even if it meant they would be on foot, leading the horses.

Maria had just hung up his freshly cleaned surcote to drip from one of the pegs, and she hummed a little tune as she went to the pot on the hearth and stirred the stew that would be their supper. He watched her covertly, the way she hung the ladle carefully on the side of the pot, how she fussed over the stacks of their belongings, which Valentine had sorted into like categories. She packed them carefully into the satchels—the poorer costumes in the worn bags, the finer things in the new. It was very domestic, and caused a stirring in Valentine that was foreign and not a little arousing. He was certain Maria would make an excellent wife, and he found himself envying the man who would soon have the right to touch this beautiful English flower.

The flower.

He reached into his bag and withdrew the little bound book of his drawings and notes, and when he unwound the string the pages fell open to reveal the dried flower pressed there. Its color was faded, its petals papery, its scent only a memory. He brushed his thumb over the petals without removing the spent bloom.

Teresa. . .

He would at last see Teresa again in Prague, kiss her and hold her in his arms. He had missed her so in the years since he'd last seen her. He hoped she had not heard of the vile things of which he had been accused since Chastellet. He cared little for what the world thought of him, but Teresa could never think him a murderer, a traitor.

"What is that?" Maria asked cheerily, drawing his attention from the image of Teresa's face in his mind and causing him to close the journal—not so quickly, though, that he would arouse Maria's suspicion.

"Nothing," he said, slipping the book back into his satchel. "Only a little journal I keep. I make notes of the places I've been, people I've met, news I've heard."

"Enemies you've made," she guessed, but it was said in a light-hearted tone and delivered with a smile.

He returned the gesture. "It is quite useful when traveling at length as I often do. Did," he amended. "I try never to make danger-ous enemies, but—" He shrugged. "It can no always be avoided."

"Like the merchant trader in Zwettl," Maria offered.

"Yes," he said. "Although I doubt his town holds much affection for him." He got up to assist Maria with setting the full bags near the door, ready for travel at a moment's notice. He liked that he'd not needed to explain that this was necessary. "For instance, I meet a friend in Paris, and we get on well, and I learn he has a brother in Brussels. Should I find myself in Brussels, I will pay this man a visit with his brother's compliments."

"But what if the brothers hate each other?" Maria asked, seeming genuinely interested.

"I should pay him a visit any matter," Valentine said, "only no di-rectly. Perhaps I ask after him, and find him in some tavern, in which case I sit nearby and loudly lament the stingy bastard who cheated me in Paris."

To his surprise, Maria laughed. "So it is a friend either way."

"Perhaps friend is too strong a word." Valentine smiled.

They came back to the low table again, and Maria cut the round of bread in half horizontally while Valentine went to the stew pot for a final stir. He carefully scooped the rich meal into the halved breads and then joined her at the table.

Maria stuck her knife tip into a chunk of turnip and held it to her lips, blowing away the curling steam. She popped it into her mouth in a moment.

"Mmm," she hummed, and then chewed while she picked around the stew. "Thank you," she said when Valentine set the silver cup of ale near her.

He took a seat on the oddly short stool—little more than a wooden cassock, really—and began his own meal. He took a generous pinch of the salt in the open bag on the table and noticed that Maria watched him closely and then mimicked his seasoning.

Did she know nothing of life?

"Do you miss . . . traveling?" she asked, lifting her cup to her lips. She sniffed the ale, then took a hesitant sip.

He shrugged. "I have missed it of late, yes. Melk is no bastion of culture."

"That's dreadful," Maria said, and Valentine looked up from his stew to find her frowning into her cup and licking her lips daintily. "Your home, then—Aragon. You miss it?" She took another drink, this one considerably larger.

"Ah, yes—Aragon I do miss," he said, before sampling the ale himself. He smacked his lips. It was quite good. "The air, the light, the food. It is like heaven."

"You've not been back since you left," she guessed.

He shook his head. "No."

Several moments passed as they ate, and Valentine could feel her curiosity rising up from her as if it had its own substance.

"Your family?" she asked in a light voice.

And there it was. "I have no family left in Aragon, Maria."

Her eyebrows rose. "Dead? But I thought—"

"To me, yes." He heard his voice growing gruffer and tried to relax. "My parents, they died many years ago, before I left. I had an older brother, a cousin I was close to at one time. . . ." He let the sentence trail away, then waved his knife in the air, as if the mention of them meant nothing.

"The ones you robbed," she noted.

Valentine took a silent breath and then another leisurely bite of stew. "I did no rob anyone, Maria," he said. "What I took did no belong to them."

She opened her mouth to, Valentine assumed, pry further, but he foiled her attempt with a question of his own.

"Have you always been with your—Agnes, is it?"

"Agnes, yes," she said. "My mother took her on as a maid soon after I was born. I was left in her care when my parents took a short voyage to Normandy together—they were only to be gone a fortnight. They never returned."

"She is like your mother, then, this nurse."

Maria nodded, swallowed. He could see the shimmer of tears in her eyes. "I miss her very much. I hope I have not worried her too terribly."

Valentine refrained from voicing his opinion that, if the woman indeed thought herself any sort of a mother to Mary, Agnes was likely beside herself.

Maria took another long drink of the purportedly dreadful ale, perhaps to compose herself before speaking again. "I've often wondered if I resemble my mother." She raised her face, and her eyes locked with Valentine's, bright with hope. "Do you think? I mean, can you recall? Probably not, I understand. It was so long ago." She dropped her eyes back to the stew, waving her knife in the air as Valentine had done earlier.

He continued eating but regarded her closely, his eyes moving over the lines of her jaw and nose, in profile to him, the curve of her ear. He searched his memory.

"You do," he said casually. "The shape of your faces are similar, your cheekbones; you have the same hair—I remember the color clearly, as it was so much lighter than the women of my family."

She raised her eyes. "Really? I look like my mother?"

"Yes," Valentine said, "but no entirely. You have your father's eyes. And his beard."

She laughed loudly, her cheeks flushing prettily in the firelight. Then she stilled, dropped her head a bit, and picked at her stew.

Valentine could tell that she was struggling with her emotions, but he could not tell of what kind, and it frustrated him, used as he was to reading others as if they were signposts. Perhaps it was the coziness of the old mill, the flicker of the hearth flames, the feigned domesticity they had shared along with the meal and the ale. Perhaps it was how beautiful she looked in the stolen black veil, the lace shadowing her face like angels' wings.

Whatever it was, it prompted Valentine to push his cup aside and reach for her hand. She let it lay limp in his grasp while he stroked the back of her palm with his thumb.

"Do no be sad, Maria," he cajoled.

"It's silly, isn't it?" she asked in a strained voice. "To miss someone you've never met?"

The firelight behind her made her silhouette glow, and he suddenly wondered what the Maria of years ago would have thought of him, his younger self, perhaps at the time when they would have met had their agreement been honored as it was intended.

"I do no think so," he said. "You did meet them. You only do no remember it."

She looked at him at last, her eyes shimmering with unshed tears. "You and I met once, too. I don't remember you either."

"This is true," he agreed lightly.

"Have you wondered?" she asked. "What it would have been like if we had—if we . . ." She let the sentence trail away, but her eyes pinned him still.

"It does no matter," he said quietly, and he realized it was true. Whatever previous fantasies he'd held of seducing Maria must be forgotten. "Maria, what might have been is a dangerous game for us to play. You are to be wed, and I am a criminal with a price on my head. If we were to be caught together, it would ruin your life, and I would most certainly hang."

"I don't believe you are a criminal," she said in a whisper.

Valentine swallowed, noticing that her fingers were now curved around his hand. "No?"

She shook her head.

"What has caused you to change your mind?" he asked.

The only sounds in the room were the crackling of the fire and the hush of the rain beyond the stone walls. He could feel her pulse quickening beneath her skin.

Then she stood up from her stool without withdrawing her hand and stepped toward him. Valentine rose automatically as she came into his arms and raised her face. He lowered his mouth to meet hers as if it was a dance they had rehearsed a thousand times, and their lips met perfectly. Maria's right arm came up around his neck and his left went easily around her waist.

Valentine heard the roar of a warm sea in his ears, tasted the sweet saltiness of her mouth, smelled the garden of her hair. His heart pounded in his chest like hoofbeats, his body pulsing with this sudden onslaught of unmistakable desire.

And then he pulled his mouth away from hers, released her, stepped away with his palms out. He placed them on his hips when he noticed their tremble.

"Maria, no. It is too dangerous."

She looked at him for several moments, her eyes flashing, her lips wet and parted from their kiss. The bodice of her gown rose and fell sharply.

"That is why I don't believe you are a criminal," she said in a breathless voice. She turned away and began clearing the remains of their forgotten supper.

He stood there for a moment and then chuckled. "It is almost charming how you think you are so clever."

"Is it?" she asked, glancing at him while she walked past him to the door to scrape the pot out.

He was waiting there when she returned and yanked the pot from her hands, tossing it to the floor with a clang. Then Valentine bent Maria over his arm while she gave a little squeal, dropping his head to hers and kissing her thoroughly. He only relented when he felt her legs give way, and then he pulled away, stood her upright, and steadied her with his hands.

"Do no think to play games with me at which you are inexperienced, Maria," he warned in a low tone. "Regardless of the romantic imaginings you have of me, my promise to Victor and my regard for your welfare will only be pushed so far." He dropped his hands and turned to the door to tend the horses.

"Do no forget my hat," he tossed over his shoulder as he left the mill.

Chapter 9

It was still quite dark when Mary followed Valentine—he leading his horse, she, hers—from the mill, through the tall grass still heavy with dew, to the road. The stars were invisible, either because of the nearing dawn or cloud cover—it was difficult to tell because Mary could not take her eyes from the horse's rump in front of her long enough to squint at the sky. The path Valentine cut was treacherous in the dark, slippery and uneven in her worn leather shoes, and Mary was looking forward to gaining the road.

Until they actually gained the road, and the thick mud oozed up over her insteps, slid inside her lacings, and insidiously packed around her feet like cold, slimy shrouds with each slipping step. Her skirts were pulled up on the sides and tucked into her belt like a field worker's, and the air on her legs was welcome, even if it was humid and clammy. By the time they had been on the road an hour, the dawn coming up red and angry, Mary had sweat through her bodice from the effort of wrenching her feet from the sucking road with every step.

Thankfully, the path joined up with a wider road via a sharp turn to the northeast, and it was not long after that when Valentine gave the signal that it was safe to mount the horses. Mary sighed with relief after he helped her into the saddle, her feet feeling as though she had giant rocks tied to them. She leaned down and picked at the sticky laces, pulling the shoes off and tying them to the back of her saddle to dry. Her linen stockings were packed through and stained an ugly brown, and so she removed those as well, undoing her skirts to hide her bare legs.

This road led them from the open country dominated by gently rolling fields into a more heavily forested land, the rises sharper and closer, with stretches of woodland crowding the valley road. She watched Valentine riding ahead of her. They hadn't said a score of words to each other combined that day, but Mary was unsure if it was because of his usual disagreement with the morning or her misstep from the night before.

She had been wrong to test him so, and she felt the familiar prickle of heat on her already rashed skin as she recalled the way she had purposely goaded him into kissing her. It was so unlike her—perhaps unlike who she used to be? But she'd needed to determine whether she was actually safe with Valentine Alesander or not. And she'd wanted to know what kissing him felt like. She knew that it had been wrong, and stupid, and yes, dangerous. What if she had been mistaken about him, and he had decided to take her mock seduction to heart, pressing her to deliver to him in full what she had presented?

It wasn't as if he hadn't shown interest in her as a woman—he in monk's robes, of all things—before they had been properly introduced in Melk. In the short time she had known him, he had barely escaped an unpaid innkeeper in the dead of night, assaulted a merchant, essentially stolen quite a large amount of very valuable goods, and broken into someone's place of business. By his own vow, he was wanted by his family, and by the Crown of England. Yes, tempting him had probably been very unwise.

But Mary felt herself changing. That time alone in Zwettl, when she'd donned Valentine's cast-off pieces of costume, had seemed to strengthen a backbone she'd not noticed she'd had before. When they'd departed, Mary had felt that she had no choice but to trust this man, a stranger and rumored bloodthirsty traitor, if she were to have any chance at all of a future as a married woman. But now that she was out from under the protection of Beckham Hall, of Agnes, away from the group of wealthy and noble pilgrims traveling largely for pleasure and comfort, after having been left alone in the hovel in Zwettl, she'd come to terms with the fact that she could very well be left to her own devices without catastrophe.

And that it need not be been quite as frightening as she had once thought.

So, yes, it was important to know the likelihood or nay of Valentine Alesander seeing her to their adventure's end fully and honorably. This man who was so full of secrets, and so adept at being whomever he needed to be at the moment that he was still largely a character in a story to Mary. But her suspicion that he was much more than he claimed to be—that there were important details to his story than he was unwilling to confide to her—was stronger than ever now, after his refusal to ravish her, and then his punishing and passionate kiss.

Valentine would protect her, she was now certain, but why? She was under no illusions that he held any sentimental feelings for her, any passion that ran deeper than the physiological fact that he was a man and she a woman. Mary knew Valentine was indebted to Father Victor for his protection, but she felt that even that obligation would only have been worth so much to a lesser man longing for freedom. Valentine owed her nothing, and by his own admission cared little for contracts and promises.

It struck Mary suddenly that she had already spent more time with Valentine Alesander than she had with her betrothed, and it caused an uncomfortable sensation in her belly. Two months ago, if her intended had asked her to embark on a journey alone with him to a foreign land, would she have accepted?

Mary slammed the door shut on that unwelcome visitor. Of course she would have accepted—the alternative was ridiculous. She planned on spending the rest of her life with that man, having his children. He was a lauded soldier. A hero. If she trusted him enough to accept his offer of marriage, she would certainly have followed him anywhere he asked her.

But would she have? The door creaked open again of its own accord, letting the thought slip through that, even after their hours of conversation in her modest third-floor hall, Mary did not know where the man had been born, if he had siblings, if his parents were still alive. They'd talked mostly of Mary, of her father, and of Beckham.

She shut the door firmly again with a shake of her head and threw the bolt. Silliness. Most men and their wives knew precious little about each other before they were wed. Indeed, hadn't Agnes told her that it was not unusual for men and women to only see each other perhaps once or twice a week once they were married? They certainly didn't share an apartment, let alone a chamber. Her husband was to be her husband, not her friend or her confidant or her traveling companion.

Up ahead, Valentine looked over his shoulder at Mary, drawing her attention from her nonsensical musings.

"Small village ahead, Maria," he called. "Do no slow."

"All right," she answered, wanting to question him as to why they could not stop to rest for the noon meal there, but not wishing to incur any further bad feelings between them. She trusted him as well as she could trust anyone—in fact, she could trust only him—and so she held her tongue and increased the pace of her mount to ride closely behind him as they passed through the small cluster of ramshackle dwellings.

Mary felt the eyes of the inhabitants watching them openly as they passed, and for a moment, she wondered about the girl she had been at Beckham Hall, and what that girl would have thought of her and Valentine had she spied them racing through the village from her window.

Right away she knew that she would have imagined they were a couple on their way to a very special meeting, and that it was important that they arrive there on time.

Mary marveled at how close to the truth that observation actually was.

Valentine felt as though he could drop from his saddle as he and Maria rode through the gates of Tábor, night firmly wrapped around the earth. He knew she was likely more tired than he, but he had pushed to gain this burg before they stopped to sleep. By tomorrow night they would be in Prague.

Maria drew her horse even with Valentine's as they rode through the wide main thoroughfare, and Maria's head seemed on a swivel, taking in the sights. Although Valentine guessed it was nearing midnight, he and Maria had no trouble navigating the streets, lit by torches and the lights from inside the many taverns, their doors thrown wide to the warm night.

Revelers spilled from the establishments and milled about the streets, where melodies from several different instruments mingled in the ale-perfumed night. Screams of laughter, shouts of argument, snippets of sung verse flew through the air like the night birds between the buildings, swooping low over the streets to pluck at the air near their ears.

Valentine rode past the majority of the rowdy taverns closest to the gate, where most travelers would stop. In other circumstances, he

would have done the same. But he was tired, and although the festiv-
ities did look amusing—as did the women in their thin, low-cut summer gowns—he wanted a peaceful night's rest at a quiet
establishment where he need not fear for Maria or their belongings.
There would be time aplenty for merrymaking after tomorrow.

He knew he had found just the place when he spied the stooped
old man pulling the door shut, a torch in his hand lighting the small
sign above, shaped like a horse's head. Valentine spurred his mount
and called out in the tongue of the land.

"Pardon, sir, pardon!" He raised a hand and then swung off his
horse, leaving Maria to sit in her saddle and watch.

The old man paused, peering around the door with not a little impatience. "Closed," he said gruffly.

"Sir, I beg of you," Valentine said, stepping forward and grabbing
the edge of the door so that the man couldn't pull it shut. "We have
been traveling since before dawn and need a reputable establishment
such as yours to rest ourselves and our horses." He cast a disparaging
glance down the street at the revelers. "One whose clientele is perhaps not so . . . enthusiastic."

"Loud," the old man snorted. "Destructive. *Pissed*," he leaned toward Valentine and whispered, glancing at pretty Maria on her saddle.

"Indeed," Valentine agreed, frowning along with the proprietor.
"We are off to Prague on the morn. Certainly I shall pay you in advance for two chambers, a simple meal, and board for the horses."

The old man shook his head. "No."

"Please, sir," Valentine said, holding the door tightly when it
would have shut on his fingers. "Consider my—" He looked back at
Maria, watching them expectantly, the slightest crease between her
brows indicating that she was unsure whether she should be concerned about the nature of the exchange she was witnessing or nay.

"Consider my wife," Valentine continued, looking back at the old
man, who seemed to be chewing on the inside of his own face for
lack of teeth to hold it taut. "This is her first time in this part of the
world, and so far she has been terrified by the . . . loudness."

The man grunted understanding.

Valentine nodded. "The destruction."

The innkeeper snorted and shook his head.

"The sheer *drunkenness* she has encountered on our journey,"
Valentine lamented. "She is . . . meek. Inexperienced."

"Right." The old man nodded, looking at Maria again. Then his eyes found Valentine's once more. "No."

Valentine struggled to keep his demeanor humble and friendly. "Are you full?"

He shook his fuzzy gray head.

"Then I fail to see why letting out two chambers would be a burden to you."

The old man sighed. "Only one left."

Valentine pressed his lips together. "Are you quite sure you have only one?" He glanced at Maria again. "My wife, she . . . she is in a delicate condition, you understand? It would be unseemly for us to—"

"One," the old man insisted. "Yes or no?"

Valentine looked over his shoulder at the crowd milling farther down the street. At least six of the men were currently engaged in a full-out brawl, and two women were going through discarded satchels beneath a torch. Valentine was fairly certain by their frantic pawing that the items they were tucking into their turned-up skirts did not belong to them. He'd seen that game run many times. Participated on more than one occasion.

He sighed. "Yes."

The old man released the door and followed Valentine to the horses, where he waited while Valentine helped Maria from her saddle with exaggerated care and took all the satchels into his own arms, leaving her empty-handed and confused. Then the innkeeper took hold of both sets of reins and gestured toward the doors with a toss of his head.

"Wait," he instructed.

"Come along, my darling," Valentine said coaxingly and began walking toward the inn. "Can you walk? Shall I carry you over the threshold?"

Maria frowned at him and then glanced over her shoulder at the old man as he disappeared with the horses into an alley at the corner of the tavern.

"What are you about now?" she demanded as she held the door wide for him and Valentine stepped through. She followed him inside and pulled the door almost to.

"Shh," Valentine hissed, looking around the empty room before he dumped his burden onto a table near a stone hearth that contained nothing but banked coals.

Maria crossed her arms and waited. "What am I today? An idiot?"

"You are my wife," Valentine said, taking in the plain but tidy common room. This was perfect. The building was made of thick stone, keeping out most of the noise from the street. The door was solid, reinforced with hammered metal and two thick beams. The room even smelled . . . well, not like vomit.

"Very amusing, Valentine. What did you tell him?"

"Maria, whether he has more or no, the man is only giving us one room," he clarified, taking his purse from his belt and looking at her levelly. "You are my *wife*."

"Oh." She closed her mouth and frowned. "But why did you treat me as if I were . . . fragile?"

"I was trying to persuade him to let us two chambers, so I told him you were—" he stopped counting out coin long enough to roll a hand in the direction of her midsection—"you know."

"Sick?"

Valentine pulled a thoughtful face. "Something similar to that, yes."

"What?" Mary said, her voice filled with confusion. "I don't . . . ?" Then she gasped and brought a hand up to her mouth while her face bloomed the color of poppies. "You told him I was *with child?* Do I *appear* to be with child to you?"

"It is nothing to be ashamed of," Valentine cajoled and couldn't help his grin. He put the coin on the table and began retying his purse. "You are a married woman, after all. And I? I am a proud papa!" If he thought her face pink before, now it was scarlet. "Do no be so upset, darling. Perhaps I will let you kiss me again later."

Maria picked up the satchel closest to her and raised it, but then the door to the inn opened and Valentine stepped to her side, wrapping one arm about her waist and pulling her tightly to him. Maria dropped the bag down near her thigh and pasted a thin smile to her mouth.

"I am so happy," he whispered sensuously into her ear.

"I hate you," she gritted between her teeth.

"Little Valentine. Or Valentina, yes?" He moved his hand as if to place it on her abdomen as the innkeeper came fully into the room, and Maria swung the saddlebag across her body and into the general vicinity of Valentine's groin. He stopped it before full impact and jerked it from her hand, slinging it onto the table.

The old man raised a hoary eyebrow in their direction before chuckling and barring the door. He pocketed the coins before taking hold of half their bags, and then jerked his head toward them as he began walking to a darkened doorway in the back of the room.

Valentine released Maria and took up the rest of the bags. "After you, *mi amor*," he said, bowing low, unable to hide his grin.

She did manage to tread on his foot as she passed him, but it only made his shoulders shake with laughter.

He followed Maria's stomping steps up the tidy stairs and then down a slanted corridor to the last door. The room was narrow, the bed more so, and it was quite a pinch with him and Maria and the curt innkeeper crowded into the little chamber. But it was clean and quiet, and the man promised to bring up a tray before he saw to the horses properly. He bowed to Maria before quitting the room, his eyes lingering on her stomach, and Maria blushed wildly again before turning away from the door.

Valentine dumped his satchels on the floor and then walked to the narrow bedstead, falling backward onto it with a groan.

"This may be the most comfortable bed I have ever lain on in the whole of my life," he vowed, his eyes still open and fixed on the ceiling. The underside was clean, straight, wooden lathe, and the packed thatching between didn't hold the slightest appearance of rot. Well built and well tended. He sighed. He would rest easy here tonight.

"Don't become overly comfortable," Maria grumbled, digging through the pile of bags to locate her own. She jerked it open and began rummaging through the contents.

Valentine rolled to his side and propped his head up with one hand. "Why no?"

She pulled out her hairbrush, tossed the bag back to the floor, and turned to flop onto the small room's only other piece of furnishing—a hard-looking wooden chair. She began tugging the ribbons from her hair. "That's my bed, isn't it?"

Valentine chuckled. "Of course it is." She began brushing her hair vigorously, and he added, "And it is my bed."

The brush paused in midstroke. "I'm not sharing that bed with you."

He shrugged. "Then you will be sleeping on the floor, I am afraid." He rolled to his back once more, folding his hands behind his head and closing his eyes with another great sigh.

"Valentine!" she insisted, and he thought that if she had been standing, she would have stomped her foot for emphasis.

"I do no know why you are so suddenly shy," he said, and then cracked one eye to peer at her across the room. "I would think after such a passionate kiss last night, you would be eager to be invited into my bed."

Her face went scarlet. "I am sorry about my behavior last night. I believe that horrid drink affected me."

"Hmm." He closed his eye again. So comfortable.

"I—I only wanted to see if I could trust you," she stammered. "If you were honorable."

"That is no a good test of honor for a nice lady to put upon a man when they are alone."

"I realize that now," she said, and to his delight, she did sound remorseful. "I exercised poor judgment."

He opened his eyes again and looked down the length of his body at her. "Well?"

"Well what?"

"Did I pass your test?"

"Yes," she said, her cheeks rosy again. "Yes, you did. And I am truly sorry."

He smiled. "Good. I accept your apology. And now it will be no trouble for both of us to take our rest here."

"No! Valentine, I—"

"Maria," he said, cutting her off and sitting up, swinging his feet over the side, "we are in a clean, respectable establishment, with a bed. We are no out of doors, in the rain, on the ground. I, for one, have missed the simple pleasure of a mattress. The proprietor thinks we are married, and no one else will ever see or know. We have been together these many days, and as of yet, the only one of us who has made an inappropriate advance upon the other is *you*."

"I'm not certain that's completely true," she argued, but she didn't look particularly happy either. He had to admit he was enjoying her discomfort.

"So," Valentine pressed, "do you trust me or no?"

Maria took a deep breath and then blew it out. She might as well have waved a flag in surrender.

"Yes," she said wearily. "I trust you."

"Good," he said as a rap sounded at the door. "Now, there is our supper. Do let him in so that we can eat and go to sleep. I am so tired, I could not ravish you even if I wanted to."

Mary stared at the blackness shadowing the ceiling, her arms crossed tightly over her bosom. The room was silent, save for Valentine's deep, even breaths. She turned her head to look at him—well, to look at the back of his head. Mary thought he had been asleep as soon as his head had touched the satchel he was using as a pillow. The outline of his shoulders was only a blacker shadow in the room. She turned her face back to regard the ceiling once more.

He had been true to his word. It hadn't seemed to stir his passions in the slightest when he'd climbed into bed beside her.

Likely because he's done it so many times with other women, she reasoned.

The thought did not help her sleeplessness. In fact, it made it worse. Although she tried to close her eyes, longed to sleep, now she was wondering just how many women Valentine Alesander had had, in rooms just like this, all across the world? How many women had he loved and then left?

And why *didn't* he want to ravish her anymore?

Chapter 10

If Mary had been surprised by the revelry in Tábor, Prague was a complete shock.

She saw the lights from the city hours before they actually entered through the wall; the glow of it against the night sky was like a little sunrise. Mary could feel Valentine's excitement the farther they went on the road, where now they were joined by scores of people heading into and out of the city, alive even in the grave of night. He showed no sign of the fatigue that had plagued him the night before, and Mary wondered crossly what he was so looking forward to.

She had been cross the entire day.

But if Valentine sensed her bad mood, he gave no indication of it, leading her from one tavern to the next, all respectable twins of the establishment they'd stayed at the night before, and like any reputable inn, already closed long ago. They clomped over narrow, cobbled streets for more than an hour before he finally turned to her with the faintest expression of irritation.

"It will be dawn soon," he said, almost to himself.

"Is there no place for us?" Mary asked. "Surely in a city so large . . . ?"

"Yes, I know a place, Maria," he said dismissively, looking at her in an intense manner, up and down her plain traveling gown. "But you will have to change."

They snuck into a sleepy stable, and Mary remained hidden behind the tall wooden boards of an empty stall while Valentine tossed her particular items of clothing over the top.

"Why can't we simply sleep here?" she asked, her voice causing the beasts in the adjoining stalls to shift and huff at the disturbance.

"Shh," Valentine warned, throwing over a gauzy-looking piece of white material. "Because, Maria, if we were found in the morning by the stablekeep, he would have us arrested and confiscate our belongings and our animals."

"What is this?" she whispered, holding up the thin garment, the sleeves only now discernable.

"We shall call it a chemise, yes? Put it on."

"I can see through it!" Mary hissed.

Valentine's head popped up over the rail. "No all the way," he argued. "I will give you an overdress, Maria. Put it on." Then he disappeared again, and in a moment the wine-colored velvet came flying in a ball into the stall. The boots came next, and Mary dodged the second one with a yelp as she rubbed the crown of her head.

"Apologies," Valentine whispered.

The scandalous excuse for a chemise and even the tall boots gave her little trouble, considering that she had nothing to lean against save the rough stall wall, but the gown was a trial. Four sets of laces held the dress together, two each to the front and back and both sides, ending in long ties below her hips, and it felt to Mary as though she struggled for a half hour before she was confident enough that she was properly covered and stepped out into the dim light cast by the cracked stable doors.

Valentine turned his face toward her, his foot propped up on a cart wheel where he had been wiping at his tooled leather boots. He wore the embroidered tunic and tight leggings she'd seen him in the morning they'd left Melk, and when he smiled at her appearance, Mary felt a flutter in her stomach.

"Very pretty, Maria," he said, walking toward her. "We need only a bit of adjustment."

"Should I wear the lace?" she asked as his hands went to the tie at her side, and expertly began tugging at the laces. She swayed with his every pull.

"What?" he asked, momentarily perplexed. He turned her halfway round and began working at her other hip. "Oh, no. No veil for you tonight. In fact—" he turned her away from him and swept her hair over her shoulder, raising gooseflesh on her arms—"I think you should put your hair up. Have you any ties?"

"Up?" she questioned, as she felt her shoulder blades drawing together. She looked down at her brown boots, which were now visible to her ankle, as was the cut work along the hem of her plain underskirt. "I think so, yes."

"Good." He turned her around to face him once more, and Mary tucked her chin to watch his nimble fingers confidently work the long ladder of her laces, starting in the middle of her chest, where only a slim band of the silk shirt could be seen. He pulled the edges apart and then went to the bow below her navel, deftly untying the strings and then drawing each rung tight until the velvet touched up to and over her rib cage. Then he moved back to the bottom, refashioning the bow before stepping away.

"There," he said. "Better."

Mary looked down and gasped, bringing her hands to splay over her bosom, which now seemed doubled in size and straining at the white silk.

"Maria, you look—" He held his open hands toward her, as if at a loss for words.

"Naked!" she hissed, and felt her cheeks stinging with heat.

He paid her little mind, though, going to his horse and reaching inside a satchel. "Hair," he reminded her over his shoulder as he rummaged.

Mary raised her hands to undo the ribbons in her plait, but then brought them back down immediately when it felt as though her breasts would spill completely out of her dress with the motion. She tentatively tried again, and miraculously, the shirt managed to contain her chest. As long as she didn't breathe.

She turned her back to him as he found whatever the dark object in his hand was and gathered her hair to the crown of her head, forming it into a long loop and then tying the ribbon around it securely. She checked to make certain her breasts were still in her gown and then turned around once more.

"Valentine, I don't know what scheme you have concocted, but I simply cannot be seen like this," she said.

He stepped toward her, and she saw that the object in his hand was his wide feathered hat. He placed it at an angle atop the knot of hair she'd created and then stepped away.

He smiled. "Now it is perfect."

"Did you *hear* me?" she demanded.

"I did," he said, already walking away from her to open the stable doors and looking cautiously in both directions before returning and holding out his hand. She took it and he led her to her horse, helped her to mount. "I would no take you to such a place had I any other choice," he explained, handing her the reins and then moving to his own horse. "But since there are no other lodgings available to us this night, I must go where I know we will both be safe." He gained his saddle and turned his horse toward the doors.

Mary followed. "I don't see how I can possibly be safe anywhere!" she called out in a loud whisper, and then kicked at her horse in order to keep up with him. "Valentine! *Valentine, where are you taking me?*"

The wooden cutout swung in a warm breeze, smelling of alcohol and cologne over the street: the outline of a fat white bird with one eye closed and a flower clasped in its beak. Black lettering was scrawled ornately across its breast.

The Snowy Owl.

The front of the tavern had no windows, only a formidable-looking wooden door reinforced with hammered black iron. It was at present flanked by two equally formidable-looking men, one of them bald as an egg, the other sporting a long red plait that hung down over his chest. A crash sounded from behind the door, causing the wood to bulge outward. The bald man turned, opened the door a bit, and reached one beefy arm inside. When he withdrew it, a limp, scrawny man dangled from his fist and was promptly flung into the street. Shrieks of laughter and song flooded the muddy walk like a bright river before the guard slammed the door shut once more.

Mary looked to Valentine, and he gave her a wink, not unlike the one sported by the tavern's mascot. On the street in front of Mary's horse, the ejected patron began crawling away, perhaps happy to have escaped.

Mary noticed that he was wearing only one boot, and no chausses at all.

"Have you brought me to a brothel?" she demanded.

Just then, one of the guards called out in a language Mary was unfamiliar with. It seemed an angry shout, but at her side, Valentine laughed. He dismounted, catching her eye.

"Only smile, Maria," he said. "You are lovely. *Smile.*" Then he turned to the bald man, clasping forearms with him, and each of them clapped each other's shoulders. They conversed in the strange tongue as the guard's eyes appraised her.

Mary tried to smile, but her lips were trembling and her heart was racing. She wondered if her breasts were betraying her.

The bald man laughed and waggled his eyebrows at Valentine, who gave a ridiculous bow before turning to Mary and helping her down.

"Stay close to me, Maria," he whispered into her ear as he held her against him and then allowed her to slide down the length of his body to the ground. It was an intimate gesture, to say the least, and Mary wasn't at all certain her legs would hold her when her feet did touch the street.

"*Comprende?*" he whispered, looking down into her face. The wide dark brim of his hat on Mary's head shielded them, and Mary thought it probably appeared to the tavern guards that they were kissing. Valentine's breath was hot against her lips. "I will secure us a room as quickly as I can, but you may see some things that will shock you. I will make it known that you are mine, but I must feel you beneath my hand at all times."

If her knees were weak before, his words made them positively nonexistent. She didn't know how she would manage to walk through the door.

What was wrong with her?

"Maria?" he insisted, giving her a little shake, and Mary realized she had yet to reply. "If you think you can no do this—if it is too much . . ."

He was too much tonight. The environment had little to do with it.

"I can do it," she said.

He ducked his head to look into her eyes. "You are sure?"

She nodded and gave him a smile. "*Vamanos.*"

She couldn't be certain, but she thought she felt his arms tighten about her the slightest bit as his smile grew wide and his dark eyes sparkled. Then he swung her around on his arm, causing her to grip his shoulders with a squeal. He swept her toward the door, the burly man with the long plait pulling it wide for them and once more letting the rush of gay sound and light loose onto the drab and dirty street.

The door closed behind them with a little push of warm air, and Mary felt as though she had been plunged into a foreign sea. The room was humid, long and low with plaster and beams running up the walls and over the ceiling. A squat stone hearth was at the far end, but it was the populace of the room itself that held Mary enthralled.

Men everywhere, seemingly from every caste, lounging on chairs or low benches, on tall stools and even the floor, surrounded by women of every shape and color imaginable. Mary saw red hair, black, blonde; skin that was the color of milk, olives, the deepest ebony; all of them in similar, ruffly, white-bodiced gowns, the skirts falling just below their knees, where they met tall boots decorated with long white feathers down the backs of the calves and across the instep.

"The Snowy Owl," Mary murmured, making fascinated sense of the costumes.

The music was lively, and several of the patrons and girls sang along to the song, in words that were foreign to Mary but whose accompanying gestures were clear enough to bring a flush to her cheeks. Especially when she saw the two women atop one of the small tables, dancing a spirited jig back-to-back, their bodices pushed down to completely reveal their breasts, bouncing in rhythm to the steps and the tempo.

Not a single head turned to see who had entered the tavern. It was as if they were invisible.

Valentine was pulling her deeper into the room, leaning toward her as if to say something, when they were both nearly knocked from their feet.

"Ballenteeeen!"

Perhaps not invisible after all.

Mary's hat fell down over her eyes as it was knocked loose by the arms flung around Valentine. She straightened it as she felt his hand slide away from her waist, and then Mary turned to look at the interloper.

She was hanging from his neck, her long dark arms shining and smooth in the candlelight, like polished wood; her mouth was pressed to his, only the high curve of her ebony cheekbone, her finely turned ear, and her close-cropped black hair was visible. Her shapely shoulder seemed to glow against the pristine white of her gown. One of her hands came up to caress Valentine's face, and Mary noted the beautiful pink nail beds, the creamy tan of her palm against the mahogany of the rest of her skin.

Just as Mary was contemplating ripping the tall woman away from him, she pulled back on her own.

"Ballenteen," she cooed again, and her straight white teeth flashed between impossibly plump, rosy lips. Her brows drew downward and she wagged a long, elegant finger before his nose. "They say you have been very naughty."

"Do no believe everything you hear," Valentine said, his smile for the woman so fond that Mary felt her teeth grinding together.

"Don't you worry—I don't!" the woman said with an unself-conscious laugh. Then she turned to Mary at last, her eyes openly curious. "And who is the beauty you bring us after so long, eh?" She still hung about his neck with one long arm, her fingers playing with his hair at the nape.

Valentine's arm snaked back around Mary's waist, pulling her into the pair so that they became a trio. "This is M—" his pause was nearly undetectable—"my Fleur."

Her eyebrows raised, her wide mouth quirked. "She is your flower, or she is called Fleur?"

Mary heard herself answering before she knew what she was doing. "Yes," she said, leaning into Valentine with a smile.

To her surprise, the dark woman laughed and then leaned forward and kissed Mary on the mouth. "Welcome, Fleur. I do fancy your hat. I know a pirate who wears a hat such as that. I hope you are staying a while." Then she stroked Mary's cheek with the back of her hand.

"Fleur, this is Brennie," Valentine said. "A room quickly, *por favor*? I would prefer we no be seen tonight."

Brennie pulled a sad face. "You will not drink with us?"

"No tonight, *mi amor*. Karl is tending our horses and will bring our things. We have traveled a long distance today and are only seek-ing a comfortable bed."

Brennie's deep eyes flashed to Mary's décolleté and she hooked a long forefinger in the top rung of her laces and gave a playful tug. "I do not blame you, with such possessions to unpack." She let go of Valentine but took hold of Mary's other hand, pulling her deeper into the room. Valentine trailed behind, never releasing Mary as they snaked through the bawdy crowd. "Come, Fleur—Brennie knows just what Ballenteen likes, and I will take very good care of you both."

Valentine worried for the construction of his chausses.

Seeing Maria in the Snowy Owl, her creamy skin flawless, with the little curling tendrils of hair over her shoulder, her clear blue eyes wide with—shock? Horror? Curiosity? Her innocence lay over her like a veil only Valentine could see while debauchery danced around her and then—in the form of lusty Brennie—marched right up to her and, throwing the veil back, kissed her on the mouth.

She didn't belong here, Valentine knew, and although he was more than comfortable in the brothel that had once been his haven, he would have paid a proper innkeeper any price to keep Maria away from such wickedness. Even in her seductive gown, with her ankles showing, she was like a patch of wildflowers growing up through scorched earth, her innocence as sweet and fresh as the blooms' scent.

But she was not afraid. And she had not hesitated, had not stepped out of character for even a moment. Feeling Maria's clasping hand, the tremble of her flesh as she clung to him, the way she had answered the question that she was his without prompting or hesitation . . .

Valentine had never wanted a woman so badly in his life.

There was no second floor at the Owl, only a maze of corridors flowing away from the back of the tavern and then behind the row of other establishments that lined the street in front. The Owl's private apartments were accessible from inside the tavern or through the narrow alley behind, a convenience for loyal patrons who would rather not be seen entering from the street, as well as men who might or might not have a price on their heads for crimes they might or might not have committed. Valentine would have gone directly to the alley, but he was no longer sure if Brennie would keep the same apartment, or if she would even still be at the Owl. She had promised to keep watch for Teresa, and Valentine had known she would do her best, but three years was a long time to wait.

The dark beauty released Maria's hand to fish a ring of keys from the fullness of her skirts, and Valentine gave a low whistle.

"Chatelaine now, Brennie?"

She flashed him a dazzling smile, full of pride. "I am Madame, Ballentine." She fit a key into a lock and turned. "Now it is in my power to give you whatever you want." She winked at Maria. "Anything at all." Brennie pushed the door open and stepped inside.

Maria looked back over her shoulder at Valentine as she moved to follow Brennie, and to his surprise, she gave him a rather impressed smile and a wink of her own.

It took all his self-control not to grab her there in the corridor.

Thankfully, Karl appeared just then at the end of the long row of doors, bearing all the satchels from their horses save the one Valentine already carried. The bald man raised a hand to indicate he saw which apartment they had been assigned. Valentine followed the women inside.

The Owl had obviously prospered in the years since Valentine had last visited. Always clean and well appointed, the room into which he followed Maria's gently swaying hips was lavishly decadent, with broad fabric panels climbing the walls fluidly to join together in an intricate knot in the middle of the ceiling over the wide, low bed. The squat plaster and stone hearth was cold but contained a lidded brazier, which Brennie went to right away, pulling a long reed from a copper cylinder nearby and lifting the lid to light the stem. She moved to two standing candle holders in opposite corners as if she had done it in the dark a hundred times, and soon the room sparkled with golden light against the shimmery fabric and upholstery of the bed and other furnishings.

The exotic woman turned on her heel and blew out the reed, then tossed it into the hearth. She held out her arms, indicating the room. "What do you think? Will it do?"

Karl was stacking the satchels in a corner behind a small round table, and he raised a hand in silent farewell as he quit the room and closed the door behind him.

"I can no believe this is the same place," Valentine said, watching Maria from the corner of his eye as she took in their accommodations. Her expression was for the most part composed, but she was standing rather stiffly in the middle of the room near the bed, and her eyes were wide. "Is this your doing, Brennie?"

The dark beauty nodded her head with a proud grin. "I brought in so much coin that Pig gave me free hand. It has served our customers—and his purse—very well."

Maria obviously realized her lack of appreciation for such plush lodgings, for she walked forward suddenly to a low upholstered chaise and ran her hand over the back of its deep incline. The arms of the chair stuck out perpendicular to the seat, rather than parallel, and ended in carved wooden knobs. "This is interesting," she said.

"You will love it," Brennie said, coming over to the chair and turning around to fall backward into it. In a blink she had raised her feathered feet and hooked her knees over the arms of the chaise, her skirts falling over her crotch with a flounce. "So comfortable."

Valentine saw Maria swallow, and then her eyes met his.

He turned away quickly and rolled his neck from side to side, shook out his arms, took a deep breath and blew it out.

Brennie laughed, and he heard her get up from the chair. "Someone is eager," she teased, coming up behind Valentine and wrapping her arms about his waist. She laid her head between his shoulder blades and then squeezed him with a happy sigh. "I am so happy to see you again, Ballentine. You cannot know."

Valentine laid his forearms over Brennie's and returned the gesture. "And I, you. That you are doing so well gladdens me. We will talk on the morrow, yes?"

"Of course." Brennie moved away, and Valentine turned to face the two women again, his libido once more in check—surely an oddity for most men after such an embrace. Brennie was appraising Maria now, as she busied herself inspecting the draperies on the side of the room farthest from the wicked chaise. "Unless you want me to stay—I must confess that your Fleur does not look at all like one of your women."

Maria's wide eyes flew to Brennie. "What do you mean?"

Brennie pursed her voluptuous lips, crossed one arm under her breasts, and then laid a fingertip to her chin, contemplating. "Your coloring—it's so pale." She dropped her arms and sashayed to stand before Maria, seizing both of her hands and holding her arms out, looking at her from side to side. "Your hips are narrow. But you are not long." She dropped one of Maria's hands to sweep the hat from her head and gasped. "Look at that hair! Very English." She smoothed a palm down the side of Maria's creamy cheek.

Maria looked at Valentine, but her words were for Brennie. "You think I am not to his liking?"

"Oh, I can tell by the way he looks at you that he likes you very much." Brennie chuckled, and Maria gave him a sly smile. "I certainly wouldn't mind having you for myself. It is only that you are not the sort of woman I would consider for Ballentine."

Valentine felt he must speak up before Brennie started trying to seduce Maria into her own apartment. "What can I say? I have changed since last we saw each other."

Maria pulled away from her new dark admirer and reclaimed his hat from Brennie's hand. She began walking toward him, and he was surprised to see that her cheeks held not the slightest hint of blush, although her lips were rosy, her eyes sparkling. She sailed his hat onto the decadent bed.

"Perhaps it is I who changed him," Maria mused aloud.

Valentine opened his arms at the last moment, when he realized Maria intended to slide her hands around his middle. She tilted her face up to his, and the scent of her made him see double for a moment. He had a perfect view of her breasts. His breathing grew shallow. His heart raced like a horse on desert sands.

"The room grows hotter." Brennie chuckled, but Valentine did not look at her. Could not look away from Maria, in this sensuous room created for making love, the air of seduction all around them, indeed, raising the temperature twofold. "How can I help bring you lovers ease?"

Maria's gaze was flitting over his face, landing on his mouth, his eyes, like physical touches. "I crave . . . a bath," she said. "Is it too late to request one, Brennie?"

"Never too late to fill the tub," Brennie replied, coming to stand behind Maria. She reached up and untied the ribbon holding her hair, and it cascaded down her back while Brennie combed it with her fingers. She leaned her lovely, pointed chin over Maria's shoulder. "I will wash you, with your man's permission."

"Sorry, Brennie, I do no share her," Valentine said hoarsely.

The dark woman clucked her tongue and stepped away, trailing her fingers through the ends of Maria's hair and then letting it fall back onto Valentine's clasped hands.

"I thought as much," she said ruefully. "But he has never been so stingy before with his sweets. I will have the water brought, *mi amor*. And some oils, so that—" She broke off with a laugh. "Well, you know what to do with them."

He heard the door open and close.

Maria remained in his arms. Her tongue peeked out over her lips.

Valentine felt drunk. So drunk that he was hallucinating. Or dreaming.

"Are we to share this bed as well?" she whispered. Maria didn't even glance at the satin-smothered mattress. "It looks very comfortable."

"Maria, I do no know that it is wise to . . . be so close to you . . . in this room."

"We are already close," she reasoned with a little shrug. "I promise I won't assault you again. But if you'd rather, I could sleep on the chaise."

He heard himself growl in his throat and dropped his head, his mouth hovering just above hers. Her head tilted, her lips parted, breathing her little breaths into his mouth.

"Are we even now?" she asked.

He paused. She was learning quickly. "I do no think so," he said. "I owe you for your performance, Maria."

"Pay me later? I have a bath coming."

"I must, *must* go. Far away."

"Quickly, please," she said, her body expressing the exact opposite sentiment.

Releasing her was like pulling great roots from the earth, and he and Maria tore away from each other, both breathing heavily, as if they had only narrowly escaped disaster.

In Valentine's mind, that was precisely what had happened.

They should have risked arrest in the stable.

"I will return within the hour," he said, giving her a shallow bow. "You will be safe here. Do no fear."

"I'm not afraid," she said, giving him a pretty smile, but her eyes still burned. "I trust you, remember?"

Chapter 11

Mary woke up the next morning feeling as though she had spent the night in heaven. The sunlight through the long shallow windows set just beneath the ceiling shone through the draped silk, giving the room a jeweled glow, and the thick mattress beneath her cradled her body as if in a giant gloved hand. She raised her arms above her head and stretched, releasing once more the perfumed scent of the oils she'd rubbed into her skin after her delicious bath in the round copper tub the night before. She turned her head to see the other side of the bed undisturbed.

Valentine had not returned before she'd fallen asleep.

Uncertainty seized her, shaking her from her languor, and she sat up in bed, clutching the light coverlet to the underdress she'd donned for sleeping.

But there he was at the little table, already dressed and stuffing what looked like the rough brown monk's habit into the satchel he was never without. He cinched the neck tight and closed the flap. Mary worried for a moment that he had left her alone in the room all night—perhaps passing the evening with the stunning Brennie—but then her eye caught the drape of a sheet over the wicked chaise in the corner.

He hadn't left her. And yet the relief of that knowledge was spoiled a little by the fact that he had preferred to sleep apart.

Her movement drew Valentine's attention, and he looked at her with what was probably the best smile he could muster so early in the day. That he smiled at all raised Mary's suspicions even further.

"Good morn, Maria," he said, setting the satchel aside and moving to a tray on the table. "Did you sleep well?" He picked up the tray and crossed the room toward her.

"I think so," she said, noticing that the words came out rather clipped. It was usually she who was bright and cheery in the mornings, but this day found her wanting only to bark and growl at the dawn, and especially at the handsome man who deposited the tray on the mattress near her hip.

"I am afraid that the Owl's patronage does no usually break the fast here, but there was this." He indicated the bread and cheese, and a squat cup containing what smelled like spiced cider.

Mary picked up the cup and sipped. "Thank you." It was quite good, but she would have rather bitten off her tongue than say so.

Where did you go last night?

Who were you with?

Why wasn't it me?

But she asked none of those things, realizing the folly in them. He was her protector on this journey, yes, and by some ancient decree they were joined to each other for the time being, but Valentine Alesander did not answer to her. He was a man with his own life, and very soon that life would not include her at all. She would be nothing more than a memory, another fabled escapade to add to his repertoire.

And she would be married to a respectable man and returned to Beckham Hall, as she wished. Where she would live the rest of her life without thievery, or evading authorities, or criminal activity of any sort. And especially no prostitutes.

But she was not cheered.

"When do we depart?" she asked, picking at the bread as Valentine returned to the table.

"Perhaps tomorrow," he said.

Mary felt one of her eyebrows arch. "Tomorrow?" Whoever he had passed his hours with last night must have pleased him very much. Probably Brennie after all.

"Or the next day," he said.

"Oh. I didn't know we were traveling for pleasure now," Mary said, picking up her cup again. She sipped, her mood gathering strength like thunderheads on the horizon. "Perhaps you have forgotten that I have somewhere to be?"

"I have no forgotten, Maria," he said with a smile that did nothing to soothe her. He picked up his satchel and slung it over his shoulder, seemingly ready to depart.

Mary set her cup aside and threw back the coverlet. "Fine. I'll only need a moment to dress. Where are we going?"

"No, no," Valentine said, holding up a palm and walking to the door. "You rest. Brennie will be about to see to your needs when she arises." He paused, quirking his mouth charmingly. "I would say around noon. You will be fine until then."

"But I want to go," Mary said, hearing with dismay the petulance in her voice. "I want to see the city."

His hand was on the latch. "Later, Maria," he promised. He opened the door and then paused. "Remember, while we are here you are my woman. Do no give us away."

"Valentine!" she insisted, punching her fist into the damnably soft bedclothes.

"Latch the door behind me," he directed and then left her.

Mary gave a growling sigh and shoved the tray away. The cider sloshed out of the cup and ruined the bread, but she didn't care. She swung her legs over the side of the low bed and her feet touched the floor.

"Mary, do this. Mary, do that," she snapped under her breath. Her entire life it seemed as though she had done nothing but follow the directions of others. The king, Agnes, Father Braund, the elderly pilgrims who had been her companions until Melk. Even her betrothed. Now it was Valentine Alesander who commanded her. *Wait for me. Behave this way. Be quiet. Smile. Pretend.*

She stood up from the bed and crossed to where she'd laid out a fresh gown over the back of a chair the night before.

Where had he gone? To gather supplies for the last part of their journey? A special merchant, perhaps. But why was he insistent that she stay behind? Likely because whomever he was meeting was a fellow criminal.

But if that were the case, why would he need his monk's robes?

No, she didn't think he would get up to anything blatantly unlawful—his caution in securing their lodgings the night before and his intention to stay in Prague for perhaps several days showed that he was being mindful not to draw attention to their presence in the city.

She pulled the gray gown over her head and cinched the simple ties in the front—no whore's costume for her this morning—and her bosom seemed sadly shallow. She picked up her discarded ribbon and began walking to the door to latch it as Valentine had commanded, gathering her hair as she went. As she reached for the metal turn, Mary heard low voices in the corridor and, letting her hair fall back around her shoulders, she placed the side of her face against the seam of the door frame and listened.

It was Valentine's voice, but he was speaking too quietly for her to make out his words, and Mary did not know to whom he was speaking. A man, she thought. Perhaps the brawny Karl from the night before. Were they discussing Valentine's intended destination? She strained to hear.

Her squinting eyes fell upon her boots and the long black lace veil peeking out from her satchel near the table, and a mad idea seized her. If she hurried . . .

By the time Valentine's footsteps were fading down the corridor, Mary was cracking open the door.

He was just disappearing around the corner of the alley when she emerged from the back of the Snowy Owl, and she skittered along the daubed wall of the buildings to peer down the street after him.

There! She caught sight of Valentine weaving through the crowd, and Mary followed, skipping several steps to close the distance between them. He crossed a wide common, skirting a bubbling fountain in the center, and disappeared into another alley. Mary dodged a meat vendor and ran amidst a little clutch of hooded old women, murmuring her apologies as she dashed through the common. As she slowed and carefully turned into the alley, Mary realized she was smiling.

She threw herself back against the stone of the building when she saw him, stopped perhaps one hundred feet from her just beyond an abandoned wooden stall that was listing to one side. A short stack of broken crates was near Mary's hip, and she slid down the wall until she was crouched behind them, peeking through the slats at Valentine.

He had hung his satchel on a peg of the stall and was now pulling out his brown robes. He looked around the alley, and for a moment it seemed that his eyes landed directly on the place where Mary was hidden and she held her breath. She released it with a giggle as he pulled the habit over his head. He attached the corded belt and then raised the wide hood. When he threw the satchel over his shoulder once more and turned to continue down the alley, Mary followed.

She trailed Valentine for what must have been nearly a half hour, dodging citizenry through the narrow, twisting streets. They crossed a wide, arching bridge over the river that divided the city, and in the moments that Mary was forced to follow Valentine in the open, her heart beat like mad, fearing he would suddenly turn and discover her. Once she had reached the other side of the bridge, though, she was accosted by a small gang of beggar children, soliciting her with plaintive, foreign words and tugging at her skirts. She pried off their hands in a panic, walking backward, explaining in her own useless tongue that she was sorry, but no, no, she had nothing, no coin, let go, *let go!*

Then she was off again, her boots flying over the cobbles, afraid for one terrifying moment that she'd lost Valentine in the crush, and then at last catching sight of his dark hood as he passed through the gates of a tall wall ahead.

The dome and steeple in the distance gave the indication that it was some sort of cathedral or religious enclosure, which made his choice of costume perfectly reasonable, and the idea that his intended destination was a church buoyed Mary's heart as she herself disappeared into the trickle of people seeking the walled garden beyond the gate.

Uncertainty struck her again soon after she came fully into the lush enclosure; the sculpted trees and beds filled with statuary and flowers were being admired by scores of individuals, more than half of whom wore the long, dark-colored robes of the religious. Valentine had vanished into the throng like a single crow into a murder.

Mary froze near the center fountain as the crowd milled around her, her eyes darting from face to face. Her gaze landed on a woman at the end of the paved walkway leading from the fountain to one of the doorways of the looming cathedral. She was clothed in the garb of a nun, her white linen headdress covering all but the perfect oval of her face. She seemed to be staring through the crowd directly at Mary, but then a robed man eclipsed the nun for a moment as he walked toward the woman. When Mary next saw her, the nun had brought both hands up to cover her mouth, and Mary glanced again at the robed man who continued his approach, his fine leather boots showing beneath his hem.

Tsk-tsk—he'd forgotten his sandals.

Mary waited until Valentine had reached the woman, both of them holding forth their hands long before they were close enough to embrace, before she began drawing closer. Valentine and the nun clasped hands but then withdrew abruptly, and Mary turned her back when Valentine's head swung around, surveying the crowd. Mary peeked sideways through her veil to see them walking to the left, behind a line of tall, sculpted evergreens. She followed, stopping on the other side of the elegant shrubs, where a stone bench like the one on which Valentine and his companion sat waited empty.

Mary could see them through the fragrant boughs—the woman was crying, but the tears ran over a face shining with joy while her arms were around Valentine's shoulders. She was serenely beautiful, with her olive coloring, dark lashes, and brows, and she spoke hushed, rapid words flavored with Valentine's own heritage. The only word Mary could make out was *Vallenteen.*

"It's *Valentine,*" she muttered crossly under her breath.

The pair drew apart, spoke for a moment over each other, laughed, and then embraced again. Mary watched the way Valentine held the woman's hands in his own, smiled at her tenderly. His voice seemed choked with emotion as he spoke in his own tongue.

And then it struck Mary as certainly as a bolt of lightning from the sky: this woman, the person Valentine had not wanted Mary to meet, was the reason Valentine had left Aragon. The reason he had not honored the agreement to take Mary as his wife. The reason he had fallen out with his family. This woman was not one of his travel conquests, no cheap companion he'd once passed a random night with. The love of Valentine's life had taken the veil.

And Valentine had dressed the woman who had been intended as his wife as a whore and left her at a brothel.

Mary sat on the bench beyond the bushes, the bright sun warming her face and hair beneath the black lace veil Valentine had given her, listening to the rapid, affectionate conversation she could not understand. Her heart ached in her chest, but she did not know why. Valentine was not hers. The only reason they were even together on this mad journey was to ensure that they had no claim to each other whatsoever, that a connection could never be drawn between them in the future. She was marrying another man in only weeks! She shouldn't care what or who was in Valentine's life, then or now.

But she did.

Mary stood up, intending to leave the garden and the estranged lovers to their privacy, but then she sat back down.

She had no idea the way back to the Snowy Owl. She'd been so in-

tent on not losing Valentine in the crowd that she'd paid little attention to the route they'd taken, beyond the fact that they had crossed a
river. But she could not very well wait for Valentine and then follow
him back. The mere idea that she risk coming face-to-face with the
woman Valentine loved brought a deep flush of shame to her face.

She would simply have to manage. It wasn't the first time she'd
been alone, after all.

Mary rose again, this time with her chin lifted, and walked directly
away from the oblivious couple hidden by the elegant landscape. She
passed the fountain, her boots crunching on the fine colored gravel,
the water bubbling merrily. She told herself that she would not cry as
she wiped her eyes with one end of the beautiful veil.

She paused for a moment outside the gate and drew a deep breath
to calm herself and get her bearings. The cathedral sat upon a hill,
and so she could clearly see the river and bridge she'd crossed below.
It would be easy enough to get to the other side, and once there, she
would hope that something seemed familiar.

Mary found she was quite thirsty, and wished she had thought
enough to grab her purse from the room before she left. She had no
coin, nothing in her possession at all.

Foolish, foolish girl. In more ways than one.

She began walking in the direction of the bridge, the buildings
lining either side of the street seeming to close over her head. She
had not gone very far when she heard a high, warbling voice calling
over the bustle of the crowd. At first she did not stop.

"Mary!"

What an odd coincidence, she thought.

"Mary! Lady Mary Beckham!"

Mary's movements froze—indeed, even her heart seemed to still
in her chest. She didn't have time to turn of her own volition, for in
the next instant her arm was seized and she was swung around.

Before her stood the Lady Elmsbeth.

"Mary!" the old woman gasped, happy tears in her eyes. She pulled
Mary to her ample bosom. "Thanks be to God, we've found you at
last!"

"I never thought to see you again," Teresa said, pressing one palm
to her chest for a moment. "There has been no word from you in almost three years—not even to Brennie. I feared you were dead."

Valentine's face ached from the wide smile he couldn't help. It was so good to see her, to hear her voice speaking their shared language. "No, not dead. It was far too dangerous to send a message to you, this last year especially."

Teresa's face lost a little of its glow. "It can't be true, what they are saying you did."

"It is and it isn't," Valentine hedged. "I did not aide the betrayal of Chastellet, and neither did the men with whom I was forced to join forces."

Concern filled her eyes. "The prisoners?"

Valentine nodded. He told her briefly how he had come to be imprisoned alongside Adrian Hailsworth and Constantine Gerard, and how Roman had freed them. "We are in hiding until our innocence can be proven." He stayed her question before she could even ask it. "I cannot tell you where."

Teresa's smile returned. "Very well. I shan't yet press you further only because I am so happy to see you at last, no matter the circumstances. But then you must tell me, why are you here in Prague now? Are your . . . friends with you?"

"They are my friends now, yes, but they are not with me." He paused, smiled, gave a little shrug. "I am with a woman."

Teresa threw back her head and laughed out loud, and Valentine's heart expanded at the sound. "Of course, it is a woman! Who is she, and what sort of trouble is she in?"

"Do you remember the tales of the English ship wrecking on our beach when I was but a boy?" At her nod, he continued. "The noble captain and his wife were aboard, and she bore their child at our villa. It happens that the infant girl and I were joined to each other."

Teresa's eyes widened. "I had forgotten! The woman you are with then—it is she?"

It was Valentine's turn to nod. "Maria—Mary," he corrected himself.

Teresa clapped her hands together. "She found you and wishes the contract to be honored!"

"What woman in possession of good sense would wish to be joined with me?" Valentine chose to ignore Teresa's chastising frown. "She needs me to disavow my claim so that she might marry another. She and I are on our way to England now."

"Are you glad for the escape?"

Valentine shrugged again. "We would not have made a good match."

"I meant from your hiding place," Teresa said with a sly grin. "But do tell me about her—I long to hear your voice."

Valentine sighed and pursed his lips for a moment. "She is innocent but curious. She's not been from her home the whole of her life. Very English, with skin like cream, and her hair is the color of the sand on our beach after a rain."

"She is not ugly, then."

"No, no—far from it. She loves the mornings—annoyingly cheerful. Her mind is very determined, and has a definite sense of what she wants, what she does not. She is trusting, perhaps overly."

"It is good that she is with you, then, yes?"

Valentine shrugged. "I do not know."

"Valentine?" Teresa tilted her head until he met her eyes again. "What is it?"

"Nothing. This taste of freedom only has me thinking mad thoughts."

"You wonder what would have been?" At his shrug, Teresa nodded and then thought a moment before speaking. "Perhaps it *is* the freedom—going where you wish after so long in hiding."

"I think so," Valentine agreed. "It must be."

"Does she love you?"

He chuckled, scoffed, "No. Of course not. She loves this other man, her betrothed. *Her lord.*" His smile fell away. "She has a grand manor for a home, a place of honor in her king's eyes. She would not give that up for a criminal with no family."

"You are not without family," Teresa reminded him.

"No," he agreed quietly, grasping her hands again. "I am not. Speaking of, let me show you what I have brought you." He pulled his satchel onto the bench between them and dug inside, pulling out a weighty sack and placing it in her hands.

"Valentine!" she gasped.

"I have been away for a long time, yes?" he said.

From above their heads, a bell began to toll with deep, melodious gongs, vibrating in Valentine's ears. Teresa pushed the bag toward him.

"You keep it for now," she said, and gained her feet. "I must go. You will come back tomorrow, won't you? Please say yes, for I, too, have some things to tell you."

Valentine stood, the bells still tolling through the garden, his brows drawing together. "Yes, I will come, but Teresa, what is it? Are you in danger?"

"No. Not yet, any matter," she said with her brown eyes sparkling above a mischievous smile and began to back away. "Come tomorrow and I will tell you. After morning prayers I can be away for an hour."

"Teresa!" He held out a hand as if he thought it would prevent her from going, but he knew it wasn't so.

"Tomorrow," she promised. "Go find your Maria. I love you, Valentine."

And then she turned and disappeared into the dark shadows of the abbey.

Valentine sighed and replaced the heavy bag of coin in his satchel before slinging it over his shoulder. He shouldn't be surprised that their time was so short today—Teresa had not expected him, and she would not risk drawing attention to his presence by neglecting her obligations. Tomorrow was not so long to wait.

He turned with a smile of his own and began walking from the garden, to find his Maria.

Chapter 12

"Lady Elmsbeth." Mary gasped. The old woman's claws pinched the tender flesh of Mary's upper arms. "I—you . . . What are you doing here?"

"What am *I* doing here?" the dowager countess demanded in her warbling voice. "What are *you* doing here, young woman? When you disappeared from Melk, we turned the village over, searching for you!"

"But your pilgrimage," Mary stammered. "You were to go on to Vienna, and then—"

"I am familiar with the itinerary we had planned," Lady Elmsbeth chastised. "But do you think I would simply abandon you to whatever fate had befallen you in Melk? I promised Father Braund—"

Just then a wheezing old man came trotting up to the dowager's side, dropping his hands to his knobby knees and panting. The fullness of his cap had drooped sideways, and Mary could see half of his shining pate.

"Lord Roscoe, are you all right?" Mary asked, fearing for the old man, who had once lorded over a small but politically important estate in England.

"By God . . . you were . . . right . . . Beth," the old man wheezed, glancing up at Mary with his rheumy blue eyes. His cheeks bore startling magenta patches on their sunken middles. "Good day . . . Lady . . . Mary."

Mary's eyes went back to the dowager as the old woman continued. "I knew we would find her in Prague. Whoever absconded with her would certainly not have been so brave as we to draw nearer to the Holy Land. Which is simply full of *authentic* criminals."

Mary frowned and glanced toward the steeple of the church. She must escape the pair before any more of their party caught up with them and Mary was overwhelmed.

"What are you talking about?" Mary demanded. "Who—?"

"The man you left with," Lady Elmsbeth said, a knowing look on her jowly, wrinkled face.

"No. Man? I don't—"

Lord Roscoe had caught his breath enough to stand erect and address her. "There is no use in denying it. One of the monks at Melk saw you. And I'm certain he wouldn't lie."

Lady Elmsbeth nodded. "He was an albino, you see," she confided. "They are touched by God."

"So who is he, young woman?" Lord Roscoe demanded.

"And *where* is he?" the dowager added. "He will answer for this depravity—to us and to the authorities of this city!"

Mary's head was spinning as her eyes flicked between the two elderly nobles. She couldn't very well tell them the truth. She thought about turning on her heel and dashing over the bridge—she was confident she could outrun them. But as soon as she did, the authorities of Prague would be searching for her as she wandered the streets seeking the Snowy Owl. Even if by some miracle she managed to locate the brothel on her own, there was no way to alert Valentine that she had been discovered and that they were both now wanted as he made his way back through the city.

It could mean his death if he were discovered.

Mary flung herself suddenly into Lady Elmsbeth's arms with a dramatic cry. "Thank God you found me!"

"Oh, there, there, dear," the dowager said happily. "All is well now. You are safe."

Mary's eyes searched the slow trickle of visitors emerging through the garden gate as she clutched at Lady Elmsbeth's rounded shoulders. "We must be away!" she wailed.

The old woman pulled back from Mary and looked keenly into her eyes. "Have you escaped? Is that why you are alone in the city?"

"Yes!" Mary said, clinging to the excuse. "I left with nothing— not even a single coin. I was . . ." Her eyes flicked to the gates again as bells began tolling. "I was going to seek help at the church."

"And dressed as a peasant, no less," the old woman said with a sniff, eyeing Mary's beautiful veil. "But do not fear, my dear, we shall provide for you, shan't we, Roscoe?"

"Indubitably," the old man agreed with a solemn frown. "But, Lady Mary, when Beth saw you, you were coming *from* the church. Did they refuse you?"

"No," Mary hedged, raising her voice over the echoing gongs that flooded between the buildings lining the narrow streets and seemed to wash away her words. "I . . . I changed my mind."

"You changed your mind?" Lord Roscoe challenged. "Without a farthing to your name, and a mad man in pursuit of you?"

"Roscoe," Lady Elmsbeth said sharply, "don't press the girl. She was clearly ashamed of her situation."

Mary quickly dropped her face, mimicking the emotion. "Yes. So ashamed."

"Oh," the old man said. "I see."

Mary frowned at the street. What did he see? Mary didn't even see.

"We shall simply not speak of it, dear," Lady Elmsbeth said in a low, quick voice. "No one ever need know, especially your betrothed. He may not even notice on your wedding night. Most men don't."

Mary's head snapped up so fast she heard the little bones in her neck pop. "What?"

Lord Roscoe appeared mortified and had turned slightly away. "As far as anyone is concerned, we made our journey as planned."

"Precisely," Lady Elmsbeth agreed. "It is very common to have last-minute fears before your wedding, Lady Mary. I certainly do not fault you for that. You suffered a terrible, childish, dangerous lapse of judgment, though. And I certainly hope that you won't pay for it any more than you already may have." The old woman looked pointedly at Mary's midsection. "It might be rather . . . difficult to explain."

Oh, my God, Mary thought to herself. *They think I ran away from Melk with a man to avoid my wedding. And that I've spent the past fortnight in his bed!*

Most of which was actually true, she realized.

The bells of the church were fading away now, and the rush of people at the gates had increased.

"I can't talk about this now," Mary said, hearing the desperation in her voice, which was there for an entirely different reason than the elderly nobles before her believed. She looked at them squarely, mustering all the anxiety she truly felt. "Can we please just go? Please?"

"Yes, of course," Lady Elmsbeth said kindly, linking her arm with

Mary's. They turned back toward the church. "Our inn is just on the other side of the cathedral."

Lord Roscoe graciously took her other elbow and the pair began leading Mary back toward the garden gates.

The old man patted her arm reassuringly. "There is a corridor through the vineyard that leads to the other street," he said. "We shall be there in a thrice."

There was nothing Mary could do but let herself be dragged up the cobbled street by her elderly captors. *I should have stayed in the room,* she berated herself. *I should have listened to Valentine.*

And then, as if her thoughts had conjured him, he appeared at the gate, drawing his hood up over his head, his satchel slung across his body. He was smiling and appeared occupied by his thoughts, and Mary feared he would walk right past them.

"Vamanos," Mary said suddenly in a loud voice.

The monk glanced up briefly, and then Valentine looked again, his head turning over his shoulder to follow Mary as she passed.

"What on earth, Lady Mary?" Lady Elmsbeth said with a frown.

"I believe it means 'thank you' in the language of Prague," Mary hedged.

Lord Roscoe was nodding. "She's quite right, Beth."

"Well, of course you are welcome, my dear," Lady Elmsbeth said. "And have no fear—we shan't let you out of our sights again, shall we, Roscoe?"

Lord Roscoe harrumphed. "Indubitably."

Valentine stopped in the street, closed his eyes, and turned his face up toward the sky with a sigh. Then he spun on his heel and began following the pair of old people who held Maria captive back through the cathedral's gate. If any of the good citizens of Prague had been able to translate the forceful and colorful curses muttered by the man in the habit, they certainly would have been shocked.

What was Maria doing on the other side of the city? Had she followed him? Valentine hadn't seen her inside the garden, but he admittedly had been distracted. Perhaps she had become lost. The old people laying such bold claim to Maria could be none other than those from the pilgrims' party she had abandoned in Melk, and Valentine could not believe their exceptional good fortune in happening upon her in Prague.

Which would have been impossible had Maria stayed at the Owl as I requested.

Never mind that now. There would be time aplenty for lectures and chastisement as soon as Valentine figured out where the old pilgrims were taking Maria and how he was to get her back.

The trio wound around the marble fountain and toward the corner of the garden opposite the public gate, where trellises of grapevines twisted overhead and created a cool, dark passage over the gravel path. The old man stepped ahead to push open a rounded, swinging wooden door, and then they stepped out onto the street beyond. Valentine averted his face as the old man let the door swing shut, and then he waited a moment before exiting the path himself.

He looked right, left, and caught sight of Maria's black lace as she was led away from the river and up the street in a diagonal line toward the buildings opposite the cathedral. Valentine hung back a bit as Maria and the old pilgrims ducked through the doorway of an elegantly façaded building, and then he followed in their footsteps.

It was a lavish inn, complete with a proper tavern, Valentine saw as he ducked into the cool, dim room. Delicious smells wafted from the open doors in the rear, and Valentine could see the elaborate outdoor kitchen beneath a deep overhang across a busy alley. Valentine was distracted from the opulent appointments at the sight of Maria in a back corner of the room, being seated at a table by the old man. Her eyes were wide, her distress clear on her pale face.

Maria saw him, then, her lips parting in an O of either surprise or dread, but to her credit, she looked away, as if he were not there. The old woman sat down next to her, her mouth moving in animated conversation, which Valentine was certain he was glad he could not hear. The old man wandered away.

Valentine spied an empty table halfway through the room and weaved his way between patrons. He chose a chair that would give him a sideways view of Maria, and yet not place his back to the door. But before his arse could connect with the wooden seat, a scrawny lad skittered around his backside to confront him.

"I think not, brother," the boy said in the language of the city. "You know him don't give charity. He'll toss you."

"I can pay," Valentine said. He pulled his satchel around and produced two small coins, which he flipped to the lad. "Be gone, and return with an ale."

The coins twinkled in the dim light before the grubby fist snatched them from the air. "He'll toss you," the boy repeated resignedly but went away, Valentine hoped, to do his bidding.

While Valentine waited for his drink, he kept a watchful eye on Maria and tried to think of how he would extricate her from the old woman, whose jowls had not stopped moving since she had placed her considerable girth in the chair. This inn must be where the pilgrims were staying, and if they secreted Maria away into a room before he could make a move, it would be much more difficult to locate her. The doorway that Valentine surmised led to the upstairs apartments was open, but a man sat to one side on a tall stool, likely to keep the upper floors sacrosanct for the inn's privileged guests.

Before he could come up with anything more, a thick, hairy palm slammed down on the tabletop before him and then lifted to reveal one of the coins Valentine had given the serving boy.

"Get out," a voice growled near his ear, and Valentine turned his head calmly to regard a wide, florid face, with red, bushy hair ringing the entirety of it, save for what was stuffed under a pointed velvet cap.

"Good day, brother," Valentine said. "Is there no ale to be had in your establishment? My coin is authentic, I assure you."

"None for the likes of you," the proprietor said through jagged teeth. "Which the boy just told you. My patrons find no ease with a man of God watching their every move, even if he be a worse sot then they. This is no church. Now get up and get out, before I have need to show you the way."

Valentine felt one of his eyebrows quirk. He would love nothing more than to grab the plum-faced man by the back of his thick neck and introduce his nose to the tabletop. Fortunately for the proprietor, Valentine could not draw that sort of attention to himself at the moment.

Then Valentine realized the man might be of use after all.

"I would not do that if I were you," Valentine said, and then glanced around the room pointedly. He gestured to the man to lean closer with a toss of his head, and he did so, albeit with obvious reluctance. "I am no monk, innkeeper."

"What kind of shite is this?" the man demanded. "I care not if you call yourself a monk, brother, father, or holiday goose."

Valentine shook his head discreetly, and then lifted up the hem of his robe to reveal his leather boot. He reached down and slid the hilt of his dagger up where the man could see it above the tooled cuff and then replaced it again. "I am no monk. See you the young lady in the back of the room? With the old woman?"

The red-haired man stood erect and turned to look boldly toward the rear of the tavern. "Yes, I see her."

"Shh!" Valentine hissed and grabbed the man's thick forearm, catching him off-balance and dragging him into a chair at the table. "The English party; they have just requested accommodations for her, yes?"

"Yes," the man said slowly with a frown. "She is to share the chamber of the lady she is with now."

Valentine let his lips press into a thin line. "Damn! Of course! I underestimated their cunning yet again." He let his eyes go to the innkeeper's confused face again, and Valentine leaned forward over the table. "Do you not find it odd that a lone young woman would suddenly appear with an aged group such as theirs—reportedly on a *pilgrimage*?"

A frown began to appear below the bushy eyebrows and his gaze flicked to the rear of the room with suspicion now. "What's this about?"

"If you wish to preserve the reputation of your fine establishment, you will listen to me carefully and do exactly as I say."

Mary stole furtive glances at Valentine as he had what at first appeared to be an altercation with the inn's proprietor, and then seemed to engage in serious conversation with the capped and aproned man. At her left, Lady Elmsbeth prattled unceasingly, but Mary could not have repeated a word of what the old woman was saying. It didn't seem to matter to the dowager that Mary contributed little to the conversation save for the occasional head nod or assenting hum.

Then, suddenly, the bearded man stood up from the table in the same moment as Valentine, and each went in opposite directions across the tavern floor—the innkeeper disappearing through an apparently guarded doorway and Valentine striding past Mary's table to exit the inn through the rear, his hood drawn up. He did not spare her even the slightest glance.

Something was afoot, but Mary had no idea what it could be, and her nerves jangled so that she felt her skin would leap from her flesh at any moment.

She did give a little jump in her chair and a gasp of surprise when the inn's proprietor suddenly reappeared at her elbow between Mary and Lady Elmsbeth.

His accent was thick. "I beg your pardon, my lady," he said to the dowager, although his eyes flicked to Mary as he spoke. "There is a small problem in moving your belongings."

"What?" Lady Elmsbeth squawked. "What problem?"

"I am not certain," the bearded man said with some difficulty, and Mary noticed the beads of sweat along his forehead, soaking into the edge of his cap and darkening the velvet. "I . . . there—"

He never got to finish his struggling explanation, as the dowager stood up from her chair with an exasperated sigh. "Never mind. I shall see to it myself. Will you be so kind as to keep watch over my ward? Do whatever you must to keep her here." She didn't bother to acknowledge the innkeeper's hasty nod but looked to Mary and pointed a gnarled finger at her. "I shall be but a moment, child. Do not move from this table, lest further misfortune befall you."

At her words, the innkeeper's eyes widened, and Mary saw him swallow. He bowed quickly, averting his horrified expression from Lady Elmsbeth as the old woman swept toward the doorway and disappeared from the common room.

Then the man stood upright and took hold of Mary's arm, helping her to stand gently but quickly. "Hurry, Your Royal Highness," he said and began pulling her toward the back of the tavern. "Your man has found you and is waiting through the back. Hurry!" he prompted. He released her at the door and then gave a grandiose bow. "Go with God, and remember with kindness me and my humble inn to your father."

Mary was not certain what game Valentine had played with the man, but she thought it best to reinforce the ruse. A long-handled dipper hung on a peg near the door and Mary grabbed it, holding it up before her face, as if it were a scepter or sword.

"Kneel, good man," she said haughtily, and the innkeeper's eyes widened as he fell to the floor. At the last moment, he swiped his cap from his head and clasped it to his chest with both fists.

"For service rendered to my family, I hereby dub you a knight of the realm, so that you may be—" Mary faltered a bit—"that you may be recognized in . . . in our land as such, and receive all applicable . . .

ah, favors due to you." She tapped him on each shoulder and then shoved the ladle into his clenched hands. "Thank you."

Before she could say anything more, someone grabbed her from behind and nearly jerked her from her feet as she was pulled from the doorway.

It was Valentine, his robes now discarded, and together they ran with linked hands down the alley toward a horse tethered to the back of a cart. Valentine released her and gathered the reins of the beast before swinging up onto its bare back. He held one hand down to her.

"Hurry, Maria," he commanded, and then yanked her up in front of him.

"How did you manage to buy a horse so quickly?" she asked as he wheeled the steed around in the close alley.

"We are no buying. We are stealing," he said, and then Mary could do nothing but cling to his arms as Valentine gave a shout and the horse leapt into a gallop, carrying them away from the inn.

They did not slow until they were across the bridge and had zigzagged over perhaps a mile of twisting streets. Then Valentine guided the horse into a stable and helped Mary to slide down before he, too, dismounted.

A young man approached and took the reins from Valentine.

Valentine fished a coin from his pack and gave it to the man. "The remainder this eve."

"Aye, milord." The young man didn't look at them twice, only led the horse away.

Then Valentine turned and left the stable, and Mary found herself skipping to keep up with him on the street.

"What are we to do with a third horse?" she asked him. "And a stolen one at that?"

He refused to look at her. "We shall no be retrieving the horse, Maria. It will be found by its owner soon enough, fed and well tended."

"Oh! I see," Mary said. "What did you tell the innkeeper? He called me 'your royal highness.'"

"I told him you were a princess who was being forced into a political foreign marriage by your aunt against your father's will. If you were no returned to him, it would start a war."

"My goodness," Mary marveled. "I'm glad I knighted him."

Valentine looked twice at her and then, as if he couldn't help himself, gave her a rueful grin. "That is what you were doing with the spoon? Knighting him?"

Mary shrugged. "It was all I could think of."

"A nice touch," Valentine conceded. "Although the party you were traveling with—I assume the English pilgrims, yes?" At her nod, he continued. "They might find the rest of their stay uncomfortable, as the innkeeper now thinks them enemies of the king of England."

Mary winced. "I feel terrible to have done that to them. They were only trying to help me."

"You *should* feel terrible," Valentine agreed. "But no for them. I must venture once more to the part of the city beyond the bridge on the morrow, and there will surely be an alarm raised to locate you. Your companions will perhaps recall me from the tavern, and so I will be forced to abandon my robes as a disguise."

He was going back to the cathedral tomorrow, to see his love again, Mary realized. And although she was sorry to have caused him the trouble of rescuing her, she was petulantly happy to have made his rendezvous difficult.

Was she *jealous*? Of a *nun*?

Mary had meant to apologize to him, but now she found she could not force the words from her throat as she recalled the loving way Valentine had looked upon the beautiful woman.

They snaked through endless alleys without speaking, and Mary was just about to voice her plea that, if they were not drawing near to the Owl, she must have something to drink. The close streets between the buildings were stifling in the afternoon heat, and the stench of the refuse along the gutters seemed to bloom with the rising temperatures.

But Valentine delayed her request by asking a question of his own. "Why did you follow me?"

Mary thought for a moment before replying. "Because I didn't want to be left alone again. And—" she thought she might as well be honest—"I wanted to see where you were going."

Valentine suddenly stopped before a wide oaken door and gave a deliberate pattern of raps with his knuckles. In a blink, Karl swung the door wide. He and Valentine exchanged words in the foreign tongue Mary did not understand, and then the big bald man handed Valentine a key.

Mary followed him down the corridor as he spoke to her over his shoulder, holding up the small piece of metal. "We are fortunate to have Brennie looking after us. In any other brothel, we would be returning to an empty room."

Mary realized that she had abandoned the room to follow Valentine with no thought for the satchels of their belongings she had left behind—including the one that contained her own purse.

"I'm sorry," she said finally, stiffly, as he fit the key into the door and then pushed it open.

He gestured for her to precede him. "Sorry for what?"

"Sorry for following you," she said, removing the lace from her head and draping it across the back of a chair.

"You are no sorry for that," Valentine argued in a monotone voice, closing the door and tossing his satchel on the table. "You got what you wanted, yes? You saw where I went?"

Mary turned to look at him. "You're right. I'm not sorry for that. I apologize for leaving the room unattended, then." She poured herself a cup of water from the fresh pitcher on a tray. Brennie was certainly anticipatory of her guests' wants. If Valentine did anything right, he made sure to surround himself with amazing women. Mary drained the cup and straightaway poured another.

Perhaps it was the residual energy left over from encountering Lady Elmsbeth; from the danger of escaping the inn on a stolen horse through a foreign city; perhaps the shock of seeing Valentine in such a way that she never had before, but Mary felt herself itching for answers. For an explanation.

She raised the cup to her lips but before drinking asked, "Is she the reason you left Aragon?" She swallowed the cool water, but Valentine only looked at her, so she pressed on. "The reason you did not honor the marriage contract?"

Mary thought he would simply refuse to answer. So it was a surprise when he said, "Yes."

Although she had already guessed as much, the admission caused Mary's heart to skip a beat, her stomach to flutter. How different would her life have been if not for the beautiful woman in the cathedral garden? Perhaps she and Valentine would have been happy. Perhaps they would have children now and be living at Beckham Hall together, or even in Valentine's homeland.

One thing she knew for certain: she would not be hiding in a brothel in Prague, trying to evade detection on her race back to England to marry a man she hardly knew.

"You love her still," Mary said, the words a statement rather than a question.

"Her name is Teresa," Valentine said. "And yes, Maria, I love her very much." He picked up the cup Mary had discarded and poured himself a drink.

Mary had known as much. But it seemed as if his matter-of-fact admission knocked upon an ancient and—up to this point in her life—very locked chamber in her heart filled with nothing but rage and resentment. The opulent room around her pulsed with her own heartbeat. Her chest tightened; her fists clenched. She watched Valentine's throat as he swallowed his drink, gulp after gulp.

Knock. Knock. Knock.

Mary walked deliberately toward Valentine Alesander and let that door swing wide, slapping him so soundly that the cup still held to his lips went flying across the room, flinging an arc of water through the air.

"You heartless bastard," she said in a low voice, her eyes boring into his. One of his eyebrows quirked, but it was the only expression of surprise as he swiped his forearm across his mouth. "I had no one. *No one.* My parents were dead; the king had forgotten me. I was alone at Beckham Hall all those years, with only a child's nurse for companion." She beat her flat palm against her chest. "When I at last find someone who wanted me, I needed your leave to gain my freedom. And what did you do in the midst of our journey? You left me in a *brothel* while you visited the woman for whom you abandoned me!"

"It is no as you think, Maria," Valentine said in a grave tone. "But even if it was, you would never have wanted a man such as me. I am no English lord."

"I am confident my parents were aware of your heritage when the contract was made," she said. "And don't tell me what I would or would not have wanted. You don't know anything about me."

"I think it is you who does no know anything about you," Valentine countered.

Mary glared at him. "What is that supposed to mean?"

"You say you want this man—this *knight*? You leave your comfortable little prison and risk your life to find me—the criminal, the reprobate—that I might rush back with you in secret and renounce my claim. No one can ever know that you were to be mine, yes? There can be no taint upon the reputation. And yet with me you tease, you play bold, you follow me. You expect me to save you, but you will throw me away when you are done."

Mary felt heat rushing up her neck and turned from him so that he could not see. "I have no choice in what I am doing. *You gave me no choice when you forgot about me!"*

"What is it, Maria?" he demanded, ignoring her accusation. "What do you expect to gain from this little game you play?"

"My life is no game!" she shouted, spinning around to face him once more. She struck her breast again, this time with both fists, her fingers clawing at the material of her bodice and hanging there tangled. She felt the shocking tracks of wetness down her heated face, but she didn't care. "I've been so lonely for so long, and I just want to have a family—a husband, children! People who are mine, who belong to me and I to them. Someone who at last doesn't find me so infinitely easy to leave behind!"

Valentine's expression was drawn, enigmatic. "And you are angry with me now because you think that I am that man?"

"No," she said at last on a shuddering breath. She sniffed, covered her eyes with her hands for a long moment, and then dropped them with a sigh. "You are not that man now. But perhaps you could have been. And I would have tried very hard to make you as happy as does your Teresa."

He walked toward her then, and Mary held out her hands to ward him off. She was so embarrassed; she did not want his pity.

"Please don't," she said.

But he ignored her, collapsing her extended arms between them as he drew her near. She turned her face away and pushed at him, but he held her firm and then took her chin in his hand and forced her to look up at him.

"Maria, you would no have to try very hard to make me happy," he said, his eyes holding no hint of amusement. "Then or now. Forgive me for ever making you think otherwise." Then he lowered his mouth to hers and kissed her as she'd wished he would a hundred times since leaving the old mill.

And he kept kissing her. Until she realized that he was no longer holding her captive, and she let her arms go around his waist to clutch at his back, pulling him closer. She felt as if she'd finally come to a place that was familiar, safe, in the embrace of this man who'd been intended to be hers but that she could now never have. He held her at her waist, at the nape of her neck, his thumb caressing her jaw. His stubble scraping her lips and chin felt both foreign and right and she breathed in the scent of him.

He finally pulled away, but only far enough to look into her eyes. "I am sorry that I left you behind, Maria," he said quietly. Mary wished she knew which instance he was referring to, but then decided it didn't matter as he continued. "I promise that I never will again before you are returned to your home. You will be at my side until that day."

Mary felt as if she might cry again, but she managed to nod.

"And although it can no change things between us now, you must never think that I abandoned you," Valentine said, still stroking her cheek with his thumb. "Teresa is my sister."

Chapter 13

Maria's lovely, tear-glistened eyes blinked. "Your sister?"

"Yes." He steadied her as they drew apart, not wishing to be without her in his arms but recognizing that if he was ever to get through the telling of this tale, they would need to be separated.

And wine. They would need wine. Perhaps a lot.

Valentine led her to the table and she sat down in a chair heavily, as if their argument had nearly been all she could physically endure. He had never intended to reveal to Maria the details of his exile from Aragon, and now he wanted to even less. It was best that she actually think the worst of him, but Maria was correct—he did owe her an explanation, and it never occurred to him to lie to her. If there was anyone on earth who deserved to know the truth about his life, it was Maria.

He retrieved the cup from the floor in a corner of the room and brought it back to the table, filling it and another from the taller decanter on the tray and setting one of them before Maria. She whispered her thanks before drinking, and then simply sat there, waiting.

"My mother bore my father seven children," he began, deciding to walk about the room as he did the telling, the memories too haunting and terrible to sit with for very long. "Two of those never drew breath; two more lived only a few days. Six boys, in all. Enrique is my older brother, by six years. When I was ten and two, Teresa was born. Her miracle, Mama called Teresa—the only girl. But Mother's body was tired, and this time it was she who nearly died instead of her babe. She was no the same after Teresa, although she would live to see her girl reach seven.

"My father was a wealthy man—a baron, I think he would be in your England. He was ruled by no man, although he renewed his fealty to Aragon's Crown every year. Enrique was always a greedy boy, pressing my father to war, to absorb some of the smaller holdings around us, but my father refused. He had his honor. When Mama died, he did no know what to do with himself. He died only a year later."

Valentine had almost forgotten Maria was present until she spoke. "And that left your brother, Enrique, the estate."

"Yes." Valentine nodded, coming back to refill his cup. "As I said, Enrique was greedy. He refused to swear allegiance to the king. And he went to war with everyone—everyone!" He gave a harsh laugh. "We lost so much—so many men, so much of our wealth. He never held anything he gained for long. He began to charge his own family a sum for coming to our villa—a tax for having the misfortune of being related to him, I suppose. Our people were beginning to refuse him service. They would no fight for such an honorless man. I, of course, would no support his lunacy."

"There was nowhere for you to go?" Maria asked. "No other family you and Teresa could turn to?"

Valentine shook his head. "Perhaps at the beginning, but even then Enrique held the purse strings tight, and there was still some hope that he would be a benefactor as my father had. Once it could no be denied that he was nothing but evil, Teresa and I were also anathema.

"But even though Enrique was evil, he was no completely stupid, and he at last found a people who would join with him—the Muslims to the south. The head of a large and powerful family, a terrible warlord, visited our villa. He became infatuated with Teresa, and so Enrique bartered our sister and a large dowry for the dog's loyalty."

Maria gasped. "But wasn't she still only a child?"

"She was ten years old," he answered quietly, recalling vividly that terrible night when Enrique had announced that Teresa was to be married. "And the man she was to marry was more than two score, with many other wives."

"What did you do?" Maria asked, a worried frown creasing her lovely forehead.

"I fought him, of course. I would have killed him, had my cousin, Francisco, not stopped me. Francisco had been right—killing Enrique would have done nothing to revoke the marriage agreement, and I would have been of no protection to Teresa if I was charged with murder. And so I waited. I made Enrique think that I was defeated. It was spring. Some of our family had traveled to our villa for Teresa's wedding and so there were many people in our home. When everyone was asleep, I killed a pig and collected the blood. Teresa gathered her things while I found the box containing the last of our family's wealth—the gold meant to be Teresa's dowry. I poured the pig's blood over Teresa's bed, the floor of her chamber.

"And then Teresa and I fled Aragon," he finished simply.

"I see," Maria said. "You wanted it to appear that Enrique had killed Teresa, invoking the warlord's wrath."

Valentine nodded. "But I was no yet as skilled as I am now. Looking back, I can no believe I did no see the flaws in my plan. When Teresa's bloody chamber was discovered, the missing girl, the missing coin, the missing brother . . ."

"They thought you killed her and absconded with the dowry," Maria finished.

"*Exactamente*. The Muslim did no care so much what had become of his child bride, but he did want his coin, which Enrique could no give him."

"Perhaps you can at least gain some satisfaction in the fact that the confrontation was uncomfortable for your brother," Maria offered.

Valentine shrugged. "It was rumored that Enrique lost part of his tongue for his deception, but I do no know that for certain."

"Did you take Teresa directly to Prague?"

"I did. The convent did no want a little Spanish orphan girl at first, but then I showed them the coin. It was the same when my friends and I arrived at Melk." Valentine could at last give Maria a grin. "Gold opens many, many doors."

She returned his smile with one of her own, albeit a sad one. "But how could you be sure they would continue to care for her?"

"I continued to bring her coin," he said.

"All these years?" Maria asked with wide eyes.

He nodded. "And that is why I could no marry, Maria—you or anyone else. Enrique, Francisco, they have been searching for me since the night I left Aragon. Although they must know by now that the amount of coin I originally left with could no sustain a man this length of time, they still crave vengeance upon me. And if I am killed, there is no one to support Teresa. That is what I was doing yesterday—bringing her the coin I had managed to save since I last saw her three years ago."

"You gave up your life for your sister," Maria said, watching him with a keen, steady gaze.

Valentine shook his head, uncomfortable with the implications her statement left hanging in the room. "I am no hero, Maria. Of course I love my sister, and I could no stand aside while Enrique sold her innocence, her childhood. But I could never have stayed in Aragon any matter. My brother was destined to fail, and it would no have been long before I had no home there. Enrique would have eventually ejected me for constantly challenging him, or the estate would have been lost."

"What happened to him?" Maria asked.

"I do no know," Valentine said with a shrug. "He was still on my trail three years ago, nearly caught me once here in Prague. After some time, I worked my way through the Holy Land, knowing that he would never follow me there."

"That was a narrow escape then, for Teresa."

"And for Brennie as well." When Maria's eyebrows rose, Valentine supplied, "She had been a slave, a gift from the warlord for Teresa. I brought her to Prague with us. Now she has power over men that most never dream of."

Maria's expression carried an atypical smirk. "But you are no hero."

"No," he said, walking back across the room toward her. "I am no."

Her gaze tracked him, her face tilted up as he passed, and Valentine had the sudden urge to kiss her again. "I wish you would have told me sooner."

"I saw no reason to," Valentine said, coming at last to sit opposite her at the small table. "Neither of us can change the past."

"No," she agreed. "But if you had come for me, perhaps you could have spared yourself the trials of Saladin's prison."

"Perhaps," he said. He poured more wine, then raised his cup toward her in salute. "I am saving you to the best of my ability now, though, yes? To your future husband." He drank, hoping that he could force the wine down his throat.

"I suppose," Maria said, her gaze still unsettling in its intensity, as if she was studying him anew. "But what if I no longer wish for you to save me for him?"

Mary held her breath as she watched Valentine lower his cup, and she tried to gauge his reaction to her impetuous words. She was likely a fool for declaring such a thing to this man, who would want nothing less than to be saddled with an inexperienced innocent who seemed to do nothing right.

"You are caught up in our journey, Maria," he said. "Our adventure. It is exciting for you. *Now*," he added quickly. "But in three months, a year, you would find little novelty with me."

His overly kind tone stung. "You mean you would find little novelty with *me* after that time, don't you? You are used to variety, scores of women at your beck and call."

He looked at her for a long moment and then shrugged, his gaze going to the cup he raised to his mouth. "Perhaps. Yes, perhaps that is what I mean." He drained the cup and set it down on the table with a sigh and met her eyes again. "Is it no kinder for me to tell you this now than to allow you to throw away a certain future?"

Mary felt her cheeks heating with embarrassment, and she wished she would have simply kept her mouth shut rather than force Valentine to try to reason her naive and sudden declaration away. But she was no prideless wretch.

"You're right, of course," she said with a sigh, and forced herself to give him a smile. She hoped it was bright enough. "After all, I never considered you as a proper husband. Thank you for sparing me that humiliation." Mary stood.

Valentine's mouth thinned for an instant, and then he gave her a tight smile that didn't quite reach his eyes. "Certainly."

Of course he was uncomfortable; they still had hundreds of miles left to travel together. He was probably worried she would romanticize over him the entire way.

She turned away toward the bed. "I think I shall lie down for a while. This morning has been a trial."

"Of course," Valentine said, and she heard the screech of chair legs behind her. "I shall leave you to your privacy."

"You needn't go," she said, turning around again and holding out her hand. "It's not as if I fear you will accost me in my sleep." She gave a little laugh, although she felt a nauseous pit in her stomach. Somehow that declaration sounded more pathetic than her earlier plea.

He shook his head as he slung his satchel over his arm and backed toward the door. "It is no trouble, Maria. There are some things I must do, any matter."

"Oh. All right, then," she said lamely as he stood with his hand on the latch. "Good-bye."

"Good-bye." He stood there a breath longer, looking at her. Then his full mouth quirked with his now familiar grin. "You will feel happier after a rest." He opened the door and was gone.

Mary stood staring at the door for a long time after she heard the lock scrape and his footfalls disappearing down the corridor. When she finally turned again toward the bed and crawled upon the mattress, it seemed all the joints of her bones creaked. She laid her head upon the silken pillow and stared across the room at Valentine's feathered hat, hanging on the arm of the chaise.

Mary wondered if she would ever feel happy again once their adventure was over.

Valentine's feet seemed to drag beneath him as he made his way to the Owl's tavern, his mind seeing over and over the look on Maria's face when he'd rejected her.

His act had convinced her, but the playing of it had cost Valentine a portion of his heart.

He pushed through the door and claimed one of the many empty tables—it was still early in the day, and the bulk of the Owl's patrons had yet to free themselves from their obligations. The common room was quiet save for the middle-aged woman propped in the corner near the stone hearth, practicing a mournful tune on her small harp. It was one of the women employed there, although no one would have recognized her as such, clothed so modestly, her hair plaited, her eyes clear and sober.

Valentine slung his satchel over the back of the chair and sat down, propping his elbows on the table and scrubbing at his face with his hands for a moment.

Slender arms snaked around his neck and Valentine caught Brennie's spicy scent before she murmured in his ear, "Good morn, *mi amor.*"

"It is past noon," he remarked as she slid from his shoulders and into the chair next to his, her long brown arm propping up her closely cropped head, her deep eyes still heavy with sleep. She wore a long belted robe with wide sleeves that slid to her elbow as she held herself up.

Her smile was lazy and indulgent when she came out of her yawn. "Yes. And I said good morn. There was a time when you, too, would only venture out of your room once the sun was already on its way back down. But by the look of you, you have been about for hours. You've been to see Teresa, I suppose?"

Valentine nodded. "Something she said has me troubled," he remarked, realizing Brennie would sense his mood, and not wishing to discuss Maria with her.

"Of course," Brennie said. "I told her you would not easily accept the news. And then to learn that she wished to marry . . ."

"What?" Valentine said.

Brennie's eyes widened, and then her lips quirked into a rueful grin. "Oh-oh. It seems as though my mouth is more awake than my wits. She didn't tell you."

"No," Valentine said through gritted teeth. "I am to meet her again on the morrow, when she will reveal some mysterious news to me."

"And now I have ruined the wonderful surprise," Brennie said with an unconvincing pout.

"Who could she possibly have found that she wants to marry while cloistered away?" Valentine demanded, refusing to engage in Brennie's play. "Some renegade priest?"

"Oh no, *mi amor*," Brennie said, shaking her head. "You'll get no more from me. You should hear it from your sister's lips."

"She can no leave," Valentine said, as if it was the end of the thing. "I can no protect her right now."

"Protect her from . . . ?"

"I have bigger predators on my scent now than Enrique could ever dream to aspire to," Valentine said. "If it was discovered that I have a sister, and if she was no protected by her asylum, I do no know what could happen to her."

"Nothing will happen to her," Brennie said in almost a bored tone. "Her man would never allow it."

"You know him?" Valentine demanded, and he leaned forward when she nodded her head lazily. "Who is he? Is he in the city? I will find him today and demand that he leave my sister in peace."

"I will not tell you who he is, but yes, he is in the city when he is not plying his trade. Did you really expect her to live her entire life as a nun? Teresa is as religious as you are."

"Brennie, had it been in my power to have chosen a different life for Teresa or myself, I would have done so long ago."

"Would you have?" Brennie said, peering into his eyes. "Since you arrived here with the lovely Fleur, I wonder." Before he could argue his point with her, she continued. "Any matter, now that you are in Prague, the man who wishes to marry your sister can at last ask your permission himself, and he and Teresa can be away from the city with your blessing."

"Never," he said, standing up from his chair and reaching around for his satchel, irritated that the day had seemed to hurry him from one disaster to the next. "And I shall make that quite clear when I see her on the morrow."

Valentine and Brennie's heads swiveled in unison as the heavy wooden entrance to the Snowy Owl burst open, and several men blustered through the doorway.

"Constable," Brennie murmured under her breath, not in the least disturbed by their intimidating appearance. But Valentine's spine stiffened. "Looking for runaways again, I'll wager." To the men now filling up the common room, she called out a friendly greeting, addressing some of the watchmen by name.

"Any new girls, Brennie?" the portly constable asked. "We've got a kidnap—an English lady by the name of Mary Beckham."

Had Valentine not known Brennie, he never would have caught the twitch of her eyebrow or the knowing gleam in her eye as she slowly, slowly turned her serene face toward Valentine. "A lady, you say? I don't know of any English girls at the Owl, and certainly no *ladies*. Did any come in last night?" she asked him, and then added pointedly, "Perhaps you could ask *Fleur*."

"Who's this now?" the constable demanded, eyeing Valentine.

Valentine shoved away his alarm to make a sweeping bow to the group. "Enrique Francisco, at your service," he said, letting his accent thicken. "Procurer of the finest specimens of womanhood the world over."

"A whoremonger," the constable snorted. "Any English ladies in your depraved band?"

"I prefer to think myself more a curator of desire," Valentine countered. "But no. They are much too reserved for a profession of such passion."

The constable snorted again and turned to Brennie once more. "We must search, you understand," he said. "There's a baroness or some such shite paying a hefty price for the lady's recovery."

"Of course," Brennie said and then looked up at Valentine again. "Go rouse the girls. I can't bear to listen to the complaints this early in the day, and what good are you if not for the ugly jobs?"

"It would be my pleasure," Valentine said with a short bow. "I shall refill the brazier in your room while I am about it."

She waved a lazy hand at him. "As you wish."

"Two moments," the constable warned, "and we shall enter each room thoroughly."

"Two moments," Valentine agreed and then turned on his heel and walked deliberately across the floor and into the back corridor.

Once the door swung shut behind him, Valentine broke into a run, pulling the key from his pouch as he swerved around crooked corners. He unlocked the door and burst into the room, already barking orders.

"Maria! Maria! Get up! Get your things, now. *Vamanos*," he said, trotting to the hearth while swinging his satchel from his shoulder. "Maria!"

"What is it?" She didn't sound as though she'd been asleep, and he heard her rustling from the bed.

"The city constable is here with a band of watchmen, seeking you by name. They are searching the rooms." He pulled forth the bag he had tried to give to Teresa and then squatted down, lifting the lid of the brazier and checking that it was cool before dropping the bag inside.

"Oh my God," she gasped from behind him, and he heard her scurrying about. "What are we going to do?"

Valentine replaced the lid and joined Maria as she looped straps over her arms, bent to scoop up her boots, her veil.

"We're going to run," Valentine said distractedly, giving the room a final quick glance. He swiped his hat from the chaise and placed it on Maria's head. If they had forgotten anything, they would have to leave it. He turned back to her and nodded toward the door. "Open it slowly."

Maria opened the door a crack and Valentine stuck his head out. He pulled it back in with a hiss as he saw the band of watchmen in the hallway, pounding on doors. "Damn!" He peeked through the crack again as he heard squeals and ribald curses in very feminine voices. Half the men disappeared into the first doorway they'd come to, and the second half of the group waited entry at the next. "Come on, come on!" If they didn't enter before the first group came out . . .

"Now!" he said to Maria, pulling her into the hallway as the last man ducked inside. He left their door swinging and pushed Maria ahead of him, toward the rectangle of light where Brennie stood, holding the exit wide. "Horses?" he called out as loudly as he dared.

"Karl's with them now," Brennie said, when they were nearly upon her. "Godspeed, *mi amor*." She smirked at Maria. "And *Lady Mary*. I do hope we meet again. Enjoy my Ballenteen."

Valentine saw the cross look Maria threw over her shoulder as he shoved her into the alley. "It's *Valentine*," she said.

"Go!" Valentine said in exasperation.

"It *is* Valentine," she insisted as they turned left and ran down the alley. "Your name begins with a V."

"Not always." Valentine pulled Maria by the crook of her elbow toward the stables just as Karl emerged into the bright sunlight, leading their horses.

He held his large arms out toward Maria as they approached, and Valentine was surprised and pleased when Maria jumped into them without question, allowing the large bald man to swung her into her saddle.

"My thanks, friend," Valentine said, seating himself and pulling up the reins as Maria took possession of hers.

"Go the southwest gate," Karl advised. "Near the abattoir at the river. Should be able to follow the stench."

Valentine winced. "Really?"

"No one ever stays there long," Karl said with a shrug.

"Valentine?" Maria said in a warbly voice, looking over her shoulder.

Valentine followed her gaze and saw the constable and his associates just coming into the alley. "What's our other option?" he asked Karl.

"The gaol," he said pointedly.

Valentine sighed. But he had little choice now, as the constable had seen him. "Do no look back, Maria," he warned.

"You! You there!" the constable called out, raising his hand in the air as he and his band approached. "Henrygay Fran . . . Franch—you, whoremonger!"

"Go ahead of me," he said through his wide smile for the constable, raising his own hand now as if in a hearty farewell. "Quickly. And whatever happens, do no stop."

Maria moved past him obediently, her horse at a trot, and Valentine fell behind her as they fled from the constable's cries.

When they reached the corner of the alley and the wide, open street, Valentine called out, *"Vamanos!"* and he overtook Maria, leading the way as they abandoned Prague.

Chapter 14

Mary wasn't exactly certain which circumstances had brought her to the point where she was once more racing along behind Valentine through city gates, but she was fairly confident that it was not good.

And she was also fairly confident that it was her fault.

She didn't know where they were going, beyond the general direction of northwest, as they swerved around and dashed past travelers in carts and on foot, leaving clouds of dust and fading curses behind them. Valentine never looked back.

How far to the next city? How long after to the sea?

How soon would this adventure end upon her own doorstep, with Valentine riding away from Beckham Hall without her, never looking back?

The road was a hilly, live thing, snaking along the river and occasionally swerving up onto the southern hillside. They charged around blind curves, through dappled and humid shadows of the forest that reached like arms over the road as if to dip its long, branch fingers into the water. The track was hard and dusty, thankfully, for their flight could spare no misstep, and the effort required to keep herself astride would not allow Mary to dwell upon the cryptic end she and Valentine were racing toward.

They slowed to a trot after perhaps a half hour, then a walk some time later, giving Mary chance to loose her arms from the satchels she carried, securing them each carefully to the saddle behind her, one at a time. Perhaps an hour passed before Valentine veered from the road toward the river, and Mary urged her horse from the track, following him into the woods along the marshy bank.

Valentine swung from his horse quickly and let the reins fall just before it tromped into the deep, reedy wet to slurp at the water. He caught the bridle of Mary's horse, preventing its advance to the shore despite its whinnying protest. Mary slid down without pause, swaying a moment as she caught her legs beneath her. Valentine's hand shot out to steady her, but she shook him off, not wanting his help.

"I'm fine," she said.

He gave a little shrug and turned to one of the wide, ancient trees. He sat down at its thick base and leaned his head against the smooth bark, closing his eyes with a sigh.

Mary mimicked his actions, although she chose a tree nearby rather than sit at his side. She took off his feathered hat and rested it in the nest created by her crossed legs.

"This is no good, Maria," he said at last.

"I know it," she snapped. "I'm not as dense as I was when first we met, Valentine. We have no food, no supplies. I'm not even certain where we are or where we're going, although I'm assuming you have our location at least somewhat generalized."

His brows lowered before he let his head fall sideways against the tree and then opened his eyes to look at her. "That is no what I meant, although our lack of supplies is a problem."

"Oh. What do you mean, then?"

"The authorities of Prague will no give you up so easily, knowing that you have a wealthy benefactor. The constable has seen us both, seen our horses. This road is no safe for us."

"You think they will pursue us?"

"It would no surprise me," he said. "We can only afford a short rest for the horses, and then we must try to stay ahead of them as much as we can."

"Is there a village nearby?"

"No any of a size that we could hope to remain invisible in." His face turned away from her, and he seemed to be admiring the leafy canopy above them. "There is a large settlement north of here, on the Elbe. Two, three days, mayhap. No ideal, but it is there we must go, I think."

"I don't see how it's so very bad, then," she said, not at all relishing the idea of such a long journey ahead of them with little to no food. "If we can make it that far undetected, the constable will have given up. Then we can resupply and be on our way."

"I am afraid it is no that simple," Valentine said. "Keeping to the road would mean venturing through villages that . . . perhaps are no so safe for us."

She glared at him. "You mean you can't show your face in them lest you be arrested."

"They are savage places," he scoffed. "Full of criminals and mercenaries."

"Don't placate me. This journey would be a lot easier if you didn't make enemies everywhere you went."

"It would be easier indeed, Maria, if you had done as I asked and stayed at the Owl."

She chose to ignore his very relevant observation. "If we can't go through the cities, what are we to do once we reach the settlement?" Mary demanded. "Grow wings and fly?"

He grinned at her. "You are very pretty when you are being sarcastic, you know?"

"Stop," she said, feeling her face heat. "And just tell me whatever horrid thing it is you are trying to distract me from."

Valentine shrugged again. "We must take the river."

Mary paused a moment and blinked. Tried to think of a way in which she had misunderstood. "You mean follow the river away from the cities?"

"No, Maria. I mean we will have to sell or trade our horses for supplies and a conveyance that is better capable of carrying us *past* the cities to the sea."

"On the river," she clarified flatly.

"Yes." He gave her an encouraging smile.

"In a boat."

He turned down his lower lip as if considering the thing. "Or something similar."

"No." She stood up and marched toward where their horses had wandered back up onto firmer land, leaving Valentine's hat lying in the dirt under the trees. *"Absolutely not,"* she muttered as she grasped wildly for the reins hanging down.

"Maria, what are you doing?" Valentine called, a hint of laughter in his voice.

"No," she repeated, throwing him a glance over her shoulder as she at last seized both straps of leather and began several false starts of trying to mount, her horse moving sideways nervously.

Valentine got up from the tree and picked up his discarded hat, heading toward her just as she finally gained her saddle. She turned the horse, but he reached her before she could move away.

"Where do you think you are going?" he asked.

"Back to Prague," she said, looking down her nose at him. "I shall surrender myself to the constable and rejoin Lady Elmsbeth's party."

"Yes?" he inquired, with seemingly great interest. "And what shall you do after, when they return you to England and you must explain to your betrothed that you are already married?"

She pursed her lips and gave a short sigh through her nose. "Then I shall join up with whatever road it is we should have rather taken and meet you wherever it is that we must meet," she said, and then paused. "What is the name of that place, exactly, so that I might ask the direction of it?"

"You will do no such thing," he said. "Maria—"

"Valentine, I cannot be on the water, in a boat, for more than a moment. Surely you know that by now. I'll die. Now, turn loose my horse."

"I understand it is uncomfortable for you—"

"It's not uncomfortable," she gritted between her teeth. "I can't breathe. I can't move. I'd as soon throw myself overboard and drown rather than be afloat for longer than a ferry crossing."

"How did you make the sea voyage to the continent?" he asked with a squint. "And how do you think you shall return to your country? By cart?"

"I stayed below decks the entire time, abed, with a special potion given me by Lady Elmsbeth," she said.

"Ah," he said. "You were drunk."

"I wasn't drunk," she argued. "It was a *potion*. Herbs? A root of some sort, perhaps."

"You were drunk," he insisted. He released the horse's bridle then and placed his hat on his head, walking away as if the subject were confidently settled in his own mind. "But we may no have the luxury of such a vessel upon our return."

"What do you mean?" she demanded, urging her horse forward to follow his tapering back.

He held up his hands. "Passage on that type of a ship—it is costly. We will most likely find ourselves aboard a humble trading vessel.

Perhaps we shall even sit upon the cargo, which does provide a lovely view of the sea should we not encounter a storm. So it is better that we accustom you to the water as soon as we are able, yes?"

"No!" she insisted. She only realized she had dismounted and was following him on foot when he turned to sit down at the base of the tree again and looked up at her expectantly, waiting for her explanation. "True, I only have a portion of coin left, but you still have a sack of—"

"Had," he interjected.

Mary cocked her head to look at him sideways. *"Had?"*

"Had. That was Teresa's coin. I left it in the brazier at the Owl, and as I have no plan to return to Prague in the near future . . ." He gave a half shrug.

"You mean until you dump me at Beckham Hall and are on your way back through to Melk."

"I would never dump you," he said with an offended air. "I will place you ever so gently in the arms of your intended if you wish it. But no, I shall no divert through Prague."

"So much for your professed love and longing for your sister, eh?"

"Bah," he scoffed. "She wishes to throw away all I have done to keep her safe by marrying some unknown man."

Mary blinked. "She wants to marry and leave the abbey?"

Valentine rolled his eyes as if it was the most absurd thing he'd ever heard.

"And you are refusing her?"

He held his hands out again in supplication. "What can I say? Her suitor had no chance to broach the subject with me before I was forced to leave the city against my will. I expressed my refusal to Brennie, though, and I am confident that she will relay my wishes along with the coin."

"Oh!" Mary shouted. "You are unbelievable! How dare you play such a game with her!"

"It is no game, Maria," he said, crossing his arms over his chest, stacking his ankles as he stretched out his legs. "I am protecting her. There is no telling what sort of criminal has thought to take advantage of her vulnerable situation."

"A criminal like yourself, you mean?" Mary countered, her hands on her hips. "It's not as if she'd planned to run away with him without your knowledge, even though she's surely of age to speak for herself. I fail to see what spoils he would gain by wooing a young woman who is cloistered, with no coin nor—" Mary broke off, realizing Teresa Alesander's good fortune.

Perhaps Valentine then also realized what he'd done, for his handsome face was slack, with a slight greenish tinge.

Mary couldn't help her chirp of laughter. "Oh, my. My, my!" She did sit at his side now, their elbows brushing. She nudged him with hers before she reclaimed the hat from his head and placed it on her own with what she was certain was a smug grin. "Perhaps someone didn't quite think his plan through."

"She would no," he said.

"No?" Mary repeated. "Hmm. Let's see—interminable amount of time in a religious cloister, or freedom with the man I love. All right, yes, I can clearly see how you would be so confident of her obedience."

"What would you do, Maria?" he asked after several moments.

"What would I do? As soon as I had the coin in hand, I would go." She paused, and saw his head drop only slightly, but for proud Valentine, it was a clear sign of dejection. "After all, she only has to pick up and be off. I . . . well, I had to come all this way to find you." She feared she had said too much and so added, "So that I could marry the . . . the man I love."

He nodded but made no reply.

"Are you reconsidering a return to Prague?" Mary asked, struggling to keep the hope from her voice. "I'm certain we could evade—"

"No," he said suddenly and heartily. He slapped his hands on his knees and then rose, holding out a hand to Mary. "You are right. What is done is done. We must be away, Maria—we have been too long here already."

He released her as soon as she gained her feet, and Mary began following him to the horses once more.

"But no river, Valentine. Valentine?"

It took two full days to reach the settlement of Drezdeny, upon the widening river Elbe, and during those two days Mary had been filled with dread. Her feeling of unease was not lessened by the sight of the savage village, its rooflines saw-toothed and asymmetrical, leaning over a river that seemed to be as broad as the Channel and twice as rough.

The streets were wide ditches, pitched with holes shimmering with steaming, putrid water. Its inhabitants, swarthy and suspicious-looking themselves, cast appraising glances at Mary and Valentine as they rode through the hazardous streets. By the time they had reached what appeared to be the village's only livery, where the street ended abruptly at the river and a ramshackle wharf, Mary had seen such a cross-section of the settlement's population that she greatly feared never escaping Drezdeny alive.

In contrast, Valentine's face was calm, and he seemed pleased, muttering, "Yes, yes. We will find what we need here."

He swung down from his horse as a thin, greasy-looking man emerged from the darkened stable and approached Valentine, the livery-man eyeing the horseflesh with blatant greed. Valentine and the man worked for a moment or two at finding a common language, although Mary could not have determined what they had agreed to speak. Their conversation seemed to deteriorate into a heated argument for several moments as they each gestured in turn to the horses and toward the river, and Mary distracted herself by studying the boats tied to the wharf.

Although the term *boats* was rather generous. There were only two proper vessels, as Mary knew the definition, but they were both long and shallow, and one was turned upside down upon the shore, a gaping hole in its side marking the end of its career. Most of the craft tethered to the tall, rough piers were crudely constructed, square rafts with a single mast at the center. The sails were patched and ragged, setting poles lashed to the masts. Some boasted a bench or stool near the center, but besides one larger raft whose mast supported a triangle of tarp perhaps meant as a makeshift shelter, it was obvious that these conveyances were for nothing more than moving goods either up or down the river short distances.

Her attention was drawn back to Valentine and the liveryman by the clinking of coins. Valentine had a distasteful expression on his face as he pulled the strings of his purse tight and began unlooping his bags from his saddle.

Mary jumped as a series of barking shouts sounded near her left side, and she turned, her hand pressed to her chest, to see the swarthy horseman glaring at her and gesturing to the street.

"My God, what does he want?" Mary asked through a strangled throat.

"He would like for you to please dismount now, Maria," Valentine said, glancing up. His brow lowered and he came around the front of the mounts, his arm out, pointing to the man and shouting in the guttural-sounding tongue.

The man grumbled something in return, and Mary gasped as Valentine drew a knife from his boot faster than she could blink and held it before the man's nose. The two shared a quiet private conversation and then the liveryman held up both hands with a grin and backed a pair of paces away.

"Today, Maria?" Valentine asked over his shoulder. "Before I am forced to let this man's blood and we must defend ourselves against the entire town."

Mary scrambled down from her horse, landing on her feet heavily, and quickly loosed her bags. Valentine was at her side in a moment, pulling her from the street while the liveryman took possession of the horses, grinning at her the entire time. A shiver ran up her spine.

She thankfully lost sight of the man as Valentine tugged her along behind him into the shade between two buildings. He released her arm and then dropped his bags onto the dirt, following them to one knee and pulling a satchel open.

"What do you have that you do no absolutely need?" he asked, his voice still gruff, Mary assumed from the conversation with the rude stableman. He dumped the contents of his bag and began sorting through the items quickly.

"Well, I don't know exactly," Mary said, watching him with wonder as he reconfigured his possessions using priorities she could not grasp. "What might I have need of?"

"My apologies, Maria," he said in a milder tone, glancing up at her with a rueful smile. The contents of his bags were redistributed now and secure, and he held out his hand. "If you will allow me?"

Mary handed him her satchels, and Valentine wasted no time in treating her own possessions in the same hasty manner, resulting in one bag that was straining at the seams and another that contained items Mary could not ascertain if he had deemed necessary or not. One of her bags was left limp and empty.

He handed her up the lighter satchel and added the other two to his own shoulder, rising to his feet. "Let us go," he said, taking her elbow and leading her back onto the street.

"Are we passing the night in this . . . place?" she asked, glancing around furtively as she let Valentine pull her along the rutted thoroughfare.

"No under the threat of certain death," Valentine muttered. "And it would likely come to that if we were to stay."

"Good." Mary sighed. "But what about our horses? Surely we cannot push them any farther this day."

"They are no our horses any longer, Maria," Valentine said as he paused before a ramshackle building, pushing aside the dirty curtain across its doorway and peeking inside. He let the curtain fall and turned back to her. "I sold them."

"To that dreadful man?"

"Yes. Come along. Stay close." He pulled the curtain aside fully and ushered her into the dark.

Valentine realized that he needn't have warned Maria to remain close to his side as soon as they stepped inside the tiny shop—she had no choice but to stay pressed to him, lest she accidentally brush against one of the countless towers of goods and be crushed to death by the ensuing avalanche. Which almost happened when two snarling, snapping, growling mouths came at them from behind a tall counter.

Valentine pushed Maria behind him and reached for his blade, crouching down and readying himself to slit at least one beast's throat before the dull clink of chain sounded and stopped the monsters' advance not a hair too soon. Maria screamed shrilly—and a bit late, Valentine thought—her voice competing with the hounds' barking in the limited space of the shop. Two huge dogs—half as tall as Valentine himself—with wiry gray hair, long square snouts, and rangy legs strained at their bonds, causing the floor beneath Valentine's feet to shudder with every hollow volley.

A wheezy voice called from behind another curtain beyond the tall bench, and a moment later a little white troll of a man appeared. His crown was bald, but the hair around the sides and back of his head was thick and white and stuck up in a rather startled manner. He wore a leather tunic and green leggings, with wide-cuffed leather boots about his skinny ankles. Many belts and straps crisscrossed his chest and the narrow circumference of his body, with a variety of locks, clasps, tassels, vials, and jewels dangling from the loops. Valentine thought he even spied the dehydrated carcass of a small mammal but wasn't sure, as it was near the man's ear, and a moment later had blended into the hair that sprouted there.

The old man whistled sharply to the hounds and they quieted, although they only slunk down into a crouch with frustrated whines rather than retreat to the counter, which would have made Valentine infinitely more comfortable.

"Good day, merchant," Valentine said in the language he had used to converse with the rat-assed liveryman. "Will you trade?"

The little man eyed Valentine with a growing sly grin that revealed a surprising row of little white teeth. "Not if you insist we conduct our business in that gutter language you're using now," the man said in perfect Spanish, and Valentine let his own grin blossom.

"We are countrymen, are we not?" the old man pressed.

"Perhaps," Valentine hedged, not wishing to reveal too much to the old man. "Are you well familiar with Seville?"

"Bah," the merchant snorted, flapping his hands at Valentine and then disappearing behind the counter, which was taller than the old man. His head appeared incrementally, as if utilizing a set of steps hidden behind the bench. "I could smell the Aragon on you as you stepped inside, boy. I think we can do business. What are your needs?"

Valentine moved to step closer to the counter but quickly retreated as the hounds regained their feet and their voices.

The old man whistled again and then clicked his tongue twice, and the two dogs at last turned tail and slunk behind the counter.

"You understand that I must preserve my interests in a place such as this," the old man explained. "I am not much for the sword any longer. Too old."

"Good merchant," Valentine began, as he strolled to the counter and braced his forearm along the top, near his own shoulder. Maria skittered along behind him, keeping a loose hold on the back of his tunic. "I am a physician, traveling with my patient to Brussels. We have worn out our horses and must travel the remainder of the way by river. I have not enough elixirs nor supplies to sustain us until we reach our destination, but I have some goods and a small amount of coin to trade."

The man's eyes narrowed. "A physician, are you?"

Valentine smiled. "Yes. That is right."

"And I am the duke of Normandy." He raised one spidery eyebrow. "I have not in my life known a proper physician to ever come out of Aragon, and none of any country has ever come through this hellish place, let alone to my donkey cock shop. What is it exactly that you are wanting, criminal?"

Valentine drew his head back and affected an offended air. "Only the typical supplies for a journey of any length—food, a bit of soap. And then a tincture of poppy mixed with a handful of other ingredients. I am more than capable of preparing the potion myself if you will only provide the components. I can assure you that I am—"

"You can assure me that you are pretending to be someone you are not in order to escape those who are pursuing you—" he edged up as if on tiptoe to look down his nose at Maria, still hiding behind him—"and the young woman cowering at your back." He looked at Valentine with a menacing frown now, like a wicked character from some childhood tale. "She is no more your patient than I, and I shall not provide such ingredients for you to render her unconscious, and possibly kill her. I'd wager she has no idea what you are even asking me for, and if she did, she would run as fast as she could. Perhaps straight into the arms of your pursuers, yes?"

"No, you do not understand," Valentine said, trying to control his impatience. He felt a tug on his tunic.

"Is everything all right?" Maria asked in a worried-sounding whisper.

"It is fine," he said over his shoulder in English. "Everything is fine." He turned back to the merchant. "Whether you believe me or not, we are in a terrible hurry."

"Oh, I am certain you are. Is she dying?" the man asked, trying to peer over Valentine again. "She appears healthy to me."

"Her illness, it is—" Valentine paused, leaned forward conspiratorially—"*mental.*"

The old man raised an eyebrow. "Good day, milady," he said in English, directly to Maria.

Maria popped her head from around Valentine's arm to look up at the troll. "Oh! Good day!" she replied with cheerful surprise, betraying what Valentine was beginning to think was an accurate diagnosis. "Your dogs are quite beautiful. Frightening but beautiful."

"You are too kind, milady. I do love them so. Traded some copper to a Gaul for them when they were only pups. They seem fearsome, but they are like kittens when we are alone."

"I'm certain they are," Maria said agreeably. "And well they should be. What line are they, do you know? I've not seen any of their kind before."

Valentine sighed and raised his voice to interrupt the merchant's animated reply. "I beg your pardon!" When Maria and the merchant both turned their faces toward him, he continued in a calmer manner. "As I said, we are in a bit of a rush. Will you trade or no?"

To Valentine's consternation, the merchant looked again to Maria. "Are you very ill, milady?"

Maria opened her mouth and then looked to Valentine.

Yes, he tried to convey to her with his eyes.

Maria appeared confused for a moment and then began a horribly false-sounding racking cough. "Yes. I *am* ill. So ill. I think I have the plague," she rasped.

Valentine rolled his eyes.

But the merchant only threw back his head and laughed, as if it was the funniest thing he'd ever heard.

"I'm certain you must, if you've cast your lot with the likes of him," he said, tossing his head toward Valentine. "What I mean to say, young woman, is: are you with this man of your own election? Do you trust him?"

Maria glanced at Valentine for a moment, as if unsure what to say. Valentine didn't think any more damage could be done unless she decided to confide in the old man the details of their adventure together.

She looked back at the merchant, and her voice was once again strong and clear. "Actually, I came a very long way to find him. And I trust him implicitly."

The merchant's eyes narrowed. "With your life?"

Maria did not look at him again, but Valentine felt the weight of her next words in the core of his heart.

"With my life, at the very least."

In moments the merchant had released his dogs and let them loose to cavort with Maria on the shop floor. The old troll beckoned to Valentine to follow him behind the curtain.

"Bring your coin and your bags."

Chapter 15

"She will be safe," the merchant advised as he let the curtain fall behind Valentine. "The villagers know to call out before they enter, and if it is a stranger who comes—well, they should not remain for very long, yes?"

The narrow room behind the curtain was dim and cramped—little more than a walkway between floor-to-ceiling shelves that held row upon row of crocks and jars and sacks and bowls.

"Let's see, let's see," the old man muttered, squinting up at the shelves. "Ah, there you are." He seized a spindly ladder and moved it across the floor in front of Valentine with a dusty scrape. *"Perdone."* Then he began to climb, the rickety thing bowing under even the merchant's slight weight. He fussed at the front of his tunic before removing one of the little vials, and then laid the cork aside and began filling the cylinder with little pinches from various containers.

"So," he said while tending to his task, "you wish her to sleep."

"Yes," Valentine replied, trying to say as little as possible to the keen old man.

The merchant paused and turned his bumpy profile over his shoulder, his fingers pinched above the vial's opening. "Ah . . . for how long?"

Valentine frowned and tried to figure the distance in his head. "A week?"

The old man turned more fully on the ladder to look sternly at Valentine.

"Off and on," he amended. "It is the river. She becomes ill."

An expression of understanding came over the merchant's face and he added the pinch still held between his fingers before grabbing

the cork and scurrying back down the ladder. "I can add no antie-
metic," he said with a tinge of regret, dragging the ladder along the
shelf by hooking his arm through it. He began climbing again, pausing to add this and that in tiny amounts during his ascent. "If I was
accompanying you to monitor the dosage, perhaps. But if she were to
ingest too much—she would not be able to rid her body of the poison, you see?"

"I do."

"Hmm. Hmm." The little troll placed a finger against his lips, surveying the pots before him. "But perhaps a little mint. You know," he
said to Valentine directly as he began to once more descend the ladder, "there was another of our countrymen in my shop some time
ago." He glanced up at Valentine before grabbing a jug from a nearby
bench and uncorking it with his perfect little teeth. He poured a small
amount of clear liquid into the vial, turning the contents a rich and
wicked brown.

"A man from Aragon, you say?" Valentine asked, trying to appear
suitably surprised.

"Or was it Seville?" the merchant goaded, recorking the jug and
then the vial and shaking the little cylinder efficiently. "I'd wager my
teeth for Aragon. He was searching for his cousin." The old man
handed the vial to Valentine and made sure to meet his eyes. "The
two of you share a resemblance."

"I have no family," Valentine said and took the vial. "How much
of this?"

"Only a finger. Perhaps a little less—she is a small woman. And
best after she's eaten a hearty meal." The man took the empty sack
Valentine offered him and began depositing little parcels of unknown
contents inside. "He seemed quite concerned for your whereabouts,
this man."

"I'm certain he was," Valentine muttered.

The old man looked around.

"A man searching for his family is usually distraught," Valentine
explained in their native tongue.

The merchant winked and then returned to filling the bag.

"'Tis true, 'tis true. If the woman is not your patient, and she
came a distance to find you, who is she?"

Valentine hesitated a moment. "She is my wife."

This gave the troll great pause. He looked at Valentine keenly for an instant and then began to chuckle. "I would sooner accept you to be her physician."

"You do not believe a woman such as she could be my wife?" Valentine asked, hearing the offense in his tone.

"I do not," the merchant admitted. "But if she were your wife, you would be a fool to give her up."

"I would be a fool to keep her," he said. "She would never be happy."

The old man reached past Valentine to push aside the curtain with the back of his gnarled fingers. He glanced out and then leaned back, nodding toward the opening.

Valentine could not control his curiosity, and so he leaned toward the curtain, peeking into the room.

Maria was propped in a corner amidst the piles of goods, a giant gray head across each of her thighs. She stroked the beasts' long foreheads from snout to ear as their wiry jowls billowed and collapsed with their snores.

"She looks happy enough to me."

Valentine stepped away from the opening, and the merchant let the curtain fall. "She . . . adapts well to bad situations," he said.

"Whatever you say, friend." The little troll handed the now bulging sack to Valentine with a knowing grin. "Here you are. I'll take your trade now."

"Do you not wish to inspect the items?" Valentine asked, holding out the bag. "How do you know my possessions are worth what you've given me?"

"I shall take it all." And he did just that. "Being the only trader in this hellish burg, I sell every manner of thing. And unless this sack contains the Holy Grail, my potion alone is worth more," the merchant said with a quirked brow. "But it is rare that I cross paths with a man of my own country, and it shall never be said that Morcillo does not help his own." He started to move past Valentine and threw over his shoulder, "Even if he is a fool." Another false start. "And a poor liar." Then he held the curtain aside for Valentine to precede him.

"I am not a poor liar," Valentine hissed as he passed.

The dogs had to be ordered from the nest of Maria's lap, and she, too, seemed sad when the animals left her. After looking at Valentine quizzically and receiving no lead to follow, she proceeded to thank the little troll and wish him and his ugly beasts every good thing she could possibly think of.

The merchant was clearly charmed, and he bowed low over Maria's hand and kissed it twice tenderly, calling down God's blessing upon her.

Mary blushed and smiled.

Valentine rolled his eyes. Then he took possession of Maria's elbow. "Many thanks," he said to the merchant with a curt bow, and then turned Maria toward the curtained entrance.

"Good luck to you," the troll called out in his and Valentine's shared tongue. "And beware—those men usually return around this time of year."

Valentine stopped abruptly, nearly pulling Maria from her feet. He turned to look at the old man. "Men? You said *man* before—one man, seeking his cousin."

"Did I?" the old troll said with a contemplative air. "Well, they ofttimes do not travel together, you see? And perhaps it was not cousin but brother. As I said, I am an old man. It should not matter to you, as you have neither, yes? Farewell!" He gave a jaunty wave and a grin.

"Well, that was a pleasant surprise," Mary said as she skipped along behind Valentine. "What a lovely little man. And he spoke English, too."

"My cousin has been to this place," Valentine said curtly, leading the way past the stable, helping Mary around the copious piles of rotting dung. "Likely my brother, too. They are still searching for me."

His words startled Mary out of her dreamy reverence for the old Spanish merchant. "It is well that we are on our way then, is it not? Did he have what we need?"

Valentine pulled the vial from his tunic and handed it to her. "Your carriage, my lady."

Mary frowned at the muddy brown liquid in the thick, bubbled glass before uncorking it and taking a tentative sniff. She gagged and took the vial away from her nose.

"This doesn't smell at all like the potion Lady Elmsbeth gave me."

Valentine took the small container back and recorked the stopper. "The potion Lady Elmsbeth gave you was most likely strong spirits," he advised, slipping the vial into his rough cowled tunic. "And while it perhaps was enough when you were sheltered within a ship, it would no work for our purposes, beyond increasing the occurrence of—" He waved one hand in the air, as if searching for the correct word.

Mary winced. "Vomiting?"

"I think yes," he said with a sage nod.

"What is it, then, if not spirits?" she asked, heaving her now much heavier satchel over her arm and following him farther along the row of rickety buildings toward the wharf.

"It is a type of—" more waving of the hand, and Mary was beginning to understand that she should take the motion as a harbinger of something dreadful—"ah, a type of poison."

Mary stopped on the first gray board of the creaking pier and waited for Valentine to turn around. *"Poison?"*

He rolled his eyes at her and shook his head, as if she was completely overreacting. "Only a tiny bit. Just enough, you see?"

"Enough to kill me?" she demanded.

He sighed and pinched the bridge of his nose. "You are no going to drink the whole thing at once, Maria."

"The way it smells, and considering it's *poison*, I doubt I shall be drinking any of it!"

He spread his arms wide and gave her a bow. "Suit yourself." Then he turned on his heel and began walking once more down the pier, his boots echoing on the raised and rotted wood. He gave a little hop over a section with missing boards, the river sloshing beneath like a fat brown ogre waiting to devour her.

"Valentine!" she demanded.

He stopped, his shoulders drawing up near his ears. He turned, leaped over the hole in the pier once more, strode up to her as if he would run her over, then stopped just as his tunic brushed her gown.

As Mary had known he would.

"If you would be so kind, Maria, as to refrain from using my given name in a place crawling with criminals, and where my family has recently been inquiring of me, you would win my undying devotion."

"Is that all I have to do?" she mused up into his face, trying to ignore her quivering knees.

"What do you want?"

"That pier doesn't look at all secure," she said.

"As you could see with your own eyes, I traversed it with no trouble."

She took a deep breath, as if in preparation to speak, but found she could say nothing, and so she continued to look up into his face.

His eyes looked into hers, his lashes twitching with the little movements of his gaze, and she saw his brow soften the tiniest bit.

"Do no be afraid, Maria," he said. "You will be fine, potion or no potion, yes?"

"Yes," she said at last, giving a shaky sigh. She was grateful he had not insisted she try to convey to him her fear of the leg of their journey that lay just ahead of them now. Not only the travel by river but the persistent and growing knowledge that the closer they came to the North Sea, the farther away Valentine moved from her. Already his past was encroaching, causing his thoughts to turn inward and then ahead of them, to the time when he would be free of her. "Can you . . . ?" She held one hand slightly away from her, palm up.

His full lips quirked, but not maliciously, and he readjusted their satchels in order to take her fingers in his warm grip. "All right now?"

She smiled as a flush crept up her neck and then nodded. Perhaps it would be different this time.

"Are you certain? We can go now?" He cocked his head, and Mary could see the sparkle return to his eyes. "You do no need a privy? A sweet?"

"I would love a sweet," she said, playing along.

He tugged her fully onto the pier, keeping her attention on his face as he continued to make light. "We shall have to see what is in the bag the little troll gave us. As soon as we are underway, yes?" He placed both hands at her waist and lifted her over the missing boards and then joined her with a fleet leap, once more taking her hand. "No, no—do no look down at the water; look at me. *Bueno.* Nearly there now."

Mary's head was already swimming when they came to a stop only a moment later. She felt as though the pier was riding the waves, the shoreline on the far side of the river undulating lazily in the heat. Her throat constricted. She felt cold little beads of sweat dotting her hairline and upper lip.

This time would be no different after all. Unless it was perhaps worse.

"Here we are," Valentine said, and Mary blinked and looked past him to discover the large raft she had seen earlier, with the triangle-shaped shelter tied to its mast.

"Maria?" Valentine called, giving her fingers a little shake. "Maria, give me your satchel." He released her and reached for the strap of her bag, and immediately Mary felt herself begin to list drunkenly.

"Oh, no." Valentine seized her arm just in time. "Find your balance once more. There you are. I'll be just a moment. All right?"

She nodded, and felt a hard little pebble at the base of her throat that she tried to swallow so she could answer him properly. But the pebble only grew larger the more she tried to force her rigid muscles to obey.

Valentine stepped nimbly onto the floating square, and up close Mary could see the threadbare material of the sail, the patches on the triangular shelter, the wet rot at the base of the little bench. Brown water sloshed over the corners of the bucking raft as Valentine walked about. He drew a length of frayed, filthy rope through the straps of their satchels and then looped the rope around the mast securely.

Mary's nostrils felt stuffed with the warm stench of dead fish and stewing vegetation. A rivulet of sweat ran down the nape of her neck and into the swampy place between her shoulder blades. The splashing of the river seemed to grow louder, a roar that pressed against her eardrums. Her mouth felt gritty, dry, and flooded with saliva in the same moment. If only she could swallow . . .

"Maria?" Valentine said, in what to Mary seemed like a whisper. She looked down and saw his handsome, concerned face looking up at her from the raft. He was holding a hand up to her, and even though she knew Valentine was standing perfectly still, his hand retreated, advanced, circled, blurred . . .

Her arm seemed like a tree trunk when she tried to raise it to take Valentine's hand, and so she attempted a tentative step closer to the edge of the pier. The wood felt spongy beneath her feet, causing her to sink ever so slightly against the horizon that was now rushing up to the sky.

She fell onto the raft, onto Valentine. She scrambled over him, her elbows bowing as the raft bucked and dirty water ran over her fingers where she gripped the side of the wood. Each wave seemed to coax another round of retching from her.

"Maria, hold on—I am going to untie us so that we might move out into the smoother water," Valentine said somewhere behind her, but she could not respond.

Her head pounded. She felt like she would suffocate between the constant bile in her throat and mouth and the horrid, humid river smell that had had permeated her entire world. After what seemed like an hour, the vomiting slowed, and she was no longer hearing her retching echo under the rickety pier.

She pushed away from the edge of the raft, the sleeves of her gown wet past her elbows, her skirts past her knees, and fell over on her side, facing the mast. Valentine pulled the setting pole out of the water and secured it. The he came to kneel at her side.

"Better?" he asked, raking her sweaty hair from her eyes.

Mary shook her head as best she could. She felt as though her guts were swirling still, seeking something—anything—to expel from her shivering body.

"Let me move you," Valentine said, reaching down and taking hold of her beneath her arms. "Perhaps if you can no see . . ."

He dragged her beneath the tarp, and Mary knew it was the most undignified she'd ever been in her life, her skirts leaving a wide, wet trail across the decking, but she couldn't care. She only hoped she would die soon.

Valentine propped her up against the pile of their bags and squatted down. "Maria?" he called gently, and even in her stupor she could see that he was trying to keep an eye on the river and the shores beyond. "There is some wine. Would you—?"

"No," she croaked. She felt better enough to shake her head properly now and hold out her hand, her fingers stretching wide, reaching. "Give me the poison."

He dug into his tunic.

"All of it," she clarified.

Chapter 16

Morcillo's potion worked.

Within moments, Maria fell into a deep sleep, her lovely face at last relaxing from the terrible grimace, her skin chalk pale, but not the sickly shade of gray it had been since stealing the raft.

Maria would likely frown at him about that little piece of information, should she find out. But the thief at the stable had not been fair with his price, knowing he was the only one in the village who could pay coin of any amount for the animals. Valentine didn't blame him, really; he was just evening out the transaction by including the man's raft in the bargain.

Valentine pushed the setting pole into the soft mud beneath the water over and over, guiding the raft with the current, stretching his muscles, as the sun dipped over the mountains behind him, and he began to breathe deeply again for the first time since leaving Prague. At this time on a different night, he would be scanning the shoreline, seeking a safe place for him and Mary to make camp. But not this night. Maria would likely sleep for several hours, and it would be difficult to carry her from the raft without overturning it. The country to either side of the Elbe was mostly marsh, and so coming ashore with even a conscious Maria would prove a challenge.

Valentine could still spy the road intermittently between the trees on the shore, and he wished to put as much distance as he could between himself and Drezdeny. The thought of Enrique and Francisco looking for him there was unsettling. It was easy to hide from them in Prague, but in a village of such small size, and with only one road or the river in and out, there was little anonymity to be had. Valentine would kill Enrique if need be—he longed for it, actually—but his cousin? Francisco had been more of a brother to Valentine than his own flesh, and it would pain Valentine to shed Francisco's blood, even after knowing he had fallen in with the enemy.

He bent slightly at the waist and peeked beneath the tarp where Maria slept on. Morcillo had traded them no lantern, so there would be no further opportunity to see her until the sun rose again. She seemed restful, the side of her face pillowed on her folded hands, her legs curled up toward her middle on the pile of their bags. She reminded Valentine of an abandoned kitten.

He looked back to the river and took another deep breath as the stars began to peek through the darkening blanket of deep velvet. Valentine felt a dull ache in his chest at the realization that Maria would soon belong to another. Likely she would revert to the woman Valentine had first met in Melk—anxious, rigid, restless. She would return to the only home she had ever known, to lie with some lauded English knight and bear his children. Her adventure, over.

Valentine would never know the part of her he longed for, the part that he had blithely taken from so many women before—her body, her passion, her love. He told himself he was a fool for not having her and being done with the mystery. She could have been his at the old mill, or in Tabor; certainly in Prague, where the fire between them in the Snowy Owl had nearly burned Valentine alive. But he would not ruin her.

Maria might think herself in love with him now, but she had nothing to compare him to. Their time together had been naught but a rousing escapade that showed her a small sliver of the world she had been denied access to her entire life. Valentine was helping her achieve what she professed to want most: a husband and children. What Maria likely felt toward him was gratitude, and an appreciation of the exciting voyage they were on, the memories of which would have to sustain her for the rest of her life.

The rest of her life, married to another man.

A man who would perhaps never know the depths of her revulsion for water travel. Or her love of millinery, and the way she flushed at the slightest hint of a compliment. Or her damnable cheerfulness at the rising of the sun. A stranger who had never seen nor known of any of Maria's family, who were dead and gone forever.

Did Valentine love her? Perhaps, he conceded to himself. Perhaps he did. After all, in attempting to think of the future, even one moment beyond the day when he would be forced to part from Maria, it was as if the world dropped off sharply into nothingness. As if half-way through a written page, the words simply ceased, disappeared, the rest of the page blank.

Such melancholy thoughts were ruining his relaxation, and so Valentine shook himself and scanned the riverbanks once more. Fatigue began to wash over him, and he thought perhaps they were far enough from the village and the road now that a safe place to put in could be found. Unless it was a trick of the moonlight, a rocky peninsula jutted out into the water a short distance ahead, a downed tree leaning over it into the river. It seemed an ideal place to drag ashore and make a fire, and he would not have to wake Maria—if that was even possible so soon after she had imbibed of Morcillo's potion.

But as Valentine drew closer to the peninsula, he saw that the spit of land was already occupied. A lone man stood in the shadow of tree branches atop the flat rock, as if waiting for Valentine to pass. His head turned slowly, slowly, tracking the raft's progress.

A chill ran up Valentine's spine, and although he knew the man could not possibly make out his features in the gloom, he reached back and pulled the cowl of his tunic up over his head. He did not turn away from the stranger as he passed, but neither did he call out, choosing to watch him as closely and silently as Valentine himself was being watched, letting the setting pole skim the water behind the raft with a little trill.

The man stood with one foot braced against the downed tree, the forearm of his same side leaning against his knee. Valentine could see the outline of his tall boots in the moonlight, the jagged points of his pleated tunic. A dark shape hung at his other hip, as if he clutched something in his hand. As Valentine slowly floated past, the man raised the shape above his head: a wide-brimmed hat, with what looked to be a long feather at the crown.

Just like Valentine's own, which Maria so fancied.

Valentine did not return the greeting, only watched the man as his own heart pounded.

The man lowered the hat and then his foot from the tree and turned, blatantly following the raft's progress.

Valentine kept his eyes on the black outline of the man, using all his will not to shove the setting pole back into the water and begin pushing with all his might, away from this stranger who was perhaps no stranger at all. But he waited. He waited until the raft eased around a bend, draping the figure of the man in night-blackened branches, and only the sparkling moonlight moved near the bank.

Then Valentine set to work again, pushing himself and Maria down the river as quickly and quietly as he could.

He might have to part from her, but it would not be this night. And it would not be until he was ready to let her go.

Mary was lost in a world of warm color, the shapes and sounds swirling around her seeming to undo the chaotic dizziness that had seized her before she had drunk the vile potion. Now she felt only like a leaf loosed by a gentle breeze, the current of air turning her lazily as she floated down, down, to land on a cool carpet of grass.

"Mary, Mary," a voice called playfully.

She sat up on one hip, her arm out to brace herself, and looked to see who had spoken. "My lord," she said, her voice echoing as she saw her betrothed sitting only paces from her. He was eating something dark clasped in his hands, a piece of bread perhaps.

Her heart shriveled a bit at the sight of him. He was here, waiting for her after all.

"Where have you been, Mary?" he asked before taking another bite of the food in his hands.

"Why, nowhere," she answered. "Nowhere at all."

He chewed noisily, his teeth crunching, crunching, and the sound caused a shiver down her spine.

"Not so, Mary," he said, his voice low with chastisement even as he smiled at her. The way he kept emphasizing her name caused her to wince. "You've been very naughty. You've betrayed me, Mary."

"I haven't," she insisted as he continued eating. "But I can't marry you."

"You will, though. You will be my wife, Mary."

"I don't love you."

"I . . . don't . . . care," he singsonged and tossed the last bit of food up into the air to catch it deftly in his mouth with a loud crunch. "You are home now and we will live together forever and ever." He turned slightly to reach behind him for another piece of whatever it was he was dining upon. "Mary." Crunch.

"Stop calling me that," she insisted. "That's not my name."

"It is your name, Mary. And this is our home, isn't it? Hasn't it always been your home?"

Mary looked around and was startled to discover that she was sitting outside the wall of Beckham Hall. Only that wall was leaning precariously now, crumbling toward her, a gaping hole near the ground where once stones had been stacked securely.

Her eyes found him again, and she realized that he was eating a piece of that very wall.

"So happy you've returned, Mary," he said and smiled at her again, this time showing his teeth—long, broken fangs. He took another crunching bite of stone.

"Stop calling me that," she repeated.

"Ma-ry," he gurgled.

"No!"

He tossed the rock aside and began scuttling toward her like some demon, his limbs a blur, his teeth gnashing. "Mary!"

"No!" she screamed, throwing her hands up in front of her face as he reared over her, his mouth yawning wide. "No!"

"Maria!"

She realized she was screaming as she opened her eyes, Valentine's worried face only inches from hers. He was gripping her upper arms, leaning over her. Her scream died and her breath left her in a rush as she sagged back against the satchels.

"Maria, what is it?" Valentine insisted. The light behind him was soft, gray. Birdsong filled the air, dancing with the hush of the river.

"Nothing," she said, hearing the tremor of her words. She moved to sit up, and Valentine assisted her. "Just a nightmare. Where are we?"

"Halfway to Hamburg," Valentine said, moving away a bit to fetch a jug and a piece of bread wrapped in a cloth. He handed her the jug, and after she had taken hold of it, he twisted out the cork. "You've been asleep for almost two days."

"Two days?" she repeated, stopping the jug halfway to her mouth.

"Perhaps a bit too much potion, yes?" he said with a grin as she drank. "I would no have woken you, but you need to eat and drink. And I need to sleep for longer than an hour."

She took the bread from him, and her hunger appeared suddenly as the last vestiges of the terrible dream wafted away like noxious smoke. "Have you brought us this far with no more rest than that?"

"I put to shore a bit last night, but it was no good for long." He moved to sit back against the mast, and she could see the fatigue around his eyes, how his skin had been burnished a deeper copper by the sun. "I think perhaps we are being followed."

She swallowed the bread. "Your brother?"

"I do no know for certain," he said with a shrug. "It does no matter, really. But we are far enough from the road now that I think we will be safe for a few hours. You can stretch your legs without fear of falling into the river while I sleep."

Mary leaned forward and peeked beyond the tarp to see that they were in a grotto of sorts, the raft pulled up onto a rocky beach. The sight of the jagged gray stones gave her a momentary shiver. She set the jug aside and took another bite of bread before scooting from beneath the tarp and standing. The raft was at a tilt but firmly aground. She realized that she desperately needed to make water.

"Do no wander far," he warned as he crawled into the spot she'd recently vacated. "Wake me if anyone approaches—no matter how harmless they seem. There is plenty to eat in the—" he yawned widely, and Mary thought that he looked quite boyish and sweet when he was tired—"in the bag."

"I will," she said, looking around her again, chewing the bread. She looked back. "Shall I make—"

But his eyes were closed, and Mary thought it very likely that he was already lost to sleep. She smiled at his figure sprawled on their bags. He had labored so diligently to bring them this far. Soon, though, he could rest.

They only had to reach Hamburg, and then they could surely relax.

Constantine Gerard stood at the end of the table nearest the tall windows in Melk's secret library, the morning light streaming through the narrow colored panes of glass behind him, turning the map spread on the tabletop into a rich mosaic. His hands were braced on the thick vellum, his eyes tracing the routes between Melk and the North Sea one by one, over and over. His mind pictured tiny figures along the map—horses and riders—while he repeatedly calculated the time passed.

"How far do you think he's gone?" Adrian Hailsworth asked from his chair, his words disturbing the dusty silence.

"I know not," Constantine said.

"You do know," Adrian challenged. "You're just not saying."

Constantine looked over his shoulder to where Adrian sat in his chair and noticed the chalice clasped in his hand. "Are you already drinking?"

"I was already thirsty," Adrian said, turning his smirk toward Constantine and raising the chalice in a mocking toast. "How far?" he repeated before bringing the cup to his lips.

Constantine turned back to the map. "Depending on the weather, the route—perhaps Leipzig. If he's had no trouble."

Adrian snorted. "Knowing Valentine, that is an impossibility."

The wall leading to the abbey's main repository swung inward, and the opening was filled with the massive bulk of Roman Berg, Lou perched on his shoulder as usual. Father Victor glided in behind them and then secured the door.

"Good morn, gentleman," Victor said, making his way around the table to take his usual seat near Constantine.

"Father," Constantine replied. Adrian only grunted and sipped at his drink.

Roman deposited Lou on his perch and adjusted the bird's hood and tie. He fished in his robes for a piece of desiccated meat and gave it to the falcon before turning toward the table.

"What's got Adrian into his cups so early?"

Constantine glanced over his shoulder again and then looked back at Roman. "He's worried about Val."

"Worried he won't come back and will send the bounty hunters to our doorstep for a coin," Adrian muttered.

"Valentine has more honor than you give him credit for," Roman said, leaning back in his own chair. Constantine heard the wood creaking under the Norseman's huge frame and saw Victor's slight wince at the sound. Roman was hard on even the abbey's sturdy furniture. "He would never betray us."

Victor leaned his forearms onto the table. "Let us pray that Roman is correct in judging Valentine's integrity, for I have just this morning received news that may place Glayer Felsteppe directly in his path."

Constantine looked up, but the old abbot had everyone's attention now.

Glayer Felsteppe. Second in command to King Baldwin, after only Constantine himself. The traitor of Chastellet.

I will see everything you love burn, Gerard.

Constantine shook himself. "Where?"

"He was tourneying with the English king in Normandy. A month ago, any matter."

"That's not good," Adrian said. "In bed with Henry now."

Victor nodded. "It would seem so. My source says that Felsteppe planned to separate from the king and go north before returning to England."

Roman tapped his fingers on the table in a rapid staccato, then seemed to catch himself and laid his palm flat. "Forgive my saying so, but 'north' is very general, Victor."

Constantine dropped his eyes back to the map, locating Normandy and tracing the larger routes north from the region while he listened to the conversation.

"The rumor is that Felsteppe has aligned himself with a reputable noble and now has the financial backing to enlarge his search for the four of you. The English king has given him leave to assemble the most talented of trackers and scatter them across the map. The rewards for your capture have increased."

"How much?" Adrian asked, dark humor and wine thickening his words.

"One thousand pieces of English silver on each of your heads," Victor replied.

Roman whistled, but Adrian gave a shout of outrage. "One thousand pieces? I'm worth at least two, if only so that my brain may be studied."

Roman laughed. "It would take that many oxen alone to transport your massive head."

Adrian saluted Roman with his cup and a black smile. "Or one rock-headed Norseman."

Constantine was in no mood to participate in the jesting. "A month ago. It's probable they will miss each other entirely. And if not, Val would hear of such a gathering, were it to take place anywhere around him. His compatriots are . . . knowledgeable about new means to gain a large sum of coin."

"His compatriots are all criminals," Adrian clarified.

"That's what I said." Constantine thought for a moment and then mused aloud. "Even if Valentine and Felsteppe should be in the same room together, neither would likely know it—Val is the only one of us who would not recognize him on sight, nor has Felsteppe laid eyes upon Val."

Roman rhythmically tapped his thick forefinger on the tabletop again, like a hammer on a tiny chisel. "You reckon that's an advantage, Stan?"

Adrian spoke before Constantine could form an answer. "It's not an advantage at all. Should Felsteppe ply just the right criminal with just enough coin, he could be led directly to Valentine, and Valentine would never see him coming."

"Adrian's right," Constantine admitted. "But I do think that Valentine will refrain from fraternizing with his usual contacts. After all, one thousand pieces of silver would sorely test most friendships."

"But," Roman argued, "Valentine doesn't know the stakes have risen."

Adrian added, "And there is no way to get word to him in time to warn him of Felsteppe's potential proximity, even if we knew exactly where he and his little English bride are."

Constantine looked up with a sigh. "We will just have to trust that Valentine's cunning will get him across the Channel safely. After he has freed himself from his connection with Lady Mary Beckham, he will be much more agile, and perhaps quicker to return." His eyes went to Victor. "When and where is this convening of mercenaries to take place?"

"Two days from now," Victor supplied. "In Hamburg."

Chapter 17

Valentine likely would have kept sailing until the Elbe dumped them out into the sea or the raft finally fell apart completely had it not been for the flashes of lightning that lit up the distinct outline of Hamburg's four castles. Thunder rumbled, temporarily deafening him to the roar of water on the river, both the current and the sheets of rain crashing into the Elbe, creating the illusion that Valentine was trying to steer the raft through a waterfall.

It had been raining for the past two days—pouring, storming so that day was barely discernable from night. He had navigated in a perpetual wet dusk, inhaling water like a fish. There had been no way to get out of the river, swollen and churning, pushing the raft along at such a pace that it was all he could do to keep the rickety wooden square to the closest approximation of the middle of the river as he could guess. And the entire time, Maria had slept on, the dreams that entertained her unconsciousness sometimes causing her to thrash and call out. Valentine was soaking wet, exhausted beyond measure, and the raft was beginning to disintegrate under the stress. If he didn't find a place to tie off soon, he feared he would look around and see that the narrow planks that made up the vessel had widened, allowing Maria to slip through the gap and into the black water to drown.

He knew the inn straddling the land between one of the main trade routes into Hamburg and a branch of the Elbe had to be close. He could see the black masts and inky hulks of the cog ships along the shore, lit up intermittently by the menacing lightning. Hamish kept a dock behind his inn for seagoing patrons and merchants, and if Valentine could find it . . .

No sooner than he'd thought it, Hamish's dock found Valentine, the wooden planks of the pier catching the cusp of his shoulder before the raft ploughed under the dock. Valentine was thrown from his feet, and as he lunged for the spindly mast and missed, the lower half of him plunged into the icy Elbe. The raft listed as Valentine caught the rough lashing between the planks with one hand and threw his other arm around a thick piling. He realized a moment later that the raft's steep angle was stopped by the vessel on the far side of the dock, and so he cried out with effort as he pulled on the lashings with all his strength, kicking his feet beneath the water and using the thick piling for leverage.

He was rewarded with a shuddering scrape of wood on wood, and the raft went horizontal once more.

"Maria!" he shouted, and his voice was amplified in the tunnel created by the pier above. "Maria, wake up!" The lightning flashed again, and he could just make her out in the lines of white light that flickered through the boards over them. He thought she might have stirred, but then again, it could have been nothing more than a trick of the shuddering light.

The rotten lashing began to loosen in his hand. "Maria!" He was afraid to throw his leg over the side and pull himself up, fearing the planks would begin to separate against the failing ties. He couldn't reach her from here, and he couldn't let go of the raft, lest it spin out from beneath the dock on the wild current and into the Elbe, washing Maria out to sea like a corpse at a Viking funeral.

He had only one choice.

"Maria!" he called out as he loosened the lashings with quick, jerking movements, letting go of the raft only for the few seconds it took to pull the ropes loose from the boards. Then he gripped the far plank again, pulling the raft straight once more. The loosened end of the decking floated toward him briefly, and then scissored against the rest of the raft as Valentine moved his way up the board to the next lashing.

Two boards, three, five—all loosened and set floating into the swollen Elbe like twigs, until nearly half of the raft was gone and Valentine seized the center mast. He would have only seconds, he knew, to make his move. Once he released the raft, it would immediately start to spin, crashing into the pier or the ship beyond before being spit out into the river. The lower half of his body was nearly numb with cold, his left arm aching with the strain of holding on to the pier, the fingers of his right hand felt frozen.

"Maria!" he shouted again as the lightning gave him the briefest glimpse of her lying atop the limp sacks. The food was gone, but he didn't know how much else he would be able to save, if anything.

"Valentine?" she at last answered.

"Do no move!" he shouted as the light stuttered again and he saw her trying to raise herself up. If she leaned toward him suddenly, she would go over the edge and into the river. "Maria, sit up slowly—can you sit up, *mi amor*?"

"Yes." Her voice was like a whisper.

"Good girl. Can you find my satchel? Grab it, Maria; put it high up on your arm."

"I think I have it. Valentine, where are we?"

"Everything is fine. Can you grab your own bag? Maria?"

The thunder shot holes in her words. "I don . . . know. I have so . . . can't see."

"Just get what you can," he shouted. "I am going to grab you in a moment, Maria. You have to come into the river with me."

"No!"

"Do no be afraid, *mi amor*," he said. "Can you swim?"

"No!" she repeated, and this time Valentine could clearly hear the fear in her words.

"It is fine," he said, trying to make his voice calm and sure. "Once you are in the water, there is a piling to hold on to. And me, you will hold on to me. I will find a way up."

"Valentine, no! I can't—"

"We have no choice, Maria," he interrupted. "When the lightning flashes again, I move." He waited a breath. "Maria?"

She said something, but the thunder stole her words.

"What?" he shouted.

"I said I trust you!"

In the next instant, the lightning flashed. Valentine released the mast of the raft and swung his body through the water as the starboard edge spun toward him and the port side—where Maria crouched—twisted away. His right arm went round her waist with some force, doubling her over his elbow, and he dragged her toward him as the raft scraped away beneath her legs.

The weight of the satchels and her soaking gown dragged her under the water immediately, and Valentine gave a mighty roar as he pulled her up once more. She sputtered and coughed and gasped, and he felt her legs kicking in the blackness beneath them. She flailed against him, trying to turn, and at last flung one arm around the piling, her other arm swinging up to snake around his neck.

"Are you all right?" he asked into her ear.

She continued to cough but managed to nod.

Valentine looked up; a pair of wooden pegs jutted out of the piling perhaps three feet above his head.

"Gracias a Dios," he whispered. He leaned forward and pressed his lips to Maria's cold, wet cheek. "Hold on, *mi amor*—I will have us out of this river in only a moment."

Mary wrapped both arms around the slick and smelly piling, as Valentine instructed, and when he moved away from her abruptly, taking his warmth and solidness and leaving her in the cold, dark, swirling waters, she knew true terror. She gripped with her knees as best she could, her skirts feeling like frozen iron around her thighs. If she slipped, she would go under the water, and Valentine would never find her.

A fall of water poured over her head and face as he tried to launch himself away from the river two, three times, his gasps and curses growing with each attempt. She stifled her scream of panic but would not close her eyes. When he rose the next time, he did not descend again, and she felt the air before her face open up as he vanished above her.

The thick pillar was coated with a wide band of slime at the waterline, and Mary felt herself sliding with each push of the current. It seemed a lifetime passed as Mary clung to the piling, her chin tilting farther and farther up to keep her face above the water, but in reality it was only a moment.

"Maria!" came Valentine's shout from above.

Lightning flashed, and she saw the outline of his hand, his fingers spread wide.

"Reach up!"

"I can't," she cried, and as if to reinforce the idea, she slipped farther into the water, the current pulling at her skirts. She spat out a mouthful of foul water. "It's too far!"

"You must," Valentine argued. "Reach up as high as you can. I will grab you."

"No!"

"I will!" he insisted. "I will no let you go. On three, now. One," he began.

In her mind, Mary could already feel her fingers sliding out of Valentine's cold, wet grasp.

"Two, *mi amor.*"

Mary decided then that, if she was going to die, it would be while reaching for Valentine.

"Three!"

She let go of the piling entirely and dove at the memory of where his hand had been. For one terrifying instant, she feared she had missed, for her fingers clawed at nothing but rain. And then a steely band clamped around her wrist.

"Help me, Maria," Valentine called out as he pulled. "The pegs!"

Mary floundered at the slick wood, her body twisting in the air, and at last she found the short grip. She could not raise her legs, trapped within the crushing weight of her skirts.

"I have it!" she shouted and strained upward with her arms, desperate to be out of the water.

She felt his other hand clamp above her elbow. Mary folded her forearm over his fingers and used his support to leverage herself up higher against the piling. His hand around her wrist released and she felt him grab a fistful of her gown between her shoulder blades, and Valentine hauled her from the river.

He fell backward, pulling Mary with him, and she landed atop him, her head low on his chest, her fingers gripping his sodden tunic. His breathing was labored enough to cause Mary's head to bounce on his muscled abdomen, but she hardly noticed through her own relieved gasps. The rain still pelted them, the lightning still flashed, but she was alive, and so was Valentine.

Once they were both sitting up, Valentine gathered Mary to him. "Are you all right?" he asked, his voice raspy and thick.

"I think so," she said. "Just cold. You?"

"I have never felt better," he said, and Mary could hear the smile in his voice. He gained his feet before helping her to stand.

Mary let the two satchels she had grabbed—she didn't know yet which ones—slide from her frozen arms to the pier. "Where are we?" she asked.

"On the edge of Hamburg, at the house of a friend." Valentine squatted down on his haunches and gathered big handfuls of her skirts, trying to wring the water from them. "Look across the river, Maria."

Mary turned her head and gasped. Perhaps it was only the lingering effects of the potion, but the lights of the city and from the lanterns hanging on the moored ships sparkled in the rain like starbursts, and lit the surface of the river like fairy fire. From her position on the dock, the Elbe seemed deceptively calm—not even a ripple could be seen on its black surface, belying the raging torrent they'd just come out of. One could only guess at its tumult by the deep bobbing of the cog ship moored on the far side of the dock.

Mary turned her head quickly the other way, toward the solid shore they had at last achieved, and saw a very different landscape—one of darkened forest and sloping field, of rough-hewn fencing like skeletal bones in the flashing lightning; squat outbuildings ringing a tall, square structure with two low wings to either side.

"What sort of friend?" she asked. "This appears to be an inn."

Valentine stood, picking up the bags as he straightened and swiped at his eyes with his forearm. "It is. For travelers who do no desire to stay in the city." He took her arm and started up the pier toward the crest of the hill. "Mostly those traveling with large parties—many horses and belongings, or much to trade. Hamish caters to the nobility—and a certain kind of criminal, it is true—so we should be quite comfortable here."

"I think I would be comfortable in a cave right now, so long as it was dry," Mary quipped, struggling to move her legs against the weight of her skirts. "Are we to play at being someones we are not?"

"Not with Hamish," Valentine said. "He owes me a favor or three."

"Ah, a fellow criminal from your colorful past," Mary said. "Why am I surprised?"

"No, no," Valentine said, helping her up the slippery grass. "His reputation in Hamburg is beyond reproach."

Mary couldn't help her laugh. Valentine always knew how to twist situations into the most favorable light.

"What of his reputation elsewhere?" she pressed.

Valentine shrugged in the darkness. "Perhaps slightly less. But I assure you, there would be few men who dared test his identity, lest they wished a quick death."

Mary winced. "I see. I simply can't wait to meet him."

Valentine laughed as he led Mary to the rear of one of the low wings of the inn. He released her hand to rap on the door with the backs of his knuckles.

Mary could have sworn she felt the ground beneath her feet vibrate with the loud stomps coming from beyond the door. She turned her head to look nervously at Valentine, but he was smiling. He glanced over at her and gave her a wink and a reassuring nod.

Unintelligible shouts grew louder as the stomping approached the other side of the door.

"—laggin' peasantry! Can't even read a flaggin' drawering, can ye?" The door swung open with a whoosh, emitting kind, golden light and delicious-smelling warmth into the wet night. "Th'inn's closed for a private party, ye flaggin' bast—*Valentine!*"

The man standing in the doorway was no taller than Mary herself, and slender, with a full head of wavy golden hair that rose in a wave from his forehead. He wore a handsome, tooled leather apron over his creamy white shirt, and his boots gleamed black in the light of the room behind him.

"Good evening, Hamish, my friend," Valentine said. "We seem to have bypassed the main entrance and so missed what I'm sure was a masterful illustration indicating that you were closed for business this night. My apologies."

"Come in, come in!" Hamish laughed, stepping back from the doorway and giving Mary a friendly smile. His bright blue eyes sparkled. "I must say I'm not surprised to see you, but my God, man—a lady with you? Good evening, milady. Welcome, welcome!" He closed the door after them.

Mary saw that they were in a busy kitchen. A wide hearth took up the entire wall toward the center of the structure, filled with a variety of metal frameworks and rotating spits. Cauldrons boiled, portions of meat glistened and sizzled, the fragrant smoke and steam stinging Mary's eyes and causing her mouth to prickle. Three long tables took up the center of the room, all surrounded by an army of white-aproned men and women, chopping and stirring and clattering wooden trenchers together. None of the kitchen workers seemed to care one whit for their entrance.

Hamish came around them and shouted to the people in a guttural language. One rotund woman swept past, carrying a large, steaming pot with the ends of her apron wrapped about the handles, and she answered him quickly and dismissively in the same language. Then Hamish gestured for them to follow him through the kitchen to a doorway at one end of the hearth. It housed a narrow stairwell, which they climbed.

"Eloise'll be so flaggin' pleased to see you, Valentine. 'Tis sorry I am that I cannot place you and yer lady in the king's apartment, but we are full up tonight with some flaggin' general's business. You can have one of our chambers above until they clear out on the morrow."

"The king's apartment?" Mary whispered over her shoulder.

Valentine shook his head with a grin. "Hamish names the chambers. He says it makes the patrons who stay here feel important."

"I see," she murmured, although she didn't.

"Everyone wants to feel they're important, milady," Hamish said cheerily above her. "Even if they've no more flaggin' pedigree than a dross mare."

"He has unusually keen hearing as well," Valentine said, quite unnecessarily at this point, Mary thought.

"Keen hearing is a necessity in my lines of work, eh?" Hamish said, coming to the top of the stairs and glancing back with a grin. He went to a door on the left and pushed it open, then popped his head in to look about, his words muffled a bit. "I demand a pretty coin for a room at the Queen, and so if a bloke is willin' to pay, well—" he took a step back into the short corridor and wrapped the hem of his leather apron around his hand before seizing one of the sconces from the wall—"he's to be treated like a flaggin' prince, 'sfar as I'm concerned. The city's bleedin' me dry for taxes—I need all the coin I can lay hand to. The only reason I agreed to shut down the Queen for the night. Every room full, the stable as well.

"Milady," Hamish said with a sweeping bow, holding the light high toward the open doorway.

Mary stepped into the room, feeling her skirts pulling on the boards behind her. "I'm sorry for the trouble when you are so harried," she said to Hamish, who was securing the sconce to a wall of the room.

"No trouble at all," he said with a bright smile. "The oldest usually sleep here, any matter, but the lot of 'em's at the cottage with their mother tonight. Be safer there, Eloise reckoned."

Valentine had deposited their bags in a corner on the floor. "How many do you number now, Hamish?"

"Our sixth was born in May."

Valentine paused and looked at his friend with what appeared to be anticipation. "Boy?"

The jolly blond man threw back his head and laughed. "Another flaggin' lass, if you can believe my poor luck! Seems I'm to be the only cock in the roost. Ah, well." Mary thought he didn't look at all disappointed. "Am I to understand that all your belongings soaked up the storm?"

"Soaked up the Elbe is more accurate," Valentine said wryly, and Mary noticed that Valentine's usually swarthy complexion had taken on a grayish cast. He was obviously exhausted.

Hamish cocked an eyebrow in surprise, and for the briefest moment, Mary could almost see his mind turning over this information behind his friendly eyes. She suspected there was much more to Hamish than his humble innkeeper façade led one to believe.

"You flaggin' despise travelin' by river!"

"Believe me, friend, I despise it even more after this night."

Hamish laughed again, and his calculating look had vanished to the point where Mary wondered if she'd even seen it in the first place. "Well, I'm lookin' forward to hearing what has turned the great horseman Alesander to sailor. There are some simple garments in the wardrobe—help yourselves."

He turned back to the door. "You can come to the main room after for food if you can keep your shadow and your woman close, which I know you can, Valentine. Flaggin' rough lot we've got in tonight. But do come for a tankard, any matter. We can reminisce a bit before they get too pissed an' I have to start cleanin' 'em out."

"My thanks, Hamish," Valentine said, turning to the large wooden box against the wall.

As soon as the door closed, Mary rushed to Valentine's side, looking over his arm as he rifled through stacks of yellowed ivory and brown wool. "All right, tell me," she said, hearing the eagerness in her own voice.

"Tell you what, *mi amor*?" he said.

"Your friend. Who is he really? He said his 'lines of work.' One line is, of course, as an innkeeper. What else?"

Valentine had collected several pieces and now turned from the wardrobe. "Well, he is obviously a breeding stallion since he has six children. I do no blame him; Eloise is—" He made a noise that was a sigh of longing.

Mary felt herself stiffen. "I see. You knew her before her husband, then."

He placed the clothes on the bed, wide and lumpy and low to the floor, and laughed. "I knew her before Hamish, yes. But I didn't *know* her, Maria. I assisted them in traveling here, to Hamburg, to start their life together. I placed myself in great danger for them, certainly. But I could never resist the pleas of two people in love."

Mary placed her hands on her hip and cocked an eyebrow. "Oh, really? And how much did he pay you for your sentimentality?"

Valentine shrugged and then tossed her an undergown that unfurled in the air. "His entire wage."

Mary caught the rough flax material in her hands. "That doesn't seem like it could have been remotely enough to risk your life for."

"Hamish is very good at what he does," Valentine conceded, as if that in itself should have been explanation enough. "And I had learned a thing or two from my terrible mistake in secreting Teresa away. Helping Eloise and Hamish escape was child's play for me."

Mary frowned for a moment. "You made it seem that Eloise was dead?"

"Yes. Are you going to change or no?" he asked.

"Yes, but—"

"Then do so, pray, *mi amor*—my throat, it is very scratchy. I am in need of dry clothes and a strong drink."

Mary huffed and went behind the wardrobe. She fought with her wet gown while she continued to ask questions. "Why would you want to make it appear that the woman Hamish loved was dead?"

"Her father never would have allowed the marriage, for one. Eloise is noble, and Hamish is . . . well, he is no so much."

She pulled the rough underdress over her head. The dryness felt heavenly. "I find it difficult to accept that her father would prefer a dead daughter over one married to a commoner. But since I have no father, I cannot know for certain. Mine shackled me to you, after all." She couldn't help but smile at her own wit.

"Maria," Valentine said in mock warning from beyond the wardrobe.

Mary removed her soaking shoes next, trying to wipe off the bits of wet leaves and debris with her ruined gown as best she could. "I've finished. Are you decent?"

"Completely nude," Valentine said.

"I'll wait." Mary picked up her sopping gown and stood behind the cabinet, biting her lower lip. She sighed, curling and uncurling her toes to help bring the feeling to them faster, trying everything she could not to imagine what Valentine looked like without his clothes. Surely he was dressed by now. She would just take a little peek.

Mary eased her head around the edge of the wardrobe slowly, her eyes going wide in anticipation of what she would see.

What she saw was Valentine Alesander, dressed in the outfit of a manservant, his arms crossed and smiling at her.

"Caught you," he said with a wink.

Mary's face whooshed with heat, but she managed to hang a frown on her mouth and stomped from the corner. "You were taking too long," she said with her chin raised. She tossed her wet things atop Valentine's own and turned to him with a flounce. She paused when she saw him crawling onto the bed.

"I thought you wanted a drink," she said.

"I do, Maria, but right now, I am no feeling so well. I think it would be better for me to lie down for a bit. I will visit with Hamish later."

Mary frowned in earnest then, and approached the bed, sitting on the side of it close to Valentine. She reached out and placed a palm along his temple; he was burning with fever.

"Valentine, I believe you are taking ill," she said.

"It is nothing," he said. "I am only tired. I have no slept."

"Tired doesn't bring on fever," she argued. "I will go below myself and solicit your friend for some food and something to drink." She fully expected him to forbid it.

He didn't say anything for several moments. And then, "All right. Something warm, *por favor*."

At that, Mary became genuinely concerned. "I will do my best."

"Gracias, mi amor."

She stood up and then paused, a thought occurring to her. "Valentine, what was the other thing?"

"What other thing, Maria?" He groaned.

"You said Eloise's father never would have allowed her to marry

Hamish because he was not noble, *for one*. What was the other reason?"

"Because Eloise's father was Hamish's employer. And Eloise? She was the mark."

Mary frowned. "I don't understand. Mark?"

Valentine rolled back toward her with an exhausted sigh, but his tone was patient. "My little Maria, I hate to completely destroy your innocence."

"Tell me," she insisted. "I vow I shan't reveal to Hamish that you did."

"I do very much doubt that he would care," Valentine said with a wry but weary grin. "Tonight we sleep in a bed belonging to one of the world's greatest assassins."

Mary smiled to herself as she stepped out into the short corridor at the top of the narrow stairs.

That cheerful little blond man a hired killer? Valentine must think her a child needing entertainment with such wild tales. Or perhaps he was trying to instill an abundance of caution in her by exaggerating Hamish's reputation. Either explanation was rather sweet, any matter, she thought.

She stepped lightly down the stairs, her bare feet making no noise on the smooth wooden treads. She had added a rough brown kirtle to the underdress, and found that she was now quite dry and alert. But she was also starving, and her mouth was sticky with dehydration. She hoped she could locate Hamish quickly in the bustling kitchen; Valentine did not look at all sound, and she wanted to care for him as well as he had done for her on those long days adrift on the river.

If it was possible, the kitchen seemed even busier than when she and Valentine had first arrived. Mary stood on tiptoe and craned her neck to look across the sea of heads bowed to their tasks, but she did not spy the Queen's proprietor. She edged around the nearest bench toward the place where the back entrance met up with another doorway, which assumedly led to the main room. Rowdy shouts and laughter burst through the opening intermittently. Mary had little desire to search for Hamish in the midst of such a disorderly company, so she would simply wait there, being as inconspicuous as possible, until he returned.

Mary didn't realize the woman's gruff shouts were directed at her until she felt the kick to her shin.

"Ow!" she shouted, bending up her knee to rub at her leg and giving the rotund cook she'd seen earlier an offended frown. "I beg your pardon!"

But she was forced to return her foot to the floor as the cook thrust a tray crowded with brimming tankards at her. Mary took them reflexively, lest they crash to the floor, and as soon as she had a firm grip, the fat woman began haranguing her in the same guttural language she'd spoken earlier, simultaneously pointing at the doorway that led to the main room.

"I'm sorry, I don't understand," Mary said, giving the woman what she hoped was a friendly smile. "I'm looking for—"

But the woman cut her off with more barking, this time enunciating slowly while doing an elaborate pantomime, as if it would help Mary to understand the foreign words she spoke. She pulled a length of what appeared at first to be a rag from her apron pocket and jerked it down over Mary's hair even as Mary tried to duck away.

It was then that Mary noticed the cook's kirtle and underdress were of the exact cut and color as the ones Mary herself currently wore. The misunderstanding became clear to her a moment later as she stood there in the kitchen in her bare feet and wet, tangled hair, the short lappets of the simple cap tickling her jaw.

"You think I came here for *work!*" she said with a relieved smile and a half laugh. "No, no—I'm a *guest.*" She tried to return the tray to the woman. "All of my own clothes were ruined and so—you don't understand me at all, do you?"

The woman responded by stepping close to Mary's side, landing a sharp pinch to the underside of her arm, and then shoving her, tray and all, through the doorway.

She barely kept her balance as she was forced to run after the precariously tilting tray, and she sighed her relief as she came to a stop along the wall of the main room and saw that the heavy tankards had kept to their bottoms. She looked around at the dark, smoky room, paneled in rich, oiled wood that flickered with the liquid gold of the oil lamps on the small tables. Another huge stone hearth made up the innermost wall, but this one contained only a small fire over which a solitary spit turned what appeared to be palm-length sausages. A young lad stood at the turn, handing out the morsels on long skewers.

The room was full of men and serving girls, dressed—to Mary's chagrin—exactly as she was. The girls floated around the tables, hosting males of seemingly every nationality and caste; some wore the fine dress of officers, some the rough costumes of the peasantry. There were those clearly hailing from foreign shores, with long, colorful robes and capes, and Mary even saw a pair of turbans bobbing above the heads of those gathered.

All of the men were heavily armed, it seemed, with long swords, curved blades, and sheaths lashed to their legs. Mary saw quivers and crossbows, bundles of unknown contents strapped across backs, satchels looped securely over torsos.

It was as if they were readying for a war.

A serving girl swept from the kitchen, bearing a full tray identical to Mary's, but paused next to her to lean close.

"You'd better move lest you find yourself out of doors on your arse without pay," the girl warned in a heavy accent, her spotty face betraying her youth. "There'll be time a plenty to choose the one you'll have for the night once they're into their cups proper. No worries—I was new once as well." And then the young servant fixed a sultry smile on her face and moved off into the crowd.

The tray was growing heavier with each passing moment, and the only thing Mary could contemplate now was relieving herself of her burden and locating Hamish. It seemed the quickest way to do that was to make her way among the patrons, who appeared to reach up for a fresh tankard at will.

"Looks as though I'm to play at being someone else after all," she muttered wryly to herself. "Valentine will be so pleased." Mary seized the handle of a tankard from her tray and drained it of its contents for courage, her stomach soon after gurgling loudly and sending up a large and certainly unladylike belch. Then she set off into the room, trying to avoid the largest puddles and grasping hands as best she could.

She at last reached the far side of the room, her tray blessedly empty, and paused near the hearth to wipe at her brow, letting the round wooden platter hang near her knee. She now had a deeper respect for those in service. In the past quarter hour, Mary had been pawed at, pinched, caressed, and spoken to in such lurid foreign tongues that she was glad she had been unable to decipher the words, although their meaning had been quite clear. Mary vowed to herself that she would more thoroughly appreciate the efforts of those waiting on her in the future.

She caught sight of Hamish, then, at a table near the center of the melee. He appeared to be engaged in a rather serious conversation with a man whose back was turned toward Mary. Her forehead wrinkled as she noted the man's flowing red hair and studded leather tunic.

Studs of that sort would twinkle in the firelight, Mary knew.

She gave a shiver, as if she'd just seen a ghost, and then laughed nervously at herself. What a ninny she was! Mary decided she would simply wait until Hamish disengaged from the man, and then she would follow the Queen's proprietor back to the kitchen.

But when Hamish stood from the table and stepped away, he walked instead to the front of the room, where a tall wooden crate had been laid down in front of the conspicuously barred entrance.

The gathering obviously did not want any surprise arrivals.

Hamish stepped up on the crate and held his hands high, calling for the room's attention.

"Welcome, friends, to the Queen's Inn," Hamish announced loudly. "It is my honor to host such an ignominious group of gentleman—and I'm sore hoping it never happens again!"

The crowd roared with laughter.

Mary looked back to the man Hamish had left, who was now standing as he adjusted his belt and sword and swept his red hair back over his shoulder with a toss of his head. Mary caught a glimpse of a craggy nose, a pointed chin . . .

The potion must have addled her brains; surely she could not be in the same room with the very man she was racing back to England to marry. She squeezed her eyes shut tightly.

When she opened them, the redheaded man had yanked a serving girl to his side and bent her back over his arm. Mary saw his face clearly before he thrust it between the wench's breasts.

Mary's breath lodged in her throat. It *was* him.

"You already know you have been summoned here to join in a special and dangerous mission," Hamish continued, "but let us now learn the details of the thing. It is with great pleasure that I introduce your most generous benefactor, the hero of both the English Crown *and* the king of Jerusalem, baron of the Cinque Ports, the lord of Beckhamshire—"

"What?" Mary gasped as her brows pulled together.

"Lord Glayer Felsteppe!"

The men erupted with calls of "Huzzah!" as Mary Beckham's betrothed stepped to the makeshift platform and raised his hands, as if displaying himself, basking in his audience's approval.

Oh my God, Mary thought, her anger turning quickly to anxiety. *If he sees me, I'm finished.* She put her head down and started to move away from the wall, attempting to keep her body angled toward the back of the room.

A hand grasped her arm and jerked her back. Mary's head snapped up, her eyes wide, but it was only the spotty young serving girl.

"No," the girl whispered, pulling Mary back against the wall. "Be still. We'll not be punished for a rest now, but we might should we interrupt."

"My esteemed colleagues," Glayer Felsteppe began in a crisp and proper accent that Mary knew all too well, and the group bellowed with laughter. Glayer's thin lips split in a wide grin. The front of his tunic was wet, likely with drink, and Mary felt suddenly nauseated.

"I am infinitely heartened by your willingness to join with me on such a perilous mission. For, as many of you already know, the men we seek are not only a danger to the rulers of the Christian world but a threat to the safety of citizens everywhere."

"We don't care what they've done," a man shouted from near the back. "Tell us who and how much, so we can get back to drinking!"

Glayer Felsteppe chuckled and held his palms toward the crowd. "I shall get to that in but a moment, good man," he promised. "I, too, have a thing or two I'd like to attend this night—a blonde and a brunette, to be precise." His audience whistled and stomped their approval.

"So much for undying devotion," Mary muttered.

The servant girl leaned toward her and whispered, "They're all pigs, ain't they?"

"Indeed," Mary said between her teeth.

"You will each receive a small stipend this evening as you formally enlist to serve the royal heads of those sponsoring you— twenty pieces of English silver, if that should suit you well enough."

The men banged their tankards on the tables and cheered until Mary's betrothed was forced to call for silence once more.

"Let that coin fund you well as you search for the criminals we seek. Whoever succeeds in capturing them, alive or dead—I recommend, of course, the latter—your reward upon their captivity or interment shall be—" he paused dramatically, and Mary saw nearly the entire crowd of men lean forward in a wave—"*one thousand* silver pieces!"

"*Each?!*" one man cried out rapturously.

"Each," Felsteppe assured with a sage nod.

If the men had been enthusiastic before, now they were shocked into murmuring silence, their heads bowing together with their compatriots, already scheming.

"They could be anywhere," Felsteppe continued. "The last reliable word we have is that one was spotted in Prague, and so they may have split their little group apart to hide solitarily."

Mary's spine stiffened. Prague?

"One is a commoner, and so may be difficult to locate if he has taken up once again with the peasantry. He is notable, though, for his size and his coloring: Roman Berg. A Norseman who has worked as a stone cutter. White-headed. Beast of a man. Strong, but largely a coward. I would not recommend engaging him alone." Glayer held out his hands and bobbled them as if they were scales while his mouth quirked. "Perhaps a group of four or five."

"No," Mary whispered to herself.

"Next: Constantine Gerard and Adrian Hailsworth—both titled nobility until quite recently." The crowd snickered at Felsteppe's sly grin. "As well as the two most likely to remain paired. Unnatural friendship, I have on good authority. Gerard has experience on the battlefield and would make a dangerous opponent if challenged. It would be best to come at him from behind if you are at all able. Hailsworth has little battle experience but is learned and cunning to the extreme. Do not underestimate him."

"Stop," Mary whispered as her eyes sought Hamish's face in the room. The blond man watched with as much interest as everyone else in the crowd. "Don't say his name."

"The final mark—" Mary's stomach flipped at the word, so recently entered into her vocabulary—"Valentine Alesander. A rogue

Spanish noble known for his talent for disguise and as an exquisite polyglot. He can fade into the citizenry of any country, a fact that was his only saving grace in Damascus. His own family has been searching for him for the past ten years, trying in vain to recover a fortune stolen after Alesander murdered his own sister. Find him and you may be rewarded with whatever gold he is carrying."

Mary felt as though she might vomit as she watched Hamish's face, his smile having faded away into an intense look of—pain? Anger? She couldn't tell.

The world's greatest assassin.

The city's bleedin' me dry for taxes—I need all the coin I can lay hand to.

Felsteppe continued. "If you have any questions, or any clues on the whereabouts of these vicious criminals that you care to share with your friends—" the men laughed—"bring them to me as you make your mark and collect your stipend. There are likenesses of the wanted in the back of the room. I think that is all. Good luck and Godspeed to you, gentlemen." He stepped down from the box and was immediately surrounded by mercenaries and the woman he had groped earlier.

Mary looked around but could no longer locate Hamish in the crowd. It was as if he had vanished.

She had to get back to Valentine, and they had to leave the Queen. *Now.* She stepped away from the wall, then stopped.

They had no coin. Their possessions were all lost, as far as Mary knew. Her eyes went to the man she was supposed to wed upon her return to England. Glayer Felsteppe had one arm wrapped around the serving wench, and no fewer than ten men were vying for his attention.

Mary recalled the night—a lifetime ago, it now seemed— when Glayer Felsteppe had shown her his purse in a hidden compartment of his tunic. And yet she hesitated. If Felsteppe caught her, if he saw her here in Hamburg, her future was no more.

But he was already flaunting her father's title, as if Beckham Hall had always belonged to him. And he was helping whoever had betrayed Chastellet and Valentine's friends. He wanted them dead.

He wanted *Valentine* dead.

Mary squared her shoulders and lifted her tray, taking a circuitous route toward where Felsteppe stood. She snatched up empty tankards as she went and placed them on the platter to hide her face, balancing the tray up on her shoulder. She came to the table at Felsteppe's back and squeezed between, pressing herself against him and then jostling the girl away from his side.

The serving girl turned her head to glare at Mary over Felsteppe's shoulder, and then snarled something quite nasty-sounding in another language before giving Mary a shove, sending the empty tankards tumbling onto the tray. Mary ducked away sheepishly as Felsteppe only glanced back at the commotion, and then skittered toward the kitchen, her eyes darting around the room for signs of Hamish.

Nothing.

She sped into the kitchen and slid the tray of tankards onto a bench atop a pile of discarded knives, withdrawing her fist quickly and shoving it down into the folds of her skirts. She ignored the fat cook's shouts as she fled the room.

Mary started up the narrow stairwell with her blood pounding in her ears, carrying a blade in one hand and Glayer Felsteppe's weighty purse in the other.

Chapter 18

Valentine dozed fitfully, each breath searing his throat and lungs, the skin of his face feeling as if it had melted into the rough coverlet of the bed. His back, arms, neck—everything ached as though in a vise.

Maria would be pleased to at last be right about something.

Her image swirled in his partial consciousness, and brought with it the olfactory hallucination of spring flowers swaying in the breeze, the auditory fantasy of her whispering his name in passionate desire as he took her in a bright field of soft grass. Her innocent, creamy skin pressed against his, cool like wet silk. That she wanted him meant that he was purged of all his past misdeeds, cleansed of his sins, made whole and honorable. *Valentine. Valentine. Val—*

"—entine!" The screeching was not at all like her voice in his dream. It was rather unpleasant, and he wished to remain in the springtime field with the naked Maria, the loving Maria, the *quiet* Maria . . .

Her palm was indeed cool, but the fantasy effect was largely lost as she slapped his cheek soundly. He struggled to raise his head.

She slapped him again.

"That was no necessary, *mi amor*," he slurred. "I am awake now."

"Get. Up." she insisted as she seized his tunic and began yanking him upright. "Getupgetupgetup!" Not happy with him sitting, she struggled to pull him from the bed completely. "Do you have your boots—yes, good. *Come on!"*

"Maria," Valentine said, holding out his palm and easing his backside down on the mattress again. "What has you so alarmed? I think you were right—I have acquired some slight illness. I am no well enough to—"

A polite rap sounded at the door, and then Hamish's voice called through the wood. "Va—" He broke off for a moment. "Er . . . my friends? May I enter?"

Valentine opened his mouth to call for his friend to come, but before he could make a sound Maria clamped one hand over his lips, the other behind his skull.

"No!" she whispered harshly. "Valentine, do not say one word!" She ran lightly to the door and leaned against it with one shoulder, holding her fist up in front of her chest.

He saw that she gripped what appeared to be a long curved kitchen knife.

"Ah . . . Hamish?" she called.

"Yes, milady?" Valentine's friend answered. "May I come in?"

"We are . . . ah, indisposed at the moment."

"Is . . . everything all right, milady?" Hamish asked, and Valentine heard the suspicion in his friend's voice.

Valentine was a bit suspicious himself at the moment.

"Oh, yes," Maria said eagerly, and then he saw her face turn bright red and she squeezed her eyes shut. "It's only . . . we're . . . we're naked."

Valentine couldn't help his hoot of laughter. He must truly be dreaming with fever.

Beyond the door, Hamish answered with his own chuckle. "I'll give you a moment, then."

"A moment?" Valentine called out in mock outrage. "Better an hour, Hamish!"

"I'll be back," Hamish assured them through the thin wood. And then, as if as an afterthought, "Do not venture below without me, though, eh?"

"Yes, yes, of course," Maria agreed.

"Now go away, you bastard!" Valentine ordered. He was feeling quite fine at the moment, although he had no idea what use Maria had for a knife. Perhaps she intended to force herself on him.

He hoped he could summon the strength. He tried sitting up straighter to test himself, but his legs above his feet felt rather rubbery, and he let himself go loose again.

No matter. Maria was an exemplary rider.

Maria seemed to listen intently at the crack of the door for Hamish's retreating footsteps before she rushed back toward him.

Valentine craned his neck to look up at her. "You can no longer resist me and wish to take advantage of my weakened state, yes?"

"What?" Her face twisted in horrified confusion.

"Very well," he said and allowed himself to fall backward onto the mattress. It caused a pain in his head, but he hoped Maria would make all discomfort go away very soon. "I surrender."

"I can't understand you when you speak Spanish," she hissed as she pulled him upright again.

His head swam. "I was speaking Spanish?" he asked and then looked at her closely. "Am I still speaking it?"

She sighed. "No. Get up. We have to leave, right now. Before Hamish returns."

Valentine shook his head. "I can no, Maria. Whatever it is, it can wait until morning. Did you happen to remember my drink?"

She dropped to her knees before him.

"Oh, ho!" he said with a smile. "The drink can wait, I think."

But Maria did not return his smile. Instead she framed his face with her palms, and through the heat of his fever, Valentine saw the tears in her big eyes.

"Valentine, please," she pleaded. "I know you are very ill. I know. But if we don't leave—*right now*—neither of us will see the morning. We'll be dead. Do you understand me? *Dead.*"

Her words sobered him slightly, but he could not seem to shake the entirety of his confusion. "Where are we to go? I have no strength. No coin. No horse. What can you expe—"

"The first thing we must do is get out of the Queen alive," she insisted. "And we must do that now. If you can help me by walking out of here with your own strength, I promise I will get you out of danger."

"But I am protecting you," he argued, and reached up to place his hand over the back of one of her palms.

She smiled at him gently, her face so full of the tenderness Valentine had craved for so many years, it almost brought a misting to his eyes.

"Not this night," she said. "Tonight, it is I who must protect you. Ready?"

Valentine turned his lips into her palm and kissed it firmly. Then he pushed her away as he stood up, swayed for a moment, the room blurring madly, and then gained his balance.

"Vamanos," he said.

Maria shot to her feet and all but flew to the corner where their bags and discarded clothes lay. She kicked the wet and ruined clothing aside before picking up the bags and swinging them over her own arm.

"Come nearer the door," she ordered. "I need to put out the light."

He obliged, and once the room was in darkness, Maria whispered, "An immediate right at the bottom of the stairs, straight through to the door we entered upon our arrival; the other entrances are barred. Do not turn your head, do not stop. If anyone calls your name, we run. Just so you are not overly shocked, if Hamish catches us, I shall have to kill him."

Then he felt her place something snug over his head, and thought it might have been the maid's cap he just realized she'd been wearing.

"All right, let's go," she said.

He followed her down the stairs toward the brightness and noise of the kitchen, wondering why she would threaten Hamish's life. Surely the food couldn't be that bad.

There was no more time for fevered musings as they swept through the kitchen. Valentine thought he heard the fat cook call after them, but they were out the door in a blink, the cool mist that had replaced the rain washing over his burning skin like angel kisses.

"Ah." He sighed, turning up his face.

"No," Maria insisted, grabbing his hand. "Come on—run!"

He tried. The best he could manage was a hitching shuffle. Valentine realized they were proceeding down the wet and slippery hill toward the Elbe once more.

"Maria," he rasped, the air doing much to clear his head. "The raft, it is no more. We can no—"

"I know," she said impatiently. "I'm not seeking the raft." Their feet clattered onto the wooden dock, and Maria released his hand when they came upon what seemed to Valentine at first to be a solid wooden wall. But then he remembered that they were on a dock jutting out into the river, so that couldn't be right.

He looked up and saw the towering mast of the cog ship upon which their raft had broken up.

When he looked back to Maria, she was climbing the short rope ladder that led to the deck above.

"Come on," she called over her shoulder.

Valentine stood there a moment, completely perplexed, watching her as she threw her leg over the side of the ship and then disappeared.

"Maria?" he called up. "Do you know? This is a boat." He shrugged and hoisted himself up onto the thick, swaying ropes.

"Valentine!" she called from beyond the deck rail.

His muscles were weak, shaking with effort. By the time he grasped the wooden rail and swung his leg over, he was sweating, shivering, and felt as though he might vomit.

He tumbled over the railing, crumpling onto the decking in a heap, only catching himself with his palms the instant before his face would have smashed into the planks. His breaths heaved in and out of him.

"I hope you know what you are doing, Maria," he rasped and with great effort raised his head to find her in the dark and the wind.

"I think she has done very well," a man's voice answered.

Valentine blinked, shook his head, tried to clear his vision. The dark mass before him wavered, doubled, then revealed itself to be Maria, being held before a man whose forearm was around her throat. His other hand apparently held Maria's arms behind her. Valentine focused on the dark oval of the man's face, hidden by the wide brim of his feathered hat.

"Francisco," Valentine whispered.

"Hello, cousin," Francisco said. "We are reunited at last. Roland," he called over his shoulder, but Valentine could feel that Francisco's eyes never left him. "Let us ensure my beloved kin does no think to part our company so soon."

A dark shape emerged from behind Francisco and Maria, and Valentine recognized the unmistakable outline of a dagger, its blade piercing the dark woolen sky, checkered by rigging.

"No!" Maria screamed. "Don't hurt him! He's—"

Valentine never heard the end of her plea. The dagger struck him in the temple and, after the blinding flash of pain behind his eyes, all was black.

Mary screamed as Valentine collapsed fully to the decking, and then she came to life, thrashing and kicking at her captor. She tossed her head back, seeking some part of him to bite, but he pushed her away from him, as if realizing her intent. She landed on the decking near Valentine's legs.

"No so loudly, Maria," Francisco said, "lest you seek to summon the guests of yonder inn. I am no willing to turn loose of Valentine now that I've only so recently caught him." He casually tossed overboard the kitchen knife he'd taken from her. "So kind of you to save me the effort of sneaking into the Queen later tonight."

Mary bent over Valentine, turning his head gently and leaning her face down close to his mouth. He was breathing easily, but she could not see where he had been struck. His servant's cap had slid off, and a quick examination with her hands found a lump at his hairline. Thankfully, it was not sticky with blood. She eased Valentine onto his back and reached out to drag the sodden satchels she'd dropped close to place under his head.

"How do you know my name?" she demanded over her shoulder.

"I have been following the pair of you since Prague," he answered simply. "Valentine is no the only Alesander who has learned to travel anonymously."

Mary made a show of checking Valentine's person as she worked her way down to his feet. Once there, she turned her back to Francisco and slipped her hand inside Valentine's boot, sliding his dagger free. Then she spun on her heel, turning and rising in one fluid motion.

She pointed the dagger at Francisco Alesander. "I hope for your sake that he is not the only one able to travel quickly, either," she said. "Call to your men to cast off. We must be away from here immediately."

The despicable Roland, who had dealt Valentine's blow, edged closer to Mary's side. "You want I should take it from her, Captain?"

Mary adjusted her stance, glancing between the two men as she swept the blade from side to side. "You stay away from me!" she shouted, realizing that her voice held no tremble, her hand was steady. "Both of you! Come near and I shall slit your throats."

Roland's eyes widened and he gave a low whistle. "Captain?"

Francisco's tone implied he was not at all concerned for the safety of his person. "By all means, Roland—let us oblige the lady."

"Aye," Roland answered and turned his back on Mary. He walked into the darkness, calling out curt orders.

Immediately, the deck of the ship seemed to come alive, shadows of coiled rope and stacks of cargo revealing the shapes of the men hidden among them. Mary stepped backward until she felt Valentine against her bare heels. She faced Francisco, who continued to watch her almost curiously, his feet braced apart and his hands on his hips.

In moments the crashing and slithering sounds of miles of rope could be heard, along with the sloshing of the waves against the hull, and Mary noticed the skyline gradually shifting. She heard shouts above her head and dared to glace up, fearing attack from above, but instead saw men about their jobs high up in the rigging. They called back and forth to one another, repeating orders, confirming tasks, and Mary looked around, taken aback at the swift response to her demand.

The ship crested a swale as it turned out into the Elbe away from the dock, causing Mary to sway and throw out her arms for balance, her stomach giving a familiar lurch.

No. Please, no. Not now.

But by the time the ship was pointed west and headed into the center of the river, Mary realized she was fine. Her feet were planted firmly, her legs limber, her head clear. Mary Beckham was standing on a moving ship, and she was fine.

In her shock, she had quite forgotten about Francisco Alesander, and when she swung her head back around to find him, the place on the deck where he'd stood was empty.

But now the ship was beginning to light up as, one by one, long torches and hanging lanterns were lit. Mary realized that no one at all was paying her any mind, and so she felt rather foolish, brandishing Valentine's dagger at the breeze. She dropped her hand to her side, the wind whipping her hair back from her face as she turned into it and looked past the aft castle of the ship to see the lights of Hamburg sliding past.

Where would Francisco Alesander take them?

"What have I done now?" she whispered.

She sighed and then dropped to her heels at Valentine's side once more. His breathing was still steady and even, but his face felt like a smooth coal—dry and searing with heat.

"Valentine," she said, running her palm over his forehead. "Valentine, can you hear me?"

"When did he take ill?"

The murmured question came from directly behind her head, and Mary jumped, whipping up the hand that still gripped Valentine's blade.

Francisco grasped her wrist before she could use it, although his grip did not twist or bruise. "I am no going to hurt you, Maria," he said. "Either of you."

She jerked her arm back and, miraculously, he let her go. "You already have hurt him," she shot back.

"I did no know he was ill," Francisco defended. "Although I should have known something was amiss when he allowed you to board an unknown ship before him. Had he been well, the only way I could keep him in one place was to render him unconscious."

Although Mary agreed, she gave no comment, only continued to watch Francisco warily. "He doesn't have any gold, if that's what you're after."

"I do no want his coin."

Mary's eyes narrowed. "And he didn't kill his sister."

At this, Francisco's handsome face broke into a gentle smile. "I know, Maria."

Mary was confused. "Then what do you want with him?"

"I will get to that later," Francisco said. "But first, let us move Valentine to a place where he can rest easily and where we can better care for him, yes?"

Mary pressed her lips together for a moment. "Are you trying to trick me?"

"I would never." His smile returned, and in it, Mary could see the ghostly outline of Valentine's own indulgent grin. "*Vamanos*, Maria."

Chapter 19

His parched throat was the first thing to come to Valentine's awareness. Indeed, the hot, sand-dry feeling seemed to fill up his mouth as well, and he tried to swallow before opening his eyes. The reflex only succeeded in triggering a hacking cough that would have brought tears had he any moisture at all in his body.

Perhaps he was dead, decomposing, like one of the many bodies he'd seen half-buried in the desert along the road from Damascus. The corpses had resembled parchment stretched over bundles of sticks.

But no—Damascus was a long time ago. He had gone on to Melk, and then—

Maria, he thought suddenly, and his eyes opened.

He saw dark planks of wood over his head—not very far above him, it seemed.

Where was he?

Where was Maria?

"Good afternoon," a man said somewhere beyond his line of vision. "Have you decided to live after all?"

Valentine turned his head very slowly to the right, and soon the blurry outline of a person rose up and drew nearer. Valentine blinked. He opened his mouth, but nothing came out save a wheezy gasp.

"Here," the man said, reaching for something and then placing his hand behind Valentine's head to raise it up. He felt a cup placed against his lips, and then cool liquid flooded his mouth.

His throat constricted painfully as he swallowed, and he coughed most of the water back up through his nose and down his chin.

"Too much?" the man asked while Valentine gasped for breath. His lungs felt afire. "Let us try again."

This time the water went down, and Valentine felt the liquid sluice through his innards like some magic elixir. The hand released him back onto whatever pallet he currently occupied and he closed his eyes again with a sigh as he wiped at his mouth.

But he forced his eyes open once more. "Francisco?" he whispered.

"*Sí,*" his cousin answered. "Do no trouble yourself to leap from your deathbed to embrace me."

"Maria," Valentine rasped.

"Maria is fine," Francisco said. "Do you know, I think she would have tried to kill me? I have a feeling that is no her nature."

"I . . . kill you," Valentine whispered.

"That is no a good plan, cousin, since you and your woman are on my ship. Have another drink instead. Then you can threaten me with a clearer voice, yes?"

Valentine nodded.

"*Bueno.*" Francisco helped Valentine to another dipperful of water. When it was empty, he let Valentine's head back down gently. "Better?"

"Where is Maria?" Valentine asked.

Francisco's face was coming into focus in the gloom of the small dark chamber. His lips were curved in the faintest of smiles.

"She is above deck," he said. "I will fetch her for you as soon as we have had our talk, yes? She is a good sailor."

Valentine watched Francisco, and for the briefest moment the fact that Valentine had missed his cousin so much overshadowed the pain of their history. Francisco had aged well—the lines on his face that of a grown man, where once an idealistic youth had looked out. Francisco appeared healthy, confident.

Of course he is confident, Valentine thought to himself. *You are clearly in no condition to best him. He can do with you what he likes now.*

Then Francisco's comment about Maria at last reached his consciousness.

"If you think she is a good sailor, you have obviously kidnapped the wrong woman. Where is Enrique?"

"Dead."

Valentine's heart skipped a beat in his chest. "When?"

"Two years." Francisco shrugged and then shook his head. "Nearly three now."

Had Valentine the strength, he would have laughed. "And look at you—even after his death, you still seek to do his dirty work. What an obedient little jackal you became."

"Valentine, I am sorry."

"No as sorry as you will be when you discover I have no coin to shower upon you. The Alesander fortune—ha!" He turned his eyes back to the planked ceiling, as foreign, unpredictable emotions welled up inside him.

"It was never about the coin," Francisco said quietly.

"No?" Valentine challenged, letting his head fall back toward Francisco again. His cousin's elbows rested on his knees, his hands clasped loosely. His head drooped, showing Valentine only the crown of his curly head. "Then what *was* it about? Your great devotion to Enrique? The man you once said had brought dishonor to our family? Did you think that by aligning with him he would make you his heir?"

"I never had any love for Enrique," Francisco said. He raised his face then, and looked Valentine in the eye. "The love I had was for Teresa."

Valentine winced. "Teresa?" he whispered. "I do no understand what you are saying."

"The night—" Francisco paused, swallowed—"the night you left, I had gone to the sheik's apartment at the villa. I was going to kill him. To save her, you see."

Valentine did not comment; he only watched his cousin closely.

"But I was only a boy. And I was a coward. I failed, and so I sought to beg Enrique one last time. But before I could find him, I saw the blood."

"It was you who discovered we were gone?"

Francisco nodded. "I knew by Enrique's panic that he had no killed Teresa. It was easy enough for him to convince me in that moment that you had—especially because you had not included me in your plan."

"As you said—you were still so much a boy," Valentine defended reluctantly. "I could no take you from your mother, and had I confided in you, Enrique never would have stopped torturing you until you told what you knew. How could you think—even for a moment—that I would do such a thing to Teresa? You were the only brother I knew, Francisco."

Francisco had been nodding his head the entirety of Valentine's speech. "All you say, it is true. But I knew how frightened for her you were. You had a better idea than I what her life would be like, and I knew that you would do anything to spare her the horrors that awaited her. You would rather see her dead."

"I did no kill Teresa, Francisco."

"I know that."

"Yes? And how did you come by this knowledge?"

"Enrique told me on his deathbed. He had located her in Prague, you see. But he could no get to her. You had secured her in a place that a reprobate such as Enrique had become could no hope to reach her. He had no fortune, no title, no lands, no reputation. He was powerless."

"A deathbed confession, eh?" Valentine whispered. "Did you absolve him of his sins?"

"It is Enrique we are speaking of. He was no looking for absolution," Francisco almost spat. "He was charging me with finding you and exacting his revenge."

"Which you are doing now, yes?" Valentine said with a shrug.

But Francisco ignored the question. "I did no believe him at first. A part of me—the part that had betrayed you—wanted it to be untrue. I went to Prague, to see with my own eyes. I found Teresa. And even before I spoke with her, I realized what a fool I had been. I understood at last what you had done. What you had sacrificed in order save her." Francisco reached out a hand and gripped Valentine's forearm. "And I am sorry that I was no there to help you. To help you both."

Valentine did not dare react to the hand on his forearm. He attributed it to his illness, but his composure was tenuous at the moment.

Thankfully, Francisco continued. "I vowed from the moment I saw her—I vowed to her and to myself—that I would find you. And that I would make amends for my terrible betrayal. But then you vanished. Before, I would perhaps hear a tale or two about where you had been. Rumors. Stories. But that was two years ago. And then—" Francisco broke off.

"Chastellet," Valentine whispered.

"Yes." Francisco paused a moment. "I never believed it, no for a moment, and neither did Teresa. I knew that my only hope for redemption was to find you and help you."

"You were going to walk to Damascus and have a talk with Saladin?"

Francisco let a grin slip over his face. "It was so much like before. But, yes. That was my intention. Only I was penniless. And so I had to find a way to make my own fortune. I took a place on a ship out of Ritzebuttel, and found I had a . . . talent for the work. Now this—" he sat up straighter and held out his arms—"this is *my* ship. *The Azure Skull*. I am no longer a boy, nor am I a coward."

Valentine felt his eyebrows rise. "You are captain of your own trading ship?"

Francisco twisted his grin into a thoughtful moue. "I do no do so much trading as acquiring."

After a moment, Valentine closed his eyes, chuckling silently. "You are a pirate," he whispered.

Francisco leaned forward with a wide smile that was so like the ones he'd worn as a boy. *"I am a pirate!"*

Valentine's mirth led to another coughing fit, and so Francisco helped him to some more water and then sat back on his stool.

"Congratulations," Valentine said, feeling the effects of the conversation dragging him down like the tide once more to sleep. But he forced himself to tread water; he desperately wanted to see Maria. He needed to see her. "Unfortunately, there is little you can do for me now. Especially since your vocation is rather—notorious, and without regard in the higher circles. I fear you have wasted your time in locating me."

"I have no," Francisco said and leaned forward once more, his expression alert, almost anticipatory. "I had greater cause to find you now than ever before. If only you had stayed in Prague another day."

"What does Prague have to do with any of this?" Valentine asked.

"I still love Teresa," Francisco said, his features softening. "And I wish your permission to marry her."

Valentine blinked. "You want . . . it is *you*? You are the man?"

Francisco nodded.

"But . . . you are a pirate," Valentine reasoned, lifting his right hand toward Francisco. "I can no have my sister married to such a criminal."

"Because two criminals in her family would be too many?" Francisco quipped. "I will no have her climbing rigging, Valentine. I have amassed such wealth that I can pursue other interests once we are wed."

Valentine's eyebrows rose again. "Truly?"

"Well, perhaps I would engage in it occasionally. As a hobby, yes? I do enjoy it, and it is a very profitable profession."

"I clearly chose the wrong path in my life's work," Valentine muttered.

"But do you no see?" Francisco insisted, leaning forward once more, his wide grin returned. "This is your opportunity, cousin!"

"Francisco, I am tired."

"I know. But only listen to me a bit longer and I will fetch your Maria." He scooted forward on his stool and held his hands out, as if the ideas he spoke of were tangible objects between his palms. "You are a terrible criminal, yes?"

"No."

"No, of course you aren't. But . . . yes."

Valentine sighed. "All right. Yes."

"You have nowhere to go once this woman you are with is returned to her home, save—I assume—the place your criminal friends are hiding, yes?"

"Correct."

"So, you do no return to those men. You come with me, learn the life, and then take the ship over when Teresa and I marry."

Valentine blinked. "You want me to become a pirate?"

"Why no?" Francisco asked, holding out his arms. "You are already a wanted man. You would have more gold than you could ever amass otherwise and the freedom of the sea. Flying under my flag, none would dare challenge you. Assume my name and none would ever know *The Azure Skull* had changed hands. It would be as if Valentine Alesander no longer existed."

The weight of his cousin's words seemed to sink into Valentine's body and spread, like a foamy wave breaking on the sand. With each moment that passed, Valentine realized Francisco's plan could actually work.

"I will have to think about it," he said.

"My proposition? Or Teresa and I marrying?"

"Both." Valentine sighed. "I do no think I can be called Francisco."

Valentine's cousin laughed as he stood. "Oh, I do no go by Francisco," he said, and then swept his feathered hat from the end of the berth with a flourish and placed it on his head. "I am *La Ave Mortal*!"

Valentine felt the corners of his mouth pull downward. "That is worse than Francisco."

His cousin held his palms up toward Valentine. "You think about it, yes? I will send down your woman."

Valentine was asleep again by the time Mary stepped carefully down the steep stairs into Francisco's cabin, easily balancing the tray of food against the rolling of the ship.

Apparently, she was her father's daughter after all.

She slid the tray over the narrow lip of the shelf on the wall and noted that he now had bright patches of color on his cheeks, where only this morning a shroud of gray had given him the disturbing appearance of lifelessness. Valentine's conversation with his cousin had obviously done much to revive him, and it gladdened Mary's heart.

The scrape of the wood caused him to stir, and his eyes found her immediately. "Maria," he whispered, his lips curving into a smile as he slid his arm away from his body on the mattress, his palm up.

Mary did not hesitate, climbing into the narrow bed and nestling against Valentine's side as if she had done it a hundred times, as if her very soul was not rocked by admission of his need for her. She wrapped her arms around his middle and pressed her face into his ribs. Mary felt his arm come around her shoulders and his lips brush the crown of her head.

"I've missed you," she said into his skin, for once not resentful of the sudden tears that leaked from her eyes.

"Mi amor . . ."

She turned her face up to his, and he kissed her forehead. Then each eye, the apples of her cheeks, and, when Mary tilted her chin up a fraction more, his lips were gentle on hers.

Only for a moment, though, and then he let his head rest fully onto the pillow again. "Tell me what happened at the Queen."

And so, after retrieving a cup of wine and a bit of bread for Valentine to eat, Mary sat on the edge of the bed and relayed every detail she could recall of that dreadful night, beginning with the moment she had entered the kitchen and had a tray thrust at her. Valentine appeared quite impressed when she revealed the large price on his head.

"In the end, I did not know if Hamish would harm you or protect you," she finished. "But you were in no condition to make that decision, and I knew if I did not err on the side of caution, we could both end up dead."

Valentine was nodding even as he swallowed the mouthful of wine. "You made the right choice, Maria. Hamish has been a good friend, but I would never ask him to choose between me and his family."

Mary gaped at him. "You would not fault him for turning you over for the silver?"

Valentine shrugged. "I do no think he would have implicated you in any way merely for being in my company," he hedged, picking off another piece of the hard bread and chewing it while he spoke. "I am certain Hamish would have seen that you were protected from the men hunting me."

Mary drew a deep breath. She had withheld from Valentine only one detail of the disaster, saving it for the very end. "It wasn't the mercenaries I worried about," she said. "Valentine, my betrothed was part of that gathering."

He stopped chewing and looked at her for a moment. He swallowed with some effort and said, "The man you are to marry? He was there?"

"Yes," she said bitterly, and then reached down into the pocket of her borrowed servant's apron and pulled out Glayer Felsteppe's weighty purse. "I stole this from him." She dropped the purse onto Valentine's stomach. "It's probably Beckham Hall's coin, any matter."

"I see," he said, picking up the bag and examining it in his palm, turning it this way and that, testing its weight. "That would have indeed changed your situation greatly, had we been discovered. At least we know there is a good possibility that we will gain England before him." Valentine gave the bag a little toss and caught it again. "Well done, Maria."

Mary nodded absently. She didn't really want to discuss anything at all having to do with Glayer Felsteppe at the moment. Soon, yes. Soon she would bring it up. But not now. Not while Valentine was still so weak and she so glad to be near him.

"Francisco seemed very happy when he came for me," she offered instead. "Did he tell you?"

"About Teresa?"

"About Teresa, about Enrique—about everything."

Valentine gave a weary smile. "Look at you, knowing so much. Yes, he did."

"It's wonderful, isn't it?"

"I do no know that it is wonderful," he said with a grimace. "But it is better than I feared when Teresa told me she wished to marry. You know he is a pirate as well, I presume."

Mary grinned. "It's very exciting. Your cousin cuts quite the dashing figure on deck."

Her heart thrilled to see Valentine's face darken. "The Deadly Bird. Bah. He is still so much a boy. Playing at pretend battles as we used to do as children."

"Oh, I don't think he's playing," Mary said, letting a touch of admiration tinge her words. "Considering the size of this ship, I can only think he's likely very good at what he does."

Valentine snorted and rolled his eyes. "I want my coin back from Teresa."

Mary struggled against her smile while she scooted closer and tucked his coverings around him. "Will you rest now?"

"I am tired," he conceded. But he grasped her wrist when she prepared to rise, and Mary's stomach jolted at the possessive gesture. "Where have you been sleeping?" he demanded. "Francisco's crew is—"

She cut off his words with a finger to his lips. "No one has offended me, Valentine. They're all quite gentlemanly." His eyes were murderous, and so she turned slightly and pointed to the narrow cot beneath the stairs. "I've been right here with you the entire time."

The fight went out of him, then, and the creases in his face rearranged into a self-deprecating smile. "Is it comfortable? That little bed?"

"It's no Snowy Owl," she admitted.

"Would you stay with me? Here, in this bed?" he clarified. "I would keep you close while we are surrounded by such brigands."

Mary's heart pounded in her chest and she leaned forward to place a brief kiss on his lips and he responded, hesitant at first, as if unsure. At last, at last . . .

"I will stay anywhere you want me," she whispered. "But first, you must tell me—what does *mi amor* mean?"

His smile was so gentle. "It means 'my donkey.'"

Mary felt her face go slack and she sat up, staring at him.

"It is a precious endearment in my country," Valentine explained, his lips twitching. "They are such sweet creatures, yes? So simple and helpless."

"I am your donkey?" Mary asked, her cheeks heating. "Your *donkey?*"

Then Valentine laughed out loud and pulled her back to him. "Oh, Maria, Maria. *Mi amor* means 'my love.' What else could you be?"

Chapter 20

The next day, Valentine felt strong enough to venture above for a slow turn about the aft castle with Maria on his arm. That night, she helped him ready a makeshift bath, although she excused herself just prior to the removal of his clothing. Valentine found that he only just stopped his request for her to stay by biting his blasted tongue. Later, she crawled into the berth with him once more, her rough servant's underdress for a nightshift, and he welcomed her into his arms, molded her warm curves and soft, unbound breasts to his body, and they fell asleep that way.

They woke in the morn with a lingering kiss, one that stretched the bounds of Valentine's will to such lengths that he feared he would go mad. But he managed to escape her before she dressed. That night, he was plagued with fiery dreams of Maria beneath him. The next morning, she was—and Valentine's hands were caressing her breasts as he came fully awake.

He dropped his head to her mouth, kissed her hard and deep, but then flung himself from the berth with a growl, grabbed his shirt and boots, and stomped above deck.

He missed her sitting up in the bed, watching him go with her fingertips pressed to her mouth, curved in a slight smile.

He was consumed with thoughts of her as he strode across the deck. Her body. Her voice. Her smell. As if to reinforce her sweetness, the bilge water below sloshed and belched up its foul stench. Valentine dropped his boots to the deck and jerked his shirt over his head and then propped his hip atop a coil while he pulled on his boots. Then he leaned against the rail and looked out at the unbroken sea, gray and reflecting the overcast sky.

"We will be in sight of land by morrow's setting sun." Francisco had come upon him silently, or perhaps Valentine was so preoccupied by the woman below that he simply had not heard his cousin approach. Either way, it increased his crossness.

Valentine made a sound in his throat to indicate he'd heard the news. It was sooner than he'd guessed, and the realization that in as few as two days he and Maria would part turned his heart to stone.

"Have you considered my offer?" Francisco asked.

"I have," Valentine said. "You have my blessing to marry Teresa. Where will the two of you go?"

"Back to Aragon," Francisco said. Valentine looked at him quickly, surprised, and his cousin continued. "We both miss it so. There are plenty of impoverished estates that I might purchase. And," he added nonchalantly, "it is a convenient place for one who makes his life on the sea, yes? Or perhaps for one who makes his life on the sea to visit?"

"That is true," Valentine agreed. Then he sighed. "Francisco, I am no seaman. And if I am caught . . ."

"You would be killed, of course," Francisco finished. "But that would happen if you were discovered on a ship or in whatever cave you and your friends have carved out for yourselves. I would wager you have better chance on a fast ship, with a crew to watch your back. You have nothing to do with those men's troubles."

"Perhaps I did not in the beginning," Valentine conceded. "But I gave my word that I would return."

Francisco shrugged, picked at his teeth with a little splinter of wood. "If not for you, they would already all be long dead."

Valentine had no reply, and so he continued to stare out at the hypnotic sea. He would soon be forced to give up Maria. Should he not, for once in his life, move toward a thing for only the good of himself?

He thought of brutish Roman and his feathered companion, Lou. The embittered and withdrawn Adrian; the quiet and steadfast Constantine. His friends now, all. Even exasperating Father Victor and the handful of monks he had come to know during his incarceration at Melk. Could he really leave all of them behind and start a new life?

He would still be just as lonely without Maria.

He would still be a wanted man with no home.

But on the sea, perhaps he could begin to forget. And if he could not forget, at least no one would be there to see him mourn.

"Yes," Valentine said suddenly.

Francisco's head swung toward him. "Yes . . . ?"

"Yes, I will take *The Skull*."

Francisco was silent for a moment, and then he gave a great whoop, wrapping his arm around Valentine's shoulder and pounding his back. "You have gladdened my heart no end, cousin! This is a new beginning for us both, do you see? The legacy we shall leave for our children—a family trade, passed down from father to son." He paused, as if thinking. "Or uncle to nephew. It does not matter!" He laughed aloud and pulled Valentine into a one-armed embrace again. "What matters is that we are reunited, reconciled, partners!" He gave a growl in the back of his throat. "I feel like stealing something!"

Francisco turned away and marched off toward the wheel, his jolly command growing fainter as he left the deck, his feather bobbing. "Roland! Roland, find me a ship!"

Valentine turned his face toward the sea again. One more night with Maria on *The Skull*. Two at most, and then they would be at her home. He would make his mark on the petition and leave her to her new life, while he departed to make a new life of his own. How would his view of the world change without her sweetness, her innocent excitement at every new thing to mellow his cynicism? Valentine doubted he would ever be at peace enough to adopt Francisco's enthusiastic abandon. Enrique's bitterness and greed came to his mind—perhaps that was his destiny, his own dark heritage. No delight, no spontaneity. What would be the point, without Maria to share it with him?

And would Maria be happy? Perhaps in time. Once she had the family she'd always yearned for. Perhaps she would forget about him, and he hoped that she would. She was too pure, too good, to be saddled with regret of any sort, and certainly not over a penniless criminal such as himself.

But Valentine knew that he meant something to Maria, even if her feelings were naïve. Their time together would forever be viewed as a turning point in her life. And so he would leave her with something positive to remember him by, if it was the only thing he could do for her save to set her free.

He pushed away from the railing and went looking for his bag.

* * *

Valentine kept to himself a large portion of the day, sitting removed from the bustle of the deck. It appeared to Mary as though he were trying to save the little journal he sometimes wrote in, which had been soaked in the Elbe. So she sought to keep herself entertained, which was not difficult once the sailor in the crow's nest called down that a ship had been spotted on their horizon.

Francisco looked through his glass for what seemed to Mary to be an hour before he lowered it with a foreign expletive and then shook his head.

"No good," he said, and then handed the long leather-wrapped cylinder to Mary. "I believe we are in the company of your future husband. Look." He helped her fit the oculus to her eye. "Up the mast—see the flag?"

"The king's?" Mary guessed, looking closely at the blurry red and gold crest.

"Aye, but not *the king's*," Francisco said. "That is the flag for those sailing under royal orders, but your king is no on that ship."

Mary lowered the glass and looked at Francisco. "Perhaps it is someone else."

Valentine's cousin shook his head. "No. It is my business to know ships, to be aware of which ones are in my presence. That is the merchant ship *Dane*; it was moored downriver from us in Hamburg."

Mary raised the glass once more and tried to discern the figures on the deck. But the distance was too great, the image too blurry. She handed the glass back to Francisco with a grimace.

"We cannot gain port before him, can we?"

Francisco shrugged, a bit of surprise in his voice. "We could overtake them, yes. But in this wind we would come close enough to shake hands with the captain. Is that a risk you wish to take?"

Mary shuddered. The thought of ever seeing Glayer Felsteppe again made her stomach turn. "No," she said. "It doesn't matter now, really."

If Francisco Alesander thought her answer strange, he did not see reason to question her.

Valentine joined her not long afterward, although he did not share with her what had kept him occupied all afternoon. They ate side by side with the entirety of the crew that night, a celebratory affair that used up the remainder of the supplies aboard ship. Once she had come close enough to land to send a small boat into town, *The Skull* would replenish her sundries and perhaps take on fresh crew before once more setting out to sea. It was far too dangerous for a notorious pirate such as Francisco to bring his ship into an English harbor.

Valentine was quiet, as was Mary, and she wondered if he, too, was feeling the shadow of their imminent parting growing shorter. But he smiled at her when she caught his eye, touched her arm, the curve of her ear; once, his hand had lingered in a caress across her back.

The food was gone now, and the crew began winnowing away the remaining drink as the music started, a motley orchestra of pipes and drum and harp when Valentine leaned close to whisper, "Do you tire, Maria?"

She was not at all tired, but she knew he was asking if she was ready to withdraw to the cabin below, and to the little narrow berth they had been sharing.

Her heartbeat quickened. She was more than ready, and so she nodded.

He stood and seized the handle of a lantern and a jug of wine with one hand and then reached for hers with the other. The crew called out good-natured taunts as they retreated to the hatch. Mary's cheeks tingled, but she didn't mind in the least.

Valentine hung the lantern from the low ceiling and then stretched out on the bed with the wine jug. Crossing his boots at his ankles and propping himself up against the smooth wood of the cabin, he tucked a forearm behind his head and watched her fidget about the small cabin.

Mary was suddenly very nervous. She'd no idea how to begin.

"I have a gift for you," he said.

Mary turned, feeling a smile upon her lips. "You do?"

"I wanted you to have something to remember our time together. Something I think perhaps only I can give you." He motioned toward a little wooden pocket affixed to the wall, where it appeared a single map was rolled loosely.

"This?" she said, taking a step toward the vellum and sliding it out. It was as long as her forearm.

Valentine nodded.

Mary tugged at the thin strand of gut holding it tight and pulled at the curl with her fingers. She turned her back to the lantern and held up the vellum.

"You made me . . . a map of Antwerp?"

Valentine's laugh was low and full of mirth. "Turn it over, Maria."

"Oh!" She laughed nervously and felt the blush come to her cheeks again as she did as Valentine instructed. Once the page was reversed, she saw that it was sideways, and so she rotated her arms to see what was drawn there.

It was a trio of small vignettes sketched diagonally across the vellum, from corner to corner. At the top right, a large bearded man walked up a beach from the sea with a helm under his arm, a listing ship and small boat riding the charcoal waves in the background. The bottom left corner held the profile of a woman who resembled Mary, but with her hair hanging in loops of plaits behind her ears.

In the middle of the vellum, the largest sketch of all showcased a woman in a lace veil, her lips parted, her eyes wide, and Mary remembered the longing with which she had looked at Valentine that night in the old mill.

But . . . she had no recollection of those other sketches . . .

I remember there was a storm, and the ship had floundered on the rocks. Your father rowed to shore himself. I was playing on the beach with my cousin when he landed.

"Valentine," she said, trying to force her voice through her constricted throat. She turned and looked at him. "Are these my parents?"

"It is the best I could do with what I remembered. The one of you, of course, is from recent memory."

Mary looked back at the vellum and sat down on the edge of the berth. The images wavered and she blinked her eyes to clear them, felt the tears splash onto her cheeks.

"Do you like it?" he asked, his voice closer to her now, and when she turned her head, she found that he had leaned up to peer over her shoulder.

"This is . . . this is priceless to me," she whispered.

He smiled and reached up with a hand to sweep a tear away with his thumb. "When you are returned, perhaps you can press it into a book. And then you can look upon them whenever you like. Perhaps even show your children one day what brave grandparents they had." He paused. "What a brave mother."

Mary let the vellum reroll gently of its own accord and her head dropped for a moment. Then she stood and replaced the portraits in the wooden pocket before turning to face the man on the bed. If she was ever to be brave, this was the moment.

Mary swallowed. "I can't marry him, Valentine."

Valentine seemed to consider this while he set the wine jug away from his hip. "No? After all we have done to come here? Why no?"

"Because—" she licked her lips—"because he was entertaining other women that night at the Queen. I saw him kissing them and . . . and touching them. And because he was already announcing himself as lord of Beckhamshire. Using my father's title. My father's coin. He is not honorable."

"Maria." Valentine sighed and reached out from the bed to take her fingers lightly into his palm. "That is the nature of men. And you are no married to him yet. Perhaps he was only—how do you say?— sowing his last wild seed before becoming your husband. You can no judge him for his behavior when he did no know you were there."

She felt her eyebrows raise.

"I am certain he would have more reason for upset at your where-abouts and actions these past months than you do for his. Have we no kissed? Have I no touched you?"

His words caused a fire to kindle in her belly. "It's different with us."

"Why?" he insisted.

"Because I love you, Valentine," she said, and felt her eyes welling with tears again. "I don't care what he does with other women. I don't want to marry him because I love *you*." She sniffed and pulled her hand away to press the tips of her fingers into the corners of her eyes. Then she let her hands fall. "I know you think that I have only been caught up in our adventure. Poor sheltered, innocent Mary. I am just another woman for you to save."

She looked at him directly and her back straightened. "But I am telling you now, even if you do not want me, I will not marry that man."

Valentine's face was that of a statue, so still were his features.

"I won't," she reiterated, her chin up.

Then Valentine nodded once, slowly. "You will."

Mary shook her head.

"You will," he insisted. He rose up on his knees and seized her hands, pulling her to the side of the bed. "You will go back to your home, your title, your country. You will marry a man who will make you a mother and give you a safe place to raise your children. If you love me as you say you do, you will obey me. You will no pine after me, some man you *think* I am. You will no follow me so that you too become a criminal and then one day watch me be cut down in the street like a dog, leaving you with nothing."

Mary was truly crying now, the truth of his words causing pain too great for her to contain any longer.

"You *will* marry him, and you will live a long and happy life. These things you will do for me. You will promise me, yes?"

She shook her head. "No," she choked.

Valentine released her left hand and grasped the back of her neck, pulling her forehead against his. Her empty fingers found his lean waist.

"You will promise me, Maria," he growled. "Because *I love you.*"

Mary's breath caught in her throat and she pulled away only far enough to look in his eyes.

"And when you love someone, you must do what is best for them, even if it means your own heart will break. I can no take you with me. And I would know that you are safe when I leave you. Please, do this for me. Please, *mi amor.*" His voice broke slightly.

"There must be some way," she began.

"There is no," Valentine interrupted. He brushed her hair away from her forehead.

Mary closed her eyes, feeling his fingers brushing her skin, the heat of him pressed to her body. He was right—of course he was right. She would only be a liability to him. But she could not simply let him go, without anything to show for the breaking of her heart.

You are Maria Alesander, a voice inside her whispered.

She opened her eyes to look directly into Valentine's. "I will promise you," she said gravely, "on one condition."

"Anything," Valentine whispered, his eyes searching her face.

"Francisco says we shall reach the port of Beckhamshire on the morrow. Until then, you are mine."

"I will always be yours," Valentine murmured.

"No," she said, placing her hand upon his chest and pressing him back into the bed. He went easily but slowly, as if wary. Mary followed him onto the mattress and then crawled up the length of him, holding herself over his chest. "You won't. I am not so naïve as to think that you will never have another woman after we part. But until you release me, I am your wife." She lowered her head and kissed his lips softly. "And tonight is our wedding night."

Chapter 21

Mary feared Valentine would refuse her after all when he interrupted their kiss by framing her face with his hands and holding her away. He looked into her eyes, his gaze intense, almost pained.

"Maria, wait. Before we continue, you must know this: never have I given myself to a woman as I give myself to you tonight. Never with love. You are the first." His thumb traced her lower lip and his gaze lingered there for a moment before coming back to her eyes. "And you will be the last."

Then he pulled her head to his again, kissing her slowly, deeply, but so differently from on the other occasions their lips had met. Mary could feel Valentine's surrender, his acceptance of the feelings they shared, and that he was offering all of himself to her.

She pulled at his loose-necked shirt, ran her palm inside across his warm, smooth shoulder. His fingers raked up through her hair, tugging it free so that it tumbled around her face and onto his chest. Then he broke their kiss to seize her upper arms and turn her to lie beneath him, his fingers hooking in the front laces of her gown and freeing the ties with a whisper of sound. He lowered his head, then turned his face to run his cheek across the skin of her breasts while he breathed deeply, his dark stubble scraping her painfully, wonderfully.

Valentine raised up on his knees, the lantern behind his head turning his body into a black outline set ablaze at the edges, like some fiery Spanish angel come down to save her. He pulled his shirt over his head and tossed it aside, while Mary pulled her arms from the slim sleeves of her gown, her eyes fixed on Valentine. She could see every curve of muscle, every chisel of flesh on the outline of his ribs and waist, and when he lowered himself onto her again, taking her breast in a gentle hand and her mouth with his own lips, Mary imagined she heard a sound like that of water dancing on hot iron.

Her gown seemed to remove itself in increments, preceding Valentine's journey down the length of her body. He branded her flesh with his squeezing hands, his hot mouth, until Mary was unconscious to the world, lost in the magic of Valentine's full attention. By the time he reached her feet, Mary's fingers were curled into the mattress, her arms straining against the thin ticking as if she would levitate up to him.

Valentine scrambled from the bed, feasting on her nude body with his eyes while he finished undressing. Mary watched him brazenly, becoming intimately educated on the perfection of his male form, his hardness in stark contrast to the infinite pliability she felt in her own flesh, eager to receive him.

She was not afraid when he rejoined her. Not afraid when he wrapped his arm beneath her lower back and lifted her to him. Not afraid when he moved over her. She welcomed the pain in her body, the searing that signified that she would never be the same. No matter what happened in the course of her life, this moment could never be repeated. This act could never be undone. She was giving the gift of her womanhood to the man she loved in this moment, the husband she was fated to call her own from almost the moment of her birth. The man charged with loving her.

Nothing had ever felt so right.

Valentine spoke to her in low throaty tones, foreign words of love that she could not translate with her mind, but their meanings were unmistakable to her heart and her body. His voice was like hot velvet, wrapping her entirely in a heady cocoon of sensation. His pace increased, his back slickened with sweat. His words of love were a hot stream of intelligible whispers in her ear.

"I love you, Valentine. I love you." The only thing Mary could think, the only thought she could voice to him.

Then his frantic pace stilled, his face pressed into her neck, and Mary held him as joyful tears slid down her face and into his hair. He gave a halting gasp, and when he moved his mouth to hers, Mary felt the wetness on his own cheeks. Their kisses were little samples, tastes, both of their lips pulled into smiles as they reveled in such exquisite happiness.

They tangled together that way until the lantern above dimmed and finally went out. And then, in the dark, they memorized each other's bodies. They whispered things of little consequence, never once treading into the ugly future, only acknowledging the present moment, the intertwining of their fingers, the caress of a palm, the sureness of an embrace somehow enough to convince them both that it was forever, even though they knew it was not.

And when the gentle dawn crept beneath the seam of the hatch, they were still wrapped in each other's arms, sleeping in peace, each of them having found respite at last. And they were blissfully unaware for the time being that the vast gray sea carried them steadily closer to the low shadow of land now laying black on the horizon, waiting for them like a patient, dangerous dragon.

Valentine was not surprised to find Maria awake when he opened his eyes. Even at sea, she greeted the dawn at its doorstep. She was watching him with a seriousness that Valentine could not find the courage to address, and so he mustered a grin for her and kissed her nose.

"Good morn, *mi amor*."

He worried for a moment when he saw the flare of her nostrils, the glistening of her eyes. But then she smiled at him. "Good morn. Do you think there is anything left to eat? I find I am quite famished."

In that moment, Valentine knew that he had been right—Mary Beckham was a brave, brave woman.

They dressed in neither hurry nor leisure and made their way to the deck as if carefully considering each action they took. Valentine did not dwell, nor did he run frantically headlong at whatever awaited them in the day. He simply was. It was a different manner for him certainly, but he relished the peace of it.

They did manage to wheedle some leathery fruit from the crew, and when they found Francisco, he was standing with one boot upon the rail with his glass raised in the direction of another, larger ship that was suddenly sharing the water with them.

Valentine heard Mary's little gasp of alarm, and for a moment he, too, wondered if the ship was the one carrying her betrothed. But the longer vessel was close enough that Valentine could see even without the benefit of a glass that it did not fly the English king's flag.

"Good morn, cousin," Valentine called up to Francisco.

"Ah, there you are!" Francisco said pleasantly, lowering the glass and looking around at them. He hopped down from his perch and held the piece to Valentine, who took it and held it to his eye. "A bright morning it certainly is. Fortune has smiled upon us today!" He then called out to the sailor manning the wheel. "All right, harder to port now. And run up *The Skull*! On your forward, dogs!"

Valentine lowered the glass. "Francisco," he said mildly, pointing toward starboard. "The harbor is—"

"Yes. I know," Francisco said, giving his cousin a smile of forced patience. Then he pointed his own long arm over the bow. "But first we will take that ship."

"Now?" Valentine felt his eyebrow raise. "Is it no dangerous to attack when we are so close to the shore?"

"A little, yes," Francisco conceded. "But that ship has been lucky—you see how low it rides? They still have all of their cargo, I would wager. Plenty to share with us, yes? And," he gave his cousin a wink as he reclaimed his glass, "if it is no at least a little dangerous, the satisfaction is no as great."

Valentine thought for a moment of arguing with his cousin, but in the end chose the distraction Francisco presented. He threw up his hands in surrender and turned away to descend into the cabin below again. He quickly laid hand to the item he sought, trying to ignore the scent of Maria lingering in the berth like cologne. Now more than ever, Valentine needed distracting from the future, and what better way to do that than by acquainting himself with his newfound criminal endeavor?

When he came back into the sunlight of the deck, Maria was arguing with Francisco in Valentine's stead.

"But we are in a terrible hurry," she insisted. "My betrothed's ship has already made port by now, certainly."

"Yes, it seems we are no the only ones to benefit from the favorable winds," Francisco allowed. "But you must understand, my crew has no taken a ship since we set sail, and while I have greatly enjoyed our journey together, I am working, Maria." He shrugged and quirked his mouth, as if it was completely out of his control, while all around them on deck, the crew scrambled to grab the wind and intercept the target. Francisco gave Maria a short bow and then leaped onto a low rig to scramble up to the wheel, shouting orders in a crazy mix of languages.

Valentine wrapped an arm about her waist and pulled her to him, unable to resist kissing her mouth. He liked the sight of her windswept curls blowing over her shoulder.

"What are we to do?" Mary sighed, running her hands over his chest.

Valentine shrugged. "I suppose we will earn our passage." He swept his hand up from his side, and Mary smiled when she saw the now battered feathered hat. He placed it on his head with a grin as above them the blue and black flag of *The Azure Skull* snapped in the wind. "*Vamanos,* Maria."

They went to the railing and watched as Francisco's ship bore down on the larger, slower vessel before them. It seemed as if they raced on wheels, and in moments, Valentine could see the scramble of crew and passengers on the deck and a white flag was run up the mast.

"Ropes!" Francisco shouted, having once more taken up his position standing on the railing with the rigging in his hand. Valentine was amused to see a blue silk scarf now fashioned into a skull cap beneath Francisco's feathered hat, one side of the silk pulled down beneath an eyebrow. His cousin looked suddenly to Valentine and gestured to the coils lined up along the railing on the deck.

"Do you mind?" he said pointedly.

Valentine laughed and began hefting the heavy cord onto his shoulder, waiting for the lead ropes that had already been cast to pull the two ships closer.

"Are you actually going to participate in this?" Maria asked.

"Yes, of course," he said. "Once Francisco and Teresa are married, I will take over *The Skull.* I must practice." Valentine spoke to Maria from the side of his mouth while he watched a handful of sailors swing down onto the other ship from long ropes. It was a great distraction from her disappointed face. He flicked the brim of his hat. "The deadly bird, yes?"

"You can't be serious," she said. "Valentine, you are no pirate."

"I could be a pirate," he argued, and as if to demonstrate, he tossed his coil of rope to the waiting hands of the sailor on the other ship. "It is very profitable work."

Maria continued to chastise from behind him. "What about your friends at Melk?"

"They do no need me," he said, grasping a part of the rigging and pulling himself up to stand on the railing as Francisco did. "I need a scarf," he muttered, then looked at Maria hopefully. "Maria, would you—?"

"No!" she replied.

They were both temporarily distracted as Francisco called out to the captain of the other ship.

"Ahoy, Captain Booley! A pleasure to meet you again!" Francisco swept his hat from his head and gave a low bow while maintaining his hold on the rigging. "Permission to come aboard?"

The request was mocking and incendiary, since ten of *The Skull's* crew were already looting the cargo on deck, tossing smaller crates across the gap of sea separating the ships or securing dangling ropes to the larger items. One of the crew seemed to be petitioning the clustered and frightened passengers for any jewels or purses on their persons, like a street performer after a demonstration.

"You go to hell, Bird," the white-haired captain spat crossly. "Be forewarned, I shall set the authorities upon your wake as soon as we reach Beckham Hall. The king's own man awaits. They'll have you this time."

Francisco blew his tongue at the old man and rolled his eyes.

Valentine couldn't help but chuckle and feel a bit of pride at his younger cousin's comportment. He only just caught a large brocade bag flung from the other ship. It appeared to be a woman's piece, and so he swung around on the rigging and tossed it to Maria.

"For you, *mi amor.*"

Mary caught the bag with a huff and strode close to the railing to raise it over her head. She heaved it toward the captured ship with a cry and then crossed her arms and looked up at Valentine with a defiant expression.

"You did no like the color?" he asked, ignoring the sting of his conscience.

"Mary? Mary!" A woman's voice cried out from across the short span of waves.

Valentine swung back toward the *Dane* and saw a rotund old woman in fine dress, one gnarled hand clutched to her bosom and the other pointing toward Maria. A stooped, hopelessly skinny old man joined the lady, his arm going somewhat about her wide waist.

"Roscoe, look—it's our Mary! She's been kidnapped by pirates!"

"Damn." Valentine jumped down from the railing and swept Maria behind his back.

"Oh, no. No, no, *no*," Maria moaned.

Valentine tried to keep his voice calm. "Maria, is that—?"

"Lady Elmsbeth," Maria confirmed dismally.

"How did she manage to match our pace from Prague?" Valentine wondered aloud.

"She is very rich," was all Maria would say.

"Lady Mary," the old man called out in a warbly voice. "Are you injured?"

Francisco, too, swung down from his perch and strode across the deck to them. "Old friends, cousin?"

"They are the nobility Maria was traveling with," Valentine admitted. "We just escaped them in Prague."

"This is no good," Francisco muttered. "We are unlikely to be pursued taking only insured cargo and a handful of personal items. But if they think we are holding a lady prisoner, they will scour the sea for us. There will be no hope of going ashore, and we must have supplies and a safe place to drop anchor until the winds turn."

Valentine looked at the other ship. The old nobles were conferring with their captain. All three were looking at the spot where Maria stood behind the two cousins.

"If I go with them," Maria said suddenly, "will they leave you alone?"

Valentine turned to look down at her. "What? Maria, no."

But Francisco acted as though Valentine had not spoken. "Hmm. I see what you are thinking. We could at least maneuver farther down the coast and send crew ashore there. Not Beckhamshire, though."

"Oxley, then," Maria suggested.

Francisco nodded, stroking his chin. "Yes. I agree. That would be a good place."

The captain called from the other ship, drawing the trio's attention just as the last of *The Skull*'s crew were reboarding their own ship.

"We will have the lady, Bird," the captain warned, the elderly nobles hovering behind him, "or your neck will stretch, and well you know it. This is her home port. I'll send up the signal, and every manned ship in the harbor will be obliged to assist."

Francisco looked at Valentine with a shrug. "She has to go, cousin."

"Francisco," Valentine began in a chiding voice, "surely you can understand that—"

"He's right," Maria interrupted and pushed her way between the two men to stand at the railing. She raised a hand to the old woman but spoke over her shoulder. "If I don't go with them now, none of us has any hope of reaching the shore for days, and that is if *The Skull* is not captured."

She turned around to lean back on the railing and face Valentine. "If my betrothed has discovered my absence, I am caught either way. But the dowager will take me straight to Beckham Hall, where I hope I still have some authority. I shall also have an irrefutable excuse for my whereabouts. You can come ashore in Oxley unseen and make your way to me. It's only a few hours, Valentine. I will be watching for you." She paused, and glanced at Francisco self-consciously before asking, "It's better this way, any matter, is it not?"

No, he wanted to say. *It's too soon.* Valentine felt that even though he would see Maria again in only hours, this was good-bye. And it was too soon.

"Let me go," she whispered. "Before I think better of it and break my promise."

She was right. If Valentine thought about it much longer himself . . .

Valentine pulled his dagger from his boot, then rushed toward Maria with a growl, lifting her around the waist with one arm as he stepped onto the railing. Maria squealed and clutched at his shoulders while he loosened a rope from its knot. He twisted the thick rough line around his forearm and grabbed at a loop and then hooked the ankle of his boot through the bottom.

"What are you doing?" Maria whispered into his face.

"Do no look down." He pulled her close and took her mouth as he kicked off the railing.

They twirled in the air as the rope lowered with a whirring of wooden pulleys, and Valentine kissed her deeply, Mary's arms entwined about his neck, her skirts blowing in the breeze above her bare feet. Her soft, unbound curls blew past Valentine's face, shielding them both from the world as they held to each other for only a moment, suspended above the sea, between the ships, beyond reality.

Valentine pulled back to look into her beautiful eyes one last private time as his boots thudded onto the *Dane*'s deck. "I love you, Maria."

Then she was ripped from his hold by the fat dowager and swung away behind the old woman. Valentine just saw the pale shock on her face, the glistening wetness on her cheeks.

"Get away from her, you filthy parasite!" the old woman screeched.

It took all of Valentine's strength of will not to reach out and snatch Maria back. To tell Francisco to sail in any direction save the one that led to Beckhamshire harbor.

Thankfully, he felt the rope drawing him back up. And so once again he mustered his gift for pretend and touched the brim of his hat with the tip of his dagger, smiling for Maria's sake. She stood on the deck, her expressionless face turned up as he rose above her, her arms hanging limp at her sides while the old woman pawed over her.

"Safe travels, *mi amor*," he called.

But Maria did not reply.

And Valentine let her go.

Chapter 22

Mary said not one word to Lady Elmsbeth, Lord Roscoe, or the captain of the passenger ship; she spoke to no one for the remainder of the journey into port. She was deposited straightaway into the captain's berth, and plied with food and drink, but Mary accepted none of it. Indeed, she stared into nothing, her eyes dry but blank.

"Poor thing," Lady Elmsbeth said to Roscoe in a not very quiet whisper. "She's likely in shock. I can only imagine the trials those criminals put her through. A lone woman aboard a pirate ship full of bloodthirsty villains. She's even without shoes." She tsked and shook her head. "I clearly saw the one who delivered her—I vow he was at the tavern in Prague, dressed as a monk, no less. Little wonder Mary acted so strangely desperate. She must have known he was there the entire time."

"We can say nothing to her betrothed, Beth," Roscoe said quietly, gravely. "You know that, don't you?"

"But Roscoe, justice must be done," the dowager cried out. "Her betrothed will pursue those dastardly men to the ends of the earth to avenge his love."

"He may, certainly," Roscoe agreed. "But think you he would still accept for his bride a woman so dreadfully used in such a way? Is that fair to Mary? That, after all this, she be turned out?"

"Oh! You're right, of course," Lady Elmsbeth fretted. "You usually are. But how are we to explain her appearance on this ship? The other passengers are to disembark at Beckham, and they all witnessed the spectacle of her release. There will be talk in the village."

Lord Roscoe was quiet for a moment. "I will speak to the captain. He will announce that Mary had been a passenger on our ship the entirety of the voyage, only away in an isolated berth, ill. She was only kidnapped at the start of the attack, but we saw her aboard before the brigands could escape with her."

"Oh, Roscoe, you *are* brilliant." Lady Elmsbeth sighed. "That is just the thing, yes." Mary heard the scrape of footsteps as Lady Elmsbeth appeared at the side of the berth. "We are only going above for a moment, dear. Have no fear—no one shall disturb you. You rest a while."

Mary continued to stare at the ceiling, so very much like the one she'd awoken beneath just that morning, after being loved by Valentine.

Lady Elmsbeth patted her arm. "Yes, then. All right."

Then she was thankfully alone, the creaking of the ship and the hush of the water against the hull the only witnesses to her grief. She fell into a defensive slumber, her dreams frightening conglomerations of Glayer Felsteppe once more feasting on Beckham Hall's curtain wall, with a burning Melk perched atop a distant hill.

Mary was drenched in her own sweat and came awake with a jolt to see Lady Elmsbeth spring back from the side of the berth, her gnarled hands clutched to her bosom.

"My goodness, you gave me a fright, Mary."

Mary blinked and stared about the small dark room, lit by two lanterns now. She had been hoping that this too was part of her nightmares. That she would be wrapped in Valentine's arms when she woke, ready to saddle the horses and set out on the road once more together, outrunning the dangers that pursued them.

But this terror was no simple bad dream—indeed, the unknown trouble that lay before her was all too real, and all too inescapable.

"I'm sorry," Mary murmured, pushing her hair back from her face. "Are we landed?"

"Yes, dear. The other passengers disembarked some time ago. Lord Roscoe and I thought perhaps it would be best if you were not available for spectacle."

Mary nodded. "Thank you."

The dowager seemed uncomfortable. "Roscoe and I shall take you straightaway to Beckham Hall ourselves. Er . . . whenever you are ready, dear."

Mary swung her legs over the side of the berth and looked down at her bare, dirty feet, the ragged hem of the servant's costume, which was the only gown she had since escaping Hamburg on Francisco

Alesander's pirate ship. She had not even a ribbon to tie back her hair with. Even though she was returning to Beckham Hall a woman who had traveled the world in a grand and harrowing adventure, loved and lost a man, known many exciting and exotic places and people and would soon become a married woman, for the first time in her life, Mary deeply felt like the abandoned orphan she was.

And then she thought of Agnes. Her nurse who was only moments away from her right now. Oh, how she longed to embrace her!

Mary stood from the berth and took the dowager's arm as if she was an invalid, all the strength and will she'd come to know in herself the past months completely vanished, and departed the cabin for the brisk night air of the deck.

The village looked so small after her journey, and the villagers she passed in the streets were strangers to her now. No one paid her any mind as she preceded the dowager and Lord Roscoe up the main thoroughfare toward the stone keep looming in the distance. She could have been a poor maidservant or a beggar. Even the few who might have recognized her face would never accept that this bed-raggled woman was their lady. And Mary took advantage of this fact, walking relentlessly toward Beckham Hall, having no care for the filth she tracked through. She didn't dwell upon what she would do if she encountered Lord Felsteppe; at the moment, she didn't care at all what he would think.

She only wanted Agnes, and her own bed.

As Mary drew near the steps to the hall, she noticed even in her daze of sorrow the lack of bustle, the absence of sound of the ever-present soldiers. There were no men milling about, no carts coming to or from the rear of the keep, where the entrance to the stores lay. The stones were gritty beneath her feet as she climbed the steps and entered the little guard house.

No guard.

She pulled at the door, some part of her worried that it would be barred to her, but it opened easily with its familiar screech.

"Mary?" Lady Elmsbeth called out in her warbly voice. "Is everything all right?"

"I don't know," Mary said. She held the door open behind her as the elderly nobles followed her into the soldier's hall.

Empty. No fire in the hearth.

She crossed the bare stones—even the rushes were gone—to the little alcove where the stairs to her personal, upper floors were defended by the heavily reinforced door Mary had opened to Glayer Felsteppe what now seemed ages ago.

The door stood open.

A chill raced up from the floor to the crown of Mary's head.

"Where *is* everyone?" Lady Elmsbeth whispered.

"Shh, Beth," Roscoe advised, and Mary heard the papery sound of his hand on the dowagers arm.

Mary climbed the steps, her heart seeming to pound one hundred times with every tread she gained. Near the top, the golden glow of flames could be seen, and the warm scent of beeswax candles filled Mary's nostrils with a familiar tingle. Agnes would be sitting before the hearth as she always was this time of night. Working at some mending or polishing, a small cup of warm milk at her side. Oh, how surprised she would be!

Mary's eyes filled with tears when she gained the top of the stairs and saw the chair pointed away from her, toward the fire. The hem of long robes, wide sleeves, draped over the edges of the chair in dark silhouette.

"Agnes," she called out, walking toward the chair, already raising her arms for the embrace she was sure would come. "Agnes, I've come home!"

The shadow jumped and then rose, turning swiftly before the fire to face her.

"Lady Mary!" Not Agnes, but Father Braund. "Praise be to God that you are safe!" He came around the chair quickly to meet her in the middle of the floor. The young priest took her hands with a gentle smile and then glanced at the pair behind her.

"I see your guardians did their job well," he said.

Mary glanced behind her to see Lady Elmsbeth open her mouth, but before she could say anything, Lord Roscoe cut in.

"Yes, she's safe and sound," Roscoe said quickly. "An astounding adventure we've all had, isn't that right, Lady Elmsbeth?"

The dowager pressed her lips together for a moment but then nodded. "Astounding, certainly."

Father Braund looked back at Mary, and she noticed the deep creases in his face that had not been there when she'd left, the sunken appearance of his eyes. He had even less hair now, and his robes seemed to hang on him.

"You've arrived just—"

"Where is everyone?" Mary interrupted. "The servants? The soldiers? Where is Agnes? I would see her immediately."

"I think we should leave Lady Mary to the care of Father Braund," Lord Roscoe announced. "Don't you, Beth?"

Lady Elmsbeth nodded, and Mary couldn't help but notice the way the dowager's eyes flitted about the room nervously. "I do. Our things have already been delivered to the inn in the village. We shall call on you on the morrow, Lady Mary, to see that you are well."

Mary blinked at them both and then looked back to Father Braund. "All right," she said. "Good night. And—" She broke off suddenly, turning once more to the elderly couple before rushing toward them and throwing her arms about the pair. "Thank you," she whispered. "Thank you both so much. I'm sorry to have caused you such trouble."

"Yes, dear—think nothing of it," Lord Roscoe said, patting Mary's back awkwardly.

"It was our pleasure," Lady Elmsbeth assured her when Mary at last pulled away. "Good night," she called over her shoulder as Roscoe escorted her back into the stairwell.

Then Father Braund was at her side, taking Mary's arm and leading her toward Agnes's chair before the hearth. "Sit down, Lady Mary. I'm afraid I only have a bit of wine at the moment. I've sent the servants home for the evening." He pressed the cup into her hand.

"Why?" Mary asked, raising the rim to her lips and gulping. She lowered the cup and gasped a little shallow breath. The wine was strong. "Is Agnes already abed? Surely she would want me to wake her."

Father Braund looked at her for a moment, seeming to gather his thoughts. "Not three days after you left Beckham Hall, a ship came into port bearing returning Crusaders. And those Crusaders brought with them a terrible sickness. The keep was quarantined, and so the illness was largely contained to the soldiers garrisoned here. Of course, many of the servants were also touched."

"But not Agnes," Mary said. "Agnes never had anything to do with the soldiers. She despised them."

"If you had not left when you did, you might have contracted the illness. It was a miracle. God's own plan," Father Braund insisted. "I barely lived myself."

Mary stood abruptly from the chair, the empty cup tumbling to the wooden floor with a clang. In some corner of her mind, she acknowledged that the thick rug that should have been there was no longer.

"Is she still ill?" Mary demanded in a shrill voice. "Who is tending her?"

"Please, sit down," Father Braund said quietly.

"No! *Where is she?*"

The priest reached out and tried to take her hand, but Mary jerked away and ran toward the shadows.

"Agnes!" she called, her bare feet flying over the smooth wood. She pulled up her skirts and raced up the dark, narrow staircase to the uppermost floor, once as familiar to her as her own appendages, but now feeling strange and cold and foreign. *"Agnes!"*

She ran across the central corridor, past the columns supporting the roof, and flung herself against Agnes's closed door. She threw it into the wall with a crash.

"Agnes?"

The moonlight shone through the single narrow window, casting its white light in a beam across the floor and in a zigzag up onto the wooden skeleton of the bed.

No crisp coverlet over a mattress. No embroidered pillow. No rug beneath the bed frame. Every inch of the room was stripped clean, empty.

Father Braund gasped to a halt behind her. Mary could hear the wheeze in his breaths, but at the moment, she was oblivious to everything save the enormous, bewildering pain in her heart.

"She's . . . dead?" Mary asked in a tiny voice. It should not have echoed in such a small chamber, but it did, reinforcing the newly realized knowledge that Mary was now completely, utterly alone in this world. "But she was always so strong. I can't recall her ever being ill."

"A fortnight after you left," Father Braund said, his breathing at last calming. "I couldn't risk sending word to . . . to where you were going. I'm sorry."

Mary couldn't seem to take her eyes from the stark frame of the bed. She realized then that everything that had touched the ill had likely been burned. "It was because I left, wasn't it? The worry of it killed her. *I killed her.*"

"No! No," Father Braund insisted. He forced her to turn away from the empty room and look at him. "Mary, I told her. The sickness, it was so strong, it overcame so quickly—I told her the mission you had undertaken. She knew, and she was *glad* for you. She was *thankful.*" He tried to give her a smile. "She said that you were so brave, and that perhaps once you had a taste of the world, you would not return. She did not begrudge you your secrecy. She knew better than any that you felt stifled here, waiting all those years for your life to begin."

"She did what she felt she must to protect me," Mary said, her words breathy with disbelief of the altered state of her home. "I realize that. But now, here I am once more." A rogue tear escaped down her cheek, hot and bitter. She swiped it away and focused her attention on the priest fully. "Where is my lord? His ship should have landed yesterday. Surely this place is not cursed now, so that no fighting men dare to sleep within its walls."

Father Braund shook his head. "He did arrive yesterday, but he did not pause at the keep. He ordered all his men to muster at a nearby estate, where one of the betrayers was rumored to be en route. He hoped to intercept him there."

"What?" Mary said, her heart stopping for an instant.

"I take it you didn't find your man," Father Braund said, his voice heavy with regret. "I'd hoped when I heard the lord was in pursuit . . . But he's gone north to Benningsgate Castle, the seat of the Earl of Chase."

"I don't understand," Mary said.

"Benningsgate is the home of Constantine Gerard. He's one of—"

"I know who he is." Now Mary's heard pounded with the intensity of a war drum. "When is Lord Felsteppe to return?"

Father Braund shook his head. "The castle is only a half-day's ride from Beckham Hall. Perhaps as early as the morning."

Mary tried to figure in her head the distance to Oxley, in the opposite direction from Benningsgate Castle. Beckham Hall lay almost precisely in the middle of the two.

Who would reach Mary first—Valentine or Glayer Felsteppe?

Only a moment ago, it seemed, Mary had wanted nothing more than to seek her own bed and cry for days. But now Valentine's safe escape from England depended on her vigilance. She must be ready for his arrival, whether before or after Glayer Felsteppe's own. If she could not secret him away without her betrothed's knowledge, Valentine could very easily wind up dead.

"I need a maid for a bath," Mary said to the priest. "Please wake one of your choosing, for her swiftness and aptitude. Tell her she may return to her bed when I have been served. I know you have been ill, but I need you to stay close to me this night, Father Braund. In the chapel below, if you would, and with my papers beneath your very hand."

"Of course, Lady Mary. But—"

"I did find my man," Mary clarified. "And if we are not very careful, everything I have done will have been for naught, and I might as well never have left Beckham Hall, for I will be as good as dead, as will be an innocent man."

The blond woman looked at Glayer Felsteppe with a haughtiness that made him itch to wipe the beautiful smirk off her face.

With a blade.

"I don't know who this Valentine Alesander is," she said, as if the name were a foul taste on her tongue. "I've never met him. The earl never mentioned him. I would not allow an unknown man into my home while my husband was away."

"I regret to report that I have heard otherwise," Glayer informed her with a slow smile. Constantine Gerard's wife was an incomparable beauty—and she clearly enjoyed the riches of her station, if her home and the perfection of her gown and jewels were any indication. She seemed no worse for the wear of not having seen her husband in two years. "Might I be so redundant as to point out that I am standing here?"

"I felt I had no choice, once I heard who you were," she allowed with a delicate arched brow. It was clear that she thought herself Glayer's better, a countess addressing the lowly soldier who accused her husband.

"True, true," Glayer conceded. "And what would you care, really? Your life has not changed since your husband all but killed his own men in Jerusalem. Betrayed the king. Here you are, outfitted as royalty."

"I care because my son has no father, and my house is now tainted by the accusations against my husband," the woman spat. "Constantine's absence has little bearing on my station. Benningsgate is my family home, whether he holds title or no. I told him not to go. But he had an overwhelming desire for one final turn on the battlefield." Her eyes sparkled, but Glayer was unsure whether it was with sorrowful tears or anger.

"So you feel he is innocent."

"Constantine may be many things," Patrice Gerard allowed wryly, "but disloyal is not one of them." She looked away for a moment, and Glayer found that the tears were sorrowful. He was disappointed. "Now, if that is all, Lord Felsteppe, it is late, and I would retire."

Glayer felt old, familiar anger bubbling up inside him at the offhand manner with which she wanted to dismiss him. As if he were nothing but another of her servants.

"Your son," he began, helping himself to a carafe of wine as if she hadn't spoken, "how old is he now?"

"That is none of your affair," Patrice said.

"If I remember correctly, he is called Christian. Rather ironic now, wouldn't you say?"

She only stared at him, loathing in her eyes. Perhaps he should have taken time to change into a richer costume. Perhaps then she would have spoken to him more kindly, as her equal.

Now she would see before the night's end that he was not her equal. He was her better.

"Get out," she said levelly.

Glayer took a large drink directly from the container and then smacked his lips with a sigh. Resting the carafe on his hip, he took a slow turn about the large drawing room, admiring the rich tapestries and furnishings.

"Any man would be a fool to leave a home such as Benningsgate," he said aloud while paying particular attention to a tall metal urn, bearing the Chase coat of arms. He tossed Patrice a smile over his shoulder. "And such a beautiful wife."

Her face showed no appreciation for his compliments, and Glayer felt his rage building, although he made very sure to keep it hidden.

"I think," he said slowly, pensively, as he completed his circuit of the room to stand before Patrice Gerard, "that perhaps Constantine *has* been here. That perhaps you are even now harboring his friend, Alesander, somewhere within Benningsgate Castle."

Patrice huffed a laugh. "That's ridiculous."

Glayer raised his eyebrows. "Is it? Who's to say? Certainly your servants would not betray you." He turned on his heel suddenly and addressed his soldiers, standing guard at the room's entrance. "Find the boy. Bring him here."

"No!" Patrice shouted. "You do not have my permission to enter my home nor to touch my son."

Glayer nodded to his soldiers. "Wait outside the doors with him until I tell you to bring him in. If any of the servants interfere, kill them."

The heretofore reserved lady flew at him then, her claws out. Glayer caught her by her wrists with a sharp jerk, and he felt and heard her left one snap in his grip. She cried out and her knees buckled. He tossed her away to let her crumple to the floor and then he squatted down on his haunches next to her.

Patrice Gerard looked up at him, and now her eyes were wide with pain and fear. But still her haughtiness prevailed. "The king shall hear of this," she vowed.

"He shall indeed. And so you had better tell me true, Lady Patrice," Glayer said almost kindly. "Have you had any word from your husband or his cohorts? Any messages? Visits?"

"No!" she screamed up at him, the cords of her delicate neck standing out. "No, no, no! I already told you—"

He gave her the back of his hand for her impertinence. It took him several long breaths to regain his control. "Well, that is too bad. Yes. Too bad indeed. For I have on good authority that Valentine Alesander has managed to make his way here in order to help an English lady. And as Adrian Hailsworth is not married, and Roman Berg is of Norse heritage, that lady can only be—" he reached out to stroke a finger down the side of her swelling face—"you." She pulled away with a wince. "He is hidden somewhere in the castle, is he not?"

"No!" she insisted, but now her indignation had deteriorated into fear. At last, she would respect him. "I swear to you, I've not heard from Constantine or any of them since the message he sent from Chastellet at the beginning of the siege. And that I already showed you."

Glayer clicked his tongue and looked askance at her.

"Please," Patrice Gerard continued. "Only think for a moment—I have no reason to shelter any of them. Constantine's return now would only be to my and Christian's detriment. I don't *want* him here."

Glayer believed her. It was well documented by his sources that the countess had plenty of lovers to entertain her in her husband's absence. She was wealthy enough in her own right.

But regardless of Lady Patrice's wishes, if Constantine was to return, all of Benningsgate's resources were technically his to command.

And that would simply not do. It would not do at all.

"Very well, Lady Patrice," he said on a sigh, and he rose to tower over her. "I would only ask one more thing of you before I leave your home."

Patrice Gerard looked up at him with great, watery cow's eyes, and bloody snot ran down her upper lip. "Anything," she sniveled.

Glayer's hands went to his belt. "Take off your gown."

The soldiers clustered around the door to the drawing room moved away at the sound of the woman's screams for help. They took the little boy, managed by some old manservant, with them. But even standing some distance down the corridor did little to quiet the hellish cries.

Some of the men blanched, but none made a move toward the drawing room doors. The little blond-headed boy seemed confused as to the happenings in his home.

Sometime later, after the screams had ceased, Glayer Felsteppe emerged through the doors, his hands stained a dull red as he tried to wipe them on what looked to be a torn piece of brocade.

"She's lying," he said to his soldiers as he came to a halt before them. His hair was damp and there was a smudge of red on his cheek. "We must teach the traitors a lesson; no place is safe for them. No one who aids them will be spared."

Felsteppe crouched down and looked at the little boy. "Your father is a very bad man, young Christian."

The boy's eyes narrowed. "You're a liar. My father is a hero."

"Hmm." Felsteppe smiled indulgently and ruffled the boy's hair as he stood. "Run along then, and see your mother."

Christian Gerard and his servant disappeared into the drawing room, and Felsteppe spoke over the boy's echoing screams. "Bar the doors and set fire to the lot of it. No one escapes. I must away to greet my bride." And he quit Benningsgate without another glance.

The soldiers did as they were commanded.

Chapter 23

Valentine rode into Beckhamshire on the back of a hay cart, his peasant garb and cap making him invisible in the morning bustle of the village. He saw the keep rising up from the edge of the town, and he looked closely at the windows.

Somewhere inside, Maria waited for him.

No, he corrected himself—Lady Mary Beckham waited. He'd left Maria on the *Dane* yesterday.

He kept a keen watch on the crowd he rolled past, noting that there seemed to be an influx of fighting men, returning from the north. And all seemed focused on Beckham Hall as their destination. Any one of them could be the man Mary was to wed, he supposed.

Tricky, Valentine thought.

He hopped off the hay cart still some distance from the keep and strolled past a market stall, his pace not slowing as he swept up an empty basket to perch on his shoulder.

Further into the village, he meandered in the crowd. His head was down, but his eyes were busy taking in the people, his ears listening for gossip. He swiped an apple from the fruiter's pile and circled around to the well. Dropping to one knee, he anchored the small fruit between his teeth while he played at reweaving a frayed spot on the side of the basket.

"—Benningsgate—"

"—just returned to Beckham."

Valentine took the apple from his mouth after a crunching bite and strode past the cluster of gossiping women toward the inn. Benningsgate, Benningsgate . . . where had he heard that name before?

A pair of wealthy-looking young men stood a short distance away from what Valentine assumed were their mounts, which appeared saddled and ready for departure. Valentine passed by the horses on the far side of the men, deftly swiping one of the bags from the saddle of the horse closest to him and tipping it into the basket. He cut directly between the two men, nodding as he went.

"Safe travels."

They only gave him irritated looks as they stepped away from each other to let peasant Valentine pass into the inn.

Young nobleman Valentine came out of the back of the inn a moment later, his basket abandoned, the bag over his shoulder now containing the peasant clothes. He set off toward Beckham Hall.

As he walked, he noticed the habit of the soldiers of carrying their bags across their backs, and so he looped the strap over his head.

Passing the rear of the bathhouse, he spied a helmet set atop a pile of clothes. He didn't break stride as he kicked at the helm with the toe of his boot, flipping it into the air. He caught it with one hand and sat it beneath his elbow.

Up the hill toward the guardhouse he went, the sun approaching noon hot on his face. A cloak hung on the end of a rickety gate, its owner busy chatting with the young maiden in the garden beyond the fence. In a blink it was draped over Valentine's shoulder as if made for him.

He glanced up at the keep, and far above on the third level, within the black square of a window, he saw a figure in a white gown.

He strode into the darkness of the hall, his senses immediately on alert for Mary's whereabouts. He was in a terrible hurry; Francisco was coming up the coast to Beckhamshire to collect him. Considering his slow journey by cart that morning, Valentine only had a pair of hours at most.

Valentine walked to the far side of the hall as if with purpose. He needed to observe the layout of the room and detect the patterns of the soldiers within, all of whom it seemed had just returned from some military exercise. He placed a boot on a bench at a table, where it appeared a meal had been finished only moments before, the diner having departed. Valentine set the helm near the plate and picked up the nearly empty goblet for a prop just as a fresh cluster of men entered the hall.

"Ah," he murmured to himself, seeing the red-haired man in the center of the group. The smug smile, the compensatingly long sword on his hip. "I must be in the presence of a general." He raised the cup as if in salute when the man and his entourage passed by the table.

And then Valentine thought he had made a terrible mistake when the man glanced twice and then stopped, backing up a step to look closely at Valentine.

"My lord?" Valentine queried in his best English.

The rather ugly man continued to study Valentine's face. "Have we met?" the man demanded. "I can't seem to remember what you are called, but you look somehow familiar to me."

Valentine gave a slow blink and bowed his head slightly, giving the impression of deference, but really his mind was whirring frantically. "John, my lord," he said, rounding out the vowels of his accent. "John Miller. I . . . ah . . . served with you last eventide."

The red-haired man frowned. "At Benningsgate?"

Valentine inclined his head again but said nothing.

"Hmm. That's probably it. I was rather preoccupied." The general pointed a gauntleted finger at Valentine. "Good work, there, Miller. Carry on."

Valentine bowed and then lifted the cup to his mouth again, watching the general as he left his men at the bottom of a hidden-away stairwell on the side of the hall. The redhead went up the steps alone.

He lowered the cup slowly. Had Valentine just come face-to-face with Mary's future husband?

Thick, hot jealousy filled him so that the wooden cup in his hand cracked. He set it down on the table when he felt the remnants of the cool liquid flow over his fingers, then wiped his hand on his cloak.

"You there—John Miller," a man called, and Valentine looked up to see three of the men who had accompanied the general approaching his table. The boldest one addressed him. "I don't recall seeing you last night at Benningsgate."

Valentine shrugged. "Neither did I see you."

One of the other men said in an aside, "I think I saw him. He was in the castle with the general."

The leader blanched. "You were inside?"

"I serve where I am commanded."

The man looked about nervously and then leaned slightly over the table toward Valentine. "Is it true? Did he really let the woman and the boy burn?"

Valentine tried to look aloof, but inside his guts roiled. "I know not what you mean."

"Oh, come on," the soldier pressed. "It will be out soon enough, any matter. So tell us then—did Lord Felsteppe really order Gerard's wife and boy to die in that fire?"

Felsteppe?

Gerard?

Benningsgate Castle.

A rushing sound filled Valentine's head, like the roar of a shell held to the ear. "Lord . . . Felsteppe?"

"Pardon me, *General* Felsteppe," the soldier said with a roll of his eyes.

"What—" Valentine broke off, cleared his throat, swallowed— "what do you think?"

"A right bastard thing to do is what I think," the man spat, standing upright once more. "You're awfully cold about it yourself, aren't you?" The soldier shook his head in disgust and started backing away, his friends going with him. "I've seen a bit of bloodshed, but to kill a woman and a little lad. Well, Lady Mary'd best be certain she doesn't anger her new husband, s'all. Good luck with your conscience, Miller."

Valentine had never before in his life fainted. Never come close, even. But in that moment, having heard that Constantine's wife and son had been murdered only hours earlier by none other than Glayer Felsteppe, who had just walked past Valentine and was now somewhere above . . .

With Valentine's Maria.

Glayer Felsteppe was going to marry Maria.

Valentine's jaw clenched. His vision wavered with angry tears. His entire body shook with such rage that he wondered that he didn't explode.

Valentine reached down into his boot to check that his dagger was still there, and then he looked toward the stairwell where Glayer Felsteppe had disappeared.

The man was armed. The entirety of the keep, as well as the village, was crawling with soldiers under Felsteppe's command. To venture up those stairs was tantamount to committing suicide.

But Maria was up there with him at this very moment, with the man who had murdered Constantine's family. Constantine, who had trusted Valentine enough to follow him to Melk. Constantine, who had welcomed a notorious loner into the group of Chastellet's survivors as if Valentine belonged with them all the while.

And then Valentine realized he *did* belong there.

Constantine, Adrian, Roman—they were his friends, his brothers. They had been damned as one to the other, and the only way they would ever put things to rights was together. Valentine would not let his friend learn of the terrible fate of his wife and son through some cryptic message sent to Victor.

Valentine might now be a penniless reprobate with no home, no title, no wealth. Indeed, his only relative of any means was a pirate. But he was not without honor, and it was a priceless thing he would not lose this day to a maggot called Glayer Felsteppe.

Valentine left all his borrowed things save the cape he still wore beside the cracked and leaking cup on the table and walked boldly to the little alcove in the only guise he thought fitting: as himself. The stairwell was clear to the daylight above. Valentine gave a quick glance around before stepping onto the bottom riser and pulling the door closed quietly behind him. He engaged all the bolts and then reached down to withdraw his dagger from his boot.

Everything and everyone he'd ever fought to save before had been so that they could be set free. Today, he would fight for those he wished to hold close to him.

Mary had been waiting the whole of the night for Valentine, but he had yet to make an appearance. Neither had Glayer Felsteppe. So after she'd had her bath and dressed for the coming battle in the simple ivory and rose gown that was to have been her wedding costume, she turned the chair in her hall toward the stairs and waited.

Then she heard footsteps on the stairs, clomping, bold, clumsy— and she knew it was not Valentine even before she saw Glayer Felsteppe's head emerge.

He stopped at the top of the stairs when he saw her, his hands at his sides, giving her an indulgent smile, as one might give a person of limited mental facilities.

"Lady Mary," he said, pulling off his gauntlets and tucking them in his belt. "How my eyes thrill at the sight of your gentle person."

"My lord," she replied, her teeth feeling as though they might crack with the pressure on her jaw.

He stood there a moment longer, and then held his arms out from his sides. "Will you not greet your husband after he has been so long away?"

Mary forced herself to rise from the chair and met him in the middle of the floor, holding out her hands reluctantly for him to clasp. Glayer Felsteppe leaned in and kissed her temple, then came away to look at her from head to toe. His eyes searched her face.

"You look . . . different, somehow, from my memory," he said with a puzzled smile.

"Much has happened since last we met," she allowed.

His eyebrows knitted together. "Indeed. I was sorry to hear of the sickness at Beckham. Thanks be to God that you were spared. Would that I had been free to hie to your side. You will forgive me of course for not coming to you straightaway upon my arrival—there was a rather ugly matter to attend to."

Mary's stomach turned. "So I've been informed."

"I hope you don't mind that I ordered my belongings deposited in your chamber," he said with a sly smile and reached out to touch her bottom lip with his thumb. It took all of Mary's self-control not to slap his hand away. "We are to be married soon. I see no reason to forestall our acquaintance."

She gave him a tight smile. "I would not risk your reputation as an honorable man. I had my own things moved to my nurse's old chamber. It is only right that you sleep in the master's apartment."

This earned her a wide smile. "Well, as you wish, I suppose." His expression grew thoughtful. "Are you certain you're well? You seem . . . rather subdued."

"I've been awaiting a visit from a friend," she said. "I'm only preoccupied."

"Well, your friend is here now, I daresay," he said, drawing her into his arms. Mary felt the woodenness of her own posture. "I do vow, you are thrice as beautiful as when I left you."

"Surely you would say the same to a serving wench," she said, unable to help herself.

Glayer Felsteppe laughed. "I promise to the bottom of my heart that my thoughts have been filled with you alone in my absence. My bed has been a lonely one."

Liar, Mary thought, before giving him a smile. "As lonely as mine, I'm sure."

His smile faltered for only an instant. "Certainly."

Mary thought she heard the cacophony echoing up from the hall below quiet, as if the door at the bottom of the stairs had been closed, but Glayer Felsteppe seemed not to notice.

"My lord," she said loudly, hoping her voice would carry. "I am sure you want to refresh yourself after such distressing duties. I will call for your bath if you leave me alone here in the hall and retire to your chamber above."

Glayer Felsteppe's eyebrows wrinkled together and he drew his head back with a perplexed smile. "No need to shout, Lady Mary."

"Yes, no need to shout," came the smooth voice from behind Lord Felsteppe, who turned with an annoyed expression as Valentine arrived in the hall. He was dressed in a fine tunic and leggings, a black velvet cape hanging over his shoulders. His dagger was in his hand. "I want him to be very aware of my presence."

Felsteppe frowned. "Miller?"

"Miller?" Mary repeated, her heart leaping into her throat as she pulled away from the redheaded man.

"Maria," Valentine murmured.

"Who's Maria?" Felsteppe asked. "Mary?"

"Valentine." Mary smiled.

"Valentine?" Glayer repeated.

"Felsteppe," Valentine growled, then raised his dagger higher.

Glayer Felsteppe blanched. "Wait. You . . . you are not one of my soldiers, John Miller? You weren't at Benningsgate with me last night?"

Valentine pursed his lips and glanced at Mary. "He is no very quick, is he?" He looked back at Felsteppe, and the certain fury in his dark eyes took Mary's breath. "Allow me to introduce myself, since we have no yet properly met: Valentine Alesander, friend to Roman Berg, Adrian Hailsworth, and—" Valentine's eyes narrowed—"Constantine Gerard. Now that we are acquainted with each other . . . it is time for you to pay for what you've done."

Felsteppe drew his sword with a ringing hiss and swept out his other arm toward Mary. "Get back, Lady Mary; in but a moment, I shall increase my wealth by one thousand pieces of silver."

But Mary ran around his outstretched arm to stand between Felsteppe and Valentine. "No. He is innocent of the crimes he has been accused of."

Glayer gave her a confused frown. "What are you doing?"

"Maria, move!" Valentine commanded.

But Mary did not budge, hoping with some small part of her that she could end this hunt here and now, and somehow convince Glayer Felsteppe to let Valentine go free. "They are all innocent. The men he spoke of were not behind the massacre at Chastellet—it was another who betrayed the king. Valentine wasn't even there."

Glayer Felsteppe seemed to be losing his patience. "What would you know of anything, you simple woman? Get out of the way." Glayer moved a step closer.

Mary threw up her hands. "No! He is innocent, I tell you!"

"Maria," Valentine said from behind her, "he knows I am innocent."

Felsteppe's eyes narrowed.

Valentine continued. "He knows all of us are innocent because it is he who betrayed Chastellet."

"What?" Mary asked and looked to Felsteppe. "Is that why it was you at the Queen's Inn? You're leading the search for them because *you* are the traitor?"

"What do you know about the Queen's Inn?" Felsteppe demanded.

"I saw you!" Mary shouted. "I heard what you said! You thief! You . . . you *liar!*"

"Come away now, *mi amor*," Valentine ordered quietly. "He will no hesitate to kill you. He has already done as much to Constantine's wife and son."

Mary gasped and backed up slowly until she was standing slightly behind Valentine. "You killed them?"

But Felsteppe's eyes were flicking from Mary to Valentine, his mind working. *"You're* the Englishwoman," he said at last. And then he roared, *"Where have you been, Mary?* What do you know?"

The sound of a door creaking filled the tense, vibrating silence, and from the direction of the chapel, Father Braund called, "Is everything all right? I heard shouting."

Glayer Felsteppe glanced over his shoulder and Valentine rushed forward, slicing at the red-haired man's sword arm. Felsteppe whipped his head around with a cry and slashed awkwardly with the sword even as blood gushed from his forearm. The blow glanced off Valentine's ribs, laying open his tunic and the skin beneath it.

Mary screamed, and then heard the chapel door slam shut.

Valentine and Felsteppe circled each other in the hall, Mary's chair between them. Felsteppe had moved his sword to his left hand, his right forearm dripping fat red splotches onto the wooden floor. Valentine pressed his left hand to his side briefly and then glanced down at his palm; it was slick with blood.

"You'll never best me with that little splinter," Felsteppe taunted, his breathing labored.

"No?" Valentine challenged. "Then why do you hesitate? Only come a bit closer and I will cut out your eyes and shove them down your throat so that you might witness your black heart as it ceases to beat, you filthy coward."

Felsteppe feinted to the left and then slashed with a backhand motion. Valentine arched his body away from the blade and skittered back.

"It is you who retreats." Felsteppe laughed. "But go on, run around like a rabbit for a while if you would. It will only tire you out more quickly."

"I can afford to bide my time," Valentine said easily, placing the chair between them. "My wound is but a scratch. You, however—" he gestured toward Felsteppe's dripping hand—"are ruining the floor with your blood."

Felsteppe's face was growing paler, in sharp contrast to his bright hair. Mary could see the fear in his eyes, and she hoped that it would be over soon.

Then a rapping sounded on the door at the bottom of the stairs.

"Lady Mary?" a warbly voice called. "Lady Mary? It's Lady Elmsbeth."

"Oh my God." Mary gasped. "That woman has the worst timing!" She turned her head to call down the stairwell while still keeping an eye on the adversaries before her. "Go away, Dowager! I'm busy!"

"I don't like the sound of your voice, young woman," Lady Elmsbeth said, her disapproval clear. "Something is wrong; I can hear it. You let me up this moment or I shall have this door broken in!"

"Go away!" Mary shouted.

"Have you a pirate up there?" the dowager demanded.

Glayer Felsteppe must have at last realized the futility of continuing the battle alone, for he cried out, "Call for the soldiers to break down the door! Beckham Hall is under attack!"

"Good heavens!" the old woman shrieked.

"This is no good, Maria," Valentine warned, still circling the chair as the first shuddering crashes against the door rang up the stairwell and filled the air of the hall.

"There are two hundred soldiers readying to cut you down, Alesander," Felsteppe said with a greasy smile. "It would be kinder to yourself to run upon my blade now. Mary might want to look away first, since she clearly has misplaced feelings for you. Don't worry— I shall rid her of them once we are wed."

"Never," Valentine vowed. "You will never touch her again."

The crashes continued, and Mary heard the sound of wood splintering, metal screeching against stone.

"Time's up, Alesander," Felsteppe said and held his arms away from his sides, his hand still dripping thick blood, as the sounds of boots pounded on the stairs.

"I think that you are right." Valentine flipped the dagger in his hand and flung it at Glayer Felsteppe.

It sank to its hilt in his upper chest with a sick thunk. Felsteppe staggered back, his eyes wide. He dropped his sword with a clang and raised his bloody hand to the dagger.

"For Stan," Valentine growled.

And then he whirled and seized Mary's hand. "Up, yes?" he said, shaking her from her horror.

They dashed past Felsteppe's crumpling form to the rear of the hall, Mary leading, and leaped onto the stairs. Behind them, the shouts of soldiers swelled, and Valentine flung the door closed behind them. Once on the third floor, they ran through the columns to the opposite corner of the keep, where another staircase nestled. They whipped around and charged up. But the flat trapdoor was stuck, and they spent precious moments trading positions while Valentine threw his shoulder into the wood.

In moments they burst into the bright sunlight of the palisade and clambered out. Valentine dropped the door and slid the bolt home. Then he spun around in place, taking in their surroundings. He pointed a long arm toward the blue water of the harbor.

"Look, Maria," he said with a grin.

She saw a familiar ship not far from shore, and although the telltale flag was not raised, Mary knew it could only be—

"*The Azure Skull*," she whispered.

"We must only reach it." Valentine glanced over the side of the battlements at the village, some fifty feet below. "Too high," he said. "Damn!"

"Wait," Mary said, "There's another stair! This way!" She grabbed his hand and they sprinted between the battlements ringing the angled roof below; one side, two sides, to the corner of the walk opposite where they had come up. Mary stepped aside while Valentine wrenched open the heavy hatch and then she climbed down.

"Where does it lead?" he asked, coming after her, lowering the door over his head.

Mary paused and looked up. "The garrison."

Valentine growled. "Why can it no lead to the kitchen? Go, go, Maria!"

They zigzagged down what seemed to Mary to be ten flights of steps, until at last they burst into the room at the dungeon level. There were indeed soldiers within, perhaps a score, but they only looked up in surprise as the lady in the fine gown and the bleeding man dashed through to the opposite flight.

They came up from the garrison in the main hall, only steps from the door that led outside, but they were halted by the formidable bulk of none other than the dowager countess.

"Mary! There you are!" Lady Elmsbeth's talons sank into her arms. The old woman looked up at Valentine, taking in his bleeding side. "Good heavens, it's *you*!"

Valentine conceded, inclining his head. "It is I."

"There's no time to explain." Mary gasped. "Tell Father Braund: Glayer Felsteppe is the traitor. He has murdered Lady Mary Beckham."

"What are you talking about, Mary?" Lady Elmsbeth demanded. "You're standing right before me!"

"Tell him," Mary insisted. "Tell him Maria Alesander told you. I will send word when it is safe." Mary leaned forward and pressed a kiss to Lady Elmsbeth's plump cheek. "Thank you again for everything."

Valentine swooped in and kissed the old woman squarely on the mouth. *"Gracias, señora."*

Lady Elmsbeth gasped and whooped. "Oh! Oh my! Oh, good heavens, go! Go! They're coming!"

Mary and Valentine rushed from Beckham Hall through the guardhouse and down the stairs. They ran from the keep straight into the milling crowd of villagers, drawing curious stares but no pursuers.

Yet.

Valentine pulled Mary to a halt near a line of horses tethered to a rail. He loosened the reins of one and then threw Mary onto its back, swinging up behind her.

"Ho, there, fellow!" an older man shouted, coming toward them with his hand raised. "That's my horse!"

"It is indeed a fine beast, friend," Valentine called, and then turned the horse toward the harbor and spurred it into a gallop down the street, sending peasantry diving for the gutters.

"How are we to get to the ship?" Mary asked over the pounding hooves.

"We will worry about that if we reach the docks," Valentine said, glancing over his shoulder.

Mary peeked under his arm past his flapping cape. Waves of soldiers were rushing from Beckham Hall into the street. "They're coming!" she shouted.

"I know!" Valentine shouted back.

They weaved among the merchants carrying their loads from the docks, leaving numerous broken crates and ribald curses in their wake.

They were running out of road.

"Valentine, look!" Mary pointed past the horse's neck to a small boat bobbing perhaps only one hundred feet beyond the end of the closest dock. Three men were aboard, one of them standing and raising his arms to signal. "It's Roland!"

Valentine yanked his mount to a sharp halt where the dock met the land, causing the horse to dance and toss its head in protest. He looked behind them, and Mary heard the shouts of the soldiers swelling as they neared. Valentine looked back to the boat, still too far away.

Roland was standing in the bow, and he waved a long arm, his meaning clear: *Come on!*

"*Mi amor,*" Valentine said calmly, "I do apologize for no mentioning it sooner—you look lovely today. But I am afraid your gown is going to get wet." Then he kicked at the horse's sides, causing it to rear with a scream before charging into a full gallop down the wooden dock.

"Valentine?" Mary asked in a shrill voice. And then her screams matched the horse's as the mount leaped from the end of the dock into the bay.

She felt Valentine's hands around her waist as he threw her away from the falling beast, and they landed in the water with a great splash. Mary came up sputtering and flailed at the water with her arms.

"*Vamanos,* Maria." Valentine gasped, wrapping his arm around her chest and dragging her through the water on her back while she clung to his wet sleeve. "There is no time for drowning."

It seemed only a moment later that she was hauled from his grasp with a great wash of water and tossed unceremoniously into the bottom of the small boat as Valentine clambered over the side.

"Heave!" Roland shouted. "Heave, you dogs!" Then Roland leaned over Mary's gasping form, his face and his grin upside down. "We keep meeting this way, you and I."

Mary laughed even as she coughed.

But there was little time for levity. As she sat up in the bottom of the lurching boat, the two men at the oars straining and moving the vessel through the water swiftly, the first wave of soldiers gained the end of the pier. A moment later, a *whipt* of sound rushed past Mary's left ear, and she saw the archers.

"Get down!" Roland shouted, and Valentine dove on top of her while Francisco's first mate commanded the men. "Heave, me hearties! *The Skull* shall cover us!"

And Roland was right. A great roar of men echoed across the water, but it was coming from the direction opposite the dock. Valentine sat up, and when Mary followed and turned her head to look up, she saw the hulk of *The Skull* looming behind them, the black and blue flag snapping high on the mast.

Francisco's crew lined the rails, their own bows raised.

A shower of arrows moved the air over their heads, and an instant later, the screams and calls of retreat from Glayer Felsteppe's soldiers answered the attack. But retreat was not forthcoming, for those who were struck, nor for the remainder of them when the overburdened dock collapsed into the bay, dumping the lot of them into the sea.

Something hairy and rough brushed Mary's dripping face and she screamed, swatting at the thing, until Valentine reached past her and seized the knotted rope. They both looked up to see Francisco Alesander smiling down at them, his boot on the rail, his arm stretched high in the rigging.

"Coming aboard?"

Valentine's grin was wide as he hoisted himself up onto the rope and then grasped Mary around her waist. It was so like the last time they had parted, only now they were leaving together.

They spun slowly through the air once more until Francisco pulled them onto the deck. "I am sorry to inform you, cousin, but *The Skull* does no employ women. *Buenos días,* Maria."

Valentine pulled Mary into his arms again, this time nothing between them. "I'll no be joining the ranks of pirates, Francisco," he said over his shoulder, his eyes crinkling at the corners and searching Mary's face. "No for a while, any matter. I have more important work yet to do."

"That is a shame," Francisco said with a tsk. "But I know that you will be back this time, yes?"

"Yes," he said. "If my wife will allow it."

Mary swallowed. "I go where you go."

"Maria, my sweet, lovely Maria—I have been a fool. I thought to protect you by letting you go, but I know now that there is no safer place for my love than at my side." He brushed her dripping hair from her eyes. "There is no bounty so high as to keep us apart, no law of man that can ever separate us. You have no home now, and I regret that I have none to offer you at the moment. But still, I beg you— please say you will be mine forever. I will never let you go again."

"Oh, Valentine." Mary smiled, reaching up to stroke his face, and then she placed her palm over his heart. "*This* is my home now." She took his hand and placed it on her own chest. "And *this* is yours. We are both home, at last. Because I have been yours my entire life—I only didn't know who you were."

He kissed her, then, with the crew of *The Skull* cheering around them, the sharp sea breeze whipping at their cold, wet clothes. They clung to each other as they sailed away from the setting sun toward the night, their lonely pasts and Beckham Hall sinking into the horizon behind them.

Epilogue

Mary waited in the luxurious library of Melk, unceremoniously barred from the secret room Valentine had disappeared into with his friends and Father Victor. It was the middle of the night, and they had only just arrived at the abbey, but Valentine could not wait, and Mary understood. She sat at a table, the light from the single candle left to her reflecting on the gleaming wood, casting the thousands of volumes around her in eerie, flickering shadows.

It was so quiet here—but not peaceful. She didn't know what Valentine's and her future held. Were they to make a temporary home at Melk? Would Father Victor allow it?

Would Valentine's friends accept her as one of the group? Especially now that she suspected she carried Valentine's baby?

A muffled roar from beyond the secret shelves pierced the unnatural stillness and made her jump; it sounded like a beast, mortally wounded. Mary's hands flew up to cover her face.

The cry could only have come from Constantine Gerard.

Mary drew a shuddering breath and sent up a silent prayer of thanksgiving that at least Glayer Felsteppe was dead.

"I will kill them all," he murmured to himself, looking out over the cold gray sea.

"What's that, milord?" the deckhand asked.

Glayer Felsteppe turned his fierce gaze toward the man, who flinched reflexively. Glayer's arm was still in a sling, his shoulder bound tightly beneath his rich clothing, else he would have strangled the scrawny man and tossed him overboard for his impertinence in daring to think Glayer had spoken to him. But the deckhand moved away without further comment, leaving Glayer in solitude, if not peace.

He was being exiled in a way. That damned priest and the fat old dowager had managed to bend the king's ear, and now unless Glayer could prove his usefulness, his claims of Chastellet would henceforth go unheard. There would be no further bounties. No Beckham Hall to draw from, now that it was suspected that Mary Beckham was dead. That lying, sneaking, thieving bitch.

He watched the foggy islands drift past, their piney, ice-crusted shores shrouded in a mystical haze, trying to calm his thrashing heart lest the wound in his chest begin to seep again.

Soon he would have all the gold he needed. Perhaps then he could petition a certain ruler on the far side of the earth for assistance in gaining his final revenge. Saladin was always eager for wealthy allies, and for useful spies. Once Glayer had earned back King Henry's trust by adding to the monarch's realm, he would court the sheik as well, and use the alliances to eradicate his enemies, one by one.

"Coming ashore, General," the first mate advised.

Glayer Felsteppe turned toward the bow to see craggy castle spires piercing the fog and snow. A strange blue-colored light seemed to emanate from the structure, like the glow of a mystical flame. Somewhere inside that ancient pile of stones lay an incomprehensible fortune and, some said, power greater than any human ruler had ever known.

Power that would soon belong to Glayer Felsteppe.

He smiled. "I will kill them all."

Please turn the page for an exciting sneak peek of
Heather Grothaus's
ADRIAN
the next novel in her Brotherhood of Fallen Angels series,
coming in December 2015!

Prologue

August 1179
Damascus

He fell to his knees on the packed road and swayed toward his long, black shadow, his bound arms affording him no leverage. At least they had finally fallen numb. His vision blurred, the pebbles and sand and slivers of dry vegetation all seeming to melt together. He expected a blow to the back of his head at any moment. Adrian Hailsworth only hoped he would be hit hard enough to kill him.

"*Get up, Adrian,*" Constantine Gerard ordered as he marched past. Only Constantine could still act the general with a pair of Saracen guards walking leisurely behind him.

Adrian tried to raise his head in time to catch Constantine's gaze—he wanted to say goodbye, here, on the road. But he was too slow, too weak, and the Saracens already blocked his line of vision. They looked back at Adrian with knowing smirks, commenting to each other in chuckling voices.

A wide, hulking shadow eclipsed Adrian's own.

"Have no worry!" a jovial voice called out from somewhere above Adrian's head. "I will allow your friend the use of my own horse so that he might join you in the city!"

Adrian let his gaze drop back to the road, his cheek twitching, the ragged strips of his once-white undershirt fluttering in the arid breeze. His chest and stomach were crusted with his own blood where Saladin's soldiers had laid beaded whips to his belly, and the hot wind tugged at the cloth where it had dried against his wounds.

The Saracen's horse clip-clopped closer so that Adrian caught a glimpse of the delicately shaped front hooves out of the corner of his right eye. Such fine horses they had here. Adrian's father and older brother would be mad to claim a pair for their stables back in England.

"Have you had enough?" the dark general asked, his voice almost kind. The tone stung Adrian's pride, as it had been none other than this very man who had ordered him whipped, bound. "Will you call out for your god to save you now?"

"I told you," Adrian rasped, his throat so dry and pinched together that the words were like blades crawling up his insides. "I am no Templar, no soldier. I am a schol—"

"I witnessed your prowess with my own eyes," the general interrupted. "It takes great skill to remove a man's head with one blow. You must have much experience."

"It takes only a sharp blade and a strong arm," Adrian choked. "My experience is limited to this day."

"Is that so?" the Saracen mused, but his words were tinged with heavy sarcasm, indicating that he did not believe Adrian's claims. "Then you should know that a soldier never forgets the face of the first man he ever kills. It pleases me to know that he will haunt your dreams. You will remember him forever."

Adrian's vision threatened to darken completely as the screams in Chastellet's bailey filled his ears once again, the sight of the wall of robed and belted Saracens advancing toward him and Constantine and the handful of Templars left standing. He felt in his numb hands the heavy hilt of the sword pressing into his flesh, slick with sweat. His friends had swung, slashed, yelled; Adrian had stood very still, his sword held before him in a two-handed grip, as the brown face rushed at him, its mouth twisted in a battle cry. The curved scimitar rising, rising . . .

One swing.

Adrian blinked, bringing himself back to the present. "Your men came into a house I built and slaughtered my friends," he rasped. Then he tilted his head and looked up at the mounted general. "I couldn't pick his head from the pile, even now."

The Saracen's boot connected with Adrian's temple, sending him into the sand at the edge of the road. He felt a faint pulling somewhere between his shoulder blades, but it was eclipsed by the blinding pain of the late sun cutting into his dry eyes.

"Though you may in time find it rather unfortunate, I remember exactly who you killed," the man said in a low, contemptuous tone, and Adrian noticed he was feeding a long coil of rope from the back of his saddle into a loop beneath his hands. "Look around you, infidel—this is *my* house. *Allah's house.* We are only ridding our pallets of vermin. With the help of one of your own," the soldier added slyly.

"That's how you knew when best to strike," Adrian commented as he struggled to come back to his knees, not in the least surprised. Adrian and Constantine had figured out as much on their own the day Chastellet had come under attack from Saladin's army—when King Baldwin and half the fighting men were away to Tiberius. "It was Felsteppe, was it not? The man who aided you?"

The Saracen clicked his tongue and shook his head, the rope in his hands now fashioned into a circlet at one end, swaying with the horse's even breaths. "So eager to turn on your brother. But no; the man who gave us the detailed plan to bring Chastellet to its knees is not called Felsteppe."

"It is," Adrian insisted. "He is one of Baldwin's generals, redheaded, and—"

"Yes, yes," the soldier interrupted agreeably. "A red haired general, his nose, long and pointy, yes?"

"Yes," Adrian said. "Glayer Felsteppe is his name."

"You are confused." The Saracen shook his head as if disappointed for Adrian. "Our mutual friend clearly stated his name was General Constantine Gerard."

"General Gerard just passed us," Adrian rasped, his muddled brain fighting to make sense of what the soldier was saying. "He is on this very road, just ahead of us."

"Is that so?" The Saracen tossed the circlet of rope. It landed expertly around Adrian's body, catching on the ties that held his arms behind him. With a sudden flick, the rope tightened, causing Adrian to realize he hadn't lost all feeling after all. He cried out in agony.

"How convenient for Baldwin that we have his traitor in our captivity. I am certain there shall be a large ransom for him."

"Constantine did not betray Chastellet," Adrian whispered, his eyes squeezed shut. He could not fathom how his arms were still attached to his torso. If he'd had any moisture left in his body, his face would have been washed with tears.

The Saracen leaned slightly toward him in the saddle, as if eager to impart a great secret. "This I, alone, know. Which is why he will not live long enough to be bought." The man regained his regal posture. "Come now, soldier—if you only ask it of Allah, he will give you the strength of ten men. You can walk into Damascus with your dignity and recover in some comfort until you are ransomed."

Adrian didn't know what the Saracen's plans for him were, but from his treatment thus far, he was very sure they would involve massive pain and torture. And Constantine was going to die. What would it matter if Adrian indulged the dark man's religious delusions with a self-preserving lie? If he played along, perhaps there would be a chance to warn Constantine. A chance to plead their cases to the triumphant Saladin. The ruler was rumored to be reasonable and fair with his prisoners.

The ones who lived, any matter.

But then Adrian's mind was filled with a memory of his father, portly, graying, his beard tugged down into a point where he worried at it with his fist. Adrian knew he bore much of the responsibility for the beard's pointedness. Rather than live a life of relative ease or take the cloth as was expected of him, Herne Hailsworth's younger son had boldly decided to leave his noble home to pursue an insatiable thirst for knowledge. Everyone had thought him a fool—his father's peers, even his own brother. Quiet, odd Adrian, with his books and his stones and his measure sticks. Adrian remembered vividly the day he'd left, when his father had taken him aside.

Always be who you are, Adrian. Dare not belittle your assets in hopes of avoiding scrutiny, for it is only in bearing his own full weight that a man grows stronger.

Adrian raised his face to look squarely at the Saracen. "*I am not a soldier.* I am a scholar. A philosopher. And if any god existed to stand before me in this moment, after all he has allowed to happen *in his house*, I would spit in his bloody face."

It was then that Adrian received the blow to his skull that he had been expecting. The hot, brown world of the Damascus Road went silent and black in an instant.

The god who did not exist was merciful in allowing unconsciousness to cling to Adrian as the Saracen soldier kept his word and used the power of his own horse to drag Adrian's limp and battered body the remainder of the way to Damascus.

* * *

The sound of ragged sobs stirred Adrian from the depths, and as he came aware of the cold stone beneath his cheek, he realized he was the source of those sobs.

His voice, cawing and raw, echoed as he writhed on the stone floor. Every inch of skin, every muscle, screamed as if they had been painstakingly scored with glowing iron. He tried to tilt his head back as he cried out again, to relieve the drawing torture on the back of his neck and spine, but he felt a wide cuff of iron dig into the base of his skull. His cry intensified.

"Adrian," a muffled voice called. "Adrian, stop. You must get hold of yourself."

Adrian thought it was perhaps Constantine who spoke, and so he tried mightily to quiet, to still, so that he could locate his friend. His cries retreated back into his throat, but he could not help the whimpers that escaped him, like dogs straining at their leads. His whole body trembled with such pain that he could not understand how he still lived.

"That's it," the voice said again, perhaps somewhere behind him. Adrian's ear canals seemed to be swollen together, muting the sounds around him but amplifying the sluggish rush of blood in his skull. "Move beyond it. Can you open your eyes? Come outside yourself."

Adrian tried to raise his eyelids, but they felt melted shut. Increasing the effort brought another round of jagged sobs, but he was rewarded with a sliver of light that made him cry out again in earnest. He felt thick wetness running down his forehead, his cheeks. He didn't know if it was blood or sweat, although he doubted the latter, as he felt as though he was in the midst of a blizzard.

Constantine? Adrian tried to say his friend's name, but all that came out was a moan of which the effort and sound pained him so that he began to weep again.

"Get hold of yourself, Adrian!" Constantine demanded, using every nuance of his military tone. "You must not surrender to it. You must fight! If you don't, you shall die."

It was his friend's last statement that brought Adrian some measure of stillness. He could not see the extent of his injuries, and he knew in some part of his fevered mind that he was only feeling a fraction of the damage that his body was suffering, but he realized that he was only hanging on to life by a fingertip. He could quiet, and then just let the pain slip away. His heart would stop beating, his pupils would contract a final time, and then Adrian Hailsworth, master architect, would simply cease to exist.

He would never again see his brother, or his father. He would never again stride through the green grass of Hereford on his visits home from his travels. He would never see the completion of the great bridge in London, the plans of which he himself had helped conceive before accepting the ill-fated charge of the great fortress Chastellet. It was to have been his final project before taking the position in Oxford, teaching generations of fresh young minds the truth about the world around them, and shining light into the darkness of superstition and myth that gripped the populous of his country.

Now that bright dream, along with his weak physical body, was flickering.

"That's right," Constantine's voice broke into his dimming thoughts once more. "Be still. Conserve your strength. You are gravely injured, it is true, but now Saladin will preserve us until we can be ransomed or traded. Kind Baldwin will not forsake us. We must have faith, Adrian."

While Constantine launched into a murmuring plea to an imaginary creator, Adrian let his friend's hopeful words reach his muddled consciousness. Ransom? Why did that sound false to his ears?

How convenient for Baldwin that we have his traitor in our captivity. He will not live long enough to be bought.

The King would be told that Constantine was the traitor of Chastellet. Perhaps the news had already spread. There would be no ransom.

But Constantine would never know that if Adrian let himself die.

Adrian tuned his ears to the sounds around him again, hearing Constantine's murmuring prayer for Adrian's failing body, for the preservation of Constantine's son and wife, awaiting what was to have been their father and husband's imminent return to England. He fought to crack open his eyes once more.

At first Adrian thought it was his damaged eyesight that made his surroundings so dim. But after a moment, he realized that it was the cell itself that was dark—blurry brown sandstone walls which appeared sueded with the orange and yellow torchlight washing over them. Perhaps it was night, but Adrian guessed that he and Constantine had been interred in some underground prison—the smooth, domed ceiling seemed to mimic Constantine's bowed form.

Adrian saw the thick metal collar around his friend's neck, and he realized then the source of the choking and pulling sensation around his own throat. But whereas Constantine was tethered to the wall behind him, preventing him from kneeling or sitting, Adrian surmised his own bond terminated on the floor nearby. He could not move anything beyond his eyeballs at the moment to test his range. Constantine's hands were free, however, and he utilized them to cross himself as he now finished his sonnet to the Great Pretend.

Adrian almost reconsidered then. What good would it do Constantine to know with certainty that he was going to die? Was it not kinder to let him believe, this last bit of time he had left, that he might be saved? That good would somehow triumph and right would win the day and he would see his little boy again? Why not let him continue in his delusion if it should bring him comfort, rather than have him die knowing that his name would be forever remembered as a traitor and a murderer?

Because it is a lie, Adrian told himself. *Because he deserves the truth. If ever an opportunity arose for Constantine to save himself before he was executed, he must be aware of the truth, else he might just wait patiently for his rescue unto the very moment of his death.*

Constantine saw then that Adrian's eyes were opened. "Adrian?" he asked hesitantly, and Adrian realized that he must look as if he had already expired.

He gave a great effort and blinked.

Constantine Gerard's broad shoulders slumped momentarily, and Adrian thought perhaps it was with relief. "We will survive this," Constantine said firmly, his posture straightening as much as his tether would allow. Even the metal restraints weren't enough to rob the commander of the Templars from his duty to lead. "God has spared us thus far—beyond the hundreds that were killed—for a purpose. And God will see us delivered."

Adrian could only stare at his friend, leashed to the prison wall. For a moment, he wanted to believe, if only to delude himself against the inevitability of the fate that awaited them both. Adrian told himself it was the pathetic condition of his physical body that caused the wetness to leak from his eyes. Or perhaps the unspeakable pity he held for the capable and honorable Constantine. But he wept quietly all the same.

The sound of footfalls shuffled dully in the space behind Adrian's head, and then the creaking of some gate being opened. Shadows interrupted the torchlight, causing Adrian to wince. A moment later, the wicked face of the Saracen general leaned into Adrian's line of vision. His smile was bright.

"You are not dead," he said with something akin to delight. "I am impressed, infidel. I have great plans for your conversion, indeed." Then the face was gone, and a pair of metal dishes were dropped inches before his face, murky water and chunks of runny, unidentifiable stuff sloshing onto the stone and splattering Adrian's cheek.

Adrian could not register any smells from the offering through his clogged nostrils, but he saw a speck of white morsel moving, wiggling within the mottled mass of gray.

Maggots.

He focused his eyes instead upon the soft-looking leather boots of the accompanying soldiers that crossed the floor beneath voluminous robes.

"Stay where you are, infidel," the general called out to Constantine from where he still stood near Adrian's form. The soldiers quickly deposited similar metal vessels on the floor at what looked to be the very limits of Constantine's restraints. But Adrian could see a wide piece of the unleavened bread popular in this part of the world, and what was perhaps a leg of meat.

When the soldiers retreated, Constantine stepped toward the food, only barely able to drag it into his reach with the toe of one boot. The dish of water trembled wildly in his hands as he picked it up and brought it to his mouth.

The Saracen's evil countenance came into Adrian's view again, and he used one hand to push the low-rimmed bowl of rotting matter closer to Adrian's face. "Here is *your* meal, infidel. Go on—eat it."

Adrian closed his eyes against the sight of the wriggling mass.

"You must have nourishment," the voice in the darkness cajoled. "To build your strength."

"Don't eat it, Adrian," Constantine called out, his anger clear in his deep voice. "Why do you give an injured man rotting foodstuffs? Have you not done enough to him that you still seek to poison him?"

"Go on," the Saracen encouraged from beyond Adrian's eyelids. "If you do not eat, I will take away your friend's food, as well."

Adrian continued to lie very still while Constantine engaged the soldier. "Take it then, for I will not eat good food while my friend is offered that which swine would refuse."

Adrian felt a painful rush of air over his skin and the Saracen's voice was directed toward the back of the cell. "Is that so? How honorable of you. Thank you for illuminating my mistake, however, this business does not concern you. It is between myself and your friend, who killed my son."

Adrian's eyes opened then, and he saw brown hands snatch the dish of water from Constantine's hands while another set whisked away the bowl of untouched food from the cell floor. His vision moved jerkily upward to see the Saracen general removing the short, beaded whip from his belt.

The man Adrian had slain at Chastellet had been the general's son?

"Will you eat, infidel?" he asked pleasantly, but now Adrian recognized the hatred burning in the man's dark eyes.

Constantine commanded, "No, Adrian. Don't."

Adrian stared at the whip, remembering its cutting song.

"Very well," the Saracen said lightly. "You leave me no choice."

In the next moment, a whistle of air preceded a clicking slap, and Adrian heard Constantine's cry escaping through clenched teeth even as he tried to contain it.

Adrian closed his eyes. Perhaps if they thought him unconscious again . . .

But only a beat of time passed before the whip's whistle and slap sounded again in the close air of the cell. Then again. And now Constantine could not withhold his shouts.

Adrian remembered the bite of the beads as they sank beneath his skin, the ripping as they retreated.

Again the whip sounded, and again Constantine screamed.

Adrian opened his eyes and saw Chastellet's general crouched against the rear wall of the cell, his forearms raised to protect his face. Adrian tried to call out for the Saracen to stop as he raised his arm again, but his throat would not work. The whip fell with a gasp, and Constantine's scream pierced Adrian's ears.

Drawing strength from an unknown source, Adrian inched his face toward the congealing mass spilled over the side of the dish before him. The scrape of the metal bowl on the sandstone floor sounded like the sharpening of a blade. He peeled his lips apart, feeling the sting of the skin as it was pulled away. For a moment he wondered that he hadn't already bitten off his tongue, for he felt nothing emerge when he willed himself to sample the rotten offering before him. But then he tasted its sour perfume, felt the liveness of the mass in his mouth, around his lips.

"Adrian, no," Constantine pleaded in a breaking voice. "It will be as poison!"

But the whip fell no more, and the Saracen's boots came into close relief as the man moved over Adrian once again and crouched down.

"Again, you surprise me, infidel," the man said, obviously pleased as he watched Adrian struggle to swallow.

Adrian gagged as the mush pushed against the sides of his throat. He fought against the urge to vomit while he held the Saracen's gaze.

"Sorry," he slurred, his voice emerging thick and garbled, unable to open his jaws wide enough to form the words properly. "Your . . . son."

The dark man blinked and his brow creased as he seemed to consider what Adrian had said. Then his eyes narrowed and he leaned forward on his haunches and spat in Adrian's face.

"Eat it," he commanded in his own raspy whisper and then shoved the dish toward Adrian's face again so that the rim bounced off of his nose and upper lip. "All of it. I want to watch you."

Adrian was thankful the Saracen was between him and Constantine so that his friend was not forced to watch the grisly meal. He hoped the dark man's chuckling laughter was loud enough to mask the retching noises coming from Adrian's body.

By the time the dish was empty, Adrian knew his mind had been broken, for he was praying for a dark angel to deliver him from the hell he had finally accepted was very real indeed.

www.ingramcontent.com/pod-product-compliance
Lightning Source LLC
Chambersburg PA
CBHW020741250626
47155CB00003B/868